Until it's Over

Until it's Over

NICCI FRENCH

MICHAEL JOSEPH
an imprint of
PENGUIN BOOKS

MICHAEL JOSEPH

Published by the Penguin Group
Penguin Books Ltd, 80 Strand, London WC2R ORL, England
Penguin Group (USA) Inc., 375 Hudson Street, New York, New York 10014, USA
Penguin Group (Canada), 90 Eglinton Avenue East, Suite 700, Toronto, Ontario, Canada M4P 2Y3
(a division of Pearson Penguin Canada Inc.)
Penguin Ireland, 25 St Stephen's Green, Dublin 2, Ireland (a division of Penguin Books Ltd)
Penguin Group (Australia), 250 Camberwell Road,
Camberwell, Victoria 3124, Australia (a division of Pearson Australia Group Pty Ltd)
Penguin Books India Pvt Ltd, 11 Community Centre,
Panchsheel Park, New Delhi – 110 017, India
Penguin Group (NZ), 67 Apollo Drive, Rosedale, North Shore 0632, New Zealand
(a division of Pearson New Zealand Ltd)
Penguin Books (South Africa) (Pty) Ltd, 24 Sturdee Avenue,
Rosebank, Johannesburg 2196, South Africa

Penguin Books Ltd, Registered Offices: 80 Strand, London WC2R ORL, England

www.penguin.com

Published in 2007
1

Set in 13.5/16pt Monotype Garamond
by Palimpsest Book Production Limited, Grangemouth, Stirlingshire
Printed in Great Britain by Clays Ltd, St Ives plc

A CIP catalogue record for this book is available from the British Library

HARDBACK ISBN: 978-0-718-14784-6
PAPERBACK ISBN: 978-0-718-14785-3

To Rafi, Martin, Tommy, Vadilson,
Arthur, Tilly and Dougie

Part One

Chapter One

I had cycled around London for week after week, month after month, and I knew that one day I would have an accident. The only question was, which kind? One of the other messengers had been heading along Regent Street at speed when a taxi had swung out to make a U-turn without looking. Or, at least, without looking for a bike, because people don't look for bikes. Don had hit the side of the taxi full on and woken up in hospital unable to recall his own name.

There's a pub, the Horse and Jockey, where a whole bunch of us despatch riders meet up on Friday evenings and drink and gossip and share stories and laugh about tumbles. But every few months or so there'd be worse news. The most recent was about the man who was cycling down near the Elephant and Castle. He was alongside a lorry that turned left without indicating and cut the corner. That's when the gap between the lorry and the kerb shrinks from about three feet to about three inches. All you can do is get off the road. But in that case there was an iron railing in the way. The next time I cycled past I saw that people had taped bunches of flowers to it.

When these accidents happen, sometimes it's the cyclist's fault and sometimes it isn't. I've heard stories of bus drivers deliberately ramming bikes. I've seen plenty of cyclists who think that traffic lights don't apply to them. But the person on the bike always comes off second best. Which is why you should wear a helmet and try to stay away from lorries and always assume that the driver is a blind, stupid psycho-path.

Even so, I knew that one day I would have an accident. There were so many different kinds, and I thought the most likely was the one that was hardest to avoid or plan against. So it proved. But I never thought it would take place within thirty yards of my own house. As I turned into Maitland Road, I was about to swing my leg over the cross-bar. I was forty-five seconds from a hot shower and in my mind I was already off the bike and indoors, after six hours in the saddle, when a car door opened into the road in front of me, like the wing of a metal bird, and I hit it.

There was no time for me to respond in any way, to swerve or to shield myself. And yet the events seemed to occur in slow motion. As my bike slammed against the door I was able to see that I was hitting it from the wrong direction: instead of pushing the door shut, I was pushing it further open. I felt it screech and bend but then stop as the momentum transferred itself from the door back to the bike and especially to the most mobile part of the bike, which was me. I remembered that my feet were in the stirrups and if they remained fastened, I would get tangled in the bike and might break both my legs. But then, as if in answer, my feet detached themselves, like two peas popped from a pod, and I flew over the door, leaving my bike behind.

It all happened so quickly that I couldn't protect myself as I fell or avoid any obstacle. At the same time it happened so slowly that I was able to think about it as it was taking place. I had many thoughts, but it wasn't clear whether they were happening one after another or all at the same time. I thought: I'm having an accident. This is what it's like to have an accident. I thought: I'm going to be hurt, probably quite badly. I thought: I'm going to have to make arrangements. It looks like I won't be at work tomorrow. I'll have to phone Campbell and let him know. Or someone will. And then I thought: How stupid. We're meeting for dinner tonight, one of those rare occasions when we all sit round the table together, and it seems like I won't be there. And I even had time to think: What will I look like, lying flung out on the road?

At which point I hit the ground. I had flipped over like an incompetent acrobat and landed on my back, hard, hitting the wind out of me, so that I made an 'oof' sound. I rolled and felt bits of me bang and scrape along the road surface. When I heard my body hit the Tarmac, there was no pain at first. It was like a bang and a bright flash. But I knew that the pain was on its way and suddenly there it was, at the centre of everything, beating against me in wave after wave, light pulsing in my eyes in reds and purples and bright yellows, each pulse a different sort of hurt. I made an attempt to move. I was in the road. The road was a dangerous place. A lorry might run over me. It didn't matter. I was incapable of movement. All I could do was swear, over and over again: 'Fuck. Shit. Fuck. Shit.'

Gradually the pain started to locate itself. It was like rain that had fallen and was now settling into puddles and rivulets. I felt dizzy but my helmet had saved my head. My upper back was numb where I had landed on it. What really hurt for the moment were lots of other places – my elbows, the side of one knee. One of my hands had been bent back and was throbbing. With the other I touched my thigh and felt sticky wetness and bits of gravel. A tiny part of my brain still had time to think: How stupid. If this had not happened, I would be in the house and everything would be normal. Now I'm here and I'm going to have to deal with it, and if only I didn't.

I lay back and the Tarmac was warm against me and I

could even smell it, oily and sharp. The sun was low and yolky in the fading blue.

A shadow fell across me, a shape blocking the sky. 'Are you all right?' it said.

'No,' I said. 'Fuck.'

'I'm so sorry,' it said. 'I opened the door. I didn't see you. I should have looked. I'm so, so sorry. Are you hurt? Shall I call an ambulance?'

Another wave of pain hit me. 'Leave me alone,' I said.

'I'm so, so sorry.'

I took a deep breath and the pain receded a little and the person came into focus. I saw the vaguely familiar face of a middle-aged woman and I saw her silver car and I saw the open door, which had been bent outwards by the impact. I took another deep breath and made the effort to say something that wasn't just whimpering or swearing. 'You should look.'

'I'm so sorry.'

I was going to tell her again to go away but suddenly felt nauseous and had to devote my energy to stopping myself vomiting in the street. I had to get home. It was only a few yards away. I felt like an animal that needed to crawl into its hole, preferably to die. With a groan, I rolled over and began to push myself up. It hurt terribly but through the fog I noticed that my limbs were functioning. Nothing was obviously shattered; no tendons had been torn.

'Astrid!'

I heard a familiar voice and, indeed, a familiar name. My own. Astrid. That was another good sign. I knew who I was. I looked up and saw a familiar face gazing down at me with concern. Then another swam into focus behind the first: two were staring at me with the same expression.

'What the hell happened?' one said.

Stupidly and inexplicably, I felt embarrassed.

'Davy,' I said. 'Dario. I just came off the bike. It's nothing. I just —'

'I opened my door,' the woman said. 'She rode into it. It was all my fault. Should I call an ambulance?'

'How's my bike?' I said.

'Don't worry about it,' said Davy, bending down, his face creased with concern. 'How are you doing?'

I sat up in the road. I flexed my jaw, felt my teeth with my tongue. I felt my tongue with my teeth.

'I think I'm all right,' I said. 'A bit shaken.' I stood up, flinched.

'Astrid?'

'What about my bike?'

Dario walked round to the other side of the car door and stood the bike up. 'It's a bit bent,' he said. He tried to push it but the front wheel was jammed in the fork.

'It looks . . .' I was trying to say that it looked the way I felt but the sentence seemed too hard to construct. Instead I said I wanted to get into the house. The woman asked again about getting an ambulance but I shook my head and groaned because my neck felt sore.

'I'll pay for the bike,' the woman said.

'Yes, you will.'

'I live just here. I'll come and see you. Is there anything else I can do now?'

I tried to say something snappy, like 'You've done enough already,' but it was too much of an effort and, anyway, she looked upset and bothered and she wasn't defending herself like some people would have done. I looked round and she was trying to close the offending door. It took two goes to get it shut. Dario picked up my bike and Davy put an arm carefully round me and led me towards our house. Dario nodded at someone.

7

'Who's that?' I said.

'Nobody,' he said. 'How's your head?'

I rubbed my temple cautiously. 'Feels a bit funny.'

'We were sitting outside on the front step,' said Dario, 'having a smoke and enjoying the evening, weren't we, Davy?'

'Right,' said Davy. 'And there was a crash and there you were.'

'Bloody stupid,' I said.

'Can you make it? It's just a few more yards.'

'It's OK,' I said, though my legs were quaking and the door seemed to be receding rather than getting closer. Davy shouted for Miles, then Dario joined in even more loudly, and the sound echoed round my skull, making me flinch. Davy led me through the gate and Miles appeared from inside at the top of the steps. When he saw the state of me, his expression was almost comic. 'What the hell happened?' he said.

'Car door,' said Davy.

I was quickly surrounded by my housemates. Davy tried to hang the bike on the hooks on the wall in the hallway. Because it was damaged it didn't fit properly. He took it down again and started to fiddle with it, getting oil on the front of his lovely white shirt. 'That's going to need some work,' he said, with relish.

Pippa came down the stairs and said something rude to Davy about how it was me that needed checking, not the bike. She gave me a very light hug, hardly touching me. Mick looked at me impassively over the banisters from the floor above.

'Bring her through,' said Miles. 'Get her downstairs.'

'I'm fine,' I said.

They insisted and I was half helped, half dragged down

the stairs into the large kitchen-dining area where we ate and talked and spent our time when we weren't in our own rooms. I was placed on the sofa near the double doors and Dario, Pippa and Miles sat staring at me, asking over and over how I was feeling. I was clear-headed now. The shock of the accident had settled into simple, ordinary pain. I knew it was going to hurt like hell the next morning but it would be all right. Dario took a cigarette from a pack in his pocket and lit it.

'We should cut her clothes off,' he said. 'The way they do in A and E departments.'

'In your dreams,' I said.

'Do you need to see a doctor?' Miles asked.

'I need a hot bath.'

'About the hot part,' said Dario. 'There might be a problem with that.'

Chapter Two

There's something satisfying about the aftermath of an accident in which you haven't really been hurt. Especially when you look worse than you feel. I felt all right, but there was a lovely bruise flowering on my calf, a raw graze down my thigh, a gash on my hand, and my left cheek had an ugly scrape. My wrist was swollen. I stung and throbbed and ached, but in a masochistically pleasurable way. I kept pressing my cuts to make sure they were still bleeding. After a shallow, tepid bath, I lay on my bed in old jogging pants and a T-shirt, and assorted members of the household strayed in to ask me if I was all right and to hear yet again how it had happened. I began to feel almost proud of myself.

'It was all in slow motion,' I repeated for the fourth time.

Davy and Dario, the two heroic rescuers, were looking down at me. Dario lit another cigarette, except it wasn't a cigarette, and a familiar illegal smell drifted across my room.

'You must have fallen in a really natural way,' said Davy. 'That's why you didn't get seriously injured. It's pretty impressive. It's the way they train paratroopers. But you did it naturally.'

'It wasn't in my control,' I said.

Dario took a huge drag on his spliff. 'Or like a really, really drunk person,' he said. 'When really drunk people fall over, they don't get injured because their body's so relaxed.'

'Let's have a look,' said Mick, sitting on the edge of the bed.

I might have made a caustic remark if someone else had said that, but with Mick you don't really make caustic remarks. He's a man of few words. It's as if it takes a painful effort for him to speak, and when he does the rest of us generally fall silent. I wanted to ask why he was more qualified than anyone else to assess the damage, but I knew he would simply shrug.

'Does this hurt?' he asked, as I flinched. 'Or this?' He pressed a hand against my ribs, then lifted each leg, one after the other, feeling along my calves over thick daubs of oil that no amount of scrubbing with warm soapy water had removed. 'Nothing broken,' he said, which I knew anyway.

Pippa appeared with a small bottle of blue liquid and a handful of cotton wool.

'Will it sting?' I asked.

'Not a bit,' she said, and applied a liberal dousing of disinfectant to my cheek.

'Shit!' I yelled, squirming away from her. 'Stop at once!'

'Be brave.'

'Why?'

'Because, because,' she said mysteriously, slapping another sodden wad of cotton wool on to my thigh.

'Have a drag on this,' said Dario, offering me his spliff. 'It's good for pain and nausea.'

'I'll pass,' I said.

'Are you all right for the meal?' said Pippa.

'I'm starving.'

'Owen's bringing it on the way back from his studio.'

He arrived with an Indian takeaway in brown-paper carrier-bags and put them on the table, then looked up and saw me at the head, in a large chair, propped up with pillows. He frowned. 'You get into a fight?'

'With a car door.'

'Those are some bruises,' he said.

'I know.'

'They'll be worse tomorrow.'

'You should have seen her,' said Davy, sitting beside me. He looked more shocked than I was. 'She flew through the air.'

'Like a human cannonball,' said Dario, taking the chair on the other side.

'Does it hurt?'

'Not so much.'

'Of course it fucking hurts,' said Pippa. 'Look at her.'

'No. Don't look at me. My nose is twice its usual size. How much do we owe for this lot, Owen?'

'Eight quid each.'

There was muttering as people fumbled in pockets and purses, counted out coins and demanded change. Dario pulled a roll of notes out of his pocket, peeled off a twenty and tossed it to Owen. 'Keep the change,' he said. 'I probably owe you anyway.'

'Did you win the lottery?' said Owen, with an expression of distrust.

Dario looked shifty. 'Someone owed me,' he said.

Everyone sat round the kitchen table and eased off the foil lids, pulled tabs on beer cans, passed round chipped plates and an odd assortment of cutlery. Pippa helped herself to Dario's spliff and took a deep drag.

'Are lawyers allowed to do that?' asked Miles.

'Not in the office,' Pippa said, and looked round the group. 'How often does this happen? It's us and just us.'

'Now we are seven,' said Dario, clinking his fork against

his plate for silence, then immediately shovelled an enormous amount of rice into his mouth and chewed for several seconds while we all waited. 'Like the Seven Dwarfs,' he said at last.

'There are certain things we need to discuss,' said Miles, rather formally. 'To start with, can I say –'

'You're Doc,' said Dario.

'What?'

'If we're like the Seven Dwarfs –'

'Which we're not.'

'– you're definitely Doc,' said Dario.

'Because I own this house? And who else is going to get the drains fixed and make sure the bills are paid?'

'The dwarfs represent the parts that make up the psyche,' said Dario.

'Is this what I flew into a car door for?' I said. The beer was making me feel mellow and the pain had receded.

'You're Angry,' said Dario to Mick.

Mick ignored him.

'Is there an Angry?' I asked. 'I don't remember him.'

'There's Grumpy,' said Davy.

'Pippa's Randy, right?' said Dario, winking across the table at Davy.

This was a reference to the fact that Pippa was not in a proper relationship, but instead had a fair amount of extremely short ones.

'Oh, boys, boys,' I said. 'That's pathetic.'

'I think we can agree that Dopey's taken,' said Pippa.

'You can have Sleepy, then,' said Dario. 'No one can sleep like you.'

This wasn't strictly fair. Pippa only sleeps at weekends, when she goes to bed in the small hours and gets up in the afternoon, looking puffy, dazed and replete. During the week she's a dutiful worker who rises at seven. Dario, on the other hand, sleeps whenever he likes.

'We're running out of the good ones,' said Davy. 'Owen can be Sneezy.'

'Why?'

Davy looked at me. 'Which leaves you and me fighting over Bashful and Happy,' he said. 'And you, Astrid Bell, are not bashful. Unless you want to be Snow White.'

'I want to be the Wicked Queen. There's a real woman.'

'You're spoiling the game,' said Dario. 'You're Happy.'

Happy. And groggy. And relaxed. I sat back in my chair. I looked round the people at the table: a motley collection who were, just at the moment, the closest I had to family. There were only three of us left who had been here from the beginning, or perhaps the real beginning was before that, when we were at university together. Miles had bought the house when he was still a post-graduate student who wanted to change the world, paying a ridiculously small amount for this rambling, run-down place at the rougher end of Hackney. Then, he had had no beard and his hair was long, often tied back in a ponytail. Now he had a closely trimmed dark blond beard and no hair at all. If I ran my hand over his head I could feel all the bumps of his velvety skull. Pippa was the other long-termer. In fact, she and I had met in my first term at university and we'd shared a house in our final year, so by the time we moved in with Miles I already knew her domestic habits well. She was tall and willowy, and had a delicate kind of beauty that could mislead people.

So we were the original trio and we'd survived, even though for a year of that time Miles and I had been sort of a couple and for another six awful months had been sort of not a couple and then definitely not a couple. Now Miles had a proper new girlfriend, Leah, and that felt good, like a fence between us. 'Good fences make good neighbours,' someone had said.

Around us, there had been various others, and the current seven was bound to change sooner or later. Mick was older than the rest of us, and carried his years as if they were a burden that weighed on his broad shoulders. He was stocky and short. He stood with his legs apart as if on the deck of a ship in stormy weather. His eyes were pale blue in a face creased by the sun and wind. He had spent years travelling restlessly round the world. I didn't know if he'd been searching for something, or even if he had found it. He never talked about it. Now he worked, doing odd jobs, and had drifted to a temporary halt in Maitland Road. When he was at home, he spent much of his time in his small room at the top of the house, though I never knew what he did up there and I'd rarely visited him. None of the doors have locks on them, but some are more firmly closed than others. Sometimes I went downstairs in the middle of the night because I couldn't sleep, and he was there, sitting quite still at the kitchen table with the steam from a mug of tea curling round his face.

We were never quite sure how Dario had come to be living here. His previous girlfriend (who I suspected was the only real girlfriend he had ever had) had rented a room for a year so he had often stayed over. Then we blinked and she was gone and somehow he was still there, digging himself into the smallest room, which was on the second floor, then gradually colonizing the empty room next door. Although he had no job and couldn't pay the rent, no one had the heart or the necessary steel to throw him out – perhaps because he didn't look much like a Dario. He had untidy ginger hair and thick freckles; his teeth were slightly crooked and when he smiled he seemed like a goofy little boy. In the end, Miles came to an agreement with him: that he should renovate the house, top to bottom, in return for living there. I don't think it was such a good deal for Miles. As far as I could tell, Dario spent most of his time smoking weed, reading astrology columns, watching daytime TV, playing games on other people's computers and doodling on walls with stiff-bristled paintbrushes that he wasn't scrupulous enough about cleaning or replacing.

Davy was the most recent member of the household, being here just a couple of months, along with Owen. He was a carpenter and builder. A real one, not like Dario. Despite the disadvantage of not being Polish, he had plenty of work. Enough of it was outside so that he was lightly tanned. He had light-coloured hair, which fell thickly over his shoulders, and grey eyes. He was good-looking, but he didn't seem to know he was, which I found charming. He had the anxious manner of a new boy in the house, but also a nice smile that crinkled the corners of his eyes, and when he arrived I had let myself think, Perhaps? and then decided probably not. Sex in the house felt like a taboo, and my experience with Miles was an awful warning.

And then there was Owen Sullivan, sitting across from me right now. With his pale skin, his straight, shoulder-length dark hair, and his wide-set, almost-black eyes, he had a faintly Oriental air, though as far as I knew all his ancestors had been Welsh. He was a photographer. He hawked his portfolio round magazines and got the occasional commission. But what he really wanted was to do his own stuff. He had once said he hated magazine work. I had giggled and said then it was lucky he got so little of it. He hadn't replied but he had given me such a sharp look that I had realized you couldn't safely tease him where his work was concerned. He used to watch people as if he was sizing them up for a photograph, checking the light, framing them. I sometimes wondered if he really saw, really listened to what they had to say.

'Seven ages of man,' said Dario, dreamily. 'Seven seas, seven continents . . .'

'That's not right.'

'Listen,' said Miles. 'I hate to break into this, but it's very rare that we're all together like this. Just the seven of us. Don't you dare start again, Dario.'

'You're right, it *is* rare,' said Davy. 'Why don't we have a group photo to mark it?'

'We even have an official photographer.'

'I don't do snaps,' said Owen, with finality.

'Let's not forget he's an artist,' I said sarcastically.

Davy just smiled. 'I'll take it,' he said.

'My camera's in the drawer over there,' said Miles, wearily.

Davy stood up and pulled it open. 'It's not here. You must have moved it.'

'Someone's nabbed it, more like, and forgotten to put it back.'

'I've got one upstairs,' said Davy.

'Let's just forget it,' Mick was starting to say, but Davy was out of the room and bounding up the stairs two at a time.

A silence settled over us. Outside, a car horn blared several times and then we heard footsteps running down the road. A door slammed upstairs.

'Who else thinks this lamb tastes like dogfood?' said Dario.

'What does dogfood taste like?'

'Like this.'

17

Dogfood or not, there was the sound of chewing and plates being scraped. There was little conversation. Everybody seemed distracted. Then Davy returned, breathless and slightly flushed, but triumphantly brandishing his camera. 'It wasn't where I thought. Now, all squash together. No, you don't have to move, Astrid. Everyone can stand round you. Owen, you're out of the picture like that. I still can't see you.'

'Good.'

'Dario, your face is hidden by Pippa's shoulder. Mick, you look a bit weird with that smile. Scary, actually. OK, ten seconds. Are you ready?'

'What about you?' said Pippa.

'Just wait.'

Davy pressed a button and ran round to join us. His foot hit the table leg so he stumbled and half fell on to the tightly massed, scowling, smiling group as the light flashed. That was how the camera caught us, a blur of flailing arms and legs, and me in the centre, mouth open in surprise in my grazed and swollen face, like the victim of a drunken attack.

'Look at us!' screamed Pippa in delight: she came out the best of us all, of course – dainty and gorgeous in the scrum.

'My eyes are shut,' groaned Dario. 'Why does that always happen?'

'Right,' said Miles, once we'd sat down again. He pushed away his plate of congealing orange curry. 'I want to say something.'

'Yes?'

'This isn't easy, but I'm giving you plenty of warning.'

'It's about the state of the bathroom, I know it.'

'Leah and I have decided to live together.'

Pippa gave a little whoop.

I frowned. 'So why the solemn face?' I asked.

'She's moving in here.'

'We can cope,' said Dario. 'Can she, though? That's the real question.'

'I mean,' said Miles, 'it will be just Leah and me.'

For a moment, nobody spoke: we stared at him while his sentence hung in the air.

'Oh,' said Mick at last.

'Fuck,' said Pippa.

'You're chucking us out?'

'Not like that,' said Miles. 'Not at once.'

'How long?' I asked. My face was starting to throb.

'A few months. Three. That's all right, isn't it? It'll give you time to settle in somewhere else.'

'I was just settling in here,' said Davy, ruefully. 'Oh, well.'

'You couldn't all stay here for ever,' said Miles.

'Why not?' Dario looked stricken. His freckles stood out in blotches.

'Because things change,' said Miles. 'Time passes.'

'Are you all right, Astrid?' Davy asked. 'You've gone a bit pale.'

'I need to go to bed,' I said. 'Or at least lie down for a bit. I feel odd.'

Pippa and Davy levered me to my feet, hands under my elbows, making tutting noises.

'I'm sorry,' said Miles, wretchedly. 'Maybe it was the wrong time.'

'There's never a right time for things like this,' said Pippa. 'Come on, Astrid, come into mine for a while. It's one less flight of stairs to manage. I can rub Deep Heat into you, if you want.'

I shuffled up the stairs, taking them one at a time, and edged my way into Pippa's room, which was thick with the smell of perfume. It was a large room at the front of the house. When we had first moved in, it was the designated sitting room, and didn't seem to have been decorated since the fifties. Pippa had done nothing to change that, just filled the space with the frippery and clutter of her life. The effect was peculiarly jarring. Two walls were a grubby mustardy yellow, and another was covered with flowery wallpaper busy enough to make your head ache and peeling at the joins. The lightbulb hanging from the centre of the ceiling had a brown paper shade, split along one side. A large bay window gave out on to the street, but Pippa kept the shutters half closed so the room was in permanent shadow.

In my woozy state, the mess she had created took on an unsettling, almost hallucinatory aspect. There was a metal bed – a large single, which was particularly inappropriate to her lifestyle – with a lusciously crimson velvet bedspread; a small divan that her grandfather had left her, which was heaped with clothes, both clean and dirty; a chest with every drawer open and underwear and shirts spilling out on to the floor; a wardrobe, similarly open, in which hung her gorgeous dresses, suits, skirts and jackets; a flimsy desk buckling under the weight of papers and files. A full-length gilt mirror was propped against one wall, and at its base were piles of makeup, bottles of body lotion and tubs of face cream, ropes of necklaces, scattered earrings, a couple of belts. Yet out of this room Pippa emerged every morning fresh and immaculate, not a hair out of place, smelling of soap and Chanel No. 5.

I pushed aside a pair of knickers and lowered myself cautiously on to the bed.

'Paracetamol?' She reached under the bed and plucked

out a box of pills. 'With whisky?' Like a magician, she produced a bottle from beneath the pile of clothes on the divan and brandished it.

'Maybe not the whisky tonight.'

'Go on.'

She shook two white tablets into my hand, then poured a couple of fingers into a tumbler and handed it across. I swallowed the paracetamol and took a sip of whisky to chase them down.

'Shall I rub your shoulders?' she asked.

'I think that might hurt too much.'

'You're not making nearly enough fuss.'

'Strange day,' I said.

I could hear voices from downstairs, then the unmistakable heavy trudge of Mick making his way to his room.

'For you, mainly,' Pippa said. She took the tumbler from me, poured herself a generous slug of whisky and tossed it expertly down her throat. 'Bastard,' she added loudly.

'Miles?'

'Who else?'

'I don't know, Pippa. It had to happen some time.'

'Bah!'

'And if he and Leah want to live on their own together ...'

'She's the one behind it.'

'You make it sound like a conspiracy.'

'Of course it's a conspiracy. So we're going to have to be the counter-conspiracy.'

She went on talking, saying something about the bump on my head making me too reasonable. But I didn't really hear the words, or make out their sense. I was feeling crashingly tired. The room swam in and out of focus. I lay back against the pillows and closed my leaden lids. 'Perhaps I'll go to sleep here tonight,' I said thickly.

Pippa grabbed my arm and pulled me into a sitting position. 'Oh, no, you don't. Not tonight, darling.'

I went crabwise up the second set of stairs, into my own room, which was white and empty after the garish mess of Pippa's: just a small double bed, a narrow wardrobe, a chest on whose surface stood all the objects I'd dug from the garden, and a big wooden rocking-chair Dario had picked out of a skip for me and I'd covered with cushions I'd bought at Camden Market. I tugged off my tracksuit trousers, then wriggled under the duvet. But I stung and throbbed, and although I was so tired, it took me a long time to sleep. I heard sounds: the front door opening and closing; voices; someone laughing; water in the tank; footsteps on the stairs; an old house breathing.

Chapter Three

I twisted and turned and slept and fretted and twisted and turned some more, and slept and woke and saw the bright sunlight shining through the curtains and gave up the fight. Besides, my body and my bike both needed checking.

In the shower – hot, this time – I examined myself. I flexed my knees and elbows. They ached but there were no cracking or scraping sounds. I needed to get moving. I also suspected this would be a fine day to be absent from the house.

Meanwhile it was good to be on my own in the kitchen. I made myself coffee and cut a grapefruit into segments. While my porridge was cooking, I went into the garden and looked at my vegetable patch. I'd never grown anything before, except maybe mustard and cress on blotting-paper when I was small, but this year I'd suddenly decided we should grow our own food. I'd gone to a car-boot sale and bought a spade, a trowel and a watering-can so nice and bright, almost new, and cheap they had clearly been stolen from someone who had forgotten to lock their garden shed. What else are car-boot sales for in Hackney? But I'd made good use of the stolen goods, measuring out a long rectangle of overgrown land, and digging it into a well-tilled plot, whose earth was loamy and rich, and studded with old coins and bits of pottery, which I collected and put on the chest in my bedroom. It was surprisingly satisfying. I relished the ache in my back, the blisters on my palms and the dirt under my fingernails. Davy offered to help with the heavy digging but I wanted it to be all my own work. I'd planted courgettes, broad beans, lettuces, beetroot and rocket – even potatoes in their own raised bed. Everyone else in the house teased me about it, but already sturdy shoots were appearing. Almost every morning and evening, I went to look at them. This morning, I had been thinking that next year I should plant sweetcorn as well, and maybe some butternut squash for soups – until I remembered that next year I wouldn't be here. It was only then I realized that I wouldn't be here this year, either, to harvest the vegetables I had tended so carefully. Miles and Leah would be picking them instead, enjoying the fruits of my labour.

I was on my second mug when Pippa came into the kitchen. She was dressed for the office in a soft grey suit and a white shirt. And she wasn't alone. A man in black trousers, a flowery shirt and leather jacket came in with the familiar mixture of sheepishness and pride you see in men in the morning. She introduced him as Jeff. He sat across the table from me and, asking if it was all right, helped himself to coffee.

I was too dumbfounded to answer. Pippa was amazing. How had she done it? Where had she produced him from? I had left her at whatever time it was last night, sitting in her room. And yet somewhere, somehow, in the middle of the night, she had found this man and smuggled him into her bed.

'Hi, Jeff,' I said, and disintegrated into a sort of stammer. 'How . . . where did you . . . ?'

'We'd arranged to meet for a drink,' said Pippa, cheerfully, 'so I said he might as well come over here. And by then it was so late that, well, you know . . .'

'Not really,' I said. 'Pippa, I wanted to ask you a professional question.'

'What?'

'Can Miles actually, legally, throw us out? Aren't we sitting tenants?'

'I don't know,' she said.

'Aren't you a lawyer?'

'Are you a lawyer?' said Jeff.

'Yes, sweetie,' said Pippa. 'Hurry and finish your coffee.' She glanced back at me. 'That doesn't mean I know anything. I'll look it up or ask someone. But don't get lawyers involved. That's the only thing I've learned.'

I nodded to Pippa and said goodbye politely to Jeff, suspecting I would never see him again. I rang Campbell at the office, and he said there would be no problem in borrowing a bike for a few days. I'd just have to pick it up from the office in Clerkenwell. Consequently, that morning I must have been the only bike messenger in London who didn't go to work on a bike. Instead I sat on the tube in tight Lycra shorts and my fluorescent yellow top, with my helmet on my lap. I couldn't have looked more ludicrous if I'd been dressed in jodhpurs and a scarlet coat.

I hardly ever went into the office. It was really nothing more than a cubby-hole where Campbell and his assistant, Becks, took orders and phoned the riders, but it was amazingly squalid, all cardboard boxes, unwashed coffee cups and unfiled files.

'Lovers' tiff?' said Campbell, as I walked into the office.

'Car door,' I said.

'Are you sure you're all right?'

I was less all right when I saw the bike he was lending me. Campbell saw my dubious expression. 'It's served me well, that bike,' he said.

'At least it's not going to get stolen,' I muttered. 'So, what's up first?'

He looked at his clipboard. 'Fancy Wardour Street to Camden Town?'

'All I fancy is you, Campbell,' I said, taking the piece of paper he was holding out. 'Now that I've seen the state of the office, I must remember to come in less often. See you at the pub later, maybe.'

It was a lovely day, the sort that made up for January, when you got wet and numb and it was dark at four o'clock, and August, when you seemed to breathe nothing but heat and car fumes. It was sunny but with a chill, and there wasn't too much traffic and I felt happy, even if I didn't know why. I darted across the map of London in straight lines. After Camden Town I went from Charlotte Street to Maida Vale, then from Soho to London Bridge. On the way back I spent too much money on an exotic sandwich at Borough Market. Then it was over the river to Old Street and thence in a long straight line to Notting Hill Gate. Cycling back into town, I stopped in St James's Park, ate my sandwich and drank a bottle of water. And so back to criss-crossing London, in and out of the photographic labs, advertising companies, editing suites, solicitors', and offices I had been in and out of for months without knowing, or needing to know, exactly what they did.

Some days it felt like I was dragging heavy weights behind the bike, but not today. The accident had clearly done me no lasting damage. My aching limbs gradually loosened up and by the evening I'd done sixty or seventy miles and I didn't even feel tired, just a pleasant ache in my calves and thighs. On the way home I stopped off at the Horse and Jockey. The pub was strictly for the cycle messengers. The motorbike messengers were large, bearded and male: they dressed in black leather and met up at the Crown just south of Oxford Street. They congregated on the pavement and whistled at women walking past and talked about cam shafts, or whatever it was that motorcycles were made of.

We cycle messengers saw each other as a more sensitive breed. We were certainly a bloody sight healthier, those of us who survived. When I cycled up, there was a small cheer from the people who were already there, clutching their bottles of beer. They gathered round to inspect my bruises and grazes and to comment that they were really nothing special. Then we got down to the more serious business. We talked about employment prospects, we gossiped and, above all, we slagged off the clients. We depended on them but that didn't mean we had to respect them. Most of the job was company work, taking envelopes from office to office, but several families had accounts with us and some of them were so rich, or at least so much richer than we were, that they thought nothing of picking up the phone to summon one of us. There was an unofficial competition about the most ludicrous request. I'd once gone on successive days to deliver a forgotten packed lunch from Primrose Hill to a girls' prep school in the West End. One messenger claimed he'd cycled to Notting Hill Gate in the rain to collect an umbrella and deliver it to a woman standing outside Fortnum & Mason. The job also gave us a chance to gawp inside some of these houses. One of the messengers said he was going to start a game: you'd get five points for a private cinema, ten for a fountain, fifty for an indoor swimming-pool.

Just as a messenger called Danny was telling me, quite falsely, about a client who fancied him, I was saved by my phone ringing. It was Davy.

'I'm at the Jockey,' I said. 'Want to meet up?'

The pub was a handy place to rendezvous in the middle of town and Pippa or Davy or Owen would occasionally join me there and attempt to blend in with the lithe, sun-tanned, lightly clad, generally god-like bodies of us messengers.

'No,' he said. 'I'm at home. Maybe you should come back.'

'Is anything wrong?'

'No, no,' he said. 'Not really. Nothing to do with us. But dramatic.'

I cycled home slowly, enjoying the amber light and the cooling air against my glowing skin. As I steered into Maitland Road, I was thinking that the one thing I mustn't do was have another stupid accident in my own road when I almost ran into a police car at the same spot where I had hit the car on the previous day. An area of pavement a few houses down from ours was taped off. Several policemen and -women were bustling around busily. One was standing by the car looking bored.

'What's up?' I asked.

'Move on, please, love,' he said.

'It's just that I live in the street.'

'It's all over.'

'What's all —?'

'Just move on.'

I felt reluctant. Something had happened almost exactly where I lived and I wanted to know about it, but the officer stared at me and I couldn't think of an excuse so I just pushed my bike along the pavement to our house.

Dario was up a ladder in the hallway painting the rose round the light. I leaned Campbell's bike against the wall. 'Someone's going to fall over that,' he said.

'It's just for today,' I said. 'What's going on outside?'

'There were more police a couple of hours ago,' he said. 'There were cars and an ambulance.'

'What happened?'

'I don't really know,' he said. 'I haven't been out. I heard that someone had been robbed.'

'Murdered,' said a voice behind me.

I turned round. It was Mick. 'Murdered?' I said. 'No! What happened?'

'Someone was being robbed in the street and they got killed. They must have tried to resist. Fucking idiot.'

Dario grinned down at me. 'Yesterday Astrid crashes into a car, today someone gets murdered. This area's getting dangerous.'

'Lucky we're getting evicted then, isn't it?' I said, and then I looked up at Dario suspiciously. 'How long have you been doing the house up?'

'I don't know,' he said.

'Were you in on Miles's plan?'

'Me?' he said. 'What would I have to gain from that?'

'I wouldn't like to think how your twisted mind works,' I said.

Chapter Four

I had a cool, very quick shower and pulled on loose-fitting clothes over my bruises and grazes, wincing. A light skirt, because outside the May evening was balmy and soft; a shirt that would cover my arms; sandals. I had a date with three old friends in Clerkenwell, and I wasn't going to get on my bike again but travel on the top of the seventy-three bus. Dario came with me, because he, too, was going out. The police were still there. There seemed to be even more of them than before, and now there was also a yellow metal sign on the pavement, just a few metres from the taped-off area, asking anyone who had witnessed anything unusual on the evening of Thursday, 10 May, to contact the police.

'Do you really think someone's been murdered?' I asked Dario.

'Definitely,' he said, with enthusiasm.

'It just says "serious incident". That could mean all sorts of things. Maybe a car crash. Or a mugging.'

'There's an awful lot of police for that,' said Dario.

We were quite used to muggings in Maitland Road, and to yellow signs asking the public for help, which rarely came. Maitland Road backed on to a rough estate. Gangs of youths roamed the street and hung out in the park, bored and belligerent, trousers dropping off their arses and cigarettes dribbling from their lower lips. They broke windows, threw bins across the road, did their drug deals in the bus shelter where we were standing now, had scuffles that could turn nasty. Where we lived was one of the roads that formed a kind of border between the well-off and the desperately poor.

When Miles, Pippa and I first moved in, many of the houses were crumbling and boarded-up. Gardens were rank with weeds, the only shops were twenty-four-hour newsagents and strange outposts of a previous civilization that sold Crimplene slacks and long johns. The sandpit in the park was full of needles and litter. It was an area that felt abandoned and unloved. Now it was being gentrified. There were still run-down terraced houses and dilapidated squats, but others had been renovated and decorated, inappropriately smart now between their dowdy neighbours. There were Volvos and BMWs as well as beaten-up old Rovers and Fords. Estate-agents' signs peppered the front gardens, builders' vans and skips squatted outside gutted houses. The brutal grey and pink blocks, with names like Morris and Ruskin House, were now grim, stubborn, neglected islands.

The bus came and I climbed up to the top deck to stare out as Hackney ended and I was into more genteel Stoke Newington, then more-genteel-still Islington, where lights glittered in terraced houses and all the expensive restaurants were full. I didn't think about the Maitland Road incident for the rest of the evening. I met my friends and we had a drink, standing outside the pub in the ebbing warmth, then going on for a cheap meal, and back to Saul's house for coffee. Everyone was tired, but because it was Friday night we lolled about, chatting idly, not willing to leave.

It was late by the time I took the night bus home. The air was cool on my skin now. I thought about sleeping late the following morning, then maybe going with Pippa to the flower market and out for lunch. And I thought, too, about the need to find a new place to live. Three months wasn't long, just until the end of the summer.

Two police cars remained in Maitland Road. Several teenage boys were standing around the first; as I passed, one kicked the front kerbside tyre, trying to be cool. When I grinned at him, he blushed, suddenly appearing much younger than he wanted to.

'Hi,' I shouted, as I pushed open the front door.

Everyone except Dario and Owen was downstairs, sitting round the kitchen table with a couple of empty wine bottles between them. Miles's girlfriend, Leah, was there as well: the cause of our eviction from the house. I would have expected there to be a certain chilliness in the air, but instead I sensed excitement

'You missed all the drama,' said Miles.

'What drama?'

'The police were round here, asking us whether we'd heard anything unusual last night.'

'Really? Did they say what had happened?'

'Mick was right,' said Miles. 'Someone was murdered.'

'In Maitland Road,' added Davy, as if that was good news.

'No!'

'Yeah.'

'God, how awful. Who was it? We don't know them, do we?'

'No,' said Pippa. She sounded almost disappointed.

'Someone called Margaret Farrell, apparently,' said Davy. 'We don't know a Margaret Farrell, do we?'

'I don't, anyway,' I said. 'Did she live near here?'

'That's the thing,' said Pippa. 'She lived just a few houses up. Number fifty-four. She was a neighbour, kind of.'

'Number fifty-four?' I said. I tried to remember which house that was and who lived there.

'The house with the dark green door and the tidy front garden,' said Miles.

'We went out to have a look at it,' added Davy.

'What time was it?' I asked. I couldn't get my head round the fact that while we had been safe and warm inside someone was being killed just a few feet from our front door.

'The police weren't sure about that. They just wanted to ask us if we'd heard anything unusual during the night.'

'Only the usual unusual,' I said. 'Shouts, people running, things being thrown.'

'That's what we said.' Davy tipped the last of the wine into his glass and held it up to the light. 'And we gave everyone's names in the house.'

'What for?'

'Routine,' said Miles, vaguely. 'I said we were all here last night. They just said we should get in touch if we remembered anything that might be helpful.'

'Margaret Farrell,' I pondered. 'Do they know why? Was she robbed – or what happened? Was it in her house?'

'No,' Davy explained. 'Apparently someone found her body where the bins go, outside the basement front. They said the binmen found her.'

'No! Just dumped with all the rubbish? That's horrible.'

'That's what I heard. It's hard to believe, isn't it?'

'But why?'

'I think she was mugged and they killed her by mistake,' said Miles.

'They?'

'It's probably the husband,' said Pippa. 'It always is, you know.'

'Do you even know she has a husband?' I asked.

'We don't really know anything,' said Miles. 'People keep

33

passing on rumours and suspicions and by now they're flying round the street, getting more and more bizarre. Everyone's talking to each other at last. Ironic, isn't it?'

'Very ironic,' agreed Leah. I started. I'd almost forgotten she was sitting there, composed and elegant, her hands lying placidly on the table.

'Scary,' I said, with a little shiver. 'Right on our door-step.'

But then the conversation drifted on to other things. Davy was doing his Portuguese homework, I picked up a magazine and started browsing through it. Miles used the remote control to turn on the TV. We watched a programme in which two experts redecorated somebody's flat and made it look much worse than before. Then we watched a cookery programme, which featured ingredients I had never even heard of. We were just starting to watch a film, the sequel to something none of us had seen, when there was a clatter on the stairs. Dario burst into the room. 'Turn the TV on!' he shouted.

Miles looked round. 'It *is* on,' he said.

'Change channel. I was watching upstairs. No, give me the fucking control.'

He changed the channel. A photograph of a woman appeared on the screen, then the picture cut to a local news-reader. I had only seen the face for a second but it was enough. 'It was –' I began.

'Shut up,' said Dario, turning up the volume so that the speaker in the television rattled with the sound.

'. . . the body of fifty-seven-year-old Margaret Farrell was found yesterday evening,' said the suddenly booming voice. 'Police have begun a murder inquiry . . .'

I heard something about appealing for witnesses and house-to-house inquiries, but we were too excited to stay quiet.

'Margaret Farrell – She's Peggy!'

'Peggy!'

'We saw her last night,' said Davy, in a voice of awe. 'Me and Dario and Astrid. We saw her.'

'What? When?'

'Peggy! But it was Peggy who knocked me off my bike.'

And so it was that the following morning, instead of having a lie-in, a hot bath, an hour in the garden tending my vegetables and a stroll down to the flower market, Dario, Davy and I found ourselves sitting in the local police station, waiting to be seen by PC Jim Prebble. The horrified euphoria of last night had died away. We were tired, the reception area was drab and depressing; outside it was drizzling. Davy had a stye under his left eye and seemed to be coming down with a cold. But Dario was in the worst state: he had had only a couple of hours' sleep and we had dragged him out this morning without even a cup of coffee. What's more, he had a paranoid dread of the police. They made him feel guilty even when he was abiding by every letter of every law. So he sat there, looking like the accused, pasty-faced and fidgeting with anxiety, his eyes glancing rapidly round him.

And when at last we were called in to see PC Prebble, in a small, square room with chairs for only two of us, and the shutters closed, it was an anticlimax. Prebble was a small, stocky man with a bumpy face, like a potato, and a bristle of grey hair. He took our names and address, and heard our account of seeing – and, in my case, being hit by – Margaret Farrell, known to us as Peggy.

'What time was this?' he asked, picking up a pencil.

'About half past seven,' said Davy. He was standing behind Dario and me.

'Around seven o'clock,' said Dario, at the same time.

'No, it was nearer eight,' I said. 'Five to, something like that. I remember because I thought I'd be late for our house meeting, which was supposed to start at eight, so I was very conscious of the time and in a rush. Which was why I hit the car door so hard.'

'So. At just before eight you saw Mrs Farrell?'

'Yes.'

'Did you speak to her?'

'Yes, well, not really. I think I swore a bit.'

'You did,' said Davy, behind me. Dario sniggered.

'And what did she say?'

'I don't really remember. Sorry. She kept saying sorry.'

'She wanted to call an ambulance,' said Davy.

'And she offered to pay for the bike,' added Dario. 'She won't do that now. You can ask her husband instead.'

'Dario!' I hissed, but Prebble didn't appear to notice.

'And that was all?' he said.

'Yes. Sorry.'

'You didn't see her after that?'

We shook our heads.

'You didn't notice what direction she went in?'

'It's a bit of a blur,' I said. 'I only remember her shoes clearly.'

'Her shoes?'

'I remember lying on the ground and seeing them coming towards me. Sensible brown lace-ups. I think I might have been a bit concussed. I remember I had this vague impression there was someone else nearby, beside Dario and Davy.'

'Nope. It was just us,' said Dario, firmly.

'So it was only the two of you?' asked PC Prebble. 'Sure?'

'Yes,' said Dario.

'Yes,' echoed Davy.

'Right. You two, then, did you see where she went after the accident?'

'We were helping Astrid into the house,' said Davy. 'I didn't really pay any attention. We wanted to get her inside so she could lie down. She was quite cut up.'

'Show him your bruises,' said Dario.

'No!'

'But you're clear it was around eight?' Prebble seemed puzzled. There was a deep ridge running between his widely spaced eyes and he ran his hand over his bristle. I watched as it flattened, then sprang back into place.

'Yes.'

'Hmm,' he said.

'We just thought we ought to report it.'

'Thank you.'

'It's probably not relevant.'

'No,' he mused, chewing the end of his pencil and gazing down at the single line of writing. 'But it's good of you. You can never tell what will be helpful and what not.'

'Have you got any idea who might . . . ?'

'We're gathering information. Did any of you know Mrs Farrell?'

'Not really,' Dario said.

'I don't remember even seeing her before,' said Davy. 'But, then, I haven't lived there long.'

'Ms Bell?'

'She was just Peggy,' I said. 'Part of the street, a bit out of place, maybe, although I think she'd lived there for ages. Much longer than all of us, at any rate.'

'In what way out of place?'

'She just looked, well, like someone who should be living

in the suburbs or something,' I said. 'In a neat house surrounded by orderly neighbours. She seemed respectable, as if she belonged to an old England that's disappeared. Certainly from round here anyway. She wore what Miles calls coffee-morning clothes.'

'Meaning?'

'Meaning clothes to go to a coffee morning in, casual but smart, you know. I don't think there are many coffee mornings round Maitland Road.'

'So she didn't belong?'

I was beginning to understand what it would feel like, being a witness in a trial. The casual, vaguely gossipy remarks we'd made about poor Peggy were being pinned down, scrutinized and given a weight they simply didn't possess.

'Maybe none of us belongs. People come and go. Everything's changing, shifting, all the time. That's why I like it. It's like a film, not a photograph. You know?'

Prebble chewed his pencil, then carefully picked fragments of wood from the tip of his tongue. 'Hmm,' he said at last. 'So are you aware of her being a victim of racist attacks?'

'No!' I wished I'd stayed silent. 'I'm not really aware of anything.' I turned in desperation to Dario. 'Are you?'

'Why me?' asked Dario, shiftily. 'Why should I know?'

'She was a neighbour,' said Davy, 'but we didn't know her. That's London for you, isn't it? We just happened to see her on the day she died.'

'Was murdered.'

'Yeah. And that's it. We're not much help.'

Prebble didn't look particularly surprised or disappointed. Just tired and a little bored. We trooped out and stood on the pavement in the drizzle.

'Well, we've done our duty, for what it's worth,' said Davy. 'Let's go and have coffee and talk about something else.'

Chapter Five

Two days later, when I returned from work, I took my bike down from the hooks and looked it over. It was a sorry sight. The front wheel was buckled and wouldn't even rotate, the front fork was bent and the chain was draped round the pedals. But that was about all. I quickly removed the damaged fork, popped it into a plastic shopping bag and cycled down to Essex Road where my friend, Gerry, ran his own bike shop. He wanted to sell me a carbon-fibre replacement that cost more than the whole bike.

'Is the other person paying?' he said.

'She said she was going to,' I said.

'Well, then,' he said.

'I'm going to have a problem collecting the money.'

He looked puzzled, then rather sad when I chose a run-of-the-mill fork off the rack. He cheered up when I bought a new wheel, a chain and a helmet as well. He said he'd put it all together for me, but I don't trust anyone else near my bike, so I wobbled home with the wheel and fork balanced precariously on Campbell's handlebars.

It was still warm and sunny, so I laid the bike down in the back garden along with the new parts and my tools. I unwound the chain from the pedals and detached it from the gears. I was going to enjoy this. Then I heard a voice: 'Need some help?'

It was Miles. He came out from the kitchen holding a bottle of beer and sat on the slightly rickety bench that Dario had promised to repair. Miles had a not very funny running joke about how impractical he was at anything mechanical or electrical. It wasn't really modest: because he worked in the City as an analyst, it was part of his pose that he lived on a superior abstract plane while the rest of us did squalid, inferior things like unblocking the lavatory and replacing the fuses.

'I could help you strip down the gears,' he said, grinning. 'They probably need realigning. I could adjust the sprockets. I'm a bit worried about your cranks.'

I looked round at him wearily. 'Are you going to keep this up all evening?'

'Sorry,' he said. 'But I like watching you work. You look so . . .' He paused, staring at me. 'So very competent. Do you want a beer?'

'I was going to have one as a reward when I finished.'

I attached the fork and, with some reluctance, got Miles to hold it while I replaced the handlebars, then the star nut, the compression bolt and the stem cap.

'How do you remember where everything fits together?' he asked.

'Because I'm interested in it,' I said.

'I just care about getting from A to B. Preferably in a car.'

'How long have we got?' I asked, as I inserted the new wheel.

'Until when?'

'Until you throw us out.'

'I'm not throwing you out.'

'Well, whatever it is you're doing to us.'

'You know,' said Miles, softly, as if he was speaking to himself, 'sometimes I find myself thinking of the alternative world I could have been living in.'

For a moment I thought he was talking in a philosophical

way, about quantum physics or something. I frowned at him.

He leaned closer towards me so that I could see my own face reflected in his dark brown eyes. I felt myself tense; it took an effort not to draw back from him or look away. 'Don't you ever feel that, Astrid?'

'Feel what?'

'You know. Haunted by what might have been, could have been.'

'No.'

'Should have been.'

'I need to finish this now.'

'That's what I used to imagine when we first moved in. We were all so poor, but it didn't matter. Do you remember the anti-war march? And we came back all triumphant and had that barbecue and lay on the grass and got stoned.'

'Apparently we failed to stop the war, though.'

'And do you remember what it was like when we were first together? We'd known each other for years and then suddenly, there we were, a couple. Astrid and Miles. Miles and Astrid. I'd know you were in the room without even turning. I'd feel you. I still do, you know. They were good times, weren't they? I still remember them and can't work out why they had to end. I always believed that one day it would be just the two of us here.'

I put down the screwdriver and stared at him. Several emotions went through my mind at the same time. The first was a kind of familiar bewilderment that we could have such different versions of what had happened. In Miles's version, we had had a passionate love affair and only my contrariness and misguided, youthful desire to be independent had thwarted it. But in my version, the relationship had been flawed from the start. When we first met, he had been some kind of eco-warrior, the first person I'd ever known who was interested in politics. He represented a new world to me, and at first he had seemed glamorous and mysterious. He fell for me because he thought I was carefree and light-hearted, then spent his time trying to turn me into a different kind of woman altogether, one who was responsible, domesticated and ready to settle down. It was as if he was trying to steer me into a future he had already planned, but I didn't want to go there. I was happy in my present.

The second emotion was anxiety, because Miles was my friend: he'd been my straightforward friend before we became lovers, and my complicated friend after we were no longer lovers, and I could see now what I had been trying to ignore for months: that I had made him suffer and was still making him suffer. When the affair was finally over, I had offered to move out but he had been adamant that it wouldn't be a problem if we didn't let it be and I had allowed myself to be persuaded. My third emotion was simple anger. That was much the easiest to cope with, so I gave way gratefully to it. 'Is this why you're throwing us out?' I said sharply. 'Because we broke up?'

'We didn't break up. You ended it. But sometimes I feel that it's not over. Not really. There's too much still there. You must feel it too. I know you do.'

'Miles, no,' I said urgently. 'Please don't do this.'

'I thought time would alter everything in the end, the way it's supposed to, but I haven't changed. Not deep down.'

'I'm sorry.'

'Just don't close the door.'

'The door closed long ago,' I said, as firmly as I could. 'And it's my fault if I didn't make that clear. Listen.' I put my hand on his arm for a moment, then hastily removed it.

'You know I'm not right for you. You could do so much better than me.'

'I don't want to do better than you.'

'You don't mean it. Look at the two of us. We live in different worlds now. You've got a job you love, a fantastic future ahead of you. You're grown-up, Miles, you know what you want to do with your life. I'm not like that. I don't know where I'm going with anything. I just cycle round London delivering parcels and waiting to find out who I am.'

'So it's just that? Our circumstances?'

'No, it's not just that. I don't understand why you're suddenly saying all of this now. You're with Leah, Miles. She's bright and beautiful and you're going to live together. You shouldn't be saying these things to me. It's not fair.'

'If you told me that there was a chance, the smallest chance, then I'd tell Leah that –'

'Hello,' said Leah, cheerfully, appearing like a gleaming apparition before us in her smart work clothes, a briefcase in one hand and a paper tucked under her arm. 'Hi, my love.' She pulled off her jacket and sat next to Miles, leaned over and kissed him lingeringly on the cheek. Then she smiled at me, her teeth white, her skin smooth. She smelled faintly of apples, while Miles smelled of beer. I smelled of sweat and bike oil. 'That looks terribly clever. I can't even repair a puncture. I just take it into the shop. I used to feel I ought to learn, and then I worked out that if I priced my time, I was actually losing money by doing repairs myself.'

'I suppose it depends how you price your time,' I said, winding the new chain round the chain-ring. I was trying not to look at her. Had she heard any of the conversation?

'Yes,' she said. 'It does.'

And that was the end of that. Miles sat and watched me

work. Leah read the paper, glancing up frequently to watch us through narrowed eyes. I felt as if I was in a cage in a zoo with people staring at me through the bars.

'You don't have to move out until you're ready,' said Miles, eventually answering the question that had sparked off his declaration to me.

'Three months, wasn't that what we agreed?' Leah spoke without raising her head from the paper.

'I don't remember,' muttered Miles.

'I mean, you're not still students,' said Leah. 'You can't go on living like this for ever. I think it's amazing that Miles has let you live here all these years.'

I didn't speak but I did cast a look towards Miles that had an element of sarcasm in it.

'Strictly speaking,' said Miles, 'they paid rent and helped out with things.'

'If you mean Dario's DIY, I'm not sure it was necessarily adding value.'

The chain was attached and I sprayed the moving parts with lube. I lifted the bike so that the back wheel was off the ground and worked the pedal so that it spun in a blur of silver. It was a beautiful sight. Time for that beer.

'What was that woman called?' said Leah. 'The one who was murdered.'

'Peggy,' I said.

'Farrell,' said Miles. 'Margaret Farrell.'

'They've arrested some people.'

Miles grabbed the paper and scanned it. 'There's not much,' he said. 'Four teenagers, who "cannot be named for legal reasons". They've been arrested in connection with the murder and robbery of Margaret Farrell. Well, it's not hard to guess where they're from.'

'Where?' asked Leah.

'They're those feral kids from the estate. They'll probably get two weeks' community service.'

'Why couldn't they just have stolen her purse?' I said. 'Why did they have to kill her?'

'That was part of the thrill,' said Miles, grimly. 'They probably filmed it on their mobiles.'

'It's funny being so close to something,' I said. 'And we don't really know anything about it and we probably never will. I guess they'll plead guilty in a few months' time and that will be that and we'll never hear anything more about it.'

'There's nothing to hear,' said Miles.

Miles was wrong and I was wrong. After three more days, cleaning, shopping, a couple of parties, a movie with Saul, and three more nights, I found myself sitting in a room with a detective. PC Prebble had met me at the desk and led me through. I sat alone in the room and looked around. There was almost nothing to see. No windows, no pictures. The walls were painted beige. There was speckled lino on the floor, the sort that is easy to clean and doesn't show dirt. There was a table with two moulded plastic chairs, and two more piled up against the wall.

The door opened and a head poked round. 'Miss Bell?'

'I'm Astrid Bell.'

The man came in. He was middle-aged, large, made larger by a grey suit very slightly too small for him. He was almost bald with his remaining hair cut very short. 'I'm Detective Inspector Mitchell,' he said. 'Thank you for coming.'

'I was surprised,' I said.

He walked over and sat opposite me. 'Why?'

'I talked to the policeman and told him I had pretty much nothing to say, and then I heard that some people had been arrested so I thought that was the last I'd hear of it all.'

He leaned back on his chair with his hands laced behind his head and looked thoughtful. 'This morning we charged the four young tearaways . . .'

'So why . . . ?'

'With breaking and entering. Namely Mrs Farrell's car.'

'If they did that, they must have killed her as well.'

'Did someone offer you coffee?'

'Yes.'

'You'll probably be asked to fill in a form so that we can improve our service to the public. It asks questions like were you made comfortable, were you offered refreshments.'

'Well, I was.'

'I'm glad to hear it.'

'You were telling me about the murder.'

'Was I?' said Mitchell. 'Oh, yes. We have CCTV cameras rigged up at various entry-points at the William Morris flats. We clocked these four gentlemen wandering past the Dyson Street camera at eleven forty p.m. on their way out of the estate, and fourteen minutes later we clocked them coming back, passing between them a bottle of Bacardi rum they had lifted from Mrs Farrell's car.'

'So they did it.'

'They didn't force entry to her car, because it seems to have been unlocked – perhaps because of damage done to it during your collision. They didn't bother with the CD player. You can't give them away now. But they emptied her shopping and took two bottles of spirits and her mobile phone, which was attached to the in-car charger.'

'It doesn't sound worth killing someone for.'

Mitchell shrugged. 'The first murder I ever worked on, a kid was killed by a classmate because he wouldn't hand over his lunch money. Anyway, the receipt was still in one of the bags. It showed that Mrs Farrell completed her purchases at Tesco at seven twenty-eight p.m. What time was it that you saw her?'

'It was a bit before eight.'

'You'll see the problem. We found Mrs Farrell's body partially concealed behind the dustbins in the area down by the basement at the front of her house. She had been strangled and there were some signs of robbery. Her purse was missing, and so, according to her husband, were her watch and necklace. She had left her car unlocked and the burglar alarm inside her house was still engaged. You see?'

'Not really,' I said.

At that moment the door opened and PC Prebble came into the room with a plastic mug of coffee. He placed it on the table with two small plastic milk capsules, two sachets of sugar and a dish on which lay two digestive biscuits. 'I didn't know if you took sugar or milk,' he said, 'or if you were hungry.'

'Just black is fine,' I said, and took a sip. It was stewed and lukewarm.

Prebble didn't leave. He took one of the seats in the corner and sat on it. Mitchell gave a sign and continued: 'At about eight o'clock, Mrs Farrell opens her car door and you collide with it. She helps you and is profusely apologetic, but your housemates appear on the scene and take over. Is that right?'

'Dario and Davy were sitting out on the steps having a . . . er . . . just chatting and they saw what happened and came and helped me.'

'Mrs Farrell has her shopping in the car. She leaves you to be helped into the house. What is she going to do next?'

'Go into her house, I suppose.'

'Collect her shopping, take it inside. But from what we can tell, she never went back to her car to take out the shopping and never opened her front door. Her husband was away that night, and the lads from the estate didn't arrive until four hours later.'

I thought for a moment. 'On the other hand, they could have attacked her, concealed her body and come back later to rob her car. Under the cover of darkness.'

Mitchell's hitherto grim face broke into a broad smile and he looked across at Prebble, who smiled back. 'It's a theory,' he said. 'It's a crap theory. But it's a theory.'

'But you probably didn't bring me in here to get my ideas about the case.'

'We're always grateful for input,' said Mitchell. 'But what really interests me is what you saw.'

'The problem,' I said, 'and I feel really bad about this, is that I didn't see anything.'

'But you were there,' said Mitchell. 'You were there when it happened.'

There was a long silence.

'I'm sorry,' I said. 'I almost want to say, "Ask me anything but that." I've got a very good memory. Ask me about my first day at primary school, every holiday I've ever been on. Next week I'll remember the colour of the tie you're wearing. But in that moment when I ran into Mrs Farrell's car door, I didn't take in anything at all. I didn't even know it was her. I hit the door, I hit the ground, I heard someone apologize and I was dragged inside. My memory's like a faded fax of a bad photocopy. You can use a magnifying-glass, but all you'll see is a mess and a blur.'

I expected Mitchell to look depressed or cross. I thought he might send me home like a bad girl. But he smiled. 'Don't worry, Miss Bell,' he said. 'Compared with some witnesses, you're like Mr Memory. I'm going to bring in another officer and you're going to say everything you know, and she'll write it down.'

'It won't take very long,' I said.

He smiled again.

'Oh, yes, it will.'

For me the police had always been vague, abstract figures. I saw them in their cars, blue lights flashing in the darkness, or walking along the street, and I felt slightly anxious, as if I might be doing something wrong without realizing it, and that when their eyes settled on my face they would see a furtive criminal. Night after night I saw them on Maitland Road and in Hackney, stopping black youths and searching them, standing in pairs with walkie-talkies crackling, shepherding the violently drunk or the stupefied stoned into the backs of their vans. Before Peggy's murder I had never been into a police station, except the one occasion when I'd reported a stolen wallet, and then I'd only got as far as the front desk. I don't know what I'd been expecting, and I was sheepishly surprised to discover they seemed quite normal, not brutal or racist or ignorant or fiendishly clever – just slightly bored and harassed men and women doing their job and thinking about what they would do once their shift was over.

Of the three of us, it was definitely Dario who was having difficulty in talking to them.

'They're not interested in you taking drugs,' said Davy, before we were all interviewed that second time. 'They're interested in who killed Peggy. Right, Astrid?'

'I know that,' said Dario. 'But I've got this feeling I'll break out in a sweat and just announce it. I won't be able to stop myself. I once heard about this guy going through

Customs. Nobody was interested in him, and he suddenly started crying and confessed he'd got cocaine in the false bottom to a set of knives and forks he was carrying.'

'Knives and forks?' said Davy.

'Yes, but that's not the point. The point is, I'm going to confess to something. I can feel it. They'll look at me and I'll break.'

'The point is,' I said, 'someone's been murdered.'

'I don't know anything. I've told them everything I know.'

'Tell them again. Then sign your name at the bottom and that'll be that.'

Of course, it could never be that simple. Someone had been killed a few yards from where we lived, a few minutes after we had spoken to her. It almost felt as if she had been killed before our very eyes, but we hadn't noticed. I knew her face, her name. Every time I passed the house, I looked down into the recess where the bins had stood, and where her body had been crammed, and imagined her there. After a couple of days, the space started to fill with flowers and messages, and after a week or so the flowers started to rot in the Cellophane wrapping, giving out a sweet stench that made me want to gag. I looked at people in the street, at the gangs of youths who hung around in the balmy evenings, and wondered if it had been any of them, or if they knew something they weren't saying. I had always thought of Maitland Road as rough and down-at-heel, but it was my home and I felt safe there. What had once seemed normal now took on an air of menace. When I heard footsteps behind me in the dark, my heart beat faster; shadows seemed to move; faces were sinister. The road hissed with rumours: the husband had been arrested and charged; the husband had been released; the police knew which of the gang from the estate had done it but had insufficient evidence; there were drugs involved; it was a mugging gone wrong; it was an accident. She had been shot, stabbed, strangled, hit over the head with a stone, raped. I even heard that one of her hands had been cut off. Everyone knew better than everyone else. Everyone knew Peggy better than everyone else. People remembered conversations they had probably never had with her. People who had never said hello to her missed her. People who had never said hello to me now sought me out because – by slamming into her open car door and landing in a dazed, cursing heap on the road – I had become a star witness, someone to know.

At the same time, another change was taking place closer to home. Suddenly we were just temporary tenants. A few days ago I'd been thinking of the seven of us as my strange rag-bag family. Now the others had reverted to a collection of individuals, and I found myself thinking: Will I still know you in a year's time? Who would I stay in touch with? I felt sure about Pippa; perhaps I would even ask her to share my next flat. And pretty sure about Miles, too – even if he was the ex-lover who harboured nostalgic desires for me and the landlord who was evicting me, even if he was a well-paid economist who was dating a well-paid architect and who owned a desirable property on the borders of Stoke Newington, while I was just a despatch rider. Dario and Davy I was less certain about. I could imagine gradually drifting apart from them, getting together for quick drinks between more important appointments, the intervals between each meeting becoming longer, the common ground dwindling into a series of anecdotes about our shared past. Eventually, perhaps, they would become people I would bump into in a pub and kiss on the cheek and say hello to and promise to give them a call soon, very soon. It was hard to believe that I would keep in touch with Mick – I didn't feel in touch with him while I was living in the same house. And as for Owen, I didn't even know if I liked him, and I was pretty sure he didn't like me. Or perhaps it was simply that he didn't see me; he couldn't even be bothered to look.

Chapter Six

The third time I felt as if I was interviewing Detective Inspector Mitchell. As he made me tell the story all over again, he shifted in his chair, fidgeted with a pen, rubbed his scalp, adjusted his tie, failed to meet my gaze.

'There we are,' I said, when I'd finished. 'The same story. Told in the same words.'

'No,' he muttered. 'It's not the same.'

'What do you mean?' I said. 'Did I get something wrong?'

He reached into a bag on the floor, removed a file and pushed it across the desk. He nodded at me, so I opened it. There was page after typewritten page. 'What's this?'

'It's the physical-traces report from the crime scene.'

'It looks very detailed.'

'If you read page four, you'll see an account of the glass fragments found on Mrs Farrell's coat.'

'So?'

'They're from a supermarket-brand vodka bottle. The fragments were scattered round her body and underneath it. Hence they became attached to the material of her coat. One such bottle is duly referred to on the receipt found in Mrs Farrell's car.'

'Well, I'm glad that's been cleared up,' I said. 'I was wondering where the bottle of vodka had got to.'

'Shut up,' said Mitchell.

'What?'

He got up and paced the room. 'I hate this fucking case,' he said.

'Why?'

'Everything's wrong,' he said. 'The yobs who stole the property aren't the people who killed her. And now this.'

'I'm sorry,' I said. 'I don't see . . .'

He sat down and jabbed a plump finger at me. 'Listen,' he said. 'You remember our scenario?'

'*Your* scenario.'

'Mrs Farrell knocks you over. She attends to you, leaving her car unlocked, her shopping inside. She is attacked, robbed, murdered, dumped. Then, some hours later, the gang from William Morris help themselves to the alcohol. As we now know, they drink the vodka on the spot and toss it down into the recess in front of number fifty-four, where it smashed.'

He paused and stared at me meaningfully.

'Is this a problem?'

'Yes,' he said. 'It's a problem. When they threw the bottle down, it should have landed on Mrs Farrell's body.'

'So it missed her.'

'What?' said Mitchell, sarcastically. 'And the fragments lifted her body and positioned themselves under it?'

'Maybe somebody else took the vodka. It could have been the same person who killed her.'

Mitchell tossed another file across the table. 'Fingerprint report,' he said. 'It was them, all right. Her body fell, or was placed there, after the bottle had been smashed.'

'If that's true, the gang could have killed her after all.'

'So she sat in her car for three hours?'

'People do strange things. She might have been locked out.'

'Oh, stop that,' said Mitchell, wearily. 'She had her keys. She wasn't in her bloody car. So where was she for those hours? With her car unlocked and her shopping in it? And why did she come back?'

'Is that what you've brought me in to ask?'

He leaned across the table. 'I want you to be sure, absolutely sure, that you've told me everything you know.'

'I have,' I said.

'All right,' he said. 'Tell me again.'

I was on my way to my room and looked up to see Dario peering down through the banisters, beckoning me, his face a parody of conspiratorial secrecy. 'What is it?'

'Up here,' he hissed.

I shrugged and made my way up to the second floor where he and Mick had rooms. As always, Mick's door was closed, but Dario's was wide open. Probably he couldn't even shut it any more: half-empty paint pots, hardened brushes, bottles of turpentine and a rusty saw blocked the entrance and spilled out into the corridor, along with the strange items he collected from skips and dumps all round East London. I stepped over a tennis racket with broken strings and made my way round a small trestle table, into the unspeakable squalor and sweet stench of the room. It was hard even to make out the bed, amid the stacks of old furniture he'd amassed: two desks, on top of each other, one without any legs; a wooden towel rack; a fraying wicker Moses basket filled to overflowing with pewter plates and mugs; a large blue trunk with brass handles; three ladder-backed chairs in various stages of disintegration; an armchair piled with clothes; a supermarket trolley on its side, one wheel missing; a little carved chest; two cardboard suitcases. Dario always said he was going to do them up and sell them.

'What's up?' I asked.

'Take a seat?'

'Where?'

'You could lie in the hammock,' he said. 'Or I've got some deckchairs I found the other day I could open up. They're a bit cobwebby, though.'

'I'll stand. What's up?'

'I just wanted to know what they were after this time?'

As I gave a brief account of Mitchell, his anguish and confusion, Dario lit a joint and took a deep drag. The sweet smell filled the room. He flicked ash on to the floor and offered it to me, but I shook my head.

'Does my head in,' he said.

'He has this feeling that we were there when it happened. I don't exactly know how. Nor does he.'

'It's going to end badly,' Dario said. 'For me probably.'

'You know,' I said, 'I've gone over and over it in my mind and I've tried and tried to remember.'

'Yeah, you said.'

'There's just one thing, but when I came off my bike and you and Davy came over, I've got some memory that someone else was there. Or maybe I was concussed.'

'That was some bang when you hit the road.'

I gave up. 'I can't think about this any more. It makes my brain hurt. I'm going to go and get myself a coffee.'

'I'll come with you,' he said, and followed me down three flights of stairs into the kitchen. Mick was sitting at the table, shelling monkey nuts and then, with a look of great determination, throwing each one high into the air and trying to catch it in his mouth. I said hello to him but he didn't stop, though a nut bounced off his nose. I went over to the back door and gazed out on to the long strip of garden. 'Let's go out somewhere, to a club or the movies or something,' I said. 'I don't feel like hanging round here talking about dead people.

But then we heard the front door opening and closing, and footsteps coming down the stairs: Miles and Leah, both cool and elegant. Leah had a couple of bottles of chilled white wine for the household, which was nice of her, but she also had one of those metal tape measures that extend for metres, then kink in the middle, and a notebook. She poured herself some wine and opened the tape measure.

'Right,' she said cheerfully. 'Let's get to work.'

'Plans?' I asked.

'We thought we could make this room really lovely,' said Leah.

'It *is* really lovely,' said Dario, dolefully. 'I've only just finished painting it.'

'It's too dark. We need to open it up, make the most of its size. It should be full of light, leading into the garden like it does,' Leah continued, as if he hadn't spoken. 'It should almost feel like being outside when you're inside.'

'Architects' fucking bollocks,' said Mick.

Leah stared at him and Mick stared back, then threw a nut at the window.

'What did he just say?' Leah asked Miles, who shrugged uncomfortably. 'As I was saying,' she continued, with a visible effort, turning away from Miles and talking to me, though I really wasn't interested in hearing her ideal-home plans. 'Then if we make that first bit of garden a patio area with benches and chairs and pots, it'll be like a continuation of the room.'

'You mean where the vegetable patch is?' I said.

'That's right.'

There was a pause, like when you're waiting for a firework to go off.

'I tell you what,' I said, getting up from my chair and putting a hand on Dario's bony shoulder, 'I think we shouldn't go to a film. I think we should go and have a picnic in the park. Right now. It's such a gorgeous evening.'

Dario, Mick and I ransacked the fridge for bits to eat. Pippa arrived with a tall man in a dark suit and a slim black briefcase, and sent him to buy more food from the corner shop. Then, as we were leaving, Davy turned up with a lovely young woman in tow. She had shoulder-length brown hair, and large brown eyes, fair skin and pink cheeks; he introduced her as Mel and she blushed, smiled and shook our hands in turn.

'Come for a picnic,' I said.

'We were going out to eat,' began Mel, hesitantly.

'Great idea,' said Davy. He grinned at Mel. 'It's an initiation rite, but I'll protect you. Let me have a shower first.'

After the world's shortest shower, Davy collected his frisbee and Dario took a large rug from Miles's room. I put plastic cups into a bag with Leah's wine. The park was just a few minutes' walk from the house, less if you climbed over the fence. It was not a very beautiful park – no ponds and walkways and landscaped views of London, no deer grazing inside well-tended enclosures – but it was beautiful this evening, green and tranquil in the dusk. There was no wind, and everything was very still, as if waiting. We made our way across the grass, strewn with plastic bags, cigarette ends, crumpled cans, to the chestnut tree, where we spread the rug and laid out our random assortment of food. As I was pouring wine into the plastic beakers I saw Owen walking towards us and raised a cup to him. He had his camera with him, and he stopped a few feet away from us and started taking photos.

'How do we look?' I called.

He lowered the camera. 'How should I know? I'm interested in that tree and its shadow.'

'Flattering,' I said.

He frowned at me, not smiling, then put away his camera, sat on the grass and pulled out a pack of cigarettes. Pippa's friend, whose name I never found out, used his briefcase as a small table on which to assemble messy sandwiches. We threw the frisbee to each other until the light became too murky to continue. Then we lounged on the grass and talked and didn't talk. Pippa and her latest sat with their legs tangled: I saw Davy and Mel shyly holding hands when they thought no one was looking. Dario lay flat on his back with a joint clamped between his lips, snorting smoke through his nostrils. He was giving a garbled account of my meeting with DI Mitchell to Mick and anyone else who would listen. Mick wasn't paying much attention but he seemed more at ease than usual. He was wearing a black singlet and I noticed for the first time that he had a tattoo on his shoulder: two intersecting spirals that moved and expanded when he flexed his muscles.

I slid over the grass towards Davy, and he and Mel moved apart.

'Sorry to butt in,' I said. 'I just wanted to ask you something. You know the police hauled me in again?'

'I heard,' said Davy. 'What's going on?'

'I think they're desperate,' I said. 'You know when you've lost something and you start looking in the places you've already looked? I think that's what they're doing. I just wanted to ask you something that's been getting on my nerves. You know when you and Dario ran out to help me in the street?'

Davy grinned. 'I'm not likely to forget it, am I?'

'I know I asked you before, but I still have this nagging impression that there was someone with you. Someone who said goodbye to Dario, or Dario said goodbye to him. Or her. Dario said there wasn't and I don't mean to doubt his word, but this is a murder we're talking about and if there's anything we can do to help . . .'

'Of course,' said Davy. I thought he looked slightly uncomfortable, but perhaps I was imagining things. 'Maybe there was someone – but if there was, Dario's the one you should ask.'

'I have asked him. You're telling me there was, aren't you?'

'I'm not telling you anything. It was sunny. I was tired. I was sitting on the steps, with my eyes closed, probably, letting everything drift over me, you know how it is.'

'Your eyes were closed?'

'I dunno. Maybe, is all I'm saying. They were open for your accident, though. It makes you realize how unreliable memory is, doesn't it? If you ask someone in advance to remember everything that happens, that's what they do. But if you ask them afterwards – well, ninety per cent has gone over their head. My head, I mean.'

'OK,' I said, not satisfied.

'What are you two conspiring about?' said Pippa. 'Are you planning to tell Miles we're sitting tenants and we're never leaving?'

'The police hauled Astrid in,' said Davy. 'Gave her the third degree yet again.'

'I should call you in as my lawyer,' I said.

'Any time, darling,' she said.

'Charge my client,' I said. 'Or let her walk.' Then a thought occurred to me. I looked round. Her partner of the evening was far enough away, pouring himself another glass of wine. I spoke to her in a quieter voice: 'Pippa, do you remember that guy who stayed over the night I had my accident?'

'Just about.' She gave a coy giggle, which irritated me.

'You might want to mention him to the police. They really want to talk to anyone who was in the area. He may have seen something when he arrived.'

Pippa's expression turned frosty. 'We didn't see anything.'

'Even so,' I said. 'It might be worth mentioning.'

'It's not really a good idea,' she said.

'Married, by any chance?' said Davy.

Pippa shot him a fierce glance. 'It would be awkward,' she said.

'Anyway,' I said, 'you didn't see anything.'

'Exactly.'

I sighed. I'd done my duty as a responsible citizen, and I didn't want to think about Peggy any more, not this evening, anyway. I went back to where I'd been sitting and lowered myself on to the grass. I lay on my back next to Owen and gazed dreamily up into the sky, which was fading from turquoise to silver grey. The trees' branches were massed darkly above me, and through them I could make out the faint outline of the half-moon. I closed my eyes.

Then Dario lobbed the frisbee towards me, spilling my wine, and the spell was broken. I sat up, cursed Dario and poured myself some more. In the thick evening light, I looked across the park. From where we were, I could see the roof of our house. Leah and Miles were there, planning how it would look once we were out of the way. They'd change bedrooms into studies and extra bathrooms, knock down walls, throw old beds and sagging sofas into a skip, paint over all the marks and stains that had accumulated through the years, until nothing would be left to show that we had lived there. Time to move on, I thought, but I'd never felt less like moving on than that evening in the park.

As the air cooled and the day faded, we saw another figure walking towards us. It was Miles. He didn't say anything, just sat down beside me, so close that our hips touched and I could feel his warmth through the material of my jeans. I poured out the dregs of the wine for him, smiling at him to make peace. He put his hand over mine and I let him, just this once.

'It's fine,' I told him. 'Like you said, we couldn't stay there for ever.'

'She's measuring windows now,' he said gloomily. 'You don't think she could by any chance be pregnant, do you?'

I didn't want the day to end. After everyone had wandered off to their own rooms, I went out into the garden. The last warmth of the day had gone and it was clear and cool. I sat on Dario's creaky little bench for a while and looked at the house: the lights in the rooms went off one by one. Only the kitchen glowed. Then I stood up and walked to the end of the garden, where I stared out over the other houses stretching in either direction, with their fences and their long gardens, and beyond them the tall, patchily illuminated tower blocks. So many people all around me; so many strangers up close. In the distance, I could hear music, the bass note jumping. Then, abruptly, it stopped and there was a sudden, unnerving silence.

I turned back to the house and started. Someone was standing a few feet away from me. 'What are you doing here?'

'You don't have exclusive rights to the garden, do you?'

'Why do you always have to be so aggressive? I'm not in the mood tonight, OK?'

Owen shrugged and struck a match; his face flared into view as he held it up to the cigarette between his lips.

'Can I have one too?'

'You don't smoke.'

'I do, sometimes.'

'Here.' He held out the packet but I stayed where I was, so he was forced to cross the patch of grass separating us. He shook out a cigarette, handed it over, then lit it for me.

I felt a violent thrill of hostility towards him. 'You won't mind, anyway,' I said, breathing a curl of smoke into his face.

'Mind what?'

'Leaving.'

'It's a pain, having to find somewhere new.'

'You've hardly made an effort to be part of the house, have you?' I continued. 'You don't see us, do you? You don't notice when we're there and when we're not. We could be anyone. There are days when I can't remember you even saying good morning or goodnight, let alone "Do you want coffee?" or "I'm going to the shop, is there anything you need?"'

'I'll try to remember.'

'Don't bother.'

He dropped his fag end and it winked like a small red eye between us. I threw mine after it. Then he put one hand against my stomach and pushed me so that I stumbled backwards. He stepped after me and pushed me once more. Now the tree was sharp against my back. I slapped his cheek and in the half-dark saw him wince. Good. He bent forward and kissed me hard. I reached up and put my hands in his thick hair and pulled him closer, tasting blood, his or mine I didn't know. Layers of clothing coming loose, buttons snapping, zips torn apart, teeth on skin, hands on each other's body, breath in gasps, muttered curses.

'Not here,' I said.

'Why not?' he said.

I couldn't think why not. Couldn't think. Now we were on the rough ground, pushed up against the fence at the back, pricked by thorns and bits of bark. It was messy and undignified. He had to tug my jeans off, and then he was against me, inside me, and all the bits of my body I'd thought were healed hurt again. Every bruise throbbed. His eyes shone in the night.

'I don't even like you,' I said, when at last we rolled away from each other.

He didn't speak for a moment, just lay with his arms outstretched, staring at the sky. Then he got to his feet, tucking his ripped shirt into his jeans.

'Goodnight,' he said, standing over me where I lay with my undone clothes and my battered body. 'Or is it good morning?'

And with that he was gone. I waited a few moments before scrambling up and leaning against the fence, touching my puffy lips with the tips of my fingers. Then I, too, went indoors, into the silent, sleeping house. Owen's light was already out when I crept up the stairs. I tugged off my clothes, washed myself in the basin, trying not to see my face in the mirror. I tumbled into my bed, and waited for sleep.

I don't know what woke me. Perhaps it was because I hadn't bothered to close my curtains, and I could see from where I lay that the sky was already getting light. Birds were singing violently outside. I turned my head and saw on my mobile that it was five o'clock. I closed my eyes again and willed myself to sink back into sleep, but it was no good. I remembered the previous night and felt heavy and sick, consumed with desire.

I swung my legs out of bed, pulled on my dressing-gown and opened the door. Not a sound from the house. Everyone was sleeping. I tiptoed along the hall, turned the handle of Owen's door with an agonizing click. He was lying with the covers pushed down to his waist and one hand dangling over the edge of the bed. I closed the door softly behind me and crossed to him. He didn't stir, until I climbed into the bed beside him and pulled the thin duvet over our two bodies and kissed his shoulder, his neck, his stomach. He gave a small groan but still kept his eyes shut and didn't speak. He turned on to his side and slid a hand between my legs. The belt of my dressing-gown tangled between us and I wriggled out of it and threw it on the floor. We were very quiet. I put a hand over his mouth when he came.

'You haven't even opened your eyes,' I said.

'Perhaps you're not who I think you are,' he said. I rolled off the bed and pulled on my dressing-gown. He opened his eyes at last and looked at me. 'And I haven't even seen you naked, Astrid Bell.'

'Nor will you. This is such a bad idea.'

'It isn't an idea at all,' Owen said. He put out a hand, ran it up my leg, and I shivered helplessly.

Chapter Seven

'That's such a nice jacket,' said Orla.

'Oh, thanks,' I said. 'I just wear it for my job.'

'You a photographer as well?'

'I'm a bike messenger,' I said. 'I'm being Owen's assistant for the afternoon. Carrying his bags and holding up the silver umbrella.'

'Where'd you get it?'

'The jacket? Another rider gave it to me,' I said. 'He was from Poland. I think he got it there.'

'Excuse me,' said Owen, with a nasty politeness. 'We haven't really got much time.'

'It's great,' said Orla. 'Poland?'

'I think so. Perhaps we should get on with the shoot, though. As Owen said, we are running a bit –'

'Is there a toilet here?' asked Orla.

Owen looked at her. His expression didn't change but I saw him clench his fists. 'Outside and up the stairs,' he said.

'Ta.'

Orla – allegedly one of the ten most promising young actresses in the UK – scampered out of the studio, pulling the door shut behind her with a loud bang. Owen rubbed his eyes with his knuckles and wandered over to the small window that gave out on to the street. He leaned his head against the pane and closed his eyes.

'Are you OK?' I asked.

'What in hell am I doing here?' he said.

'It's not that bad. It's going to be fine.'

'The picture editor wants "vivacious".'

That morning, Owen had phoned me as I was cycling past King's Cross and asked me if I would help him out. He didn't ask me very politely and he made no reference at all to the fact that in the past few hours we'd had sex twice. 'Say "please",' I said sweetly.

'Please,' he muttered.

I told myself it would be a change from delivering packages, anyway, and called Campbell to inform him that I wouldn't be available for the afternoon. As a last-minute stand-in, Owen had been commissioned to take a portrait for a feature on young British talent. Nineteen-year-old Orla Porter, rake-thin, pasty and pouty, had been the star of a TV soap I had never seen and she was apparently about to become famous in a film that hadn't come out yet. But she wasn't a real star yet. She didn't have an entourage, a press representative, a makeup artist. She had just shown up at Owen's friend's studio and said she had to, absolutely had to, leave by four. And she hadn't looked vivacious once, except on the subject of my jacket.

'Ah,' I said. 'I see. Vivacious. I see.'

'She looks depressed,' said Owen. 'Depressed and ill. She looks like a rubber band. There's no life in her. I hate jobs like this – artificial photographs of fake celebrities wearing too much makeup and too few clothes, who've been spoilt rotten by attention but who'll get dumped next season. Look at the pages of the magazines – these women all end up looking the same. You can hardly tell them apart. And that's what everyone wants. They don't want a real photograph. It's just a con and I'm part of the whole stupid process.' He turned away from the window and faced me. 'Why the fuck am I doing it?'

'For the money?'

'Yeah. *Money.*' He snarled the word at me, as if it was an obviously bad thing.

'What's the problem? Don't take yourself so seriously, Owen.'

'That's it. I'm out of here.'

And he actually started picking up his equipment and stuffing it clumsily into bags. I put my hand on his forearm, but he pulled away. 'Fuck off,' he said. 'You're just like the rest.'

'The rest of what? The capitalist system? Humanity?'

I tugged at the bag he was holding but he wrenched it back and it fell with a thud. A zoom lens rolled across the floor. 'Have you any idea what that costs?'

'I'm just a stupid bike messenger, remember? But it doesn't matter, does it? It's just money, after all.'

He gripped me by the forearm; I could feel his fingers digging into my flesh.

'You're hurting.'

'You're asking to be hurt.'

'I never ask to be hurt.'

'Oh, excuse me.' Orla's drawl made us spring apart. 'Am I interrupting something here?'

'Nothing at all,' I said brightly.

Owen muttered something and retrieved the lens. I had thought Orla might have gone to the toilet to snort some coke. No such luck. She was as lackadaisical as ever, and asked if she could have something to drink before we resumed. 'Sure,' I said. 'Coffee, tea, water, orange juice, cranberry?'

'Do you have mint tea?'

'No, sorry.'

'Or camomile?'

'Just Tetley's.'

She winced. 'Is the coffee decaffeinated?'

'Not as such.'

'What kind of water?'

'Tap,' I said.

She made another disgusted face. 'I've got a headache,' she said.

'Do you want a paracetamol?'

'No.'

'Would you like to reschedule this for tomorrow?' asked Owen. His voice was soft and creepy.

It didn't bother Orla, though. 'I'm on set tomorrow,' she said.

'Then we'll just have to do it now, won't we?'

'S'pose.'

Owen unscrewed his camera from the stand and walked over to her. 'I'd like to make things a bit more casual, less posed,' he said. 'But you know that the magazine wants you animated, happy. Do you think you could manage that?'

Orla just shrugged and stayed in exactly the same position, staring into the lens. Owen took some photographs and Orla was as unresponsive as it was possible to look. She didn't even glower.

'Orla,' said Owen, eventually. I could see a muscle working in his jaw.

'Yeah?'

'You're an actress, aren't you? Can't you manage one small smile? Look at you – you could be made of wax. Not my idea of sexy at all.'

'There's no need to be so rude. I think I'm going to call my agent and ask for someone else to photograph me.'

I looked at Owen, standing there clutching his camera as

69

if he was about to bludgeon her with it. Then I nodded at Orla. 'Can I have a moment?' I said.

'Astrid?' said Owen. 'You want a fucking girls' chat now? You want to find out how she puts on her makeup?'

'Behave,' I said. I signalled to Orla to follow me across to the far side of the huge studio. We were standing by a window, latticed with steel bars, that looked out over the canal. It was raining, the drops dimpling the surface of the grey water. I took my jacket off.

'You said you liked it,' I said. 'I want to give it to you.'

'Are you sure?' she said, unsurprised. 'That's really kind of you.'

'It'll suit you,' I said.

She pulled on the jacket with the eagerness of a small child.

'Could you do me a favour in return?' I said.

She stood in front of a full-length mirror on the wall opposite the window and admired herself. 'What?'

'Like Owen said, you're an actress,' I said. 'I know it's grim and you're tired, but for the next five minutes, could you play the part of a person who's happy and vivacious and having a really great time?'

Orla's expression was thoughtful, then she looked round at me and smiled, her eyes suddenly illuminated as if from the inside, her thin face radiant and sweet with imitation joy. 'Sure,' she said. 'What's the problem?'

'Astrid?'

We were walking back along the canal, through the gathering rain, both carrying a bag with Owen's cameras and equipment.

'Yeah?'

'Thanks.'

'You're welcome.'

'Except that I hate myself for not kicking her out on her little arse.'

'Don't hate yourself.'

'I'll buy you another jacket.'

'I didn't even like it that much.'

'And you're getting wet and cold. Put this on.'

He took off his own and put it over my shoulders. 'Are you always this forgiving?' he asked.

'Of you or her?'

'Doesn't matter.'

The rain was heavy now, ploughing up the canal and pattering in the leaves of the trees. It trickled down my neck and bounced off my nose. I could hear the water squelching in my shoes. Owen's hair was plastered to his skull and his shirt was wet through.

'Dario will have used up all the hot water,' I said.

'Do you want to get a bus or a cab?'

'Not unless you do.'

'I quite enjoy walking in the rain.'

We walked in silence, taking care not to touch and not looking at each other but staring ahead at the muddy path, the grey water. I was hot and cold at the same time.

We went under a bridge and in the half-light, without knowing we were going to, we stopped and kissed urgently, pressed up against the damp wall, water dripping from our hair and running down our cheeks like tears. Our wet clothes clung to us. Then we moved apart and set off along the canal again. Owen hadn't even let go of his bag full of equipment.

'Do you like being a despatch rider?' he said.

'Kind of. I don't want to do it for ever. Who wants to be a despatch rider when they're sixty? I've already been doing

71

it longer than I thought I would. I thought it was just for a few weeks in the summer while I made up my mind what I wanted to do next, and that was a year ago.'

'So why did you continue?'

'Because I never made up my mind what I wanted to do next. I was studying law, you know. That's how I met Pippa. But I never really knew why I was doing it. I went travelling instead, worked abroad. It's been fun, but at some point I guess I'll have to get a grown-up job. It's odd, isn't it? I mean, I look at someone like Miles. When I first met him he was radical and dangerous. He was always going on about individual freedom and the way the system imprisons you. But what was I expecting? That Miles should still be chaining himself to trees and Dario should do botched painting jobs and get stoned and I should cycle round London until I drop dead in the saddle? And that we should all live like students in Maitland Road for ever and ever? Maybe that's why we're upset about moving. Because it means we have to look at our lives.'

'Maybe.'

'Are we having a conversation?'

'I don't know. Perhaps not. You're doing most of the talking: I'm just letting you.'

'Oh. Well, I won't say anything else, then.'

But he took me by the wrist, pulled me to a halt again and stared at me in the streaming rain. 'Listen. You know you said I didn't even see you. It's not true. I see you. Here, look at your cheekbones, you could be from Lapland. Your eyes are set wide apart. You've got quite a sharp collarbone' – with one finger, he traced it – 'and strong arms and a flat stomach. On your shoulders, under your shirt, you've got small prominent knots of muscle. But then you've got these full breasts and –'

'You're talking about me as if I wasn't here. I don't like it. Stop it.'

'I'd like to photograph you.'

'I don't know if that's such a good idea.'

'All the contradictions.'

'Didn't you hear me? I'm not one of your subjects.'

'A beautiful object, an object of desire.'

'Oh, please.'

'Black-and-white. By a window.'

'I don't think so.'

He put his hands on my shoulders and looked at me. 'I'd like to photograph you, Astrid,' he said softly. 'Please?'

'I tell you what. Let me look at your other pictures and then I'll see.'

'Come on, then.'

He set off at a stride, and I had to almost run to keep up, the heavy bag bumping against my shins. We got to the house and he took it from me, then helped me out of his sodden jacket. There was the tinny sound of a radio coming from the top floor, but otherwise it seemed empty. We went up the stairs together. He opened the door of his room and looked at me.

'Now?' I asked, running my hands through my dripping hair and feeling my jeans cling to my legs.

'Unless you don't want to.'

'Of course I want to,' I said crossly. 'I'm just wet through and – oh, never mind. Show me.'

Owen's room looked different now, in the daytime, when I was fully conscious. The previous tenant, a friend of a friend of Miles, had been called Annette. She was an insomniac accountant who used to make cakes in the middle of the night, and who'd left to move in with her boyfriend when she got pregnant. She had almost parodically female tastes: the walls had been pink, the curtains lilac, with a frilly valance round the bed to match; there was a dressing-table with a folding mirror in the corner – I hadn't known anyone of our age ever had things like that – and several soft toys heaped up in the armchair. It was very different now. The pink had been painted over with pale grey; the bed had been replaced by a futon, there were dark blinds instead of curtains; a dressmaker's dummy stood in one corner, draped with scarves, and photographs hung on the walls.

'Yours?' I asked Owen.

'Only that one.' He pointed at a black-and-white picture of a swimmer, her body almost entirely submerged; the water, and the light that bounced off it, distorted the figure into a series of impossible angles, so that the image became almost abstract. 'The others are by friends.'

There were photographs leaning against every wall, and more stacked on the table under the window. I felt apprehensive and self-conscious.

'Why don't you sit there?' he said, gesturing to the chair by the side of the table. 'Here, rub your hair with this towel.'

I sat down awkwardly. Owen picked up a stack of photographs and put them in front of me.

'This is some of my more recent work,' he said formally.

I stifled the impulse to giggle or run away. 'Right,' I said.

'I've been working on them during the last couple of weeks. I'm trying to put together a portfolio.'

I turned the first one and was relieved: it was simply of water, full of ripples and glancing light – like the image on the wall, but without the human figure. Then I felt a quiver of shock run through me. It wasn't just water after all: there was a face beneath the dislocated surface, barely visible, eyes staring up, hair spread out like weeds. Like a suggestion of a drowned woman's face.

I turned over the next one. A naked woman was lying on a stained mattress, as white and flawless as a marble statue, her long hair rippling over her face so that it was only possible to see her open mouth. One hand was flung over the mattress and open, with writing on the palm that I couldn't decipher; the other was between her legs. It was both erotic and impersonal and I shivered in my clammy clothes.

'Your women don't have faces,' I said.

Owen didn't reply, just turned over the next picture for me.

A stubby thorn bush in winter, looking as unyielding as metal. That was all right.

Another naked woman – the same as the first? – this time just standing very straight and letting herself be scrutinized by the camera lens.

The same woman, her hands tied with rope, a calm smile on her face.

'Who is she?' I asked.

'Her's name's Andrea. We studied photography together.'

I felt a jab of something. Was it jealousy? 'Does she have a problem doing these?'

'Why?' said Owen. 'Would you?'

'I don't know what to make of them,' I said. 'I mean, they're powerful, but I don't know.'

'They're just exercises,' said Owen, pulling out another print.

A foot, twice the size of real life. You could see every detail – the chipped nail, the hairs on the toes, the tiny specks of dirt.

Like a slap in the face, a sudden flamboyance of colour and life: an ordinary street scene, but Owen had made it look like an exotic carnival, as if Hackney was Brazil. I smiled.

Black-and-white again. A woman sitting by a window, her back to the camera, her head completely bald, her spine running in a knotted track up her smooth back.

The same woman close-up and facing the lens, with her eyes unnaturally wide. In them I could clearly see the reflection of the photographer. I put out a finger and touched it.

'You,' I said.

'Self-portrait.'

Another tree, charred but with shoots growing from its blackened stump.

'Trees, water and naked women,' I said. 'Lots of your photographs don't look like photographs.'

'What do they look like?'

'Paintings. Sculptures. I don't know.'

'Do you want to see any more?'

'Bring it on.'

He put several more prints on the table. I worked my way through them, and it felt like work, under his unblinking gaze. I laid the final one aside and swivelled round in the chair.

'Well?' he asked.

'They're troubling.'

'They're meant to be troubling. At least you didn't just say they were nice.'

I pulled my shirt over my head. 'No,' I said slowly. 'They're not nice.'

I unclipped my bra and dropped it on the floor. Owen was looking at me with an intensity I'd never seen before, even from him. I kicked off my shoes and peeled off my wet jeans and knickers.

'You want me to photograph you?' he said.

I shook my head.

Afterwards he lay beside me on the bed, stroking my stomach.

'So is it still a no?' he said.

'That's right.'

'Don't be such a prude.'

I shook myself free of his touch, got out of his bed and started to pull my clothes on. I had the impulse to shout at him but I resisted it and when I spoke it was in a calm tone. 'We live in the same house, but until yesterday we'd scarcely exchanged a word. Then in the last twenty-four hours we've – what? We've fucked. Three times, though the first time it was like a fight and the second time you had your eyes shut all the way through, and then there was this. I have no idea what you think of me. Maybe you dislike me. Maybe you have contempt for me. Maybe you don't think about me at all. I would feel really uncomfortable letting you stare at me through the lens of your camera in the way you've stared at these other women.'

Owen just looked at me. I thought I could detect the hint of a smile.

A door opened and shut downstairs and Davy called, 'Hello!' I shivered.

'Is that it, then?' I asked.

'Is what it?'

'With us – it's finished, is it?'

'It? I didn't know *it* had ever actually begun,' he said, in an indifferent voice.

'No?' I put my hands on either side of his beautiful, hurt

77

face and kissed his angry mouth hard. 'Then how can it be over?'

That night, I stood by the window and wondered what Owen was doing in his room, just a few feet away from me. But Pippa interrupted my reverie. As always, she didn't knock or call, just pushed my door open and sat on the side of my bed. Her cheeks glowed. 'Hey! Guess what?'

'What?'

'Mick used to be in the army.'

'Did he? That makes a kind of sense, doesn't it? It explains how he can cook meals for large numbers of people, anyway. Why's he so secretive about it?'

'He was in the first Gulf War and he left after. He doesn't like talking about it.'

'Clearly.'

'After he left, he just travelled for years. I don't think he has a clue what to do with the rest of his life.'

'How do you know all this?'

'Oh.' Pippa gave a little giggle and threw me a coy look.

'No! You didn't?' I said, dismayed at the thought of all that was going on in the house.

'I did.'

'You had sex with him? Just now?'

'I thought he looked sad and I was curious about him. I thought it might cheer him up.'

'You make it sound like half a pint down the pub.'

'It wasn't the most intense experience of my entire life. Nice, though.'

'Did you just knock on his door and ask him if he wanted to have sex?'

'Not quite. I went to his room. God, Astrid, it's completely bare. There's nothing in there at all. It's like he's still in the army. Just a bed and a chest and that cupboard we hauled up from the junk room, nothing else. No personal touches. Anyway, I poked my head round and asked him if he wanted a cup of tea or a beer or something. And when he said no, I just kind of went in. And one thing led to another.'

'God,' I said. 'Mick.'

'Mick.' Pippa grinned.

'Will you do it again?'

'I shouldn't think so. It wasn't like that. It was just fun.'

'Won't it be awkward between you?'

'Why should it?'

I found it difficult to answer. 'It would be awkward for me, I guess.'

'I just thought you'd want to know.'

'Yes,' I said dubiously.

'How about you?'

'Me?'

'Your love life.'

'I don't have a love life at present.'

'No?'

'No!'

'Then you're going to, aren't you?'

'I don't know what you're on about.'

'Come on, Astrid. Owen. I saw the way you were looking this morning. And then not looking. I could have sworn you two had . . .'

I felt I was being cajoled into sharing confidences. But I wasn't in the mood for bantering and giggling.

'There isn't any "you two", and I wasn't looking like anything. I was helping Mick make bacon butties.'

'This is me you're talking to, world champion at deciphering erotic glances in the morning. He's gorgeous and

79

he's free. Why don't you pounce? I would. Hey, can I borrow this shirt tomorrow?'

'All right.'

'Mick's got a huge scar on his back. That was rather thrilling.'

Chapter Eight

Some days you draw the short straw. I got up just before seven, ignored Owen, dodged Miles, stepped round Davy, who was dismantling a crooked lintel and muttering something about 'resident cowboys', grabbed a piece of toast on my way out, switched on my radio – and immediately there was a message from Campbell telling me to pick up a package in Canonbury and take it to Camden Town. Twenty minutes later, as I was slogging along Hampstead Road on an empty stomach with car fumes in my face, the radio crackled again and he told me I might as well go straight from Camden Town up to Highgate to collect a package. Highgate is up a steep hill. It was a house I'd been to before and it was as high as it was possible to get in London.

Once, on the way up, I had passed a sign helpfully informing me that I was as high as the tip of St Paul's Cathedral. The woman who lived there was wealthy and chic and I thought she was one of those people who doesn't see poverty or disease or tramps in doorways. She lived in a different world, one of entitlement, and she treated us messengers like servants, which is, I suppose, what we were. She never recognized me. I was just part of the crowd of people who smoothed her way. One of the stories I told the gang at the Horse and Jockey was how I had been summoned once to collect a Japanese takeaway at the bottom of the hill and take it up to the top. As I handed it over, puffing and sweating while she was immaculate in her linen and her jewellery, I had thought that this was the sort of thing that provoked revolutions.

'Why me?' I asked, into the radio.

'Because you're there.'

So I dropped off the package in Camden Town, grabbed a sweet crêpe and a coffee from the stand in the high street, and set off in the faint drizzle. There were seriously rich people in Hampstead and Highgate, tasteful shops, expensive restaurants, exclusive schools where girls in pork-pie hats and boys in blazers got dropped off by mothers in four-wheel drives, tall and gracious houses with walled gardens and alarms blinking over their front doors, golf courses. The house was set back from the road. A tulip tree was flowering in the front garden and a pruned wisteria over the decorative porch, two huge empty earthenware pots standing at either side of it. I had never gone inside and only ever glimpsed the hall, which was twice the size of my bedroom and smelled of polish, paint, leather and money.

I swung myself off my bike, leaned it carefully against one of the porch's pillars, and rang the doorbell. I waited for thirty seconds or so, heard nothing, then rang again, for longer this time, and stepped back. Nobody came. A satisfying little bubble of anger formed in my chest. They make some poor sod cycle all the way up the hill at whim, then can't be bothered to be there.

I pulled out my mobile, noting the time, nine forty-one, and called Campbell to check there wasn't some kind of mistake, but the line was busy. I rapped the door knocker hard.

Again, nothing. I knelt down in front of the letterbox and prised it open. It was one of those that are angled in such a way that you can only make out a small strip of the interior. I peered through and saw the first few carpeted steps of the stairs. I twisted my head so my nose was pushed against the aperture and made out the glossy wooden floor-boards of the hall. And something else besides. I squinted and squashed my face closer into the door. Something smooth, pale brown. It looked like skin, a segment of an arm. I half stood, bending at a painful angle to get a better look. A segment of forearm becoming a wrist, and then, no matter how I twisted my face, I could see no further.

I called through the letterbox. I could hear my voice bounce round the clean empty spaces of the house. 'Can you hear me?'

The arm, if that was what it was, remained still. I scrambled to my feet and hammered at the door with both fists, then pressed the bell once more, its discreet chime repeating. I looked again through the letterbox. There was no movement.

There was only one thing to do. For the first time in my life I dialled 999. A voice answered. 'Which service, please?'

I had to make myself think.

'Ambulance, I guess. I think someone might be hurt or ill. Someone's lying on the other side of the door. I can see the arm.'

I gave the address and said I would wait until they arrived, then walked up and down the small stretch of grass, not knowing what to do with myself. Maybe whoever it was had had a heart-attack or a stroke. Or had fallen down the stairs and knocked herself unconscious. Or maybe it wasn't an arm at all, I thought, and someone would stroll up the road just as the ambulance arrived with its blue lights flashing and I would look like the idiot of the year.

But if it really was something like a heart-attack, shouldn't I do something about it right now? Or if she'd cut herself and was bleeding profusely, wasn't it important to tie a tourniquet round her? Didn't every second count? I should have asked them on the phone. Who would know? I thought of calling Mick – if he'd been in the army, surely he'd know things like that – but quickly changed my mind. Mick was probably at work, but if he wasn't he was at the top of the house and never answered the phone. I'd get Dario instead.

I rattled the door. I stood back and searched the upper floor for an open window I could climb through. I pulled my tool-kit out of my pannier: screwdrivers, adaptable spanners, inner tube, Swiss Army pen-knife. Useless. Before I fully understood what I was doing I picked up my entire bike and swung it against the large window to the left of the porch. The glass shattered and there was a violent shriek of a burglar alarm.

With my gloved hand, I knocked the remaining jagged pieces of glass from the frame so that I could climb through. I was standing in an opulently furnished living room. I walked through it and out into the hall. On the gleaming boards a woman lay face down. One arm was flung above her head, and one knee was bent. For a moment, I simply stood and stared down at her, unable to move, with the alarm throbbing in my eardrums. Bobbed blonde hair, expensively highlighted. Tanned skin. A blue silk dressing-gown riding up over her slim, impeccably waxed legs. I crouched beside the figure and, with a feeling of absolute dread, put a hand out to touch her arm. It was still warm. I gasped with relief, then tried to pull the motionless body on to its back. I jerked back in horror, letting go of her as I did so. Her head hit the floor with a thump. It wasn't just the eyes, open and glassy, staring upwards. Or the lips, swollen and blue. Her smooth face looked as if it had been drawn on with a red pen. But then I saw that the lines weren't drawn but incised, slashes on her cheek and forehead and even across one eye. The iris was crushed, something white oozing out from it.

I thought I should do something, press the chest, give mouth-to-mouth resuscitation and then I saw the sightless eyes, eyes with nothing behind them. It was pointless.

I stood up and pressed myself against the front door, my hand over my mouth, the body on the floor filling my vision. The alarm swelled in the air and in my skull. I tried to make myself feel that this couldn't be happening. It was a dream, an aberration. I'd blink and find myself back in my ordinary life, cycling up a hill in the rain on the way to collect a package. My mind focused on other things. I thought about how neat the house was, hardly a speck of dust in sight. How many hours did some cleaner work each week to make everything look as if it was in a magazine? I imagined myself telling the story later, to the house, and I already knew that I would do so with a kind of horrified excitement. I thought about my irritation with this woman, or people like her, as I had hammered at the door, and the way we messengers had bitched about her, and should I feel guilty about that? I vaguely wondered about getting my hair cut. I remembered that it was Miles's birthday next week and I needed to buy him a present but I didn't have a clue what. Something for his house – a sharp little reminder that we were leaving it? And that made me think about having to start flat-hunting soon, rather than leave it to the last minute – though I knew quite well that I probably would leave it to the last minute anyway, whatever my resolutions, and spend weeks sleeping on friends' floors and living out of suitcases. I wondered if my hearing would be damaged by the blasting throb of the alarm, and then I wondered if it was a way of sending people mad, subjecting them to this kind of noise. I decided it would be better to go and wait outside; after all, there was nothing I could do here and it seemed indecent to be standing staring at the flimsily dressed body of a woman who had seemed so impregnable in life. But I couldn't seem to make myself move. I thought how amazing it was that your brain can hold so many disparate feelings and ideas at once. And all the time I was staring at the impossible dead body on the floor, just a few feet from where I stood.

I fished out my mobile once more, noticing that my hands were trembling, but I didn't dial because at that moment I heard, behind the house alarm, the sound of a siren. The ambulance at last. I turned and pulled open the door to see it draw up outside the house. People had already started to gather in the road. I watched as a man and a woman jumped down and ran towards me as I lifted up my hand to beckon them on. Then, as they came into the garden and I saw their eyes move from me to the body that was lying behind me in the hall, I turned and vomited into one of the earthenware pots.

Chapter Nine

'Did you touch the body?'

'Yes,' I said.

The police officer looked disappointed. 'You shouldn't have done that.'

'I didn't know she was dead,' I said. 'I thought she might be injured. I thought she might need help.'

His expression softened. 'I can see that.' He stepped closer. 'Are you all right? Would you like to talk to a WPC?'

'What for?'

'They're trained,' he said.

There was a long pause.

'The window,' he said. 'That was you?'

'Yes.'

'You've caused quite a disturbance.'

'As I said, I thought she might be ill. It seemed urgent.'

He looked round at the shattered window. 'Looks a bit drastic,' he said.

'I couldn't think of anything else.' Behind him, the hallway was crowded. There were other police officers, people dressed in white like doctors. Outside, vehicles were coming and going.

'So, Miss erm . . .'

'Bell.'

'Why were you here, Miss Bell?'

'I'm just a bike messenger,' I said. 'That's my bike outside.'

'Do you know this woman?' he said.

'No,' I said. 'I've been to the house a few times.'

'Why did you come today?'

'The office rang me about a package.' There was a silence. 'I'm sorry. I've got nothing else to say. I mean, I can't think of anything.'

The officer rubbed his chin as if he was trying to think of another question but couldn't. 'I know that this has been a terribly shocking experience for you. But we're going to ask you to come in with us and give a full statement.' He looked at me, surprised by my expression. 'I'm sorry, is there something funny about that?'

'No, no,' I said. 'Not at all. I was just startled. I'd never talked to a policeman before. And now I've given two statements in a month.'

'Really?' said the officer. 'What about?'

So I had to tell him about my bike accident and my encounter with Peggy Farrell. I thought he'd find it curious, funny even in a grim kind of way, but almost immediately his face become serious and he told me to stop and wait and he left the room.

I was becoming an expert on police interview rooms. Two officers drove me down the hill to another police station. They wouldn't let me ride my bike. It would be brought, I was told. They drove into the rear car park and I was led in through a back entrance. I was met by a WPC, who took me through to my next interview room. There wasn't much to tell it apart from the other. Instead of beige walls, it had institutional light green. I sat on a plastic chair and was left alone. I took out my phone. There were about ninety-seven messages from Campbell and others. I rang Campbell.

'What the hell's going on?' he said.

'I'm sorry,' I said. 'I arrived at the house and she was dead. I'm in a police station.' There was complete silence at the other end of the line. 'Are you still there?'

'What?' said Campbell.

'I'll call you later,' I said. I broke off the call, switched off the phone and started to cry. This won't do, I thought, but I hadn't completely pulled myself together when the door opened and a man in a suit came in.

He was middle-aged with untidy greying hair that was thinning at the front. He was carrying two files under his arm. He stopped suddenly and looked at me. 'What the hell are you wearing?' he said.

'I'm a bike messenger,' I said.

'Are you the one who found the body?'

'Yes.'

'Oh, for fuck's sake,' he said, and walked out of the room. I heard indistinct shouting outside, which got more distant. I felt furious with myself that he'd seen me crying. That wasn't me. The man came back in, accompanied by two officers. One, a WPC, was carrying a bundle of clothes in her arms. The other had a tray with tea on it.

'Put this on,' said the detective.

'I'm not cold,' I said.

'That's an order,' he said. 'You may well be in shock. And when I find the police officer who left you like that, I'm going to give him such a kick up the arse.'

The clothes were ridiculous. There was a torn navy blue sweatshirt, a woolly jumper and a pair of jeans that were about five sizes too big. The WPC bent down and rolled up the legs.

'I don't think these do much for me,' I said.

The man handed me a mug of tea. I sipped it and grimaced. 'I don't take sugar,' I said.

'You do this time,' he said. 'We're going to stand here and watch you drink it.'

I felt the tea sinking into my empty stomach. 'Is there anything to eat?' I said.

The detective looked at the WPC. 'You heard her.'

The WPC looked startled. 'Can I get you a sandwich, love?'

'Anything.'

'At the double,' said the detective.

The two officers scuttled out of the room. The detective gestured at me to sit down. He placed the two files on the table one beside the other. 'I'm Detective Chief Inspector Paul Kamsky,' he said. 'How are you doing?'

'I'll be fine,' I said.

'This isn't really by the book. I know you haven't given a statement yet, but as soon as I heard, I had to come and talk to you myself.' He gave a baffled smile. 'I had to ask, what the hell is going on?'

'What do you mean?'

He picked up a file – green cardboard – and opened it.

'On Thursday, the tenth of May, you were the last person to see one Margaret Farrell alive.'

'Me and a couple of my friends, yes.'

He put the file down and picked up the other one – brown cardboard, this time. 'And now, a little over three weeks later, you are the person who finds the body of Ingrid de Soto. I wondered if you had any comment to make.'

'For what it's worth, I'm a bit shaken by it.'

'So am I, Miss Bell. Anything else?'

'Like what?'

He paused for a moment.' 'Miss Bell, I'm not sure if

you're entirely recognizing the oddity of the situation.'

'I am fucking recognizing it. It's a horrible, horrible coincidence and it's not nice being the victim.'

'You're the witness, not the victim.'

'That's what I was trying to say.'

'I could put it this way. I've been a copper for twenty-eight years and the only time I've ever found someone on two murder scenes within a month is because they were the murderer.'

'You're not saying . . . ?'

'No, no, of course not. But I'm afraid we're going to have to ask you to be here for a while. These statements take a ridiculously long time. But I'm just here to ask a couple of very simple questions.'

'Like what?'

'Like, can you think of any connection between these two women?'

'Don't be ridiculous,' I said. 'There's no connection at all.'

'Well, there's one,' he said.

'What's that?'

'You.'

'That's mad.'

'Please, Miss Bell. Help me. Tell me about your relation to these women.'

'Honestly, there is no relation. Margaret Farrell lived in the same street I do, a few doors along. But this is London. I knew her face but I'd never really met her until I ran into her car.'

'You ran into her car?'

'Well, pedalled. It probably says that in the file.' For the millionth time, I gave an account of what had happened. 'But that was it. I didn't know her. And I was in a shocked state, so I can't even remember saying anything coherent to her.'

'What about Ingrid de Soto?'

I started to shiver violently.

'I'm sorry,' I said, my teeth chattering. 'I'm not thinking in the clearest way.'

Kamsky leaned forward with a concerned expression on his face. 'Do you need a doctor?' he said.

'Seeing her body,' I said. 'I've never seen a dead body before.'

'And not arranged like that,' he said. 'Some of my young constables were pretty shaken as well. Do you want to stop for a bit?'

'No, I'm all right. What was it you wanted to know?'

'Ingrid de Soto. Tell me about her.'

'I didn't even remember her full name. Maybe I saw it on a package.'

'Why did you go to the house?'

'I wasn't planning it. My boss rang me. He could have rung anybody.'

'How many others?'

'Five or six.'

'Had you been to the house before?'

'A few times.'

'Can you think why anyone would want to kill this woman?'

'Which woman?'

'Mrs de Soto. Do you know anything about her?'

'No. I'm not her doctor, not her neighbour, not her friend. I deliver packages and take them away. Usually I don't even know their names.'

'Anything?'

'She's rich. She *was* rich.'

'That's something,' he said.

'She's rich, so someone may have killed her for her money. As part of a robbery.'

'My colleagues are still checking the scene. They haven't managed to contact her husband . . .'

'Her husband,' I said. 'Oh, I'm sorry. They both had husbands.'

'There we are. There's something else. But what I was saying is that, so far as we know, nothing was stolen. This was a murder done for other reasons.'

'Like what?'

'That's something we'll be considering.'

There was a long silence. Kamsky put his elbows on the table and rested his head on his hands.

'I don't understand this,' he said, 'and that irritates me. I've got a horrible feeling that this might be a coincidence.'

'I agree . . .'

'But that's not going to stop me.' He looked up suddenly. 'Where's the package?' he asked.

'Sorry?'

'The package you were supposed to be collecting.'

'I don't know. It wasn't on my list of priorities after I'd broken in.'

'The house was secure and the alarm on when you broke in?'

'Yes,' I began. 'It went off when I broke the window . . .'

But he was really talking to himself, not me. He chewed his lower lip thoughtfully. 'Right. After you've signed your statement I'll have someone drive you home, Ms Bell. I must ask you not to tell anyone the details of what you saw. Do you understand? Nothing about the method of killing and nothing about the marks on her face.' I nodded. 'Two officers are going to interview you and I'm afraid you're going to give a statement and you're going to say everything that comes into your mind, if it takes all day and all night.'

Chapter Ten

A police constable dropped me back at the house and left me on the front steps, fumbling the key into the lock with hands that wouldn't stop shaking, and dropping it twice before I managed to push open the door. It was only after the car had turned and driven away that it occurred to me my bike was still at the station, but I couldn't bring myself to care. I felt oddly sluggish, and very cold in spite of the borrowed clothes I was bundled up in. I was intending to creep in quietly and sneak up to my own room, where I could lie down and pull the duvet over my head, but as I pushed the door shut I heard excitable voices downstairs, and then Pippa shouted: 'Astrid? Is that you? Come here, will you? We need you.'

So I made my way downstairs, where I found the entire household gathered, plus Leah. Everyone was sitting round the table, speaking loudly and at once, and I could only pick out fragments, many of which were expletives. I sank into the armchair, away from the group, and sighed.

'Astrid can say what she thinks about it,' said Davy. 'She's pretty reasonable.'

'You think so?' said Owen. He looked at me as if he were sizing me up.

'Reasonable?' Leah snorted. 'I hardly agree.'

'What about all the work she's done in the garden?' said Dario. 'Surely that counts for something?'

'What's going on?' I asked.

'What are you wearing?' asked Pippa. 'Is this the latest bike-messenger uniform?'

'No –' I began.

'Can we stick to the point?' said Miles.

'We need some kind of mediator,' said Davy. 'It's hard for us to be objective. We don't want to end up enemies.'

'Too late,' said Dario.

'I'm a solicitor,' said Pippa. 'I can be objective.'

Leah snorted again, louder this time.

'Shut her up,' Mick said, in a low, controlled voice. A vein was pulsing in his temple.

'Leah,' said Miles. 'Please. You're not helping.'

I was surprised he didn't shrivel up under the force of her glare.

'I'm simply saying all the things you think but are too cowardly to say yourself. You want me to do your dirty work for you. Then they can blame it all on Leah, the Wicked Witch of the North.'

'Of the West, actually,' said Dario.

'Please, what's going on?' I said again.

'Bad stuff,' said Dario.

'Can I explain?' Pippa leaned towards me. 'I was the one who called this meeting. I thought it would be a good idea to discuss the terms of our eviction.'

'I'm not evicting you,' said Miles. I could tell from the way he said it that he had said this many times already.

'We have rights,' said Dario. 'Don't we, Pip?'

'Miles has already been generous,' said Leah.

'Generous how?' asked Owen. 'Generous in telling us to go? Generous in giving us a paltry few weeks to find somewhere else to live?'

'I'm a sitting tenant,' said Dario. 'Correct, Pip?'

'Well . . .' began Pippa.

'Can I say something?' Miles interjected.

I almost felt sorry for him.

'Not if you're going to give way even more,' said Leah. 'This has gone far enough.'

Davy got up from his chair and came and squatted down at my feet. 'Are you all right, Astrid?' he mumbled. 'You seem a bit out of it.'

I smiled gratefully at him and opened my mouth to speak, but closed it again. I couldn't bear to talk about it. Not yet. I didn't want this rabble turning their attention on me and showering me with their questions.

'. . . in the light of rising house prices and tenants' rights . . .'

'I'll tell you later,' I mouthed.

'. . . we need to reach an agreement on how much money is fair and reasonable,' Pippa was saying. She sounded suddenly like a different person. Someone bureaucratic and pedantic.

'You want him to pay you off,' said Leah. 'I might have known it would come down to money in the end.'

'Oh, sorry,' said Pippa. 'How vulgar to mention it.'

'I want to be fair,' said Miles. He half turned and flung me a look of such desperate appeal that on another day I might have come to his rescue. Instead, I sat limply in the armchair and thought of Ingrid de Soto's mutilated face and felt nausea rise in me.

'We have to work out a ratio,' said Pippa, 'depending on how long we've each been here.'

'You would say that, wouldn't you?' said Leah. 'You've been here the longest.'

'What about all the work I've done on the house?' put in Dario.

Beside me, Davy made a huffing sound and said something about damp courses.

'What about the fact that you've paid no rent since you

97

moved in?' snapped Leah. 'And it all needs redoing anyway.'

'Are you sure you want to be alone with this lady, Miles?' asked Dario.

'I've not been here very long,' said Davy.

'You and me both, mate,' said Owen.

'No one's going to lose out,' said Miles. 'How about fifteen thousand?'

'Are you mad?' exclaimed Leah. 'Listen, Miles, you don't have to give them anything at all. They haven't got a leg to stand on and they know it. Don't be intimidated.'

'They're my friends,' said Miles. 'Don't interfere. Or don't you want me to have friends? Is that it?'

'Don't be ridiculous.'

'Fifteen thousand each?' said Pippa.

'Pippa, you know I can't afford anything like – '

'Because a fifteen-thousand-pound lump sum, to be shared out between us, is insulting. We've lived here for years. We've helped you pay your mortgage. Now we have to find somewhere else to live. We have to put down deposits and buy furniture and begin again. Meanwhile, the value of your house has gone up tenfold.'

'Twenty, then. In instalments.'

'We all chipped in for the boiler,' said Dario. 'That cost loads.'

'Yeah,' said Pippa. 'Even though some of us, not to mention names, Mick and Dario, get more benefit from it than others.'

'If you don't like my painting,' said Dario, sulkily, 'what about Astrid's garden? She's spent days, weeks, on that.'

'Nobody asked her to do it,' said Leah. 'We're having it dug up.'

At last I spoke. 'What a cunt you are,' I said.

Leah turned and stared at me. Her beautiful eyes were hard. 'The cunt who got your man, though.'

'Whoa,' said Davy. He looked startled.

'Have you never heard the word before?' Leah asked brightly. 'Up north, did they never . . . ?'

'Cunt,' said Mick loudly. Everyone stared at him. Who was he talking to? Then Pippa gave a tiny giggle, and smacked a hand over her mouth.

'Stop now,' pleaded Miles. 'This isn't how to do anything.'

'Why? I'm just starting to enjoy myself,' said Leah.

'I don't care about the money,' I said. 'You can have mine, if you want. This is just really, really horrible.'

Silence fell on the room. For a moment, the expression on each face was frozen. Then the anger and self-righteousness turned into shame. Miles put his head in his hands for a moment, then lifted it again, meeting my eyes. 'I wish this wasn't happening,' he said. 'I wish I could turn back the clock.'

'You can,' said Dario, eagerly. 'You can, mate. Just say the word.'

'Let's go to the pub,' said Davy. 'Get out of here. Talk about it later. Not rush into anything. Yes? What do you say?'

'There's nothing to talk about,' said Leah, but nobody took any notice of her.

'Good idea,' said Dario. 'The most sensible thing I've heard for hours. The first round's on me, except I don't have any money on me, now I come to think of it. Don't know where it's gone. Come on, Miles, don't look so wretched. Nobody's died.'

'I don't want to dig up your garden, Astrid,' Miles said to me.

'I can always make another.'

'I tell you what, Pippa.' Miles turned to her. 'I should get the house valued, then come up with a proposal. Maybe I'll get outside advice, just so we can try to keep everything as neutral as possible. I want to be fair. I hope you know I'm not out to rip you lot off.'

'But are they out to rip you off?' muttered Leah. 'That's what you're not considering.'

Miles ignored her. 'Perhaps we shouldn't always have the whole household in on the discussions. It gets so heated. If you and I discuss things first, Pippa, then put it to the group ... What d'you say?'

'OK,' said Pippa. 'Why are you wearing those clothes, anyway, Astrid? Where did you get them from? A skip?'

'I got them from the police,' I said reluctantly.

It was a very strange sensation. It was as if I was suddenly a magnet drawing each element in the room towards me. Everyone turned to me, waiting for me to continue.

'There was an accident,' I said, then paused to consider the word. 'Not an accident,' I corrected myself. 'There was a death. Someone died. I saw her. She was ... she was dead in front of me.'

'Again?' breathed Davy.

'What do you mean, not an accident?'

'She was murdered,' I said. 'I saw her through the letterbox and I smashed the window and climbed in and she was lying on the floor. I touched her.' I gave a little shudder. 'I touched her and then I turned her over and her face was all ...'

'It's all right,' said Davy. 'It's all right. You don't need to say.'

'Cut up,' I finished. 'I've never seen a dead body close up before.'

'But —' began Miles.

'Oh, fuck,' breathed Dario.

'You poor, poor thing,' said Pippa.

'I don't want to talk about it any more,' I said. 'I just want to go to sleep.'

'It's still daytime,' said Dario. 'And we're going to the pub.'

Davy cast him a ferocious look.

'Who was she?' asked Owen. The expression on his face was one of curiosity. 'Did you know her?'

'What?' I shook my head. 'No, I didn't know her. I'd seen her before. She was just a client.'

'Wow,' said Dario. 'Blimey. First Peggy and now this woman. What is it with you?'

'Shut up, Dario,' Pippa said. 'Have a bit of tact.'

'It doesn't matter. He's only repeating what the police have been saying half the day.'

'It must have been terrifying,' said Davy.

'Yes.'

A brief silence fell. I could see that everyone was struggling to find the right questions without seeming too ghoulish.

'You lot go to the pub,' I said. 'I'm not really in the mood.'

'I'll stay with you,' said Pippa.

'No. You go. I'd quite like to be alone for a bit.'

Chapter Eleven

I was summoned again to be interviewed. It sounded urgent and I had to cycle up to Kentish Town in the middle of a working day, infuriating Campbell. But after I had locked my bike and been signed in, there wasn't much of an interview. Kamsky asked me a few questions but I had nothing new to say and mainly he walked up and down in silence. When he said something it was as much to himself as to me.

'These are the essential questions,' he said. 'One: why did the house show no sign of forced entry, unless Mrs de Soto knew her killer? Two: where was the package you were supposed to collect? Three: why were you present at both murders?'

'I wasn't present.'

'Four,' he continued, showing no sign of having heard me. 'Who else knew that you were going to Mrs de Soto's house?'

'Nobody. Campbell. I don't know. I've told you everything.'

'I don't think so. I think you know something but you don't know you know it.'

'That sounds too clever for me.'

'What were you doing the day before yesterday?' I asked Owen, as we walked towards the Downs. The men of the house were going to play football with a team who called themselves the Hackney Empire against another team from

Enfield. Pippa, Mel and I were going to watch. I had planned to spend the entire day in bed, trying to shut out the horror of the day before yesterday, but the familiarity of the outing was comforting. It was like going back to a time before the horrible things started happening. Except that walking there with Owen was unsettling. I wasn't like Pippa: I couldn't just go back to being a friend as if nothing had happened, as if sex was like a day we'd spent at the seaside. I was trying to act casually, speak to him in a friendly and neutral fashion, but my throat felt dry and my stomach lurched when I looked at him. Everything about him, which had been so familiar for months, now seemed mysterious to me. He'd become a beautiful stranger, grim and infinitely desirable. But I still wasn't going to take my clothes off and sit in front of him while he took unsettling photographs that turned me into an inanimate, tortured object.

'The day before yesterday?'

'Were you busy?'

'Why?'

'The police will probably ask. You'll need an answer.'

'I was at a magazine in the morning with the picture editor and –'

'Which magazine?'

'*Bella.*'

'Fake alibi?' said Davy, cheerfully, appearing at my side with Mel in tow.

'Don't be ridiculous.' But I could feel myself blush.

'I was with Mel, so I've got a witness,' continued Davy.

Mel giggled shyly and put her arm through his.

'Here,' said Davy, 'can you lend me a fiver, Astrid? I've left my wallet at home and I want to pick up a paper or two.'

I fished my purse out of my bag and opened it. 'I've only

got some change. I thought I had loads of money. I only took some out a couple of days ago.'

'Never mind.'

'I've got money,' said Mel. She was ridiculously eager to please, like a little panting dog. A sleek, pretty dog with large, woebegone eyes.

'Thanks.' He pocketed the note and bounded into the newsagent on the corner.

We loitered outside, while Pippa, Mick, Miles and Dario ambled towards us. Dario fished a packet of cigarettes out of his back pocket and stuck one in the corner of his mouth.

'Doesn't it make your chest hurt during football?' asked Mel.

'Sure,' said Dario. 'If I run.'

'Dario doesn't run much,' explained Pippa. 'He kind of loiters and puts his foot out to trip people up.'

Dario ignored them. He looked at me. 'I was thinking, I don't know which is worse. If it's a coincidence or if it's not a coincidence.'

'If it isn't a coincidence,' said Miles. 'That's clearly worse.'

'It can't not be a coincidence,' I said.

'Unless you killed them both,' said Dario, drawing deeply on his cigarette and cackling at the same time. 'No, no, don't worry, Astrid, I was just winding you up.'

'I'm glad someone can laugh at it,' I said.

'It can be to do with a sort of energy,' said Dario.

'What?' I said.

'It's like a forcefield,' said Dario, 'where terrible things happen, or have happened, or are going to happen. They're like a kind of spiritual magnetism and certain very sensitive people – such as you – are attracted to them.'

'I collided with her car,' I said.

'Exactly,' said Dario.

'And I wasn't exactly attracted to the other woman. My boss radioed me and asked me to collect a package.'

Dario took another deep drag and looked mysterious.

'The attraction doesn't have to be direct,' he said. 'There are collections of forces and they act on particular people. There's something special about you, Astrid. An aura. We might not be able to see it, but we can feel it.' I heard Owen give a small sound, almost like a snort, and turned to glare at him, but he looked away. Dario took a last drag on the cigarette and dropped it on the pavement, grinding his heel into it as Davy came out of the shop carrying a bulging plastic bag.

'Have you thought you might be in danger?' Mick said suddenly.

We stared at him and he stared back, his pale blue eyes unblinking.

'I thought it briefly,' I said finally, 'after I hit the door of Peggy's car and I was flying through the air.'

'What danger could she possibly be in?' said Davy.

Mick just shrugged.

'You're a bloody idiot,' Davy said, with unaccustomed ferocity. 'It's bad enough for Astrid as it is.'

'Thanks, Davy,' I said. 'But I'm OK.'

On the Downs we sat on the warm grass while we waited for the match to start. Davy pulled a bundle of papers out of the plastic bag and tossed them towards me. 'Something to read while we're playing,' he said.

'Why so many?' I asked, or started to ask, but then I saw the headlines.

'I thought you should be informed,' said Davy, awkwardly. 'Was I wrong?'

'No,' I said slowly. 'No, I guess not.'

We picked up papers and rifled through them, skimming the front news stories, the features and the comment pieces, avidly swapping bits of information. Of course, I should have expected a lot of coverage of Ingrid de Soto's murder, but even so I was taken aback by quite how much there was. Much more than Peggy's, but then, as Miles remarked acidly, Peggy had been a middle-aged, unphotogenic housewife in Hackney, whereas Ingrid de Soto was blonde, glamorous, rich and the right side of forty. 'Money, sex and death,' he said. 'All that's missing is religion.'

It was true that money and sex featured in many of the stories, and even God slipped in once or twice, via an interview with a local vicar, who'd clearly never met Ingrid de Soto but was eloquent about the nature of good and evil and the decline of traditional values in our celebrity-obsessed and faith-deprived contemporary culture.

The football started. There was a lot of yelling and grown men rolling over pretending to be hurt. People kept shouting, 'Ref,' and holding up a finger. Mick scored two goals, one with his head. Dario lurked by the touchline. Mel went away and came back with three ice-cream cones for Pippa, me and herself. Owen got hit by a high tackle and I saw a bruise shaped like an egg form on his shin.

While it went on, I learned a great deal about the dead woman that I hadn't known. I found out that she was thirty-two (I'd always fancied her to be older, because of her chilly, well-bred politeness, and her tall, co-ordinated house, which had the kind of affluent respectability that seemed horribly grown-up to someone like me). That she had moved from Hong Kong to London, and to Highgate, seven years ago. That her husband, Andrew de Soto, was the manager of a hedge fund, whatever that was. He was reported to be devastated by his wife's death. But Ingrid de Soto was rich through her father as well as her husband: William Hamilton was in oil, a millionaire many times over. She was his only child and he was flying to London to see her body. She had no children (I'd known that – no house could ever look so flawless with a child). Highgate neighbours were 'shocked and appalled'. Friends were shocked and appalled too. They described her as 'lovely' and 'smart'. She had no enemies, apparently: everyone liked her.

'They didn't talk to any of us despatch riders, did they?' I said.

'Did you dislike her, then?' asked Mel, her eyes round with horror.

'We dislike everybody,' I said. 'The whole world is basically against us. "Horror on the Hill",' I read from a headline.

'Hey, what's this?' Pippa shook her paper in front of me. '"Ingrid de Soto's body was found at her exclusive Highgate home by bike messenger, Alice Bell . . ."'

'Alice?'

'". . . Alice Bell, who is said to be very traumatized by her experience."'

I grabbed the paper from Pippa's hands. 'Where?'

'It must be a later edition.'

'Who said I was very upset?'

'Well, you were, weren't you?'

'Of course I was. Am. That's not the point. How do they know about me?'

'Alice,' said Pippa.

'Why would they tell them my name – not my name, as it happens?'

'It doesn't really matter, does it?' asked Mel.

'I don't know. It feels odd, that's all. Everything feels odd at the moment. It feels like everything's gathering a momentum of its own.'

'I've got something to say,' announced Davy, as we sat round with bottles of water and cans of beer after the match had finished, no one really wanting to return to the house.

'Go on, then,' said Pippa.

'Really, Dario's got something to say,' said Davy.

'Have I? I don't think so.'

'Yeah. Sorry, Dario, but you have.'

'I don't know what you're on about.'

'I'm sure it'll turn out to be nothing. But someone died. Two people died. And you've got to come clean.'

Dario spluttered.

'Come on, mate,' said Davy. I could see he was nervous. Making a stand like this wasn't in character for him.

Dario stubbed out his cigarette, ground it, then lit another. We waited in silence. 'I've got nothing to hide,' he said eventually. 'It's true that Astrid was right when she thought she saw someone. It was a guy who lives round the corner. He dropped round. He was on his way out when you appeared.'

'Why was he there?' asked Miles.

Another silence. Dario gulped. 'Just collecting something.'

'What?'

'Is that any of your business?'

'Dario?' I said. 'Just tell us.'

'I'd got some stuff for him. And he came over to collect it.'

'Stuff?' Miles's voice had sunk to a kind of growl.

'Yeah. Stuff.'

'As in what? Weed?'

108

'I've had some cash-flow problems. I needed some money to see me through. So. As you see, it wasn't relevant. But I didn't want to shout about it in front of the police. And don't blame Davy. I asked him not to tell you.'

'You fucking idiot,' said Miles.

'What?' said Dario.

'You've been dealing out of this house?' he said.

'It was just a favour for a friend.'

'How dare you?' Miles said.

'I'm sorry,' said Dario. 'I didn't realize there was a house rule.'

A row of some kind started. I heard it as if it was the wind blowing through the trees, but I paid no attention to the meaning. I was trying to think and for a moment I put my hands over my ears. Then I made my mind up. 'What's his name?' I said.

'What?'

'Your druggie friend.'

'He's not a druggie. He works in advertising.'

'What's his name?'

'Lee.'

'You know where he lives?'

'I've got his number somewhere.'

'You should call him.'

'You don't know what you're asking.'

'I do. And, Pippa —'

'Oh, for God's sake,' said Pippa, 'what is this? The Inquisition? OK, OK, I'll tell the police about Jeff. Happy now?'

Chapter Twelve

Monday morning, and I was wheeling my bike along the alley beside the house when something flashed. I blinked, looked up and it happened again. Then I realized two men were standing on the pavement outside the house, and one was taking photographs. Taking photographs of me. I put up a hand to shield my eyes and stared at them.

'Miss Bell?' one called.

'Alice?' shouted the other.

'Oh, for God's sake,' I muttered under my breath. 'It's *Astrid*,' I said. 'Astrid Bell. Where did you get the Alice from, anyway?'

The man without a camera shrugged. 'You found the body, right?'

Something about the language made me wince. The body. As if the poor woman was just a thing, a meaningless object I had happened to stumble across. There was a short silence. The photographer raised his camera again and fired off a few shots.

'I didn't say you could do that,' I told him. 'And you can't.'

'What was it like?' asked the reporter.

'How did you get my name?'

'Is it true you broke in through the window?'

'Did the police tell you?'

'Can I say at least that you were very shocked?'

'Of course she was bloody shocked.'

Dario had appeared at my side. He was wearing grubby

purple tracksuit trousers and a bright yellow anorak with arms that hardly reached his elbows. The two men stared at him.

'Don't you dare take a photo of him,' I said grimly, but too late.

'Wouldn't you be shocked if you were at the murder scenes of two women in just weeks?' Dario continued. 'You'd think it was bad karma, wouldn't you?'

I groaned out loud.

'You said two women?'

'Right,' said Dario. 'First Peggy Farrell and then this other one.'

A look of bewildered fascination appeared on the reporter's face. 'Bloody hell,' he said. 'Astrid. Miss Bell.'

But I had swung my leg over my bike and mounted. I cycled away to the sound of the camera clicking and Dario calling my name.

That evening after work I met Pippa in the Horse and Jockey for a drink. We made an odd pair: she in her trim suit and sensible shoes, her hair coiled neatly at the back of her head, little earrings in her lobes, carefully invisible makeup, and a leather briefcase, me in my black Lycra and scuffed boots, sweaty and grimy. As if conforming to our parts, she ordered white wine while I had half a pint of lager.

'So,' she said, taking off her jacket, unpinning her hair and having a hearty swig of wine. 'First of all, money. I wanted to talk to you about it before speaking to the others. You know what those big group discussions can get like.'

I nodded.

'I got an email from Miles today at work. I've printed it out so you can have a look at it, but basically what he proposes is that each individual gets paid according to the amount of time he or she has lived in the house. So you and I get the most, and Davy and Owen the least. But he's also suggesting that since that might end up being a bit unfair on them, he should give us each a lump sum, then top it up with an adjustable amount. So it's x plus y times t.'

'What?'

'That's how Miles puts it – x is one sum, y another, and t is time.'

'Ah,' I said. 'Right. Has he mentioned actual figures, or are we stuck in Algebra Land?'

'He suggests that x equals seven and a half thousand, y equals two and t is a year or part of a year.'

'So you and I, for instance – that's seven and a half add two, times – what is it? Four and a half years, that's five – so plus ten thousand, makes seventeen and a half.'

'Right. While Davy and Owen get nine and a half.'

'Which is also an awful lot of money. How much is Miles going to shell out altogether?'

'Lots.'

'Leah won't be pleased.'

'I know, but it's based on how much the value of the property has risen, which you wouldn't believe.'

'Try me.'

'He bought it five years ago for about a quarter of a million. Guess how much it's worth now?'

'I've no idea.'

'Try.'

'Let's see. Seven bedrooms, big garden. Um – five hundred thousand?'

'More.'

'OK, six hundred.'

'More.'

'More?'

'Eight hundred.'

'Fuck. For that? Even after Dario's work?'

'So you don't need to worry he's being too generous.'

'Do you think he's offering about the right amount?'

'It seems fair enough.'

'Will the others think so?'

'Dario won't. But Dario thinks he's committing a terrible crime by throwing us out in the first place and no amount of money could compensate for that betrayal. We're all the family Dario's ever had, remember. It's like a divorce.'

'But the others?'

'Who knows? Money makes people act in all sorts of strange ways. You wouldn't believe the kinds of behaviour I come across at work. It's cash, by the way. Strictly under the table.'

'You mean, he'd pay us in cash?'

'I think the idea is that he'd pay you and you'd hand it out.'

'Me?'

'Yeah.'

'Why?'

'I think he doesn't want to face any more of it.'

'Sounds like Miles.'

'Do you want another drink?'

'Go on, then.'

I watched her as she made her way to the bar. Men stood aside to let her by, then closed in again, following her with their eyes. She appeared not to notice.

'What's happening with Owen?' she asked, as she sat down.

'Nothing. Anyhow, he's away at the moment on some photo-shoot. More importantly, what's happening with Jeff?'

'Jeff?' She stared at me, wrinkling her brow. 'Jeff, as in . . . ?'

'Jeff as in Jeff-who-stayed-with-you-on-the-night-of-Peggy's-murder.'

'Oh, that Jeff.'

'Yes, that Jeff.'

'I know what you're going to say. And you don't need to say it –' But at that moment she was interrupted.

'It's the attractive and visibly distraught Ms Astrid Bell,' cried a voice, and I turned to see Saul's beaming face.

I had known Saul since I was fifteen. We met at a party, where we spent three hours sitting on the staircase and talking about music and movies, and had been friends ever since. It was Saul who got me my job with Campbell; he had been a despatch rider for nearly seven years now, and every month he swears will be his last. 'What are you on about?'

'Don't you know?'

'Know what?'

'That you're the enigma at the heart of the mystery.'

'You're drunk.'

'You're the key, but where's the lock?'

'Saul!'

'You really don't know?'

'I really don't know – I don't even know what it is I don't know.'

'Look! Hot off the press.'

He pulled the local newspaper out of his messenger bag and flung it on the table. It took me a few seconds to realize what I was looking at. There I was, standing outside our house holding my bike, one hand raised and my jaw jutting out. I was wearing the same gear I had on today and looked both thuggish and mildly pornographic. But that was nothing compared to Dario, who was in the background and weirdly shrunk by the angle of the camera lens. In his ill-fitting yellow anorak and trousers, with his hair half over his face and his mouth open, he had the appearance of an evil dwarf.

Pippa gave a horrified giggle.

'"Messenger Murder Mystery",' I read from the head-line.

'You should see the puns,' said Saul, who was tremen-dously cheerful about the whole affair. 'Look here: "cycle-ogical thriller". You're at the centre of something weird.'

'It's not that big a deal,' I insisted, but I shivered. It was as if a cloud had passed in front of the sun, turning the warm, crowded room cold and dark.

Chapter Thirteen

I stepped out of my room and almost collided with Owen, weighed down with his camera bags and tripod from a shoot. His face looked smooth and young. 'Astrid,' he said.

I needed to say something. I took a step towards him, or perhaps he took a step towards me, then brisk steps coming up the stairs halted us. It was Leah, looking mildly impatient. 'There you are,' she said.

'What is it?'

'Someone to see you downstairs,' she said.

'Who?' I said.

'If you go down, you'll find out,' she said.

I shrugged, glanced at Owen, and walked down the stairs. Detective Chief Inspector Paul Kamsky was in the hallway. Miles was standing next to him but they weren't speaking. Kamsky caught sight of me.

'Sorry to drop in unannounced,' he said.

'That's all right.'

'Is there anywhere we can talk?'

'You could go downstairs to the kitchen,' said Miles.

'It's not very private,' I said.

'It doesn't matter,' said Kamsky.

'We'll keep out of the way,' said Miles. 'I'll make some coffee.'

As Kamsky sat down at the kitchen table, he looked around with a smile. 'How many of you are there?'

'It's a bit of a floating population,' I said. 'People come and go.'

'Like a commune?'

'It's just a house-share.'

'I couldn't manage that,' he said. 'I like my own space.'

'I know what you mean.'

Miles put coffee mugs on the table. Kamsky took his and contemplated it, then looked up at me. 'It's the package,' he said.

'You never found it?'

'Did you ever have an itch that you couldn't scratch because you didn't know exactly where it was?'

'No.'

'There are several things about this case that bother me,' he said.

'That's what Mitchell said.'

'I know,' said Kamsky. 'He's not a happy man.'

'What about you?' I said. 'Are you happy?'

'There's your involvement,' he said. 'And the fact that you gave an interview about your involvement.'

'It wasn't exactly an interview,' I said. 'I shouted something at a reporter.'

'A dignified "no comment" is usually the best policy,' Kamsky said.

'I wasn't thinking clearly.'

'And most of all I'm bothered by what was taken.'

'I didn't think anything was taken.'

'I'm going to tell you something we haven't released. Please don't mention it to any reporters. As you saw, Mrs de Soto was wearing expensive jewellery, a necklace, rings, a bracelet. Perhaps you noticed that one earring was missing.'

'No, I didn't.'

'Just one. It had been pulled out, ripping through the earlobe.'

I flinched.

'Don't worry,' said Kamsky. 'It was probably done after she was dead. My psychiatric colleague tells me it was probably taken as a trophy.'

'A trophy?'

'A souvenir. By the way, he's keen to talk to you as well.'

'I don't think I'll be much help.'

'We'll see,' said Kamsky. He paused and took a slow gulp of his coffee. 'You might have picked it up and put it in your satchel.'

'The package? That's crazy. I broke into her house and found her lying dead. I didn't stop to collect a package.'

'As far as I can see, there are three possibilities. Either there was no package, or you took it, or whoever killed her took it.'

'Have you looked for it properly?' I asked. 'Sometimes when I arrive to pick something up, they haven't got it ready. It's bloody irritating. I arrive and then they go off and get whatever it is and find something to put it in. Maybe she hadn't wrapped it up yet.'

'That's a possibility,' said Kamsky. 'Another possibility is that the package was something valuable. Or perhaps it was something particular that he was after.'

'That's not possible,' I said.

'Why?'

'She only booked the pick-up half an hour earlier. The guy happens to steal something in the last few minutes it's going to be in the house. Is that another coincidence?'

'No,' said Kamsky. 'I'm getting allergic to coincidences. But the murderer kills the woman and takes only two objects: an earring and the package you're about to collect. Doesn't that strike you as interesting?'

'Strange, maybe.'

'Did you have any idea what you were going to collect?'

'No. When people call us, they only have to specify the size of the package. If it's a grand piano, they generally don't send me on my pushbike. But you should talk to my boss about that.'

'I did,' said Kamsky, with a frown. 'I don't think his record-keeping is entirely satisfactory.'

'Tell me about it,' I said. 'One day the Inland Revenue are going to descend on him and take that place apart.'

'Hello,' said Pippa, from the doorway. 'You must introduce me to your guest.'

'Pippa, this is Detective Inspector Kamsky,' I said.

'Er, Detective *Chief* Inspector,' he said. 'Not that it matters particularly.'

'And this is Pippa. She's one of the many people who live here.'

Pippa's eyes lit up and she came and sat at the table.

'Be careful what you say,' I said to Kamsky. 'She's also a lawyer.'

'But a nice person anyway, I'm sure,' said Kamsky.

'Are you in charge of the investigation of the murders?' said Pippa.

'I'm heading the Ingrid de Soto inquiry. I'm in informal touch with the team working on the Margaret Farrell killing. As yet there's no official connection between the two murders.'

'Of course there bloody is,' said Pippa.

'What's the connection?' asked Kamsky.

'Astrid,' said a voice from behind. I didn't need to turn round. Bloody Dario, bloody stoned. I could hear it in his voice and see it in his eyes. He opened the fridge, took out a beer bottle and flicked off the cap with his thumb. 'You want to watch her. Isn't there a rule about the person who reports a murder always being the prime suspect?'

'It's not exactly a rule,' said Kamsky.

Dario sat down next to me and took a swig of his beer. 'There's motive,' he said. 'Peggy Farrell opened her car door in front of Astrid. And then that other woman. Making Astrid cycle all the way up Highgate West Hill. If that isn't a motive for murder, I don't know what is.'

'This is Dario,' I said. 'Another housemate.'

Suddenly the room seemed to be full. The word of Kamsky's presence had spread and everybody was gathering to have a look at him. Davy and Mel came in, hand in hand, revoltingly in love. Owen arrived and sat beside me. Even he couldn't resist it. Leah, the hostess, pulled the cork out of a bottle of wine. She came forward with a clutch of glasses. She offered one to Kamsky and he nodded.

'Aren't you meant to say, "Not when I'm on duty"?' asked Dario, then gave a bark of hilarity.

Kamsky looked at his watch. 'I'm not actually on duty,' he said. 'Cheers.'

Now everybody pulled chairs up to the table and crammed around, as if it were a child's party and we were going to sing 'Happy Birthday' and blow out the candles. Kamsky seemed rather bemused at being the centre of attention.

'So how is it going?' asked Mel. 'I'm sorry to be nosy but I've never met a real detective before.'

'Are you another housemate?' asked Kamsky.

'She's with me,' said Davy.

'It's difficult to keep track,' Kamsky said.

'You wait,' I said. 'It gets worse.'

'Are you here to take statements?' said Davy.

'Why?' said Kamsky. 'Have you got something you want to say?'

'Not exactly,' said Davy.

'But some people have,' said Leah.

There was a silence. Kamsky shifted awkwardly in his chair. 'What do you mean?' he asked.

Leah looked around the table.

'Is it true,' she said, 'that anyone who was near the scene when the murder happened should come forward?'

'Well . . .' Kamsky began.

'Leah,' said Miles, in a warning tone.

'I just think that people should do what they said they would do.'

There was a flurry of voices around the table. Pippa held up her hand for silence. She spoke with an icy calm. 'I wouldn't have thought this was the time or the place but Leah has a fierce commitment to legal principle. Though the heavens fall. What she was hinting at was that I had a friend staying on the night of Peggy Farrell's murder. He's a little hard to trace but he will come forward and make a statement, if required. But this probably isn't of much interest to you.'

'What about you, Dario?' said Leah, triumphantly.

The scene would have been comic if it hadn't been so horribly embarrassing, with Leah turning the screw of humiliation tighter and tighter. Dario's face had gone a fierce red. 'Leah, I dunno, I . . .' He stammered to a halt.

'Dario, what's the problem?' asked Leah, brightly.

Miles flicked me an anxious glance, then flicked it away when he saw the expression on my face.

'I need to be given a bit of time,' Dario said. 'It's compli-cated. I've got to –'

'Oh, for fuck's sake,' said Leah, got up and walked out of the room. We heard the sound of footsteps making their way loudly up the stairs. People exchanged puzzled glances around the table.

'This isn't typical,' said Davy to Kamsky. 'We usually get on quite well. There've been some personality clashes.'

'You can say that again,' said Dario.

There was another rattle of footsteps on the stairs, and a visible flinching as everyone waited for the tornado to arrive. Leah strode in. 'This is from Dario's room,' she said, tossing something on to the middle of the table.

You could see the blood leaving Dario's face, as if someone had pulled a plug. On the table was a small transparent polythene bag with something brown inside.

'Dario has gone all shy,' said Leah, 'because shortly before Margaret Farrell died – *very* shortly – he was out on the front step with someone as yet to be contacted, doing one of his little dope deals.'

There was a terrible, terrible silence around the table. I'd already called her a cunt, so there was nothing left to say to her. I might have been tempted to hit her but a detective was present. I looked around the table at the shocked faces. I have a phobia about silences. Whenever one occurs, I have to break it. I looked at Leah. 'Is that your plan?' I said. 'If you can get Dario arrested, you won't have to pay him off?'

'Grow up, Astrid,' she said.

'What did you say?'

Kamsky leaned over, picked up the bag and tossed it to Dario. 'Try not to use too much of this stuff,' he said. 'It's not just that it's bad for you. People who smoke it become so boring. Look, I'm conducting a murder inquiry. If you're dealing a bit of cannabis, I don't care.' He looked at Pippa. 'If you're sleeping with your best friend's husband, I don't care. What you need to do is come forward. If you know any witnesses, tell them to come forward as well.' Kamsky stood up. 'But not to me. This isn't my inquiry. Tell them to contact DI Mitchell.' He looked at me with a smile. 'I suppose Miss Bell can give you his number.'

'Won't you stay for dinner?' asked Pippa.

Was Pippa going to start hitting on him as well? Was there no limit? Was nothing sacred? But he smiled and shook his head. 'You're a lawyer?' he said to Pippa.

'That's right.'

'It sounds like this household could do with one.'

And with that he went and left us to it.

Chapter Fourteen

No one spoke. I could hear the cars in the street outside, the house's ancient pipes grumbling, a blackbird chirruping in the garden. I could hear Dario breathing heavily. Leah's painted nails tapped rhythmically on the table. I looked up at her: her face was smooth, unconcerned. I looked at Miles, but he was staring down at his hands, which were plaited together on his lap, and I couldn't make out his expression.

At last Davy coughed nervously and spoke. 'That was pretty clear,' he said, 'and no real harm done, eh, Dario?' His voice trailed away.

Dario twisted his head. 'What?' he said. He sounded dazed. 'No harm?'

'I mean –'

'Shut up, will you, Davy?' interrupted Pippa. She put a hand on Dario's shoulder and looked across at Leah. Even I was alarmed at the icy rage in her eyes. Leah, however, didn't flinch. 'It's pretty clear, don't you think,' Pippa continued, 'that Leah's behaviour was unacceptable to the entire household?'

'Who wants some whisky?' asked Owen. 'I do. Or I could do with some of Dario's dope. Do you want to roll a joint, Dario?'

'Unacceptable?' said Dario, finding his voice. 'That's not the word I'd use. I'd say –'

'I don't think I should be here for this,' said Mel, in a small voice. 'It's private, between you lot.'

'Stay.' Davy wrapped his arm round her to prevent her moving.

'I'd say,' went on Dario, his voice growing stronger, 'that she's poison. Poison. Everything was all right before she came. We were happy. She's like a nasty, toxic stain seeping over everything.'

'Miles?' said Pippa. 'Are you going to say anything?'

Miles shifted uncomfortably, still not lifting his head. 'What do you want me to say? It's very unfortunate but –'

'Do you really think everything was all right before I came on the scene?' said Leah. Her eyes were bright. I wondered if she was almost enjoying herself.

'Don't ask her what she means,' I was starting to say, but Davy got there first.

'What do you mean?' he asked.

'Well, look at you all,' said Leah. 'There's you, Dario. How old are you? Thirty? Older? You don't have a job. You don't have a relationship. You don't have any ambitions. As far as I know, you have no real qualifications, except for being a petty criminal, and you're not even very good at that.'

Dario spluttered and his freckled face turned an unlovely red.

'Then there's Mick.' She gave a mirthless laugh. 'Would you describe him as a fully functional member of society?'

'Leave Mick out of it,' said Davy, unexpectedly assertive. 'He's not here to answer back.'

'You, then, Davy. What's the point of you?'

'That's not fair,' said Mel, her face flushing.

'And look at Astrid.'

'Look at me instead,' said Owen, and she swung her gaze to him. I saw their eyes locked and for a moment her expression grew speculative. Leah loved beautiful things. 'And now listen,' he continued.

125

'I'm listening.' She folded her arms.

'You're a bully and you're not welcome here.'

'I don't think that's for you to say, is it?'

'You're not welcome.'

'Miles?' said Pippa. 'Are you just going to sit there?'

'I only want . . .' he started miserably, but stopped as Mick came into the room, still in his jacket, eating fish and chips out of a brown-paper bag.

'You are, aren't you?' Pippa continued. 'Right, speaking as a lawyer, I'd like to say this first. Negotiations are off.'

'What?' asked Mick, a chip half-way to his open mouth, his eyes bulging.

'Off,' said Dario, banging his fist on the table. 'Yup. Off.'

'Have I missed something?' said Mick.

'Pippa,' said Miles, pleadingly, 'don't react like this. We had an agreement and it was in everyone's interests.'

'I don't see what all the fuss is about,' said Leah, calmly. 'I told the detective chief inspector what he needed to know. This is a murder inquiry, you know, and you're all behaving as if you're sitting at the back of a classroom. You're not at school, guys – this is real life.'

This was uncomfortably close to my own attitude. And she wasn't entirely wrong about Dario. And I sometimes felt as if Mick and Davy were people I'd run into on a railway platform while they were waiting to change trains. I thought I ought to say something but couldn't think exactly what. My contribution wasn't missed, though. Dario was angrily shouting that he wouldn't continue with his work on the house.

'I don't think that's a great loss,' said Leah.

'You haven't seen what I've started to do to your en-suite bathroom this evening,' said Dario, 'have you?'

'No.'

'I was working on it when that inspector-person arrived. There's no lavatory in there.' He sniggered. 'Just a big hole. And the plumbing's turned off.'

'Dario,' said Miles, 'don't be ridiculous.'

'Oi!' said Mick. 'Can anyone hear me? Or maybe I'm simply dreaming.' He pinched his cheek exaggeratedly. I watched, fascinated, as a red mark blossomed between his fingers, but he didn't seem to feel the pain. 'Nope, not dreaming.'

'We're not doing anything else, either,' said Dario. 'Not a thing. Look.' He picked up a can and tipped out the remaining beer into a puddle on the floor. 'I'm not cleaning that up,' he said triumphantly.

'Oh, for God's sake,' snapped Leah, 'don't be such a baby.'

'Or this,' said Dario, and turned an overflowing ashtray upside-down.

Leah scraped her chair violently back, stood up and strode from the room.

'Here, who wants some?' asked Owen, laconically, holding out a jumbo-sized joint.

'Me,' said Dario.

'She never said what was wrong with me,' said Pippa. 'Pity.'

The door opened and Leah's voice came through it: 'You behave like a slag.'

Two red spots appeared on Pippa's cheeks, but she laughed lightly. 'Thank God for feminism and the pill,' she said.

Davy stood up quietly, kissed the top of Mel's head, then fetched a cloth from the sink and started mopping up Dario's spilt beer.

'Miles,' I said.

'Yeah.'

'What are you going to do?'

'Do?'

'We can't live like this.'

'It'll die down.'

'You think?' asked Pippa scornfully. 'You mean, if we all pretend nothing happened then we can go back to the way things were before Leah betrayed us.'

'We have to deal with this,' I continued.

'We'll have no-go areas,' said Dario.

He rushed from the room and we watched him go in bewilderment.

'He's very upset,' said Davy, rinsing the cloth in the sink, then drying his hands. 'It's –'

'Don't,' I said.

'Don't what?' said Davy, puzzled.

'Don't say it'll be all right. That we can talk it over.'

While Davy looked disappointed, Dario reappeared, carrying a pot of paint in one hand and a large paintbrush in the other. He dumped them on the floor just inside the door and levered off the lid. The paint inside was a deep green.

'What?' said Miles, as Dario lunged the brush into the paint and started drawing a thick, messy line across the kitchen floor.

'She can only stay on her side of the line,' he said. 'I'm not having her crossing over.'

'Wow!' said Pippa, giggling. 'Look at that. She can't get to the cooker, she can't get into the garden – except by the side alley, I guess. And she can't sit down at the table. All she can do is walk in a line towards the cupboard with the light-bulbs in it.'

'You've stepped in it,' I said.

'I'm not sure this is going to be enforceable,' said Davy. 'What do you reckon, Pippa?'

'Not enforceable, but fun,' she said.

'Give that brush to me.' Miles was on his feet and holding out his hand. At last he was angry, rather than embarrassed and defeated. 'Now!'

'Come and get it.' Dario waved the brush in the air and green spots of paint spattered everywhere.

'Maybe I should make tea,' said Mel. 'That's what we need.'

Now Miles had hold of the brush as well and the two men were struggling over it. Tiny speckles of green paint covered them like duckweed, and they were panting. Then the brush slipped from their hands and landed wetly on the floor. A sudden silence gripped the room. Miles stared round at all of us, opened his mouth, closed it again, and left. For a moment, I thought of going after him because the look on his face had been so wretched, but Pippa put out a hand and restrained me. 'Not now,' she said.

'Don't start feeling sorry for him,' said Dario. His eyes glittered in his green face.

I got up and went to look out into the garden, which lay quiet and still in the evening light.

'What is it, Astrid?' asked Pippa.

'You know, you can get so caught up in the rightness of your own position that you say and feel all sorts of terrible things,' I said. 'And then it's too late and you can't go back.'

'Go back?' asked Davy.

'We were all friends.'

'He's got to choose between her and us,' said Dario.

'There you are,' I said. 'That's what I mean.'

* * *

'We seem to have got things the wrong way round,' I said.

'What do you mean?' asked Owen.

'We never do anything normal, like go to a movie or have a meal or hold hands in front of other people.'

'Is that what you want?'

I ran my hand down his smooth body and he shivered and I was filled with an unsettling joy: he seemed so invulnerable, yet when I touched him, he shivered. After the awfulness downstairs, the meanness, the violence, it had seemed natural to walk upstairs together, to hold each other. At the same time, I felt I was giving in. 'You were good down there,' I said. 'Not everybody was. I'm not sure what I want. Just don't talk crap to me. Don't start saying things like you're not ready for a relationship.'

He didn't say that. He didn't say anything. He pulled me towards him until my head was on his chest, his chin was on my hair, our legs were tangled under the covers, our hearts were beating together and I couldn't tell which was mine and which his. We drifted off to sleep like that, until I woke in the darkness and sneaked away, like a thief.

The next two days were strange and unhappy ones in the house. An air of foreboding hung over everything. I tried to be there as little as possible, and spent more time than usual in my own room. Even so, it was impossible not to be aware of the feuds and factions, the whispering in corners, the slamming of doors, the sudden chill silences that would fall if Leah came into the kitchen.

Every so often one of the group would draw me aside to tell me what was happening or who had said what to whom. Pippa told me that she was now asking for more money from Miles. Miles told me that he was unable to go any higher in his offer and, anyway, he didn't see why he should, and please could I act as a mediator? Leah told me she wasn't going to let Miles give us any money at all and that Dario would be chucked out if (a) he didn't start paying rent and (b) he didn't replace the lavatory at once. Dario said he was never going to replace the lavatory, nor would he wash up, rinse out the bath after use, put out the bin bags, vacuum the carpet or do any other household duties, which, as far as I knew, he never did anyway. He said we should go on strike. Mick said nothing, but scowled more than ever. Davy said Miles should be given a way out, not be painted into a corner. I came in and found Davy replacing the lavatory.

'Properly, this time,' he said. 'That Dario. I'm surprised we haven't got cholera.'

Owen went away again, to Milan this time and for longer. Perhaps that was just as well. I tried to stay out of it all, but found myself drawn in when I reminded Dario that he still had to find his friend, Lee, and make him contact the police, and he told me I should watch out or I'd turn into Leah mark two.

A few days after Ingrid de Soto's murder, I received a phone call. I was about to leave the house and Davy called me back, holding out the phone.

'I'm late,' I mouthed.

He covered the mouthpiece. 'I think it might be important,' he said.

I sighed and took the phone from him.

'Hello?'

'Is that Astrid Bell?' A man's voice that I didn't recognize: gravelly, self-assured, with a slight American drawl.

'Yes,' I replied warily.

'My name is William Hamilton.'

For a moment my mind was blank.

'I'm sorry, I . . .' And then I remembered. Ingrid's father. I felt a rush of emotion and took a deep breath. 'I'm so terribly sorry for your loss.'

'I'd like to meet you.'

'I understand why, of course, but you should know there's nothing really that I can –'

'With my son-in-law, Andrew de Soto,' he cut in. Then: 'Please, Miss Bell. We won't take up too much of your time.'

'Of course I'll meet you,' I said, although it was the last thing in the world I wanted. 'When's good for you?'

And so it was that at three o'clock that afternoon I found myself walking into the foyer of a tasteful, expensive hotel in Covent Garden – so tasteful and expensive that the doorman didn't blink at my Lycra shorts and stained top, but took my bike pannier and helmet from my sweaty grip and ushered me politely into a side room where the two men were sitting, a tray of tea things on the low table between them that remained untouched throughout our meeting.

'Ms Bell,' said William Hamilton, rising to his feet. He was a tall, burly man, with thick white hair, ferocious silver eyebrows over bloodshot eyes, and liver spots on the back of his hands. He wore a dark suit that had probably cost more than all the clothes I owned put together, but he didn't seem to notice my outfit, shaking my hand firmly and gesturing me to an armchair. 'Thank you for coming.'

Andrew de Soto was much smaller than his father-in-law. With wiry greying hair, cut short, and pouches under his eyes, he wasn't at all the kind of man I would have imagined with Ingrid. He looked dazed, exhausted, and I noticed that his white shirt was buttoned wrongly,

'I wish there was something I could do to help,' I said lamely.

'We realize, of course, that you have given your statement to the police,' said William Hamilton, 'but because you were the person to find ...' He stopped. I saw his large hands grip the chair arms. 'You were the person who ...'

'Yes,' I said. 'I was. I came to collect the package.'

'The package. Yes. I know that. The package that wasn't.' He scrutinized my face, then carefully cracked the knuckles on both his hands. 'I'm a wealthy man, Ms Bell.'

I didn't know what to say to that, so remained silent. Across from me, Andrew de Soto gave a single sharp cough.

'Ingrid was my only child,' he continued. 'I will spare no expense to catch the person who killed her.'

'What are you saying?'

'Saying? Nothing. Nothing.' He leaned forward. 'What do you know, Ms Bell?'

'Nothing,' I said despairingly. 'I didn't know your daughter, Mr Hamilton. I never talked to her. I was just a messenger. It could have been anyone else who found her. It was chance that it was me. I saw her lying on the floor, I called nine-nine-nine, I smashed the window. That's all. I can't imagine what you must be going through, but there's nothing I can tell you that the police haven't told you already and nothing I know that you don't.'

He rubbed his face with his hands. 'It seemed important to see you, yet why? What did I expect to discover?'

'Did she look peaceful?' This was from Andrew de Soto.

I cast him a confused glance. Didn't he know that his wife had been brutally murdered? Hadn't they told him how her face had been slashed?

'Yes,' I muttered. 'She did.'

'Excuse me for one moment,' said William Hamilton. He heaved himself out of his low armchair and made his way towards the lavatories.

As soon as he was out of the room, his son-in law leaned forward in his chair, jolting the low table. 'She was having an affair,' he whispered.

'What?'

'She was having an affair.'

'Listen, I don't know anything about that. Really. You have to tell the police and –'

'I don't have proof. Don't you think I've searched for it? But I'm not stupid. I know.'

'I'm sorry,' I said. It seemed to be the only phrase left in my vocabulary.

'And now someone's killed her.'

Later I told the house about the meeting, but I wished I hadn't. It made it sound somehow darkly funny, when it wasn't at all.

It was my favourite time of year, late May, then early June, with the leaves fresh and bright on the trees, the sky a clear blue, the evenings long and soft and warm. I hated being unable to enjoy it properly. A whole part of my life seemed to be coming to an end, and coming to an end in a sour and messy way. Sometimes I would come home and not even go into the house, but retreat at once to the garden, where my vegetables were pushing their way up, sappy little shoots lying in neat rows along the plot I'd spent so many hours digging and weeding. And it was out here, four days after Kamsky's visit, that I heard yet more noise erupting from the house. I laid down my trowel, wiped my hands along the grass to clear off the worst of the soil, and listened, trying to make out what was going on. At first I assumed it was one household member yelling at another, but I didn't recognize the voice and couldn't make out many of the words – just an obscenity here and there.

Then Davy emerged from the kitchen and made his way up the garden. He looked tired. 'What on earth's going on?' I asked.

'I think Pippa might need you,' he said.

I ran down the side alley to the front of the house. The 'fucks' grew louder and I could make out other words, like 'How dare you?', 'interfering', 'spiteful' and 'ball-breaking'. At first I didn't recognize him because he was standing at the top of the steps that led up to the front door and I couldn't see his face, though I could see Pippa's, on the other side of the door, looking shocked but defiant. But something about his tall, narrow figure was familiar.

'Hello, Jeff,' I said.

He wheeled round. 'Oh, you.'

'Jeff's had a visit from the police,' said Pippa, demurely. 'He wasn't in, but his wife was.'

'They should have been more tactful.'

'Who asked you?' said Jeff, bitterly.

'I told you to go to the police yourself,' said Pippa. 'Then none of this would have happened.'

'I was going to. When I had time.'

'With murder, the police get a bit impatient.'

'You didn't care what happened to me.'

'Oh, grow up.'

'Hang on, now,' said Davy. 'You're creating a bit of a scene.'

Dario put his head out of an upstairs window. 'What's going on?' he called. 'Shall I pour boiling pitch over his head, Pippa?'

'Better not. You might miss and hit Astrid instead.'

'That's it.' Jeff's face became apoplectic with rage. Stooping, he picked up half a brick from the path and hurled it. It arced through the air and struck the large window to the left of the front door, shattering it on impact. We all stared in fascination. Leah's face appeared in the large, jagged hole it had left.

Chapter Fifteen

'Do you know who I am?'

'You're Hal Bradshaw.'

'No, no. Do you know who I *am*?'

I looked around his consulting room. There was a whole wall of books: Freud, Jung, poetry, art books, catalogues. A variety of small sculptures was arranged on the mantelpiece and on two glass tables, small figures in soapstone, marble and bronze with several antique medicine bottles, a block of quartz. Through french windows I could see a large, colourful Hampstead garden. Dr Hal Bradshaw was dressed in faded jeans and a shirt decorated with splashes of colour, like a child's drawing. It looked expensive. He was in his forties, with long, untidy, curly black hair and a couple of days of stubble. He wore spectacles, black plastic frames, narrow rectangles, like a welder's goggles.

'Kamsky told me you were a psychological expert on this sort of stuff.'

'You could say that. Sit down.'

He waved me towards a high-backed wicker chair. When I sat on it, it crackled disconcertingly. 'I don't really understand why you want to talk to me,' I said. 'I don't know much and what I do know is in the statements I gave.'

'I've read them,' he said dismissively. 'That sort of thing doesn't interest me. I invited you here because I wanted to smell you.' He gave a sniff, like some snuffly animal.

'What?' I said, alarmed.

'Not literally,' he said, 'although I'm sure you smell very nice.'

'Not when I'm riding round London.'

'I need to get a feel for the case. I need to plug into it. Into its vibrations. There are people in white booties who go around Ingrid de Soto's house with their tweezers and their little plastic bags. I don't do that. I make imaginative leaps. I lie in the dark and think about it. I dream about it. Have you dreamed about it, Astrid?'

'No,' I said. 'Well, not as far as I know. I don't remember my dreams on the whole.'

'That's interesting,' he said, padding around the room, stopping every so often to look at me. 'Forgetting can be our way of telling ourselves what we need to know.'

'I'm sorry,' I said. 'I don't know what that means.'

'Tell me what you dreamed last night.'

'I can't. I don't remember.'

'Were you upset by what you saw?'

'Yes.'

'Tell me about it.'

I paused for a moment. 'I found a woman who had been murdered and mutilated,' I said, 'and you want me to tell you why I was upset by it?'

'What did you think when you saw her body?'

'It wasn't about thinking. I was shocked. Then I called the police. And an ambulance, too, I think.'

'You think?'

'It's a bit of a blur.'

'"Blur". That's an interesting word.'

'No, it isn't.'

'Really?' said Dr Bradshaw. 'Why not?'

'It's a cliché,' I said. 'It's what people say after a shocking experience. They say: "It was a blur."'

'Why do they say it, then?'

'Because it's true. Because it's a blur.'

Bradshaw looked dissatisfied. He walked up and down, then stopped abruptly in front of me. 'Astrid, why do people commit murders in front of you?'

'I think it's just a coincidence.'

'From God's point of view there are no coincidences.'

'I'm not sure what that means,' I said. 'But the bit of it I understand, I don't agree with.'

'We need to tell a story that links them,' said Dr Bradshaw.

'A true story?' I asked doubtfully.

'Murderers are storytellers,' said Dr Bradshaw. 'Murder scenes are their stories, their works of art. Our job is to decode them. We analyse their signature, we understand them.'

'Do you catch them?'

Dr Bradshaw gave me a look of distaste as if that were a shallow and vulgar concern. 'Astrid, let me tell you one possible story. Some murders are acts, some are statements, some are displays, some are offerings. The detectives are baffled about what could link these two murders to you. Let us imagine them as offerings. My cat is called Ariel.'

'After the soap powder.'

'After the Shakespearean character. He brings in mice and lays them by my bed. They are offerings. Imagine these murders as declarations of love.' Dr Bradshaw leaned over me. 'I love you, Astrid.'

'What?'

'I'm telling a story. I love you, Astrid, and here is the body of Margaret Farrell, the woman who almost killed you.'

'It was an accident.'

'Does it matter? And now here is the body of a beautiful,

rich woman, laid out for you. I have mutilated her face to show that nobody can compare to you.' He leaned closer still. I could smell his breath: coffee, cigarettes. 'Mmm?'

I moved away. 'It seems a bit far-fetched to me.'

'We'll see,' said Dr Bradshaw, with a smile. He picked a small wooden sculpture from a table and began to finger it delicately. 'Do you have a boyfriend, Astrid?'

'No,' I said.

'You hesitated before you said that. Why?'

'Perhaps because I can't see what business it is of yours.'

'I think there's someone, even if he's not a boyfriend yet.'

'Maybe.'

'You like him. Does he like you?'

'I don't know,' I said.

'Do you have ex-boyfriends?'

'I really don't think this is relevant.'

'Please, Astrid. Do you?'

'Well, of course.'

'Are you on good terms with them?' he asked.

It was terrible but I couldn't stop myself smiling, then regretted it instantly because Dr Bradshaw pounced. 'Yes?' he said.

'Who's on good terms with their exes?' I asked.

Dr Bradshaw walked across the room, picked up a piece of paper from his desk and read it. 'And yet one of them is your landlord. Miles Thornton.'

'I take it you've read my statement?'

'I'm part of the investigation. I read everything.'

'I think you're wasting your time.'

Dr Bradshaw replaced the paper on the desk and walked back towards me. He pulled a wooden chair across the floor and placed it opposite the wicker one in which I was sitting and just a few feet in front. He sat and faced me. 'The police are bustling around,' he said. 'They're knocking at doors. They're stopping people in the street. They're putting up those funny yellow signs asking for witnesses. They're looking through microscopes at fibres and grains of dust and samples of skin. They're checking phone records. Maybe they'll find a match somewhere and make an arrest, but it's looking less and less likely. On the other hand, I have this feeling that if we look at your life, at its details and its characters, at your hopes and your fears and your fantasies, then somewhere in there we'll find the answer to all of this. So, what do you say to that?'

'I wonder if you're like the others,' I said.

'What others?'

'I'm like a celebrity,' I said. 'I'm like someone who's won the lottery or starred in a soap. People want to talk to me and take photographs of me. Reporters come up to me in the street. I've had notes pushed through the door by people saying they want to give me a chance to tell my side of the story. As if I even have a side of the story. A woman journalist phoned me up saying that I could use my experience to help other women and that it was my duty to give her an interview.'

'Why are you telling me this?'

'I feel like I'm someone who's been exposed to radioactivity,' I said. 'Except it's a kind of radioactivity that everybody's attracted to. I've been close to a murder and people think that by talking to me, by being close to me, they can feel some of its heat. Isn't that a bit like what you were talking about when you said you needed to see me because you could somehow smell the murder on me? I've become a bit famous and people are attracted to it.'

'I'm a scientist,' said Dr Bradshaw. 'A scientist who tells stories. I couldn't care less about celebrity.'

'What about your TV work?' I said. 'DCI Kamsky told me you did a series about famous murders.'

'That was education,' said Dr Bradshaw, evidently irritated. 'Did you see any of them?'

'No.'

'They showed them ridiculously late at night. But don't you want to help find this killer?'

'Killers,' I said.

'Maybe,' said Dr Bradshaw.

'What do you want from me?' I said. 'I don't get it.'

'I want you to talk.'

'What about?'

'Everything. Leave nothing out. Spare me nothing.'

I thought for a moment. 'Kamsky said that you do profiles for them,' I said. 'Wouldn't it be a good idea if you told me the sort of person you have in mind? Then if I know someone like that, I could tell you.'

Bradshaw stood up and a smile spread slowly across his face.

'A white man,' he said. 'Early thirties. Over six feet tall, strongly built. Lives alone. Sexually isolated. Possibly with some sort of disfigurement. He works with tools: a carpenter or a plumber or a leather worker.'

'Why a leather worker?'

'Someone who works with incising tools – it was his natural way of expressing himself.'

'How do you know the rest of it?'

He gave a shrug. 'It's just a hypothesis,' he said. 'Serial killers choose victims of the same racial group as themselves. I suspect that Margaret Farrell was opportunistic, but he chose Ingrid de Soto. She was his age but otherwise everything that he wasn't: rich, beautiful, married. He was able to overpower Margaret Farrell and kill her in a matter of seconds in the street. That suggests a degree of physical strength.'

'And the disfigurement?'

'The way he cut Ingrid de Soto. That represented both his sexual frustration and, I suspect, his own sense of being mutilated. He wanted to make her like himself.' Dr Bradshaw folded his arms with obvious satisfaction. 'Even when they think they're concealing themselves, they're leaving traces, signatures, clues.'

'Well, I don't know any disfigured leather workers,' I said.

'I don't want you to be a detective,' said Dr Bradshaw. 'I just want you to talk. I don't want your theories. I want to know everything you know.'

I couldn't stop myself sighing. It was clear that another Saturday was going to be wasted.

'I've got something for you,' said Davy. 'I thought it might cheer you up.'

We were sitting in his room, which was on the floor above mine, overlooking the street. It was one of the few bedrooms in the house that felt restful to be in. When Davy moved in, he had painted it a grey-green colour, sanded the boards and put up shelves, though there weren't many books on them. He had a futon, a large chest of drawers, which he had painted white, the swivel chair I was sitting on, and a square blue rug on the floor. The room felt light and airy. Since Mel had arrived on the scene, there was also a large wooden wind chime hanging from the ceiling, which gave out a liquid booming if you knocked into it, and flowers on the mantelpiece above the fireplace that was never used.

Today, a giant red peony was wilting in its vase. It seemed a shame he'd put so much effort into making it so nice only to be moved on.

'Do I seem like I need cheering up?'

'If it was me, I'd need cheering up,' he replied. 'Anyway, it's for me as well. I thought it would be a treat. These people I was putting a staircase in for – illegally, I might add, I'm sure it breaks safety regulations and they're probably giving me this as a bribe – they had a pair of tickets going spare. For the Chelsea Flower Show. I thought we could go together. You like gardens.'

He beamed at me, pleased with himself.

'Oh?' I felt a bit taken aback. 'Wow! Do I have to wear a hat?'

'It's not Ascot.'

'That's really lovely,' I said, making myself smile hugely. 'Thanks, Davy.'

On an impulse I kissed his cheek and saw him flush up to the roots of his wavy brown hair.

'You're welcome,' he said.

'When is it?'

'About ten day's time. Is that OK?'

'Great,' I said, though my heart was sinking at the thought. A day of having to spend time with someone I didn't especially want to spend time with. A day of being on my best behaviour. It was like being a child again, visiting an unfavourite aunt.

'Can you get time off work?'

'If I warn Campbell.'

'We can have a picnic first.'

'Lovely. I really appreciate it, Davy.'

'Well.' He shrugged. 'You've been having a tough time.'

'Yeah,' I said. 'It'll pass, I guess. I don't want to think about it right now, though. I've had enough for one day.'

I picked up a beautiful glass paperweight that was on the mantelpiece, and passed it from hand to hand, looking at how the light caught in it. 'Paperweights never have paper underneath them, do they?'

'Oh,' he said, apparently disconcerted. 'I've never thought about it.'

'Sorry, I'm changing the subject. The thing I really need, Davy, is to find somewhere else to live.'

'No luck?'

'No – which isn't surprising, really, since I haven't started looking. I keep putting it off. What about you?'

'I've put out a few feelers.'

There was a silence, and I put the paperweight carefully back in its place. 'I should be on my way, I guess. I'm going dancing.'

'Nice,' he said, a bit wistfully.

I considered inviting him along too, but then dismissed the idea. I wanted to get away from the household, rather than take it with me.

I came home very late that night, with music still pounding in my ears. The house was dark, and I fumbled with my key in the lock. Then I heard a tiny whimper, coming from one side of the steps, and froze. What was it? A cat? I peered down and saw a huddled shape, a patch of pale flesh. For a moment I couldn't breathe or move. My keys clattered to the ground and bounced down the steps to lie by the shape. The whimper came again; not a cat but a human voice.

'Who is it?' I asked, my voice dry with fear.

'Help.'

'*Dario?*'

I ran down the steps, half tripping, and crouched beside

the figure on the ground. He was lying curled up tightly, like a foetus, with his arms protectively round his head. When I touched him my hands came away sticky with blood.

'Christ, Dario, what's happened? Hang on, I'm going to call an ambulance. Don't move. Just stay there.'

'No ambulance. No police. Don't!'

He moved an arm from his head and clutched at me with his fingers.

'Hang on, I'm going to call the others at least. One second, Dario. It's all right.'

I picked up my keys and bounded back up the steps, opened the door and bellowed into the darkness: 'Help! Pippa! Miles! Mick! Davy!'

I thought I heard someone groan, but that was it.

I hammered on Miles's bedroom door and pushed it open, turning on the light and seeing Leah emerge from the covers like a mermaid coming out of the waves.

'What –' she began.

'Miles!'

'What's up? Astrid? Astrid!'

'Come and help *now*. It's urgent. Dario's hurt. Leah, get the others. We're outside the front door. Come on!'

I left them, hammered at Pippa's door and yelled her name again, then ran out of the front door, leaving it open so that the light fell on where Dario lay.

He'd moved now, and was sitting huddled on the bottom step, his face in his lap and his arms wrapped round his body. I sat beside him and put an arm around his shoulder. 'If you can move, let's get you inside.'

He muttered something unintelligible into his knees.

'I really think I ought to call an ambulance.'

'No!'

He half sat up as he said this and I gasped as I saw his

face. One eye was closed, his nose was swollen and shapeless, and blood smeared his chin and ran in gobbets from his mouth. 'Can't see properly.'

'Here, take my arm.'

'Dario.'

It was Miles, and behind him I saw Davy, then Mel, in bright pink pyjamas, her hair in plaits.

'Help me get him inside.'

Davy took one arm and Miles the other. Mel cooed and tutted beside them. Pippa appeared in boxer shorts and an old T-shirt.

'Where's Mick?' I asked. 'He knows about things like this.'

'I'll get him,' said Mel, eagerly.

'Have you called the ambulance?' asked Davy.

'No ambulance!' gasped Dario.

'What happened, mate?'

'Nothing,' said Dario, as he was hauled into the hall. Blood dripped on to the floorboards. Leah stood in the doorway of Miles's room, watching. I saw her eyes widen as she saw the mess of his face.

'Let's get him downstairs,' said Miles.

'I can walk now.' But he staggered. Davy steadied him and guided him down into the kitchen.

'Hot tea,' I said, and they lowered him into the armchair. 'With sugar for the shock.'

'I'll do it,' said Mel, reappearing with Mick, who was wearing jogging pants and nothing else.

'Whisky,' said Miles.

'You were beaten up, weren't you?' asked Davy, frowning with concern. 'You really can't just leave that, you know.'

'I'll be all right.' But he was crying, his tears running into the blood. One of his teeth was missing; his ginger hair was plastered to his head. He looked about seven years old, scrawny, defeated and utterly woebegone. I squatted down and put a hand on his knee.

'Oh, Dario,' I said, and he wept harder. 'Tell us.'

'They wouldn't stop,' he gasped.

'Who?' asked Miles. 'Who did this to you?'

I turned away and went to where Mel was making tea. I soaked kitchen towels in warm water and took the disinfectant from the cupboard underneath the sink.

'How do you put up with us all?' I asked her. 'You must think you've wandered into a madhouse.'

She smiled at me shyly, her cheeks pink. 'I like being with you. I never had a family of my own.'

'My God, Mel! Is this your idea of a family? Hold on, Dario, I'm coming to clean you up a bit.'

Pippa and I washed his grazes and dabbed on disinfectant. Mick examined him to see if he'd broken anything. He howled and blubbered a bit more, held my hand, and repeated that nobody must know.

'Was it Lee?' asked Davy.

But he wouldn't give names, and in the end we gave up. Mick lifted him like a baby and carried him to his room, where he laid him on his bed and Pippa and I put extra blankets over him. Mel plumped up his pillow and put her smooth little hand on his sweaty forehead. His sobs were little whimpers now, and then, suddenly, he was fast asleep, his mashed-up face peaceful at last.

It was nearly dawn before I got to bed that night. After Dario had fallen asleep, the rest of the household sat in the kitchen, drank whisky and talked, endlessly repeating themselves, about Dario. For that brief time our group was oddly companionable again, drawn together by the experience.

One by one, people peeled away, until at last only Pippa and I were left at the table with our glasses.

'I'm not really tired now,' I said.

'Nor me.'

'Want a sandwich or something?'

'Go on, then. We haven't had a midnight feast for ages.'

I opened the fridge and peered inside. There wasn't much in it. 'I think it's a choice between a cheese sandwich or a melted cheese sandwich.'

'The second one. Comfort food.'

'OK.' I cut two thick slices of bread and put them in the toaster. 'Pippa?'

'Mmm.'

'Can I ask you something?'

'Sure – as long as it's not for a loan. I've got an overdraft of eight hundred and twenty-seven pounds at the moment.'

'Nothing like that.' I spread butter on the slices, then sprinkled grated cheese on them and slid them under the grill. 'Why do you sleep with so many men?'

Pippa gave a gurgle that could either have been merriment or dismay. 'First Leah,' she said. 'Now you. You think I'm a slag.'

'No, I don't. It's just that I've never quite got it. I'm not exactly saving myself for my wedding day, but hasn't it got to mean something? It's not like having coffee with someone . . . I don't think I'm putting this very well.'

'The cheese is ready.'

'Here you are. It's probably very hot. It's just – well, there are so many of them. It's a bit bewildering sometimes.'

'Why not?' she said lightly, and bit into her toast; strings of melted cheese clung to her chin. 'This is perfect. Just the thing after a mugging.'

'Is that it, then? Why not?'

'I guess.'

'Do you enjoy it?'

'Enjoy?' She paused with her toast half-way to her mouth and considered.

'So?'

'You really want the answer? Because it's the one thing men really want. They might deny it, but no man – however moral, however married – will turn you down if you offer them sex.' There was a silence. 'Are you shocked?'

'I was just thinking,' I said. 'I don't know whether you love men or you have contempt for them.'

Pippa thought about it. 'Can't I do both?'

Chapter Sixteen

I only found out that we were going to have a sale when I arrived home in the evening and read about it on the large cardboard sign that someone had tacked on to the tree at the front.

'House-clearance sale,' it read in large letters. I recognized the paint as the deep green that Dario had been using to paint the upstairs hall, before he laid down his brush and went on strike. 'Thursday 6 p.m.' Underneath, in the bathroom's stone blue, was written in a large, childlike hand, 'Bargains!!!'

'House-clearance sale?' I asked Davy, when I went into the kitchen. He was sitting at the table failing to do the crossword, and I could see that someone had already started putting old pots and pans into cardboard boxes while piles of chipped plates, discoloured mugs, ugly vases, a broken toaster minus its plug and a food mixer that had long ago stopped working cluttered all the surfaces.

'Apparently.'

'But we still live here. We're not moving for weeks yet.'

'We're not getting rid of everything. Just the things we don't need and know we don't want.'

'We need plates.' I stared around the room. 'Those are my mother's old teacups. You can't just chuck them out.'

'It was Pippa's idea. She said we should liquidate our assets.'

'What's this?'

He peered at it, frowning. 'I think it's an old pasta-maker, minus the handle thing. It's a bit rusty, isn't it? And that's the bottom half of an ice-cream maker. Dario couldn't find the top.'

'Right. Assets, Pippa said?'

Davy gave a little giggle. He's one of the few men I know who giggles like a girl.

'Hi, Astrid.'

I turned. Mel stood in the doorway, her soft brown hair falling over her face. She was wearing a green skirt and a sleeveless white top and looked fresh and eager. I smiled at her. 'Hello there.'

'I've just been down to the shops. I was going to make us an omelette. Do you want one as well?'

'No, I'm fine. I'll get myself something later.'

'If you change your mind . . .' She set down her shopping and rummaged among the boxes for a frying-pan.

'What does Miles think about the sale?'

'I'm not entirely sure that anyone's told him. He's not come home yet.'

'I see.' Suddenly there was a tremendous banging sound from overhead. It felt as though the ceiling might crumble at any minute. 'What the hell's that?'

'Um.' Davy pulled a wry face at me. 'I think that might be Dario and Mick. Asset-stripping.'

'Christ,' I said. 'But at least Dario's cheered up. He was even boasting about being beaten up, as if it gave him some sort of street cred. Men, eh?'

'Not this man,' said Davy, wryly. 'I'd leg it. Do you want to hear who's called you today?'

'Apart from journalists?'

He pulled a piece of paper out of his pocket. 'Dr Hal Bradshaw and someone called Rachel Lembas, who's a clair-voyant.'

'I'll pretend you didn't give me the message.' I watched as Mel broke two eggs into a bowl and began whisking with a fork. She had managed to create a tranquil domestic space in the mayhem of our crumbling household. There was a another violent bang from overhead, then a rude yell.

I went outside, into the lovely warmth of the evening, and walked into the garden to my vegetable plot. It was ridiculous, but the thing I felt saddest about leaving was this. I thought of the work I'd put into it, in the rain and the cold, and the idea that Miles and Leah would be the only ones to eat my lettuce, my beetroot and my broad beans filled me with sadness. I squatted and started to pull weeds out of the soil. I didn't hear anyone, and only when a shadow fell over me did I look up and see Miles.

'Hi,' I said, and when he didn't reply, just started gloomily down at me, I went on: 'These are courgettes. They're very easy to grow. You just have to keep the soil moist. Miles? Miles!'

'What?'

'What's up?'

He sighed and lowered himself on to the grass beside me, not worrying about his lovely dark suit. He looked hot. Little beads of sweat prickled on his shaved head and there was a moustache of perspiration above his upper lip. 'What should I do, Astrid?'

'What should you do?' I carefully eased a dandelion out of the earth, shaking its roots free of soil. 'What do you mean, do?'

'I mean, *do*. Should I tell everyone it was all a mistake and they can stay after all? Should I evict everyone right now? Should I chuck Dario out, at least, for making my life a nightmare at every turn? Should I tell Leah it's all over between us? Should Leah and I go away and leave you here, in this house that's turned into a kind of hell-hole? Should we all just –'

'Stop there, Miles. Too many choices.'

'Is it so wrong of me to want to live with just Leah?'

'No,' I said. 'Admittedly I'm tired of falling over bags of her stuff in the hall.'

'I'm sorry,' said Miles. 'We haven't decided where to stow it. I'll tell her to get it out of the way.'

'Don't worry,' I said. 'And it's not wrong.'

'So what should I have done?'

'I don't know.'

'Should I never move on but always stay in some commune of perpetual adolescence?'

'Is that what we are?'

'Don't you agree that the way Pippa, for example, has deliberately –'

'I don't want to take sides, Miles. I know that no one's behaved terribly well. But that includes you. And Leah.'

'Especially Leah,' he said.

'You can't hide behind her.'

'I used to love coming home but now I feel everyone hates me,' he said.

'I don't hate you.'

'Astrid.' His voice became soft and tender.

'No. Don't.'

'Don't what?'

'You know.'

'This thing with Leah. I think I've made a terrible mistake.'

'Then unmake it, if that's what you want. But don't involve me. It's not fair on her.'

'She doesn't worry about not being fair to you.'

'That's her business.'

'The things she says about you . . .'

'I don't want to know.'

'If it wasn't for Leah, we could go back to the way things were.'

'For a clever man you really are stupid sometimes. Don't you see that we can never go back to the way things were? That's over, safely in the past. And don't go blaming Leah for everything.'

'How come you're so wise and saintly all of a sudden?'

'I'm not.'

He brushed some grass blades from his trousers. 'By the way, what's going on with Owen?'

'Nothing. Not that it's any of your business.'

'I've seen the way you look at each other. Have you –'

'Stop it, Miles.'

'I don't want to butt in. When does he get back from his trip, anyway?'

'I don't know,' I said, with studied indifference. 'Thursday, I think.' I knew very well it was Thursday. I lay in bed at night thinking about him, remembering the feel of his hands on my body, counting the hours to when we'd creep upstairs like thieves in the night and close the door and climb beneath the sheets, our hands over each other's mouths so no one would hear.

'He's not good enough for you.'

'I'm not doing this, Miles. Either help me pull out the weeds or bugger off.'

The evening of the house sale was warm and muggy, with an occasional heavy raindrop falling from the low grey skies. Dario and Mick had carried out two tables and arranged them in front of the house, and Pippa and Davy had both taken half a day off work to sort stuff out as well. Campbell sent me over to Stockwell in the afternoon and I didn't get home until twenty to six, by which time it looked as if the entire contents of the house had been disgorged into the front garden. The tables were piled high with junk, and larger items – among which I made out an old bike, a couple of wooden chairs missing slats and a vast armchair with the stuffing spilling out, a nasty metal bookcase, a wooden lampstand, an old mattress, a fold-up canvas camp bed that looked as if it had been used in the First World War, a nasty oil painting whose glass was cracked. They were the desirable objects, I realized, when I saw what Dario and Mick were hauling out of the house now: a flimsy plastic bathtub with a crack running all the way down one side that we'd had in the cellar since we moved in; a roll of chicken wire, a rake whose teeth were almost all missing; a box of spare roof tiles; single wellington boots; half a fishing rod; the guitar Mick had trodden on ages ago and was now just a splintered wooden carcass with a few strings hanging off it.

'Blimey!' I said, as Owen staggered out, hauling a stained canvas bag. He'd returned from Italy that morning and when I'd got home from work he was entering into the spirit of the sale with a vigour that surprised me. 'What's that?'

'A tent,' he said. 'It leaks. It's always leaked. It leaks so badly that it's like sleeping under a gutter.'

'Right. But you can't throw away Miles's shoe rack. He uses it. Where are the shoes that go in it?'

Owen shrugged and tugged his tent past me, scattering bent pegs as he went. But then he stopped and gave me a look that turned my stomach to liquid.

'Hi, Astrid,' said Pippa, appearing in the doorway. Her hair was piled messily on top of her head and there was a smudge of dirt on her cheek. She glittered with energy. 'If you want to get rid of stuff you'd better hurry. People are arriving in fifteen minutes.'

'Nobody'll buy any of this.'

'Want to bet?'

'Where's Miles anyway?'

'I think he and Leah are keeping out of the way.'

'And Davy?'

'He's gone to get beer for all of us.'

I leaned my bike against the wall of the house and went over to the table. There were books (cookery books, novels, biographies, dictionaries, atlases, travel books, books about mathematics and economics, music and law, books that belonged to libraries and even schools); there were kitchen utensils, videos and DVDs, beaded cushions, a rug, a lumpy old duvet, ripped sheets, a mop, a hairdryer in the shape of a duck, a shoebox full of wind chimes, empty biscuit tins, and several packs of cards, which I was almost certain were incomplete.

'These are nice.' I bent over a small box of jewellery. 'Are these yours, Pippa?'

'I never wear them any more,' she said airily.

'Some are lovely. You can't sell these beads.'

'I can.'

'I'll buy them.'

'We're supposed to be getting rid of things, Astrid!' said Dario.

I stopped him and examined his face. He was still bruised and swollen, his speech muffled. 'How are you doing?' I asked.

'Fine.'

'You should be taking it easy.'

'No,' he said. 'I need to do this.'

Davy arrived, carrying a bag bulging with cans, which he

started handing out. I took mine and went into my bedroom, to see if there was anything I could throw out. But while Pippa's room is like an Aladdin's cave, mine is rather minimalist. I sat on my bed and stared around, realizing how little I owned.

I heard footsteps bounding up the stairs, and then they stopped. There was a knock at my door. 'Who is it?'

'Me. Owen.'

Oh.' I got up from my bed and ran my fingers through my hair. 'Come in.'

The door opened and Owen entered, pushing it shut behind him.

'I brought you something.' He held out a little box. 'From Milan.'

'For me? I don't know what to say. Thank you.'

'You have to open it.'

'Right.'

I pushed up the lid and there was a pair of small silver earrings, round and with spokes, like two tiny bicycle wheels. 'You'll spot a connection.'

I unhooked the earrings I was wearing and put them on. 'What do you think?'

'They seem good,' he said. 'But what do I know?' There was a pause. 'I'd better go. Things to carry.'

There were already about a dozen people clustering round the tables. I didn't recognize most of them. It sometimes dismayed me: I'd been living in the house for years but most of the people who lived in the street were still strangers.

I walked up to the tables and looked at the detritus of our lives together, now being pawed over by our neighbours. Soon it would be scattered and we would scatter with it.

Pippa and Dario were unpacking some clothes from a

box and draping them over one end of the table. I walked over and picked up a long flowery skirt and ran my fingers through the soft fabric. 'Some of this stuff really isn't bad,' I said. 'Why are you getting rid of it?'

Pippa gave me a challenging look, which seemed to suggest I didn't understand the ways of clothes and fashion. 'I've got a rule,' she said. 'Every so often I go through my stuff and if I find something I haven't worn for six months, out it goes, however much I think I like it. Because if I'm not wearing it, there must be something wrong.'

'Well, I haven't seen you wear any of this,' I said. 'I'm not exactly in the money at the moment but I might pick up a couple of things. How much are they?'

'A fiver each,' said Dario.

'Really?' said a voice from behind me. I looked round and saw a flamboyantly dressed woman with long dark curly hair. 'All of it?'

'Priced to sell,' said Dario.

The woman sorted eagerly through the clothes, cramming dresses, skirts and blouses under her arm. Her eagerness was contagious, setting off a frenzy among the other women who were gathered around. I still had the skirt in my hand and I managed to grab a beautiful black Victorian-style top with a lace collar. Everything else was gone in seconds and the women of Maitland Street and beyond were frantically proffering bundles of banknotes at an almost alarmed Dario and Pippa. I handed over my own ten-pound note and took my haul back to my room, squeezing past Mick who was manoeuvring a standard lamp out of the door.

'Are there any lights left?' I said.

'It's summer,' said Mick.

By the time I re-emerged, word had got round and the crowd of customers had grown quite large. The only item of clothing left was an army greatcoat that had been left by a previous tenant. But there was still plenty to fight for. People were paying money for objects that we would have had trouble persuading the dustmen to take away. Dario had priced the non-functioning toaster at fifteen pence. An old man offered him five and Dario told him he had a deal. I was rather touched by the idea of our crap toaster being lovingly repaired and having a new life making toast for him. It was like a horse finally reaching an animal sanctuary after a lifetime of grinding toil. Only the handleless pasta machine stood untouched, unbought and unloved.

'Are you Astrid Bell?' a voice said.

I looked round. The speaker was a man in his early sixties, wearing a grey suit, a tie and black shoes. He was balding and wore glasses.

'That's right,' I said.

'You were the last person who saw my wife,' he said.

I was going to say, 'Not the *last*' but didn't, because it sounded like heartless quibbling over words.

'Are you ... ?'

'I'm Joe Farrell,' he said. 'Peggy's husband.'

'I'm sorry,' I said. 'I was so shocked and upset by what happened.'

'You see that lad over there?' he said, pointing at a teenage boy who was trying on an old Walkman Dario was selling.

'I don't know him,' I said.

'I don't either,' he said. 'But I know who he is. He's one of the gang who robbed my wife after she was dead.'

'The ones who broke into your car?'

'That's right.'

'How do you know?'

'They called me into the police station and showed me photographs. He was one.'

He took a handkerchief from his pocket and blew his nose loudly. Knowing who he was, I looked at him searchingly. His face was grey with grief, if that wasn't my imagination. He had missed a patch of stubble along his jawline with his razor, now that there was nobody to notice for him. I dimly remembered that he had been brought in for questioning, not just as a witness. Did the police think he might have murdered his wife?

'They only charged them with theft,' he said. 'They're out on bail now, would you believe it? And now here he is. What do you think about that for a nerve?'

I couldn't think what to say. Everything seemed wrong. I could have said that this was where the boy lived and that it wasn't so surprising, but that might seem unsympathetic. 'It was terrible what they did,' I said. 'There's no excuse for it. But they weren't involved with your wife's death. They didn't know about it. They were stupid kids breaking into a car.'

'That's what the police told me,' said Farrell. 'How do we know they're right? They could have mugged her in the street, left her for dead, then come back and broken into the car when it was dark.'

'Did the police consider that?'

'I don't know. I told them about it and they said they'd investigate but I don't think they paid much attention. They mainly asked me about how often my wife and I argued and whether I suspected her of being unfaithful. I knew what they meant. They even got me to talk to a bloody psychiatrist. He asked me about my mother.'

'Yes,' I said. 'I met him as well.'

Farrell paid no attention to what I'd said. It was clear he just needed somebody to talk to. The words gushed out as if they had built up in the weeks since his wife's murder.

'What's all this?' he said, looking at the frenzied scenes in front of us.

'Most of us are moving out,' I said, 'so some of the guys in the house decided to have a clear-out.'

Farrell gave a loud sniff. 'You're doing the right thing,' he said. 'I'd get out of this area if I could. I've lived here for more than thirty years. They say it's coming up. But scum like that are still here.'

I didn't speak. I was a bit worried that the boy he was talking about might hear and there'd be more trouble.

'Peggy was old-fashioned,' said Farrell. 'She believed in being a proper neighbour. That's why you all knew her, isn't it?'

I murmured something unintelligible in response. I didn't want to tell him that I hadn't known his wife. That the first time I'd heard her full name had been when she was dead.

'She noticed things,' said Farrell, 'and she believed in getting involved. Those kids from the flats, they go around late at night kicking bins over and breaking windows and jostling people in the street. Other people ignored it but she used to say things to them and she rang the police about them. Not that they did anything. But those kids knew she wasn't someone who would just let something go. So they did something about it.'

'I hope the police find who did it,' I said.

'They've given up,' he said. 'I keep phoning up and they say the investigation is proceeding. But when did you last see a policeman down here?'

I didn't answer because I thought it would only confuse matters.

'Look at that kid,' said Farrell. 'He's pocketing that radio. I'm not going to let him get away with it.' I clutched at his sleeve to stop him.

'Don't,' I said. 'He'll get it home and then he'll discover it doesn't work. That'll be punishment enough.'

Farrell looked at me awkwardly. He was clearly about to go. 'If you ever want to pop round for a cup of tea,' he said, 'you know, to talk about things, I'm usually in in the evenings. And at weekends. Before you move away.'

'That would be lovely,' I said.

'Biscuits as well,' he said.

'Great.'

He moved away. 'I'll hold you to that,' he said, and I watched him edge his way through the crowd and walk alone along the pavement.

Suddenly I wanted to get away from the bustle and the noise, so I went back into the house, where I met Leah in the hallway outside Miles's bedroom.

'I didn't know you were here,' I said.

'I just got in,' she said. 'That's a squalid little scene out there.'

'I think it's quite fun,' I said. 'You wouldn't believe the things people have bought.'

She frowned. 'Oh, by the way, Astrid, Miles brought a bag of my clothes over this morning. Have you seen them?'

Chapter Seventeen

I contemplated making a dash for it, but Leah was standing in my way and to get past her I would have to knock her over.

'I don't know anything about a bag,' I said. 'I haven't been here, you see. Hardly at all. Can I come by now?'

She shrugged and stood aside, and I charged past her. As I got to my room, I heard her clipping across the hall and opening the front door. I sat on my bed and picked up my new blouse, pressing my face into its softness. It had a familiar, expensive smell. I sighed and waited for the hubbub to begin.

It wasn't long. First there was a shout, 'Hey!' in a voice I didn't recognize, then a truly ear-splitting shriek of rage.

I stood up, laying my shirt carefully on the pillow.

Then lots of voices shouting, I couldn't make out the words, followed by a crash and more screaming.

Very slowly I went down the stairs. The front door was wide open and through it I could see a wild scene taking place. Both tables seemed to have been pushed over, and the objects that had been on them were scattered across the front garden and even on the pavement. Youths were rummaging through everything in a kind of frenzy and more people were pouring in through the gate. As I looked, a very large woman, wearing tatty jeans, an old sweater and over it a glorious orange silk shirt that was several sizes too small, rushed past. There was a further yelp. I thought I recognized

Pippa's voice, but she was out of sight. Somebody was laughing and clapping.

Perhaps, I thought, I could go back into the house without being seen, creep downstairs into the basement, from there get into the garden, then sneak up the alley and be away. But even as I was thinking this, I was stepping outside and gazing at the wreckage that lay before me. The boys from the estate were picking up as much of the debris as they could hold and as I watched two started having a tug of war over the old lampstand. A group of girls were parading around with lacy knickers – Leah's, I assumed – on their heads, taking photos of each other with their mobile phones. Leah was in the corner, wrestling with the large woman whose orange shirt was now ripped from armpit to hem. Davy was with them, hopping from one foot to the other and occasionally trying to pull them apart, but although he's fairly strong, their rage was stronger and he didn't stand a chance. A few residents of the street stood in a bewildered huddle, some clutching bright garments, and stared at the mayhem, while out on the pavement a crowd was gathering. A boy hurtled past me, holding the lampstand, followed by his rival.

I turned to Leah, who now had the remnants of her shirt in her hands and was striding towards a small group of bewildered middle-aged women standing near the side alley. 'Hand them over,' she said.

They looked at her as though she was mad and backed away. 'My clothes,' said Leah.

'We bought them,' said one, nervously.

'Yes, proper money,' said another. 'This cost me five pounds.' And she held up a military-style jacket with a red lining.

I felt a nudge as Davy arrived at my side. He was panting

and there was a scratch on his cheek. I tucked my arm through his. 'How did this happen? No, don't tell me. Let me guess. Pippa and Dario.'

He didn't reply.

'Don't worry, you don't have to say. Let's try and sort this mess out.'

I walked over to Leah and the women, stepping over a boy who was scrabbling on the ground for scattered bits of jewellery. I tried to adopt an official tone. 'I'm afraid there's been a misunderstanding, and those clothes you have aren't for sale.'

'We bought them.'

'It was a mistake. You'll get your money back.'

'I don't want it back.'

'That's right.'

Leah made a strangled noise beside me. I could feel the heat rising off her.

'Just return the clothes, we'll return your money. Simple.'

'What about the others who've already left with theirs?'

'I'll get the money,' I said. 'Five pounds for each item, right?'

Again, Leah gave a whimper of rage.

'Where's the money, then? Davy?'

'What?'

'All the money, where is it?'

'Money?'

'The takings,' I said, as patiently as I could.

'It was in a box,' he said, looking around desperately. 'On the table.'

'Right.'

'And then . . . you know.'

'Right.' The front garden was littered with rubbish and people. There was still an audience on the pavement and among them, Owen was clicking away as if he was in a war zone. His camera was like a talisman, shielding him from any involvement in the disaster. I looked back at the house and saw three faces gazing out of a second-floor window: Dario, Pippa and Mick.

'So we've sold off the contents of the house,' I said, 'and Leah's wardrobe. And the money's gone.'

'It looks like it,' said Davy.

'Do you think it's funny?'

'No.' He gave a little snort and I felt my own lips curl.

'Are you laughing?' screamed Leah, into my face.

'Of course not,' I managed.

I thought she was going to fly at me, the only person she could get her hands on.

'You fucking are! You sell off my clothes and then giggle like a spiteful little schoolgirl! How would you feel if it had happened to you?'

'It has,' I said.

'What?' asked Davy.

'My bike. I left it leaning against the house. It's gone.'

Davy went over to the wall as if it would magically reappear if he gazed hard enough at the spot.

'I've spent years putting that bike together.'

The conspirators – Dario, Pippa and Mick – were advancing towards us, wearing the same expression of inno-cent surprise, which didn't suit Dario's swollen face.

'We were inside having a bit of a rest,' said Dario, 'and we heard all the noise.'

Behind us, the women dissolved away and a few seconds later I saw them jogging down the road, still clutching Leah's gorgeous clothes.

'Some of Leah's clothes have been sold,' said Davy.

'Oh dear,' said Pippa.

'Oh dear,' said Dario.

Mick shuffled from foot to foot.

'How could that have happened? We just put out all the bags of clothes we could see.' Pippa raised her eyebrows even higher. 'Didn't we, Dario?'

'Yes.' He put a hand over his mouth in a parody of dismay. 'God, I hope we didn't put yours out by mistake.'

Leah stared at them with contempt.

'Astrid's bike's been taken as well,' said Davy, but no one seemed to hear him. They were locked in their own little world of rage and revenge.

'And the money box,' I added.

They heard that. All heads turned to me.

'What?' said Mick.

'The money box has gone,' I repeated.

'How?'

'What do you mean, how? How do you think? I wasn't here. You three ran away, Leah got into a fight, Davy tried to break it up, and Owen was busy taking pictures.'

I twisted my head to look for Owen. He was talking to another man with a camera. My heart sank further: I recognized him as one of the photographers who'd been stalking me since I'd found Ingrid de Soto's body. 'That's all I need.'

'What?'

'We'll probably be able to read about ourselves in the local papers tomorrow. And here comes Miles, to make the happy family complete.'

We watched him as he walked along the street. He looked smart and cool, but as he drew nearer, puzzlement appeared on his face and his steps quickened, until he was nearly running to join us. 'What's happened?' he asked, as he came into the garden. 'Tell me there's not been another –'

'No, no,' said Davy. 'It was just –' He stopped and frowned. 'Just something,' he said.

'Have you called the police? What's going on *now*?'

'I'll tell you what's going on,' began Leah. 'And what your *friends* have been up to.'

'Not now,' I said sharply.

'It was your idea, wasn't it?' Leah said, turning on me.

'I'm the one trying to sort things out.'

'It was a mistake,' said Pippa.

'A mistake,' echoed Dario, nodding vigorously.

'Can we deal with all of this first, before the post-mortem?' I said. 'We've got to get everyone out of our garden.'

'It was just going to be a sale,' said Miles, in a dazed voice. 'I don't understand.'

'Wait,' I said. 'Just help me get them out. Davy, Mick?'

'I'll help,' said Pippa, brightly.

'You've done enough for one day.'

'Oh, don't you go all disapproving on me. It was a mistake.'

'Yeah, right.'

'Lots of money was in that box,' said Dario, gloomily. 'I can't believe it disappeared as soon as we turned our backs.'

'So surprising,' I said acidly. 'Now, why don't you get rid of those girls there?'

'What are you going to do?'

I didn't reply, but walked towards Owen and the other photographer.

'Got a bit out of hand, did it, Miss Bell?' the man said cheerily.

'Go away.'

'I'm sorry?'

'You heard. Go away. We don't want you here.'

'I'm not on your property. I'm on the street.'

'Leave.'

'But –'

'Or I'll call the police and say you're harassing me. Don't you believe me?' I fished out my phone and started dialling.

'Sparky girl you've got there, Owen.'

'I'm not a girl and he hasn't got me.'

Gradually people were dispersing. I joined Pippa and Dario, who were puffing at cigarettes amid the debris.

'Where's Leah gone?' I asked.

'Inside.' Dario tossed his stub on to the ground. 'She's a bit angry.'

'Are you surprised?'

'I'm angry too.'

'What about?'

'I was counting on that money.'

'You know what I think?' said Pippa. 'She has to leave the house and not come back until we're all out. This can't go on.'

'I certainly agree with the last bit.'

She looked at me. 'So will you tell her?'

'Me?'

'It'd be better coming from you.'

'She hates me,' I said, 'and she thinks I'm trying to steal Miles from her.'

'Miles would listen to you,' said Pippa, vaguely.

'Anyway, why should she leave? She's the landlord's girlfriend, remember?'

'Maybe Miles should leave as well. They could both go,' said Dario.

'Brilliant,' I said.

'No need to be sarcastic.'

'I can't go on living like this,' I said. 'Maybe we should move out now, sleep on friends' floors, anything.'

'Then she'll have won,' said Pippa.

'Won? This isn't a game. Look, why don't you two just apologize?'

'Apologize?' said Dario, with a hurt expression.

'It wasn't my fault Miles left a bag of her stuff hanging around,' said Pippa, primly, although she looked uncomfortable. 'But if it makes things easier, I'll say I'm sorry her things happened to get sold.'

The apology didn't quite go as planned. Leah was no longer heated: she was icily calm and there was a glint in her eye that made me apprehensive.

'Listen,' began Pippa. 'I just wanted to say that –'

'No, you listen,' interrupted Leah.

'Let's discuss this calmly,' said Davy.

'I agree,' said Miles.

'People are feeling anger,' said Davy.

'Who cares what they're feeling?' said Leah. 'It's what they've done.'

'But –'

'I don't think you're helping, Davy,' said Pippa.

'Is this a dream?' said Dario. 'It might be. That would explain everything.'

'I wish it was a dream,' muttered Miles, 'and that now I could wake up. Astrid, what have you got to say?'

'Why ask her?' said Leah. 'You all do that, the whole bloody household. It's Astrid says this and Astrid would do that and I'll just go and ask Astrid before I know what to think myself.'

'That's not fair.'

'You all talk to her behind each other's backs. Astrid-the-ex-lover, Astrid-the-future-lover, Astrid-the-confessor, Astrid-the-best-friend. But there are still some things she doesn't know. Aren't there, Pippa?'

'What's this about?' Pippa said sharply.

'Don't you know? Maybe Owen does, then. Owen?'

Owen stared at her, his expression hardening.

'No? How odd. I would have thought it was obvious.'

'What are you saying, Leah?' asked Miles.

'Don't ask her,' I said. 'Don't get involved.'

'You don't want to know?' asked Leah, turning towards me.

I ignored her, getting up from the table and picking up my jacket.

'After all, Pippa's been your friend for ages,' she continued. 'I thought she confided in you, especially about her love life.'

'Leah,' said Miles.

'Diversionary tactics,' hissed Dario in my ear. 'Pay no attention.'

'I'm not,' I said. I smiled at Pippa but she didn't seem to be smiling back.

'Pippa and Owen. Didn't you know? They didn't tell you about their little fling?'

I fixed a small, hard smile on my face and stared her down. 'Why would they?' I said.

Her air of triumph wavered slightly. 'I thought you and Owen . . .' she began.

'Then you were wrong.' Owen and I exchanged a glance. 'Anything else?'

'You're a bitch, Leah,' said Pippa.

'Cow,' barked Mick, then folded his arms across his chest and sat back.

'That's called shooting the messenger,' said Miles.

'And that's what I always am, isn't it, Miles?' said Leah. 'Your messenger.' Then she stalked out of the room.

I put on my jacket and did it up with trembling hands. I was trying to look dignified and undistressed.

'Astrid . . .'

'No, Pippa. Don't say anything. It's fine. There's nothing wrong. I just need a bit of fresh air.'

'We were a bit drunk. It was only once.'

'It doesn't matter,' I said. 'It's nothing to do with me.'

'Are you all right?' asked Miles, standing up and putting a hand on my shoulder, which I shrugged off.

'For God's sake, I'm fine. Why shouldn't I be?'

'Don't leave like this,' said Davy. 'Don't you think we should talk it through?'

'No, Davy, I don't. Funnily enough, I don't really feel like some group-therapy session about it.'

'Where are you going?' asked Miles.

'Out. For a bike ride.'

'You don't have a bike.'

'Then I'll walk.'

'Can I come?' asked Pippa.

'Not just now.'

'Astrid . . .'

'Don't say *Astrid* like that. Nothing's wrong. I just don't want to sit around here discussing it.'

'If you want company . . .' said Miles.

I looked around the room.

'No,' I said. 'That's the last thing I want.'

I walked a long way, through the soft warmth of the evening, and didn't stop until I reached Hackney Marshes. There were several teams out playing football on the pitches, but further on it was uncannily quiet and deserted. You could almost feel you were not in London any more, but somewhere near the sea. Somewhere wonderfully far away from the hot, nasty squabbles of home.

Chapter Eighteen

'How did you get here, Astrid?'

Kamsky was looking into my eyes. His lips seemed to be out of synch with what he was saying. And although he was so close to me that I could smell the coffee on his breath, he also seemed far away, separated from me, as if through glass. I felt like a fish in an aquarium and he was on the other side of the glass, staring through it at me. There seemed no immediate point in replying to him. And though it seemed like a dream, it wasn't a dream. It was real and I would have to start dealing with that.

'That's all right,' he said. 'You take your time, Astrid. We'll get someone to talk to you. Would you like some tea? Some nice, warm, sweet tea?'

He moved out of my vision. I looked around the room. There was a coffee mug on the mantelpiece, a cupboard door was open. It was as if she had just stepped out, but only for a few seconds, because she was going to come back and finish the coffee before it was cold and close the cupboard, because she wouldn't be the kind of person who would tolerate open cupboard doors. Through the cupboard door I could see a black coat and a woollen jacket, a boot, a canvas bag. Not many clothes, because most of her clothes were walking around Hackney being worn by other people. On the sofa there was a flowery silk dressing-gown and a paperback lying open. On the floor there was a cardboard box and several plastic bags. The box contained plates, jugs and a cafetière. The bags contained sheets, towels, pillows.

On the walls I could see the light rectangles and hooks where the pictures had been removed. They were now leaning against a wall. I could see only the outer one, a framed photograph of a man in a suit and a woman in a long dress, staring stiffly at the camera. Her grandparents. Maybe great-grandparents. I don't know the names of mine. They had lived and married and produced children and died, and fifty years later their great-granddaughter didn't even know their names. Was one of them called William?

The flat was crowded now.

'Do you know who I am?' said a man.

'Yes,' I said. 'You're Dr Bradshaw. Dr Hal Bradshaw. You're the psychiatrist.'

'Very good, Astrid,' he said.

'You got here quickly,' I said. 'Are you like a fireman?'

'What?' he said.

'You got here quickly,' I said. 'Like a fireman. To a fire, I mean.'

'There's a woman here,' he said. 'She'd like to take a swab from your hands. Is that all right?'

A woman leaned down in front of me. She wore a fawn-coloured sweater. A tiny crucifix swung out from her neck on a chain as she bent forward. She wore plastic gloves. She took my left hand and turned it palm upwards. I looked down.

'Oh, Jesus,' I said. 'Oh, sorry. Oh, God.'

The hand was splashed with blood. I felt something cold on it as the woman wiped it with a cloth. She placed the cloth in a plastic bag. She took a cotton bud and moved it on my fingertips so that it almost tickled. 'Do you mind?' she said, and before I spoke she examined my fingernails. 'You'll need to keep still.'

She took a shiny metal implement, like half of a pair of tweezers, and scraped under the nails one by one. I felt as if I was being cleaned, then scoured. Then she did the same for the other hand. As if by magic, DCI Kamsky was there again. 'Astrid,' he said. 'Was there a weapon?'

'What?'

'A knife. By the body. Or on the table.'

I shook my head.

'Astrid,' he said, slightly too loudly, as if I were deep in a cave or up on a ledge. 'There's a WPC here. WPC Lynch. We're going to leave her with you and you're going to take your clothes off. All of your clothes and any jewellery and accessories. We've got another set of clothes for you to put on. Do you understand?'

I flinched. The idea seemed obscene. 'Not here,' I said. 'I can't.'

'I'm sorry,' he said. 'It's important.'

The men left, looking embarrassed. WPC Lynch smiled. 'Call me Gina,' she said. 'It's procedure. Just pop that lot off and we'll get you into there and you can have a cup of tea as a reward.'

I looked around. 'Can you close the curtains?' I said.

'I'm not allowed to touch anything,' she said. 'Don't worry. Nobody can see in.'

WPC Gina Lynch unfolded what looked like a polythene laundry bag. I kicked my shoes off and pulled my socks down and over my feet. I lifted my bright yellow T-shirt over my head.

'It's a bit sweaty,' I said. 'I've been riding for hours.'

She snapped some surgical gloves on before she picked them up. It made me feel I was infected with something. Perhaps I was. 'It'll be returned to you,' she said.

I rolled my black cycling shorts down my legs and over my feet and handed them to her. I held my hand out for the tracksuit bottoms.

'I'm sorry,' she said.

'Oh, for God's sake,' I said. 'You're not serious?'

I unfastened my bra and slipped it over my arms. Then pulled my knickers down and slipped them over my feet. She put them in a smaller bag and I was standing naked in that terrible place. If she could see me now. WPC Lynch started rummaging in a satchel of the sort that postmen carry and produced a pair of grey-blue knickers and handed them to me.

'I won't even ask who these belong to,' I said.

'They're perfectly clean,' said Lynch.

I pulled them up.

'No bra, I'm afraid,' she said, and handed me a white T-shirt. I put it on, then a blue sweatshirt and red tracksuit bottoms.

She rummaged in another bag. She handed me a pair of socks rolled into a ball and a pair of black trainers.

'I'm building up a bit of a collection,' I said.

'What?'

'It doesn't matter.'

'We weren't sure of your shoe size but they'll get you home. I'm sorry, Astrid, but I'll need your earrings, the necklace and that ring.'

I quickly unclipped the earrings and unfastened the little blue-beaded necklace I'd bought in Camden Lock the previous summer. 'I don't know about the ring,' I said. 'A boyfriend gave it to me when I was nineteen. I've never taken it off.'

'If it's a problem, we can get someone to cut it off.'

'All right, all right,' I said.

I tugged at it. I couldn't get it over the knuckle but I licked the finger, then pulled until my eyes watered and my knuckle gave up, surrendering the ring. Where was Tom now? I wondered. As I handed it over I felt that I had been stripped of everything that made me me. I pulled the trainers on. They fitted well enough.

'You'll get a receipt for these,' said Lynch, 'and they'll be returned to you in due course.'

When Kamsky and Bradshaw came back in, I expected them to make some sort of joshing comment about the ridiculous clothes I was wearing but both looked serious. Kamsky nodded at Bradshaw, suggesting something prearranged between them. Kamsky handed me a mug of tea. I wondered where they'd got it. Had they made it in her kitchen? I sipped at it and flinched.

'Drink it,' said Kamsky, leaning over me like a parent urging a toddler. 'I've seen people like you faint. It'll do you good.'

A part of me rebelled against this. There was something horribly English about it. It didn't matter what it was – a natural disaster, a crime scene, the Blitz – it would be solved by a nice hot cup of tea. But I did feel weak and confused and I sipped at the horrible sweet drink to give me time to think and to pull myself together. Every time I paused, Kamsky would nod at me, urging me on, and I would take another gulp until the mug was empty and I handed it back to him like a good girl. He nodded across at Bradshaw, who nodded back.

'How are you feeling, Astrid?' he asked.

'Better,' I said. 'I was a bit shaken. Well, you know . . .'

'Yes,' he said. 'We know. Do you feel dizzy, sick, anything like that?'

'I'm all right.'

'Do you know where you are?' he said.

'What do you mean?' I said. 'Of course I do.'

'I'm sorry,' he said, 'but I've got to ask some stupid-sounding questions. I've got to assess whether you're in a fit state to be interviewed. So, you're perfectly clear about who we are?'

'I've got a rough idea,' I said.

'No, really. Do you know who we are?'

'Yes, I do.'

He looked across at Kamsky.

'What do you think?' said Kamsky, as if I wasn't there.

'It should be all right,' said Bradshaw. 'But I should be present.'

'All right,' said Kamsky. He looked at an officer standing by the door. 'You can get Frank now.'

The officer left the room and Kamsky and Bradshaw waited in silence until a man came in. He wore a grey suit and was a few years older than Kamsky, balding across the crown with silver-grey hair cut very short. He looked at Kamsky and then at me without any expression.

'Astrid,' said Kamsky, 'this is Detective Chief Inspector Frank McBride.'

'Hello,' I said.

McBride didn't answer. He just looked down at me.

'Matters are very urgent,' said Kamsky. 'You understand that, don't you?'

'Yes, I do.'

'But I need to remind you that you are entitled to have a lawyer present, if you want one.'

'What for?'

'And I need to warn you that, obviously enough, anything you say may be used as evidence and in court proceedings.'

'Obviously,' I said. 'Why else would I say it?'

'Exactly,' said Kamsky, with a smile. He stole a glance at McBride and then looked back at me. 'I'm afraid you're going to be giving more statements. We'll take you back to the station and there'll be tape-recorders and lawyers and lots of red tape.'

'I'm getting used to that,' I said.

More exchanged looks. As he started to speak, Kamsky seemed embarrassed. 'What we really wanted to say, Astrid, is that if you've anything to tell us, now would be a good time.'

'I don't understand,' I said. 'What do you mean?'

'I'll try to put this as plainly as I can,' said Kamsky. 'There are experts going over every inch of this scene. We're going to find the truth of what happened here. Leah Peterson's body is still lying ten yards away from where we're talking. Wouldn't it be good to put an end to all of this?'

I really had thought I was beyond feeling anything more but now I realized something of what was being said. It was as if a newly formed bruise was being punched repeatedly.

'I don't understand the question,' I said numbly. 'I really think you should say what you mean.'

'Let's not mess about,' said Kamsky. 'There's going to be a very large and detailed investigation. It's only just beginning. But if you have anything material to offer, it might be a good idea if you could do it now. If you have any involvement in what has happened, if you know anything, if you suspect anything, I can promise you, Astrid, that it would be better in every imaginable way if you told us now.'

'Are you insane?' I said. 'I was the one who called you. Do you think I have anything at all to do with this nightmare?'

Kamsky looked across at McBride and gave a helpless shrug, as if asking for help. McBride took hold of one of the dining chairs, pulled it across and sat down in front of me.

'Well, yes, we do,' he said. He had a light Scottish accent. 'You saw the body?'

'I was the one who called the police.'

'But you saw it properly?'

'Look,' I said, holding up my hands. McBride pulled a face.

'For God's sake,' he said, 'why hasn't someone dealt with that?'

'They took swabs.'

'That's not what I meant. Anyway, did the state of Leah Peterson's body remind you of anything?'

'It was just like Ingrid de Soto's body. Obviously. What do you want me to say?'

McBride took a small notebook out of his pocket and looked at it.

'So why were you here?'

'To collect a package.'

'People are going to stop asking you to collect their packages, Miss Bell. They'll start to think you bring bad luck.'

I didn't reply.

'Were you surprised to be called to the flat of someone you know?'

'I didn't know she lived here.'

'This is the home address of your ex-boyfriend's fiancée?'

'Yes.'

'DCI Kamsky called your office. Again. They're getting used to hearing from him. He asked for a written record of the transaction. Unfortunately they don't have one.'

'Sometimes we do jobs for cash,' I said. 'Off the books. It's better for everyone.'

'Not necessarily,' said McBride. 'And why you?'

'They asked for me specifically.'

'Is that unusual?'

'Yes. But I think Campbell said something about the woman being scared of men coming to the house. You'll have to talk to him about it.'

'You can be sure we will,' Kamsky said grimly.

Now there was a long pause.

'Miss Bell,' said McBride, finally, 'is there something you want to tell us? Something that might save us all a great deal of trouble.'

'I don't know what you mean,' I said.

McBride looked at Kamsky, then back at me. 'All right,' he said. 'Let me put it like this. How would you describe your relationship with Leah Peterson?'

Chapter Nineteen

I stared at McBride, who looked back at me without expression. Outside I could hear a bird singing and I thought it was probably the blackbird I had seen perched on the tree just outside the house when I arrived. That seemed a long time ago now, a world glimpsed through the wrong end of a telescope. I thought how all the ordinary things of life can often become moments of happiness when you look back at them. You don't understand that at the time.

'My relationship with Leah Peterson,' I repeated, in a voice that didn't sound like my own. Leah Peterson: how formal that sounded.

'Not here, Frank,' said Kamsky. 'Not like this.'

McBride shrugged. 'OK then.'

Kamsky put a hand under my elbow and pulled me to my feet where I stood, swaying slightly. 'Come on,' he said.

'What? Where are we going?'

'To the police station.'

'I want to go home,' I said, although it wasn't true. I didn't want to go home if that meant going back into the disintegrating wreckage of Maitland Road. And suddenly, as clearly as if he had been standing in front of me, I saw Miles's face, his smooth, veined skull and his brown eyes. I gasped and put a hand to my chest.

'What?' asked Kamsky, sharply.

'Do they know?'

'Who?'

'Miles. All of them.'

'You don't need to think about that at the moment,' said Bradshaw, in the kind of reassuring voice that made me want to punch him.

'But I –'

'Astrid,' Kamsky interrupted, and something in his tone made me feel cold, 'do you understand your position?'

'My position? I understand that Leah's dead.'

'Yes,' he said. 'Margaret Farrell, Ingrid de Soto, Leah Peterson. All dead.'

'What are you . . . ?'

'And all last seen by you.'

'The car's waiting outside,' said McBride. 'Let's get this started properly. Hal, follow after us, if you would.'

They led me through the hall and out of the house into the warm, blue day. There was an ambulance, three police cars and already a gathering crowd. I had the sense that I was on a stage: everything that was happening was unreal – the clothes that had been put on to me were a costume, the audience of avid passers-by the extras in a crowd scene; the body lying in the house was just pretending to be a corpse. I looked down at the pavement, trying to avoid the bright, curious eyes of the woman nearest the car, and allowed myself to be levered into it. Kamsky sat beside me and McBride in the front passenger seat. I stared at the back of the driver's neck: pink and spotty beneath his close-cropped hair.

'My bike,' I started to say. 'Well, it's not mine. Campbell lent it to me and . . .' But I stopped abruptly. 'It doesn't matter,' I said, and turned my head to the window so I didn't have to see Kamsky's grave face watching me. I looked at the blur of the world passing: cars and houses and people spooling past. I tried not to think about Leah's slashed face and her eyes, shallow and glassy, staring blindly up at me.

'Here we are,' said Kamsky. The policeman who'd been driving opened the door for me. He avoided my eyes as I stepped out and walked into the police station I knew too well, McBride on one side of me and Kamsky on the other as if they feared I might make a dash for it. A middle-aged woman in a long skirt was kneeling in the foyer, whimpering and scrabbling for all the objects that must have rolled out of her bag, but Kamsky steered me round her as if she was a bollard in the road, and straight into a bare room, with a table in the centre and plastic chairs placed round it. 'Take a seat,' he said, and I lowered myself into one. McBride closed the door and drew another opposite me, folding his arms.

'Aren't you going to offer me another tea for shock?' I asked Kamsky. 'That's what you usually do when I'm here.'

'Listen, Astrid, would you like to have a solicitor present?'

'What?'

'Would you like . . . ?'

'I heard what you said. I just meant, you know – *What?*

'It's your right,' said McBride.

A young woman came in with a tape-recorder and put it on the desk. Kamsky leaned forward and turned it on.

'Why on earth should I want a solicitor? I haven't done anything wrong. I found Leah dead and I called you and then I waited until you arrived.' I shivered. 'Sitting by her body. It changed even in that short time. It got deader, if you see what I mean. Colder and greyer and harder.'

'Am I to understand that you do not want a solicitor?'

'That's right. I don't want one and I don't know why you should think I do, and in any case what I want to ask you –'

'Ms Bell,' said McBride, in his soft Scottish voice. 'It is us who would like to ask some things of you.'

'A few weeks ago,' I said, 'I'd never seen a single dead person. Not even lying by the side of the road after a crash.'

'I want to return to the question I asked you at the house. What was your relationship with Leah Peterson?'

'She was the partner of Miles, who's the landlord of the house I live in.'

'But you knew her?'

'Kind of.'

'Would you describe her as your friend?'

'No.'

'Were you on friendly terms with her?'

I glanced at Kamsky, whose face was impassive. 'No.'

'You were on unfriendly terms with her?'

'That makes it sound wrong.'

'Had you had an argument with her?'

'You could say that. She was an easy person to argue with. She went out of her way to antagonize us. Ask him.' I nodded towards Kamsky. 'Why, the whole household –'

'We'll come to the whole household later. Answer the question. Had you had a specific argument with her?'

'Yes.' I took a deep breath. 'More than one.'

'Over what?'

'She was getting us ejected from the house.' I paused. 'That's not right. Miles was kicking us out because he's the landlord. But it was Leah who wanted us to go and I can understand that. The way she did it felt wrong. Miles hid behind her and let her do his dirty work.' I looked at Kamsky. 'You saw her at work. Then there's the fact that I used to go out with Miles. That didn't help. And then –' I hesitated, coughed, continued: 'Then she tried to create an argument

187

between me and Pippa, the other woman in the house and my friend, by telling me that Pippa and Owen had had a – what would you call it? "Sexual relationship". Yes. And what's more . . .' I was suddenly unable to go on. 'You get the drift,' I said miserably.

'Let me get this straight,' said McBride, his voice softer than ever. 'You were all being evicted from your house by Leah Peterson?'

'She was the driving force.'

'She was also the current girlfriend of the landlord, with whom you were once intimately involved.'

'Yes.'

'She taunted you with information concerning your current boyfriend and another woman in the house.'

'He's not my boyfriend.' I paused and rubbed my face with the hand that wasn't still bloody. 'He was something to me, though,' I added softly. 'Leah knew that. Or sensed it.'

'You argued last night?'

'Yes.'

'Were you angry with her?'

'Yes. And humiliated, I guess.'

'And now she's dead.'

'Yes.'

'And you discov –'

'I've changed my mind.'

'I'm sorry?'

'I would like a solicitor to be present.'

There was a silence. They both stared at me.

'Very well. Do you have your own solicitor or would you like us to contact one for you?'

'I don't know. I've never been in this position before. I don't know what I'm supposed to do. But no, no – I have someone I can call.'

Kamsky leaned back from his chair and reached over for the cordless phone on the shelf behind him. He handed it over.

'Can I do it privately? No, don't bother to answer that.'

'Nine for an outside line.'

I turned away from the two men and punched the numbers in. My fingers seemed too big for the buttons and several times I had to begin again. Outside, the sun went behind a cloud and the room suddenly darkened. I heard the ringing tone and then a chirpy voice: 'Rathbone and Hurst.'

'Hello,' I said. 'Could I please speak to Philippa Walfisch? Tell her it's Astrid Bell.'

'I'll just try and put you through. Hold on one minute.'

There was a pause. The sun came out again and the room lightened. My hand was slippery on the phone.

'Astrid, thank God you've rung. I've been trying your mobile for hours – I wanted to say how sorry I am. I'm stupid and thoughtless and crap, but I hope you know I'd never do anything to hurt you and if I'd thought for one moment that –'

It felt almost too much of an effort to interrupt her and tell her it wasn't about that and that I needed her help.

'Yes, anything,' she said eagerly. 'Just tell me and I'll do it.'

'I'm at the police station in Hackney. I think I need a solicitor.'

'I'll be there. I'm running out of the door right now. Just tell me what it's about.'

I stared at the receiver, then opened my mouth. I heard the words coming out but they still didn't make it seem any more real. 'Leah's dead. Murdered.'

There was complete silence. I pressed the phone to my ear but I couldn't even hear her breathing. 'I'm sorry,' I added miserably.

'Dead?' Pippa managed at last.

'Yes.'

'Leah?'

'Yes.'

'I don't understand. Why are you with the police?'

'I – I found her, Pippa. I found the body.'

'Jesus,' I heard her whisper. 'Jesus Christ. What's going on?'

'Can you come and help me? I'm scared.'

'I can't,' she said. 'I'm involved.'

'Oh,' I said dully. 'So what do I do?'

'Sit tight. I'm going to get in touch with someone. He's called Seth Langley and he's a friend of mine. Don't say anything until he arrives.'

'What if he can't?'

'Don't worry about that. He can come instead of having lunch with me.'

'Seth Langley?'

'That's right.'

'Pippa?'

'What?'

'It's all turned into a nightmare.'

Seth Langley arrived. He was very black, very tall, very calm. He asked Kamsky if he could have a minute alone with me. Kamsky frowned but he agreed.

'How are you?' Seth said.

'A bit shocked,' I said.

'Is there anything you need to tell me?' he said.

'The only thing I need to tell you is that I've got nothing to do with any of these crimes.'

'That's not entirely true,' Langley said. 'I talked to Pippa before coming in.'

'I mean criminally involved.'

'Is there anything you'd like to tell me?'

'Like what?'

'If I'm going to represent you, it's helpful if the nasty surprises come at the beginning.'

'I told you, I've got no connection to the murders.'

'That's not what I mean,' said Langley. 'Is there anything you've kept secret, because you thought it might be awkward?'

'It's awkward enough as it is,' I said. 'I was involved in a big row with Leah. Kamsky, the detective, even witnessed part of it.'

'If there's anything else to come out, I can assure you that it's better to admit it to me now than to wait for a journalist or the police to find it next week.'

'There's nothing else,' I said. 'I've got nothing to hide.'

'Not many people can say that,' said Langley. 'Then let's call them back in.'

He called me his client and sat beside me, speaking slowly and clearly, as if I was hard of hearing. Sometimes he would let me speak and sometimes he told me not to answer a question. They asked me the same things over and over again – times, places, names, actions – and jumped on every slip, confusion and contradiction. I had the feeling that words had turned into traps that could spring shut on me without warning.

They seemed especially interested in my relationship with Miles. How long had it lasted? How close had we been? How had we broken up? Had I been jealous of Leah? Had Leah been jealous of me? Had I had feelings of animosity towards Leah?

'Yes,' I replied, before Seth could stop me.

'You wished her ill?' asked McBride, leaning forward.

'Of course I wished her ill. I wanted her to suffer and feel guilt. There were times I hated her almost more than I can remember hating anyone. I wanted to wipe the smug expression off her face.'

'Astrid,' warned Seth.

'No, listen. So what? There are plenty of people I don't like, who I hate even, but that doesn't mean I want them dead. Or even if I did want them dead, it doesn't mean I'd do anything about it. It's ridiculous.'

And then: what were my feelings on discovering my sometime-lover — and yes, I said miserably, I had had sexual intercourse on more than one occasion with Owen — had slept with my friend? And more: if he had slept with Pippa, was it possible he had also slept with Leah? Is that what I had discovered last night?

'It's not like that,' I said.

'Let's see,' said McBride, leafing through notes he'd scribbled down. 'You had an affair with Miles Thornton, your landlord and partner of Ms Peterson. Then there's this Owen Sullivan, who lives in the house. You've been sexually involved with him, and he had also had an affair with another of the residents, Philippa Walfisch.'

'It wasn't really an affair,' I interrupted.

'Well, it sounds like fun, anyway.'

'That's not the word I'd choose.'

'I was asking if Ms Peterson and your boyfriend —'

'Who's not my boyfriend.'

'— if they had perhaps had a sexual relationship.'

'That's ridiculous.'

'For what reason?'

'Owen hates her, for a start.'

McBride looked up from his notebook.

'Enough to kill her?' he said.

I couldn't think of a reply that wouldn't make matters worse and we took a break. I had stewed coffee that made me feel sick and a cigarette that made me feel sicker. Seth made phone calls. Outside, the sky was now an unbroken blue. I looked at the clock on the interview room's wall: it was half past two. What was happening now at Maitland Road? Did they now know Leah was dead? I rubbed my sore eyes with my fists: I felt gritty and a kind of drab weariness had set in.

We began again – 'recommenced', as McBride put it. This time Hal Bradshaw was there as well, with his sympathetic face. I preferred Kamsky's inscrutability or even McBride's hostility to the way he looked at me as if he knew exactly what was going on inside my head. How could he know? I didn't know myself. He asked what I felt about Leah. He asked how I was, as if he was my doctor, as if he was my friend. I gave brief, uninformative replies. He was on their side. After it became clear that his tactic of getting me to talk, to free-associate, to give myself away, wasn't working, he looked helplessly at Kamsky.

'You're going round in circles,' said Langley. 'You're wasting Miss Bell's time.'

'Wasting time?' said Kamsky, with a flash of anger. 'There have been three murders. Your client is connected to them.'

'She's been perfectly willing to answer your questions at every stage. If you need any information, just ask her. Otherwise I think we should bring this interview to a close.'

I expected Kamsky to get angry, to shout, but he just looked weary. He turned to McBride. 'Can you leave us for a moment?' he said.

McBride glanced contemptuously at Langley and me, then left, slamming the door. Kamsky didn't hurry to speak. He ran a fingernail between a gap in his teeth as if he was trying to remove a trapped fragment of food.

'I hope your solicitor has given you good advice,' he said. He pronounced the word 'solicitor' in a slightly sarcastic tone, as if Langley was only pretending to be one and I'd obtained him under false pretences. 'You saw that the victim's face was mutilated in the same way as Mrs de Soto's.'

'Yes.'

'But we haven't found the knife. Who did you tell about Ingrid de Soto's face?'

'No one.'

'Sure?'

'Yes.'

'I'll spell it out as clearly as I can, so we all know what we're dealing with here. One, you bump into Margaret Farrell's car door and a few minutes later, if that, she's murdered. There is the minor detail that her body seems to have vanished for a period of hours, then reappeared where it was discovered. Two, you're sent to collect a package from Ingrid de Soto's house and you arrive to find that, just a few minutes before, she has been killed and mutilated. There is no sign of a forced entry, no weapon on the scene, and there is no package to be collected. Three, you are then sent to collect another package from a house, and when you arrive you discover that, just a few minutes before, Leah Peterson has been murdered and mutilated in a manner similar to that of Ingrid de Soto. Again, there is no package and no knife on the scene. You can't blame us for wanting to question you.'

'I know,' I said wearily.

'People behave unexpectedly under extreme circumstances,' said Kamsky, gently now. 'They remember the strangest things and they forget the strangest things. They do the strangest things. It's almost an accident. It's as if they've turned into someone else. They're not themselves.'

'Look,' I said, 'you don't need to do clever things to get me to talk. You don't need to coax me into agreeing with some scenario or other. I can't believe I need to say these words, but here goes: I didn't kill Leah or have anything to do with her death. I didn't kill Ingrid de Soto, or have anything to do with *her* death. I didn't kill Peggy either. But I'll stay here as long as you want. I'll answer anything you want.'

There was a silence now, which was only broken when Kamsky laced his hands behind his head, leaned back in his chair and gave a huge yawn. 'You'll remember,' he said, 'back in those days when there were only two murders, we wondered if they were connected. It seemed possible, because of your – well, what shall we say? Presence? Proximity? They didn't seem to have any other connection. Only you.'

'Is there a question coming?' asked Langley.

'And now we have the murder of Leah Peterson. It's as if God has opened the clouds and is yelling down at me personally, saying; "You want a connection? All right, here's a fucking connection you can't miss."'

'Please,' said Langley.

'I suppose I ought to be careful,' said Kamsky. 'I don't want to get on the wrong side of you.'

'And why is that?'

'Look at the evidence. Margaret Farrell injures you –'

'She didn't injure me.'

'Ingrid de Soto irritates you.'

'She didn't irritate me. I didn't really know her.'

'And you have a falling-out with Leah.'

'Everyone fell out with Leah.'

'Two alternatives strike me,' said Kamsky. 'Either you killed these women, which doesn't seem very likely, or someone wanted you to find them. I take it you won't mind if we go through your room?'

Langley gestured Kamsky away, then leaned close to me so that he could speak in a whisper. 'Think before agreeing to this,' he said. 'You don't have to let them go on a fishing expedition. But they'll get a warrant.'

'It doesn't matter,' I said.

'You're sure there is nothing in your possession that might be problematic?'

I shook my head and spoke directly to Kamsky. 'Just tidy up after you,' I said.

Chapter Twenty

When I was dropped back at the house, dazed from the repetition of my story, I felt like a traveller who had returned home after many years to find everything different. Mick was in the hall when I arrived. He looked at me with concern. 'Police?' he said.

'Yes,' I said. 'They'll be wanting to talk to all of you in the house. So you'd better come up with a good story about where you were at about ten this morning.'

'I didn't get in until three,' said Mick. 'So I was asleep.'

'Can anyone vouch for that?'

'No.'

'That's not exactly watertight.'

'I'll see you,' said Mick, and walked past me out of the front door.

I knocked on Pippa's door and she waved me inside without a word. She took a half-bottle of Scotch and a tumbler from a shelf, then glanced around. There was another tumbler on her desk, next to her opened laptop. It was filled with pens, pencils, a chain of paperclips. She emptied them out with a clatter. 'Don't worry,' she said. 'I'll have this one.'

She pulled the front of her T-shirt out from under her belt and used it to wipe the tumbler. Then she tipped Scotch into both. 'Water?' she said.

'This'll do fine,' I said.

'I'm tempted to say that we need clear heads,' said Pippa. 'But on second thoughts, I don't see the point. Cheers.'

We gulped at the Scotch a little too deeply and both flinched, as if in pain, at the same time. Pippa smiled. 'Was Seth all right?'

'He spent half his time trying to shut me up. But thanks. What's happening?'

'Gnashing of teeth,' said Pippa. 'Wailing. Rending of garments. What do you expect?'

'Who's in?'

'I came home early. I haven't seen Mick or Owen, though I believe they're both here somewhere. Miles was around, looking like a ghost. Whimpering. Dario freaked out. I went up to see him and he was scrubbing his room with bleach, terrified that Forensics were going to find traces of drugs. I tried to explain that the police would find traces of bleach more suspicious. He started raving about what he should do to get rid of the bleach. I stumbled on Mel sobbing in the kitchen with Davy comforting her. That's suspicious behaviour for a start. Anyone who's upset about Leah really must have a screw loose.'

'Pippa, for Christ's sake,' I said, 'she was murdered today. You can't mean that.'

Pippa took a sip of her drink. She didn't seem particularly chastened by what I'd said. 'It's a strange kind of guilt,' she said. 'You wish someone ill and they get more ill than you wanted.'

'I know.'

Pippa lit a cigarette and took a drag. 'I'm sorry she died,' she said. 'And shocked. But I'm not going to pretend I didn't hate her.'

'Don't you think life's too short to waste on hating people?'

'That's a bit Zen for me,' said Pippa.

'Were the police round?'

'A couple of officers were holed up with Miles for ages. They left just before you arrived. They'll be interviewing the rest of us tomorrow. Unsurprisingly.'

'Right.'

'I've been planning my alibi. I was at work. What's yours?'

'It's that I found her body but didn't kill her.'

'Your friend Campbell phoned. They pulled him in for questioning too.'

'Why?'

'He's the one who keeps sending you to stumble over corpses.'

'I don't think he has much of a motive,' I said, 'except for hating the clients. Which we all do. Anyway, that doesn't explain Peggy Farrell.'

'All roads lead to this house,' said Pippa.

'Except for Ingrid de Soto.'

'It's you, isn't it?' said Pippa, thoughtfully. 'The only thing they have in common is you. Do you think someone is killing people who get on your nerves? As a sort of favour?'

'Thanks,' I said. 'But the police are already on to that one.'

I looked down at the tumbler. It was empty. How had I managed that?

'What's going to happen?' I said.

'What do you mean?' said Pippa. 'To us? To the world?'

'Us. This house.'

'I'm going to pack tomorrow,' said Pippa.

'Do you know where you're going?'

'I'm making inquiries. By the way, I'm sorry.'

'What about?'

'Owen.'

'Oh, that. It all seems a long time ago. You slept with Owen, I slept with Owen. What's to apologize about?'

I walked into the kitchen and saw Davy, Mel and Miles in a huddle around the table.

'Was it horrible?' asked Davy.

'Next stupid question,' I said.

'The police are going to talk to all of us,' said Mel.

'I know.'

'We were shopping,' she said. 'Will they want to know that?'

'I'm sure they will. Anyway, that lets you off the hook,' I said. I really wasn't interested in hearing everybody's alibis.

Miles stood up. He looked years older; his face had lines and creases in it that I'd never seen before. I walked over to him and hugged him hard. His arms went round me, and as he held me, I felt his entire body shake. After a few moments we stepped back from each other. He started to speak but his voice cracked and he didn't manage anything intelligible.

'I'm so sorry,' I said.

Miles stared at me, still unable to speak. He swallowed. 'Our last words were bitter ones,' he said. 'Whenever I try and remember her, I think of that.'

'It's not the last moments that count,' I said helplessly. 'It's all of it.'

He shook his head from side to side, like a wounded animal. 'You saw her?'

'Yes.'

'Did she look . . . ?' He stopped.

'She looked quite peaceful,' I said, as I had said to Andrew de Soto about Ingrid. It's what you're meant to say about dead people. It comforts the living, supposedly.

'I can't believe she's gone.' Tears welled in his eyes. 'She was so . . . so alive. So forceful.'

'That's true.'

'I've got something for you.' He tugged a fat envelope out of his pocket and looked at it as if he was surprised to see it, then glanced at Davy and Mel. 'I wanted to ask you a favour.'

'Of course, Miles.'

'Not here,' he said. He led me out of the kitchen and up the stairs. When we reached the hallway he took a deep breath. 'I don't know if everything has changed. I can't think properly. But I've done this. Leah said I had to. It was the last thing she said, almost. It was what we were arguing about.'

'What? What is it?'

'Here,' he said. He pushed the envelope into my hands.

I opened it and saw it was bulging with money. I looked more closely: they were fifty-pound notes. Lots of them, thick like a paperback book.

'What's this?'

'It's the twenty thousand pounds,' he said. 'It's for you all. A sort of down-payment. Maybe you should all stay. I don't know anything. Take it anyway. I don't care any more. I didn't know who to give it to.'

'I can't take twenty thousand in cash, Miles!'

'You share it out. I don't care how you do it.'

'But it's ridiculous. I can't walk around with all this money. I've never seen so much.' Miles didn't seem as if he was really listening to me. 'I'll put it somewhere,' I said, 'and then we can talk. You shouldn't be thinking about this now. You shouldn't be making decisions about anything.'

'I feel like a murderer,' he said.

'Don't. We all behaved badly but –'

I stopped when I heard footsteps on the stairs. I closed the envelope and Miles and I stood silently, like two people with a guilty secret, as Davy and Mel pushed their way past us.

'Everything all right?' asked Davy.

'I'll tell you later,' I said.

'If there's anything . . .'

'Yes,' I said, too quickly. 'Yes, thanks.'

Mick came past. He didn't say anything, but his feet echoed loudly on the uncarpeted stairs.

Chapter Twenty-one

I returned to my room and sat on my bed and contemplated the envelope full of money. I lifted it to my nose. It had a sour odour as if the notes had been contaminated by all the unclean fingers that had grasped them. How many were there? I tried to do the sum in my head and kept failing, then finally got it right: four hundred fifty-pound notes in a plump, bendy, scary pile. I looked around the room. Where could I put it? A drawer, behind the books, in the box of tissues, under my mattress? They all seemed hopeless and then I thought of Dario, bleaching his room in anticipation of the police search that would be coming any time now. If I hid the money in my room, the police would inevitably find it and then what? Was it a crime to have that much cash? Would I be legally obliged to explain it? They might think it was the contents of the missing package from Ingrid de Soto's house. Of course, Miles could explain what the money was for but, still, it wouldn't look good.

I tucked the money into the inside pocket of my jacket. It was ridiculous. I couldn't walk around with it like that. I could almost feel it hot against my chest. I needed to sort this out as quickly as possible, before everybody dispersed. I sat on my bed for a few moments, putting my head in my hands and trying not to see the faces of Ingrid de Soto and Leah – both faces beautiful and mutilated, with eyes that had stared accusingly up at me. I thought of Kamsky ('You want a connection?') and of Ingrid de Soto's father ('What do you know, Ms Bell?') and my brain fizzed uselessly. If I was the connection, then how – why? If I knew something without knowing it, what could it be? Was it somehow, beyond the shores of my comprehension, my fault?

I needed to speak to someone. That wasn't right. I needed to speak to Owen. No one else would do. I stood up from the bed, suddenly realizing how exhausted I felt – hollow and shaky with tiredness – and stepped out of my room, where I almost collided with Dario who was manoeuvring a large cardboard box along the corridor.

'What are you doing?' I said.

'I told Miles I was moving out,' he said, his eyes darting around him nervously. 'I can't be in this place any more. But he said I had to get rid of my stuff first. I said he could keep it but he didn't want any of it. It's going to take days, and I don't have days. I don't have hours. Anything could happen. Everybody's after me. They're getting me one by one.'

'I'm not after you,' I said.

'What time was it?' he said.

'What do you mean?'

'When you found it. I mean her, Leah.'

'About half past ten.'

I saw an expression of intense concentration on his face. 'I think I saw Mick,' he said.

'Mick told me he was asleep.'

'I was doing stuff in the house,' said Dario, frantically. 'Everyone had gone to work. I met the postman. He made me sign for something.'

'I don't care, Dario. Tell the police, not me,' I said. 'By the way, I've got the money. I'll give you your share before you go.'

Dario's whole expression changed. 'Really?'

'I've got to work out the exact amount. By the way, have you seen Owen?'

'He just got in.'

It took a few seconds of hovering nervously outside Owen's door before I steeled myself to knock. There was no reply, but I pushed open the door. A travelling bag was gaping wide, with clothes spilling out. The doors of the wardrobe were ajar, revealing rows of empty hangers. Photographs that had been stacked along the walls were now in piles on the large desk. I sat down beside them, and idly lifted a few while I was waiting. Some I had seen before, others were unfamiliar. One, near the bottom of the pile, made me gasp. I put my hand against my heart. There was a sharp pain in my chest and for a few seconds I could do nothing but breathe raggedly.

The image was of the same woman Owen had photographed several times: perfectly bald, with a high-cheekboned unsmiling face and close-set eyes. But this time the eyes were shut. She was arranged like a corpse and on her face were marks. I stared while the image blurred, then resolved. Slashes scored firmly over her alabaster skin. Unequivocally like the slashes ... Bile rose in my throat.

'Hello.'

I spun round, letting the photos drop back on to the table and fan out.

'Owen,' I said. Fear was rippling through me and my mouth was dry.

'You look done in.' He gave me a smile that at any other time would have filled me with pleasure.

'Yes.'

'Horrible,' he said. 'I mean for you.'

'You mean for her.'

'For you. Do you want to tell me?'

'No.' I felt cold to the bone. Cold, tired, scared, wretched and sick. I wrapped my arms round my body and hugged myself.

'Sometimes it's better to . . .'

'No.'

'All right.'

'Owen, I want to show you something.' I shuffled through the photos on his desk, noticing that my hands were trembling, until I came to the one of the slashed face. 'There.'

'So?' He looked at me, his face hardening.

'Is that all you have to say?'

'What do you want me to say?'

'I want you to tell me – to tell me –' I found I was having difficulty in forming words; they felt thick and unwieldy in my mouth. I pressed my hands together and continued: 'To tell me why the marks on this woman's face match the marks on the faces of Ingrid de Soto and Leah.'

There was an absolute silence. His face grew grim, as if the lighting had been turned down in the room, and he stared at me.

'Well?' I asked at last.

He took a step forward and, though I shrank back, he grasped my arms so hard that I felt his fingers digging painfully into my skin. 'What are you saying?'

'They were mutilated like that,' I whispered.

'Leah and the other?'

'Yes. Let go, you're hurting.'

He dropped his hands but didn't move away.

'Nobody knows. I wasn't allowed to tell. How did you know?'

'Shut up for a moment. Let me think.'

'You must have known. Unless.' I stopped.

'Unless it was me?'

'Yes.'

He gave a sour smile. 'You think I took the photographs, then went and killed a woman – no, *two* women to make them look like that. Do you want to make a run for it now, before I attack you too?'

'Stop it, Owen. Tell me.'

'What?' He gave a short, mirthless laugh. 'Tell you I didn't kill them? That would be enough for you, would it? A denial?'

'They're identical.'

'You need to decide whether or not you trust me.'

Without knowing what I was going to do, I lifted my hand and gave him a stinging slap on his cheek and he reeled back, lifting a fist. 'This isn't about us, you idiot,' I said. 'This is about women who are being murdered. You have to explain.'

Owen looked at me. He lowered his fist, unclenched it, and took a step backwards. His face lost its hard look, and instead became weary and bleak. 'Yes,' he said. 'You're right.'

'So?'

'I don't know.'

'You don't know?'

'The only explanation I can think of is that it's a nasty coincidence. But I guess you're sick of coincidences.'

'If I were a detective, I'd want to know when you took the photograph. What day, what time.'

'If you were a detective, I'd tell you I don't know,' said Owen. 'I could tell you within a few days.'

'Isn't the time printed on the image?'

'I don't use digital for this. We were both shooting dozens of rolls of film, day after day. This one was taken . . .' Owen paused for thought '. . . between something like the beginning of May and a week or two ago.'

'That's not good enough. Would . . .' I hesitated and pretended to search for the name of the woman I'd seen in his photographs '. . . Andrea remember more precisely?'

'I doubt it.' He crossed to the window and stared out. 'You say exactly the same?'

'Pretty much.'

He picked up the photograph, looked at it, then said, 'I guess I have to take this to the police, don't I?'

'Yes.'

'I'm going out now,' he said. 'I might be some time.'

'Owen?'

'Mmm?'

'Who else has seen these, apart from me?'

'Nobody. Not even my agent. Not even Andrea. They've been here in the folders.'

'I guess it could be a coincidence,' I said doubtfully.

'Maybe it's just the way men see women,' said Owen. 'That's what you think, anyway, isn't it?'

I frowned at him. 'Do you think this is funny?'

'No, I don't. Why do you think I'm leaving?' He gestured towards his overflowing suitcase. 'You should leave too.'

'You think so?'

'There's a curse on this house.'

I shivered. 'Sometimes I'm so scared I can't breathe,' I said. 'And sometimes it doesn't seem real and I tell myself that soon I'll wake up and none of it will have happened.'

'So who can you trust? Astrid, who do you trust?'

I stared at him for a moment and he stared back. Something about him seemed different, darker than I'd known. 'Terrible coincidences happen, don't they?' I said.

Owen took a step towards me and scrutinized me. It was as if he was trying to see something that even I didn't know was there. 'I'm sorry,' he said.

'But . . .'

'About Pippa.'

'Things like that don't mean anything to Pippa,' I said. 'But they do to me, and I thought . . .' I stopped and turned away from his burning gaze.

'You thought they did to me too?'

'I guess.'

'If you need to know,' he said, 'it was before anything happened between us. I wanted you to know that. It's important to me.'

'I knew that,' I said. 'For what it's worth.'

'Right, I'm off to the police with this. Why don't you start packing?'

Chapter Twenty-two

'Don't you get it yet, Mel? They think it's one of us.'

I stood outside the kitchen, my hand lifted half-way to the door, listening to his words. The fear that was always inside me seemed to swell now, blocking off my passageways, preventing me breathing or uttering a sound.

'But how can they . . . ?'

'And that's not all.' Davy's voice, more authoritative than I'd ever heard it, cut off Mel's wail. 'That's why Owen's packing his bag. That's why Dario's running round like a headless chicken. That's why Miles was throwing up in the bathroom and putting all those letters from Leah into the garbage before he's marched off to the police station. That's why Astrid looks completely distraught.'

I put my hand on the slightly open door, waiting to push it.

'But the police are wrong,' cried Mel, her voice cracking in distress.

'Are they?'

'Yes, of course they are. What are you saying, Davy? You don't mean this. You can't. This is horrible, just horrible.'

'We have to look at it clearly, my love, and if that means . . .'

'I heard what you were saying,' I said to Davy.

'I didn't mean to make this worse.'

'No. I agree with you. That's what the police think and that's what we're all trying not to think but thinking anyway.'

'Are the police treating you properly?'

I shrugged. 'That's hardly the point. It's like a frenzy down at the station. There's an incident room and photos and charts everywhere, and about thirty police officers charging around. Have you seen Miles?'

'I think he's in his room. Packing, or clearing stuff out or something. We're all being interviewed soon. But everyone's locked away in their own private space, as if that's the only place they're safe.'

'Except you.'

'I've got Mel.'

'Lucky you,' I said. 'What are your plans? Are you moving out?'

Davy and Mel exchanged a glance.

'We're working on it,' said Davy. 'What about you?'

'I think I'd better make some calls,' I said. 'I thought it would end badly. But even so . . .'

I left them to their arrangements and went to find Pippa. As I passed Miles's room I stopped and listened. I heard things being moved around. For a moment I thought I would go in and try to comfort him. He was my friend and once he'd been more. But as Owen had asked me, who did I trust? Not Miles, not any more. Not Miles or Mick or Dario or Owen, though if Owen knocked on my door I would let him in; I would pull the covers over us and in the darkness I would hold him against me. I carried on to Pippa's door and, at the sound of her voice, pushed it open and stepped inside.

If her room had been a mess before, now it was in a new phase of chaos. Any clothes that had been in drawers or cupboards had been pulled out and lay in colourful heaps. Any books that had been in piles or on shelves were scattered. Folders were splayed open and papers lay across the floor like leaves in autumn. It took me a moment to find Pippa in the wreckage. She was sitting cross-legged by the side of the mirror, rummaging through a capacious makeup case, tossing stubs of lipstick and cakes of eye-shadow into a bin bag.

'Hi,' I said, lowering myself to the floor beside her.

'Rough time?'

'Pretty rough.'

'Do you want to tell me?'

'No, I don't think so. There's nothing left to tell. Everything I say I've already said a hundred times before. It all feels like a lie now. Does this additional layer of chaos mean you're packing?'

'Yup. I'm going to Ned's tomorrow evening.'

I didn't ask who Ned was. Instead I picked up a fringed shawl and held it against my cheek, closing my eyes for a second.

'I've ordered a skip,' continued Pippa. 'We can dump the stuff we don't want into it.'

'Is there anything left after your yard sale?'

Pippa and I looked at each other and didn't smile. The memory wasn't so funny now.

'You'd be surprised,' she said.

'The police might object,' I said. 'Disposing of evidence.'

She pulled a face.

'Maybe they can take everything away,' she said, 'on condition they don't bring it back.'

'I've got the money,' I said.

'Where?'

'Here.' I tapped my pocket.

'Christ! You're just carrying it around with you?'

'I didn't know where else to put it. The police are about to descend on us and go through everything. I thought it would look odd if they found twenty thousand quid in my knicker drawer.'

'Is there anything that doesn't look odd?'

'I want to divide it up. Can you work out who gets what?'

'All right,' said Pippa, vaguely. She picked up a pair of tights and started to ravel it up in her hands, then stretch it out again to check for ladders.

'Soon?'

'Fine.'

I remembered this house when we'd first moved in, every room clean, empty and full of possibility, the floorboards echoing when we trod on them, the light streaming in through the uncurtained windows. Gradually it had filled up – with objects, with people, with noise and with history – until it had become overloaded, like a boat buckling and tipping under the weight of too many passengers. But now we set about stripping it down again, and returning it to its original state. Rooms were being emptied, occupants were departing. Pictures were lifted down from walls, leaving patches behind them that Dario had never got round to painting. Hairballs and dust floated in the corners. The skip filled with the rubbish that had been too worthless even to put out for the yard sale, and I went and looked over its yellow rim at odd socks, cracked plates, torn sheets, a broken chair, a twisted bicycle wheel, yellowing newspapers: everything chipped, ripped, wrecked and unloved lay in the bottom. It was like a tide, I thought, that had swept in over the years, carrying us with it, and now was inexorably sweeping out again. Soon all that would be left in the house was the debris, the flotsam and jetsam of the life we'd led there.

As we were preparing to go, so the police arrived. Some were in plain clothes and would be conducting interviews with the occupants of seventy-two Maitland Road – DCI McBride and Paul Kamsky were there, and I thought I saw PC Jim Prebble, like a potato-faced hallucination from earlier days, but I didn't recognize anyone else. Others came in uniform, carrying bags and cameras, not looking us in the eye; they would be picking their way through each room and even, it became apparent, through the skip and the bin bags into which we'd so hurriedly been pouring our unwanted objects. If it felt like an invasion, that was because it *was* an invasion. They poured over our threshold like a conquering army, with their IDs, their titles, their notebooks, their evidence kits and their suspicions. I saw the house through their eyes and it was full of dark and ugly secrets; I saw us through their eyes and we were a motley tribe, nervous, defensive and scared. It had become impossible to behave naturally or innocently, or to feel that way.

I watched Dario as he led a male and female officer up the stairs towards his room; he was ashen and red-eyed. Mick scowled at them so that his forehead corrugated and a vein pulsed in his temple. He wasn't angry, I knew, he was full of terror and uncertainty, and probably all the nightmares from his past were crowding around him again. Only Pippa seemed quite cool, almost interested. She was used to things like this. She moved in the world of law and knew its language.

I went slowly down the stairs and stood in the hall, outside Pippa's and Miles's rooms. As I did so, a policeman came up the stairs from the kitchen and knocked heavily on Miles's door. After a few seconds, Miles opened it. He was dressed in an oddly formal way, in a dark suit with a white linen shirt I had given him a long time ago. His face looked thinner than it had just a few hours ago, and older as well. He stood back and the police officer entered the room. Miles stared at me for a moment, his eyes glittering. Then he smiled faintly and turned away.

'Astrid?'

I looked round. 'Well, if it isn't Detective Chief Inspector Kamsky. You don't need to interview me again, do you?'

We walked out into the back garden together. I took him to my vegetable patch and pointed. 'Broad beans, runner beans, potatoes,' I said. 'Those ones there are asparagus, but it takes two years to grow, so I doubt if any of us will be eating it. I'm moving out, you know.'

'You'll need to inform us of your —'

'Yeah, yeah,' I said. 'I won't run away. I'm going to stay with my friend Saul, not far from here.'

Kamsky didn't reply. He seemed preoccupied with things he couldn't say.

'When will this be over?' I asked.

'All I can say is what I tell the team, and that is . . .'

But I never did find out what he told the team, for at that moment a police officer came walking across the grass towards us and Kamsky stepped away from me. The officer said something, and I saw Kamsky's face become expressionless. A feeling of absolute foreboding descended on me.

'Don't let anyone else in,' I heard him say, as the officer turned away. Then he looked back at me. 'You'll have to excuse me,' he said, with a curious little bow, as if he was deserting me on a polished dance-floor.

'What is it? Have they found something?'

'Yes,' he said. 'They have.'

Chapter Twenty-three

From that moment everything changed. Suddenly I was shut on the outside looking in, not able to see. I asked Kamsky what had happened, what had been found, but he shook his head. He was an impersonal official now, estranged from me. He said it was part of an ongoing investigation and he couldn't reveal any details. I said I didn't understand. Were they going to arrest somebody? We were still standing out there in the garden, by my doomed vegetable patch. Kamsky started to speak, then hesitated, then spoke again. 'I think it's likely that charges are imminent,' he said.

'Who?' I said. 'Who's being charged?'

'We'll see,' he said, then nodded. 'Come with me.'

Then things happened quickly. A process was under way and we, the residents of seventy-two Maitland Road, were swept along helplessly in it. The house wasn't ours any more. It had changed even in the time that Kamsky and I had been in the garden. It looked like the site of a sinister biological accident. People were wandering around in white coats with their shoes wrapped in white nylon bags. The rooms on the ground floor were being sealed off with tape.

'We'd like you all to come into the station with us,' said Kamsky.

'Can I fetch something from my room?' I asked.

'I'm sorry,' said Kamsky. 'You can't. This is a crime scene now.'

'What do you mean, a crime scene?' I said. 'What crime?'

Dario was being led down the stairs by the two officers I'd seen him with before.

'Astrid,' he said. 'They're taking us in.'

'Quiet,' said Kamsky. 'I don't want you to confer.'

So Dario gestured at me helplessly, almost comically, as he was led past me and out into the street. Two men came in carrying arc-lights on metal stands. At the same time I was thinking urgently. In my pockets I had the bundle of money. Was I a suspect? Would I be searched at the police station? Would I have to surrender all the contents of my pockets? Probably not, unless I was the one who was going to be charged. In which case it would look very bad indeed. If there was any chance of it being found, it would be prudent to tell them in advance. But I couldn't think of a way of saying it that wouldn't sound strange. 'Detective Chief Inspector Kamsky, I think I ought to mention that I've got twenty thousand pounds in cash in my pocket. It's not at all relevant to the case, but I thought you might want to know.'

I felt a touch on my arm and started. It was Kamsky. 'We're leaving now, if that's all right,' he said.

'Can I take my bike, at least?' I asked. 'It belongs to Campbell – and it's my livelihood.'

He shrugged. 'Go on, then. A police car will follow you.'

As we were led out, I saw that the street now seemed to be jammed with police vehicles, the brightly coloured cars and vans and then more unmarked vans. Lines of tape sealed off a whole section of Maitland Road in front of our house. Behind the tape a crowd of people was staring. Did they think I was being arrested? That I was a suspect? Was I a suspect? It suddenly occurred to me that I ought to compose my face into a suitable expression. I mustn't smile. That would look insensitive. I mustn't cover my face, seem angry or evasive. I needed to look businesslike, every inch the woman who was helping the police with their inquiries. Except that everyone knows that 'helping police with their inquiries' is the euphemism for being the main suspect who hasn't yet been charged. I had to look self-consciously unselfconscious, like the person who really was helping the police with their inquiries. Which is what I was, wasn't I?

People from the crowd shouted my name as I walked out. I looked around reflexively. They weren't neighbours or friends. This was London, after all, where you don't know your neighbours. These were the journalists and photographers who already knew me. What did they think, seeing me with an officer at my elbow? The headline that accompanied the photograph would be the thing that everyone remembered, whatever else happened.

My return to the police station, to the interview room, the plastic moulded chairs, the linoleum, the pimpled wallpaper, was like a recurring dream, coming back to the same place, telling the same story, filling in the gaps in response to the same questions. Except this time I knew that Mick and Davy and Mel and Pippa and Owen and Miles and Dario were sitting in other interview rooms or on benches waiting their turn. For a few minutes I was left alone in the room and I could almost feel their proximity. I felt as if it wasn't just that we were separating, leaving the house and each other. It was as if one of those wrecking balls had swung into the house and smashed away a whole wall. I thought of half-demolished buildings, where you could see the wallpaper exposed to the rain, and all the innards, the wires and beams and joists, like bones and muscles and tendons spilling out of a wound.

The process of giving the statement was long and it was

boring, but I noticed gradually that it lacked the hostility of my earlier interviews. A junior detective of about my own age took the statement, and he was so ill-briefed that I had to prompt some of his questions. I knew my part so well now. I was numbed by it, but he was clearly excited to be involved. When there was really nothing more to be said, he left me alone once more. After a few minutes the inter-view-room door opened and Kamsky came in. I saw a new brightness in his eyes as he sat down opposite me. 'You all right?' he asked.

'Just knackered,' I said.

'You can leave now,' he said. 'I'm afraid you can't go back to the house. Have you got somewhere you can stay?'

'Yes – my friend Saul, remember? But –'

'You'll need to keep us informed of your whereabouts,' he said.

'Aren't you done?'

'Not entirely,' he said, and then his face broke into a smile. 'We have found evidence – blood, hair, trophies taken from the dead women. Perhaps I shouldn't be telling you this, but we're about to call a press conference at which we'll announce that we're charging Miles Rowland Thornton with the murders of Margaret Farrell, Ingrid de Soto and Leah Peterson.'

At which point I thought two things more or less simul-taneously. I thought: No, oh, no, please, no. And I thought: He never told me he was called Rowland. I didn't know I was crying until Kamsky pressed a tissue into my hand. Because, in spite of everything, Miles was my friend.

'Tell me about it,' I said at last. 'Tell me everything.'

As Kamsky kept saying, evidence was evidence. Motives might be incomprehensible, explanations hard to find, but the fact was that they had evidence that tied Miles to the deaths of Margaret Farrell, Ingrid de Soto and Leah Peterson.

'No,' I said. 'How? All three?'

'All three.'

'What?'

'A murder weapon for one. And bodily samples for another,' he said, with grotesque delicacy. 'Tissue and hair from Margaret Farrell, if you want me to be precise. Don't you see? It's perfect.' He was actually smiling. 'It solves the problem of Margaret Farrell's body. Her body was kept in Mr Thornton's room. She may have been killed there. What is certain is that her body was kept there, then dumped later at the site where it was found. What's more, there were also objects hidden in his room. Trophies, we assume.'

'Trophies? Like what?'

'You'll hear soon enough.'

'I just don't get it. Why? I mean, I can understand Leah. Not understand-understand, but grasp it. He knew her. He was her lover. But the others. Peggy, for God's sake, he hardly knew her. She was just a harmless woman who lived down the road.'

At this Kamsky gave a knowing smile. 'He killed her, though. In his own room.'

'And what about Ingrid de Soto? There's no possible connection.'

'There was an invitation from Mrs de Soto in Mr Thornton's possession.'

'What?' I stared at Kamsky for a moment. Then I remembered Andrew de Soto in the hotel, his wretched, creased face. 'Her husband thought she was having an affair,' I said slowly. 'You mean, she was having an affair with Miles?'

'We don't know about that yet,' he said. 'We've only just started.'

I wanted to say that Miles wouldn't have had an affair with someone like Ingrid de Soto, but what did I know? Nothing had ever been the way it seemed.

'I feel a bit sick,' I said.

'I can imagine.'

'I don't think you can, actually.'

'All I can say, Astrid, is that you may never understand. Sometimes questions don't have answers.'

'Right,' I said.

'You should go home now.'

'You're forgetting. I don't have one any more.'

Chapter Twenty-four

I think none of us really wanted to leave and go our separate ways, because that would be the end. We'd be scattered, blown in different directions, like the seeds of a dandelion clock. After we'd met outside the station, after the fragmented explanations, the arguments, the disbelief, the tears, the hugs, we walked slowly down the street, me pushing Campbell's crappy bike, and stopped at the first pub we came to. It was dark and hot inside, with music playing too loudly. The men squeezed round a table near the window while Pippa and I went to get drinks. I felt as though I was moving under water, sluggish with tiredness and shock. As we were watching the man behind the bar pulling pints, another horrible thought came into my mind and I did something I never do, which is to ask someone about their sex life: 'Did you ever sleep with him?'

'Who?'

'Miles.'

'Once. Twice, maybe.'

'Oh, for God's sake, Pippa.'

'It was after you'd finished with him, if that's what you're wondering, but before Leah. I wanted to cheer him up, comfort him.'

'So you slept with him. You couldn't just buy him a drink, have a chat?'

'It was a way of holding him through the dark hours, I suppose. So, I've slept with a murderer. That's a first.'

'Not the most lovable thing you've ever said.'

'Sorry.' Then she looked at me. 'He adored you. Maybe he went mad because of it. People do, you know. He's sick in the head.'

'What is it with you, Pippa? Is it an animal thing, like spraying on your territory?'

The barman interrupted us. 'Excuse me. That'll be ten pounds thirty, ladies.'

'Here.' I pulled the money out of my purse and slid it across.

'Why did you never say?' I asked Pippa, after collecting the change.

'I just did.'

I started to say something, then gave up. What was the point? The world was full of secrets, each of us hiding our real self from everybody else, even those we called friends.

I managed to pick up three of the pints and walked across to the table where the others were sitting.

'Cheers,' I said, raising a glass. 'Here's to . . . well, what? What are we drinking to?'

'Friendship,' said Davy, with no trace of irony in his voice.

Pippa spluttered.

'No, I'm serious,' said Davy. 'This has been shocking, more for Astrid and Pippa than the rest of us, I know, but we're left, aren't we? The six of us.'

'At least we know we can trust each other,' added Pippa, with another snort. Davy frowned at her. I gave her a disbelieving look too.

'Cheers, anyway,' he said and lifted his glass.

'Yeah,' said Dario.

So we toasted each other. I took a cautious sip. I didn't need alcohol: the world was already unsteady around me. Nothing real or solid.

What was happening to Miles now? Was he still in the police station, with his solicitor, maybe? Were they questioning him at this very moment, capturing his words on a tape-recorder? Or was he sitting alone in a cell? Did his parents know yet? I'd met his mother several times and his father once, but my imagination balked when I tried to picture them hearing that their clever son was accused of murder. I heard Owen saying my name, but all I could see were images: Ingrid's slashed face; Leah's; Miles's soft brown eyes looking into mine.

'Don't cry,' said Davy. 'You never cry.'

'Sorry,' I said. 'Sorry.'

'Astrid?' Owen said. 'It's OK. Cry if you want.'

And in front of everyone, he put his hand over mine and lifted it to his lips.

'Hey! What's going on?' Dario's eyes were bulging.

'Shut up,' said Owen.

But I leaned across the table, took Owen's thin face between my hands and kissed him full on the lips. 'It's all right,' I said.

Of course, it wasn't all right, but the drink started to take hold and we ordered more and, in a slightly hysterical way, started to talk about old times and even to laugh a bit. It was mostly a performance but it helped us get through the evening until it was time for us to part. Just as we were starting to shift in our seats and nod our good-byes, I remembered something. I took the cash out of my pocket.

'This is probably evidence of some kind,' I said. 'Before the police grab it, we should share it out.'

But Davy stopped me. 'For goodness' sake, Astrid, people are already looking at us. Don't flash money around in a place like this.'

It was probably more to do with embarrassment than fear but I gave a shrug.

'I'll do the maths,' said Pippa. 'Then we can arrange to meet tomorrow somewhere a bit more salubrious. It'll be an excuse for another farewell drink.'

There were nods all round as we stood up, buttoned our jackets and went out into the street together. The rain had stopped and darkness fallen, though the last traces of day still glowed on the horizon. The air was warm and beneath the petrol fumes and curry I could smell blossom.

'Don't you love London?' I said dreamily, to no one in particular. Then: 'Oh, fuck, someone's slashed both my bike tyres.'

'How mean,' said Pippa indignantly. 'Can you mend them?'

'Not without my repair kit. Never mind. I'll just have to leave the bike here and come back tomorrow.' I looked at them all, grouped on the pavement. 'Well, this is it, then.'

'Till tomorrow.'

I hugged Pippa, gripped the others by the arm. Owen stopped me. 'Astrid,' he said, in a low voice. 'Don't go just yet. Please.'

I hesitated, then took his hand. 'Saul's expecting me,' I said. 'And besides – well, this is the wrong time for anything except sleep. Maybe it will always be the wrong time – after this.'

'Don't say that.'

'We'll see each other tomorrow, Owen. I'm not going anywhere.'

'You're right. Try to rest. I hope your dreams are peaceful.'

I found it hard to go. I knew we were meeting the next day, and yet it felt that this was the last time I would see them. At last, with a final wave, I was gone from them. I looked back once to see them dispersing, a group breaking up into its individual parts, then walked along the street in the direction of the underground station. A police car passed me from the opposite direction, but for once it had nothing to do with me – some other victim and some other crime. And as I walked, past the crowded bars and the closed-up shops, through the pools of light cast by street-lamps, under the narrow bridge where a couple stood entwined and pigeons nested, the horror thinned. For a few moments I thought only of the sound my feet made on the pavement, felt only the last heat of the day on my face, saw only the road in front of me as it curved round the corner. The story was over, but summer had only just begun.

Part Two

Chapter Twenty-five

Astrid was the last obstacle. Once she was dead I'd be free. And it wouldn't be so hard. There wasn't much to it. The trick was learning that there was no trick.

Killing the first time was like losing my virginity. I had broken through. I had stepped into a new world of adulthood and I expected people to be able to see it in me, a new glow in the eyes, a sense of power. But they couldn't and that was good too. It was like losing my virginity in other ways as well: a messy, almost farcical fumbling, a struggle on a sofa, a sort of embarrassment and disbelief. A stickiness. She was called Jenny. The first I had sex with, I mean; not the first I killed. She was fifteen, she was folded up against me, half dressed, her cheek stained. Suddenly she felt heavy. I remember wishing that she would just go away. Which she couldn't, because it was at her parents' house. And it was like that with the killing as well, because after it had happened, after the spasm, after the thrill and the intimacy, my main thought was: Is that it? Is that all? Is it as easy as that?

I looked at Jenny, lying against me, one breast exposed, nuzzling into me. It was the first time for her as well. Really, she was the one who had started it, squeezing my hand at a party, even giving me a Valentine, inviting me to the house when her mum was out. I saw now that she really cared, cared about what had happened, cared about me. Now she leaned over to me and kissed my cheek and I was really quite fascinated. This was going to be the story of her first time, maybe even of her first love, and I had felt nothing at all. While it was taking its course, I had felt we were like two actors playing a scene and playing it badly. And then I realized that Jenny didn't know she was an actress. She thought it was real.

It's like the cat we had when I was little. We only had a postage stamp of a garden, with the railway embankment behind it. But when he wasn't asleep, he spent his whole life out there, staring into a bush. I never saw him catch anything but we'd find the evidence under the kitchen table. Small birds without heads, a mole, the bottom half of a rat. He was a pathetic pet cat fed from a tin, he had been bred for hundreds of years just to be a sort of fluffy toy, but somewhere, deep down, he still thought he was a lion prowling through the jungle.

Sometimes, when I was growing up, I wanted to shout at people: 'You don't think any of this is real, do you?' I hardly ever did, though, hardly more than just once. I was eleven years old and in my first year of secondary school. Some of us were sitting at the back of the class during a boring maths lesson and a boy called Daniel Benton was sticking the sharp end of a compass into his arm. Paul Leigh said he could make himself bleed and he pushed the point into his forearm. We leaned over and saw a little red full stop on his white skin.

I laughed and Paul Leigh whispered furiously at me that I wouldn't dare do that. Immediately I felt a sense of power. 'Give me the compass, then,' I said. 'Give me it and I'll show you.'

It was a once-in-a-lifetime, never-to-be-repeated show. Things quickly got hazy but I remember someone started to cry and a desk got knocked over and there was a bustle and I was dragged out of the room, leaving a red smear behind me.

When you do something like that, you don't even get into trouble. It's too big. It doesn't fit into the system of punishments. After the nurse and the day in Casualty, I was summoned to see my form teacher and the headmaster at the same time. They talked to me in subdued, sympathetic voices. When I came out of the office, my mum was sitting on the bench, crying. I hugged her while looking over her shoulder, hoping I wouldn't be spotted by anybody I knew.

In the end, I was sent to see a doctor. He wore a sweater and had a room with brightly coloured posters on the wall and toys on the floor. He got me to look at pictures and talk about them, and then he asked me about my life. I was only eleven but I think I saw quickly what the rules were. He wasn't a real doctor – he didn't want to help me or to make me better. He wanted to test me to see if I'd give myself away, to show that I wasn't like the others. It was like the bit in science-fiction films where you have someone who might be an android or might be a human being and you've got to ask them questions to see if you can tell the difference. That's what he was doing with me. In the pictures there were two people or three people, and he wanted me to talk about the relationship between them. It was obvious that I was meant to see them as nice and normal. So I said about the first one that it looked like a mother and a child and that maybe she had just collected him from school. He asked where I thought the father was and I said he was probably at work. I looked at the doctor and he smiled and nodded.

What is strange, when I look back, is that I clearly knew what not to say to the doctor. I told him that the stuff with the compass had been a mistake. I didn't know what had come over me. That wasn't a total lie. It *had* been a mistake.

For once, I had let the mask slip. I had done something real. I had broken through the pretend game that everyone was playing and showed them blood and bone and they hadn't liked what they saw.

The doctor asked me about my father. He'd probably read my school file. I could see that the point was to seem sad but not too sad, to miss my father but not miss him too much. I said it had been a long time ago. That seemed good enough. One of the photographs showed a small child with a cat. He asked me if I had a cat. Even at that age, I knew what he was trying to get me to say. He wanted to know if I was cruel to my cat. I wasn't, but even if I had been, I wouldn't have told him. I just told him the truth, which was that I once had a cat and that I used to look after him and feed him and sometimes he would come and sleep on my bed. Then he changed the subject and starting asking me about other things, like hobbies and whether I had friends. I could see his interest gradually fading. He was looking for something juicy and I had to make sure he didn't find anything. I needed to be normal and boring.

I was always good at hiding, especially from my mum – though as time went on I could never be quite sure what she saw and what she didn't. Sometimes I thought she was stupid: a big-boned, slow-moving woman with a large lap, thick hair coarse and pale like straw, a round face and a soft voice that had a kind of drawl to it because she came from Somerset. But there were other times when I'd look at her and see in those grey eyes an expression that gave me an itchy, uncomfortable feeling, as if, all of a sudden, my clothes were too tight.

She was called Mary. She had left school when she met my dad and she had me before she was twenty, so she must have been young, really, but I always thought of her as old. Old and boring. So it was a shock when I heard Jerry Barker telling a mate of his outside the newsagent that she was a bit of all right. I remember that like yesterday: a bit of all right. I tried to see her through Jerry's eyes, but it was no good. She was on the big side, she never wore makeup or had her hair done nicely, and she wore these clothes that hid her, like a tent. From what people said, my dad hadn't been much of a catch, but she couldn't even keep him for long. It was just her and me, day after day and week after week, and the dreary years went by. She worked at the florist's during the day and at night she did other people's ironing. She cooked meals with her coat still on but sat down with me to eat and tried to ask me about my day. I always told her what she wanted to hear, and then I could turn on the TV and pretend she wasn't there, looking at me with her pale eyes. 'What are you thinking about?' she'd ask, in that soft voice of hers. And I'd always say, 'I'm not thinking about anything at all, Mum,' though I was, of course – I was thinking she had a face like a fish; I was thinking I'd like her to shut the fuck up and leave me in peace. She had a cough that wouldn't go away. I could hear it when I lay in bed. Cough-cough-cough from downstairs where she was ironing; cough-cough-cough upstairs, in the little room opposite my bigger one.

I tried. I really tried to be who she wanted me to be. Of course I always remembered her birthday but I remembered other things as well. Her wedding anniversary, plus the date he had gone. The anniversary of her dad's death. I wrote them down, although I didn't really need to. I have a good memory. Sometimes, when I can't sleep, I lie in my bed and go over things in my mind to make sure I've got them clear. Other people's birthdays, where they were born, their phone numbers, their favourite food and songs and TV programmes, silly things they're scared of, stories they'd told me or I'd overheard. You never know when you'll need things. You have to be ready, all the time.

When I went to see the doctor, I had already stolen quite a bit of money but he didn't know that. Not just money. I couldn't leave a shop without putting a bar of chocolate into my pocket or slipping a magazine under my jacket. It wasn't because I needed stuff or felt entitled to it. I took far more than I could get away with at home, but it didn't stop me. Sometimes I'd dump a T-shirt in a bin outside the shop. I never got caught. I don't know why. It's not as if I was clever or had worked out a brilliant system. Maybe people just don't notice me. Whatever it was, the buzz faded. I preferred it with people. Even then, the people I'd taken money from didn't realize they had been robbed. That was the trick – to take just the right amount, so that they didn't understand that anything was missing. Sometimes they would look a bit confused as they went through their pockets and wallets. 'Where does it all go?' they might say. But it was just a few coins here, a note there.

I started with my mother. The first time I took a fiver from her bag. It was like a test, to see what would happen. Nothing did. So I edged up, bit by bit. Once, when I wanted to buy a pair of trainers, I took twenty and that evening when I showed them to her, I said I'd got them from a market stall for a tenner. I moved on to other people, but I was always very careful. It was hard work. Like being a spy.

You decide what you're going to do and then you do it. It can be that simple. I had a list of things I had to do. One was to have sex with a girl before I was seventeen. I did that. One was to be good at football. I used to take my ball to the bit of land by the railway and kick it against a wall and practise keeping the ball up in the air. Hour after hour. I was never going to be one of the best, but I was in the school team, which was good enough. It meant I belonged. I was one of the team. I was cool. I had gelled hair and scars on my legs and girls liked me, or said they did. Everyone's faking it. The difference between them and me is that they don't realize it. I do. That puts me ahead. I'm more honest than other people. I know who I am and I know that I'm alone.

I always had friends and I even had a best friend, Jonathan Whiteley. I still keep in touch with him. He still lives in Sheffield. We phone each other up and text each other, and when we meet, we reminisce about the good old days. How we used to play tennis against the wall of his house. How we got drunk on cider when we were twelve. How we used to play up in maths. The time we went camping and he got chased by a ram; the time we went to the pop festival and lived on beer, crisps and marshmallows for three days; the time we set off the fire extinguisher on the school trip. But not the time I nicked his sister's credit card. Or the time I lobbed a stone through his window late one night after an argument that I can't even remember now. Or the time I took his favourite T-shirt, balled up in my school bag between my physics and my art, and never let on. I've still got it. It's one of my favourites. It doesn't smell of Jonathan any more. It smells of me.

I get headaches sometimes. I didn't have the first until I was thirteen, and I didn't know then what was wrong with me. Later, of course, I came to recognize the feeling and would know an attack was coming by the prickling of my skin, a tenderness in my body that made it hurt if anyone touched me. But with the first one, it started with a waiting feeling – not a headache, exactly, but knowing that a headache was creeping up on me. Then a sick throbbing above my left eye, as if something was being screwed into my temple. A clammy, shivery sensation that thickened into feeling sick. Lights flashing on and off. The pain got thicker and I had to lie on my bed with the curtains closed and press my arm over my eyes, but even so I could feel my eyeballs hammering in their sockets. In the end I got to sleep and when I woke the pain had melted away and I felt powerful, clean, more alert than ever before.

For about three years, I used to have headaches once or twice a month and I looked forward to them because of the way I felt afterwards, like I was glowing. Bit by bit, they got less common. Now it's only about twice a year that I get the pain and welcome the surge of energy it flushes round my body. I like having the headaches. I'm good at pain. That's one of my secrets. I carry it with me and nobody knows. People are blind; they're blind because they don't want to see. People are fools; they're fools because they don't want to know. I like to be reborn.

Chapter Twenty-six

At last, after waiting so long, after years of training and knocking around, I was here. I was twenty-one and I was off and out. People come from all over the world to get to London. They escape on rickety boats, hide under trains and inside lorries. Not to get to Europe, not to England, but London, because in London you can either find people like you, whoever you are, whatever you're like, or you can lose yourself. People arrive at Heathrow airport and rip up their identifying documents so they can't be sent back. I'd have done that if I'd known how. I'd like to have washed up in London, naked and nameless, so I could have given myself a new name and created a new identity. Instead I got off the train at Euston and started again.

One cold Friday evening, just a few days into the new year, I was sitting in a pub on the basin of the canal at King's Cross. I was on my third pint of lager and starting to feel woozy. Then I saw my mate Duncan coming towards me with a girl I'd never met before. I saw immediately that she was the kind of girl who made me virtually unable to string together consecutive words. She was tall, with long legs and strong, slender arms, and in spite of the winter weather she was dressed in shorts and a brightly coloured T-shirt. She was tanned and her face was freckled from the wind and sun. Her curly dark hair was tied back off her face. She had very striking dark eyes, which shone with laughter at something Duncan was saying that I couldn't quite hear. She was carrying a bottle of beer in one hand, a satchel and a riding helmet. They approached the table.

'This is Astrid Bell,' said Duncan. He looked at her. 'This is the guy I was telling you about.'

'Hi,' said Astrid. 'Duncan says you're looking for somewhere to live.'

Astrid wasn't like any of the girls I had met before. She didn't flirt or flatter people. She wasn't tremulous, devious or eager to please. She didn't care if I liked her or not. I don't mean she was unfriendly; far from it. She just knew who she was and she wasn't going to try to be anyone else. There was no side to her and no trickery. I could see that she would never pretend to have heard of a band that didn't exist, or laugh at a joke she didn't understand, or act coy to get her own way. I could tell that about her even before she sat down at the table opposite me, cupping her chin in her hands and looking at me with her clear, dark eyes. I watched her at the bar as she ordered us drinks, ignoring all the men who were ogling her. And I watched her as she made her way back to me, holding the two glasses carefully so she didn't slop them, turning her head to grin and say something to a friend who called to her from the cigarette machine. There was a clean-limbed gracefulness about her, in spite of her skimpy cyclist clothes. It seemed to me that she was more clearly outlined than anyone else in the pub, as if she was backlit, or the central focus of a photograph in which all the other characters were marginal and slightly blurred.

'Cheers,' she said, taking a sip of her beer and wiping foam from her upper lip. 'So, you're looking for somewhere to live.'

'Yes,' I managed. 'The place I've been staying in isn't available any longer. I need to be out of there as soon as possible.'

'This is a house in Hackney – is Hackney central enough

for you? It's a lovely house, really, a bit run-down maybe, with a big garden. There are six of us at the moment and we're looking for a seventh.'

'Is it you who owns it?'

She laughed at that, throwing her head back. I saw her white teeth and the pink inside of her mouth. 'Do I look like I own a seven-bedroom house? I'm a despatch rider, for God's sake. All I own is my bike and a few changes of clothes. No, it belongs to Miles. He's got a real job but you don't need to be alarmed. He's cool. Or coolish.'

I tried to think of grown-up questions to ask. 'How much does it cost?'

'Fifty a week. Which is nothing. But we share the upkeep, the bills, stuff like that. Even some decorating. Gentlemen's agreement. Could you hack that?'

'Sounds good,' I said. 'What about things like mealtimes? Do you eat together?'

'It's not like the army. There aren't many rules . . . Perhaps there ought to be more. But it's worked so far. And it's fun. Mainly. Are you interested?'

'Yeah, definitely.'

'You'd have to meet everyone, of course. First, though, can I ask you a few questions?'

'Like what?' I felt nervous and dry-mouthed, but I tried to appear relaxed, pretending to take a sip of my beer. I didn't want any more to drink just yet. I needed to be alert, vigilant.

'What kind of work do you do?'

'I've not been in London that long. I've been doing odd bits of –'

Just then her mobile rang. She took it out of her pocket and flicked it open. 'Hi, Miles.'

She looked at me and smiled. 'I think I've found someone

for the room. Yes. I'm with him now in the Rising Sun . . .
That's the one – down by the canal . . . He seems all right
to me, on the whole.' She looked at me again. 'You're all
right, aren't you?'

'Yes,' I said. 'I think so.'

'Trustworthy?'

'For what?'

She laughed and resumed talking into the phone. 'Why
don't you come and meet him?' She raised her eyebrows
questioningly at me, and I nodded vigorously. 'Ten minutes,
then.' There was a pause and she listened, frowning. 'Better
and better. Bring her along. 'Bye.'

She shut her phone and turned to me. 'There. The big
boss is stopping by. I hope that's all right with you.'

'Fine,' I said. 'Is someone else coming?'

'Pippa. She lives in the house. The three of us – Pippa,
Miles and I – have been there from the beginning. Everyone
else kind of comes and goes, but we endure.'

'So it's like an interview?'

'We're not very frightening.'

But she was wrong. She didn't understand how someone
like her could make a person feel small and scared.

I knew it was them as soon as they came in. He was tall
and rangy, with a closely trimmed beard, more like stubble,
and a bald head that shone beneath the lights. He was
wearing a suit of soft, dark material that looked expensive,
with an overcoat on top, and carried a slim briefcase. He
had a firm handshake, but his eyes only met mine for a
second before he glanced at Astrid. He kissed her cheek
and I saw how his face softened. I stored away the information: he fancied her. It was written all over him. But she
didn't fancy him. I was sure of it.

The woman – Pippa – didn't bother to shake my hand.

Instead she touched my arm with the tips of her fingers and widened her eyes, smiling with perfectly painted pink lips. I could smell her perfume. I'm good at smells. I remember them. My mother smelled of grass. Pippa was as tall as Astrid, maybe taller, but fairer, slimmer, breakable like porcelain. She was wearing a cream suit and high heels. Her long hair was coiled on top of her head and every so often she would touch it delicately, checking it was still in place. She looked so demure, but 'You must be fucking crazy,' were her first words.

'I'm sorry?'

'To want to live in our madhouse.'

'Don't pay any attention to her,' said Astrid.

I offered to buy them a drink, thinking it would be money spent in a good cause, and as I stood at the bar I cast glances back at them. They leaned towards each other round the table and I heard a burst of laughter. Were they talking about me? Laughing at me?

They asked me questions. I smiled and nodded and told them the things they wanted to hear. Yes, I was pretty easygoing. Yes, I had friends in London. Yes, I could pay the rent each month. No, I didn't mind clearing up. And no, I had no intention of moving on in a few months' time.

'Do you like curry?' asked Pippa, abruptly.

'Yes. Love it,' I replied, though I don't. Too greasy and salty.

'Let's get a takeaway and go back to Maitland Road,' she said. 'Then you can meet the others. What do you say?'

'Have I passed?'

'She was meant to consult with Astrid and me first,' said Miles, in a bit of a sour voice.

'Sorry,' said Pippa, and winked at me.

'Shall I leave you to talk about me among yourselves for a few minutes?'

'No need,' said Astrid, standing up and pulling on a leather jacket. 'You three go ahead. I'll bike and meet you at the house.'

We walked outside, into the darkness. I watched Astrid as she stood under the street-lamp to unlock her bike. She clipped on her helmet, hung her canvas satchel over her shoulder and swung one slim leg over the cross-bar. Her breath smoked in the air. Everything about her was fluid and streamlined. Then I saw that Miles was watching her too.

We took a cab. Miles phoned for the takeaway from the taxi, and we stopped a few streets from the house to collect it. We walked back together with two paper carrier-bags steaming with food and two bottles of wine that I insisted on buying from a shop we passed. I had never been to this part of London before and I looked around me, trying to get a sense of it. The road we were on was one of those arterial routes that cut through the city, full of traffic-lights and clogged with cars and lorries. I could tell at once that it was a run-down area, the kind I'd come to London to get away from. The shops were strange and old and several were boarded-up; there were high-rise blocks on either side of us. I noticed that many faces were black. But the streets running off this road looked a mixture of raffish and rich, lined with tall old houses behind their iron gates and little front gardens.

'Nearly there,' said Pippa.

We turned down a long, tree-shaded street, then off it on to another, where a group of teenage boys were kicking a ball in and out of pools of light and parked cars. Ahead, a high-rise cut off the horizon. To the left was the entrance to a scruffy park.

'Here we are!'

The house must have been grand when it was built. It was three storeys high and double-fronted, with bay windows, a small garden at the front and wide steps leading up to the door. But I could tell at once that it needed a lot of work doing to it. Pointing, for a start. And slates were coming off the roof. The window-frames were cracked, the paint peeling. Years of neglect had eaten into the structure, rotting the house like an illness. I saw all of this even as I was saying, in a polite voice, what a great place it was.

'Don't mind the mess,' said Miles, as he opened the front door.

'We're here!' yelled Pippa. 'With food!'

Astrid came down the stairs. She had changed into jeans and a pale green T-shirt. Her feet were bare and I saw that her toenails were painted orange and she had a silver chain round her left ankle. 'I beat you to it,' she said. 'And everyone's here. I've told them about you.'

'Right,' I said. 'Good.'

'Are you nervous?'

'A bit,' I said. 'I'd like to live here. That puts me in a weak position.'

It was the right answer; I'd thought it would be. She looked at me appreciatively and put one hand briefly on my shoulder. 'Come into the lion's den.'

We trooped down the stairs in single file. I could hear male voices and I suddenly realized I hadn't asked anything about the other occupants. But it was too late now because there we were, standing in the large, messy semi-basement where three men were sitting round the long table, and Astrid was introducing me, while Pippa slid chipped and unmatching plates round the table, then dumped a handful of cutlery in the middle.

'Right, everyone,' said Astrid, and silence fell. Everyone

looked at me. This first impression would be important, I knew.

'Hi,' I said, and raised a hand.

'This,' she said, 'is Davy.'

I knew that first impressions would be important. I smiled at each of them. I looked each of them in the eye. I made mental notes.

'First of all,' Astrid said, turning to a scrawny, freckly man, who looked like the carrot-headed runt in my class at secondary school whom everyone had picked on, 'this is Dario.'

'Hi, Dario,' I said. 'Pleased to meet you.'

'Are you?' His pupils were dilated and his words ran into each other. Stoned, I thought.

'What? Well, yes. At least, I will be if you decide I can live here.' There was a ripple of amusement and I felt my confidence grow.

'And this . . .' Astrid gestured towards a slightly older man with a buzzcut, who was wearing a thin grey T-shirt that seemed too tight for his stocky body. Something about his pale-blue gaze made me feel uneasy. 'This is Mick.'

He grunted something. That was all I'd get.

'And last but not least . . .'

I turned towards the third man, smiling and holding out my hand. I knew at once that I didn't like him, not one bit. I didn't like his long dark hair, or his high cheekbones, or the hooded lids over his dark, secretive eyes. I didn't like his fucking beauty or the way he looked dreamy, as if he was seeing something I couldn't. And I didn't like the way Astrid was staring at him now; there was a sudden glow about her that was like heat being given off. Nor the way he looked back, a glance passing between them and electricity in the air.

We shook hands.

'Owen,' he said.

'Hello, Owen.'

I took a seat between Astrid and Dario, uncorked the two bottles of wine and poured everyone a glass. Pippa lit three stubby white candles. I listened, nodded, laughed in all the right places. I was modest, appreciative. I patted Dario on the back when his prawn went down the wrong way. I helped Astrid clear away the foil containers. I said I wouldn't mind dealing with the wasps' nest under the eaves when summer came. It turned out to be as simple as that. I was in.

Chapter Twenty-seven

I arrived the following Saturday morning. Miles took me up to show me my room, which had been rejected by six other people. It was right at the top of the house, overlooking the street.

'It's a bit bare,' said Miles. 'We haven't really got round to doing it up. Dario promised but . . . you know . . .'

It was extremely bare and, because the radiator hadn't been turned on for weeks or months, cold. There was a threadbare carpet, a bed with just a mattress, a bare bulb hanging from the ceiling, a curtain rail with no curtains.

'It's perfect,' I said, because it was. Previously I'd been staying in different places. Squatting with workmates. Sometimes even on site in a sleeping-bag.

'Have you got much stuff?' Miles asked.

'A few things.'

I had a laundry bag full of clothes and that was about it. So I went to the high street and found a funny old housing-supply shop where I bought a duvet and a cover to wrap round it, a pillow and a pillow-case to wrap round it, a sheet, a towel. Then I walked along the street and went into a little bookshop. I browsed through a section devoted to psychology, religion, self-help and gardening and found a book called *Success in Friendship: A User's Manual*. When I handed it to the girl at the counter she looked at me curiously.

'It's for a friend,' I said.

'Really?' she said.

'That was a joke.'

'It's seven ninety-nine,' she said, not laughing.

I didn't really care whether or not she thought I was the sort of person who needed a book to tell him how to find friends. That wasn't what I wanted it for or, at least, not exactly. I wanted to leave my old life behind and to do that I didn't have to create a fake birth certificate and steal someone's name. It was very simple. All I needed was never to go home again, never to phone home again. What was the problem with that? In the end my old life would catch up with me, the way it generally does, like something stuck to your shoe, but in the meantime Maitland Road was going to be my experiment. I was going to impersonate a normal housemate who got on with everybody. I was going to treat it like a technical exercise. That was why I needed a book. It would give me a part to play.

I made up my bed, hung my towel on a hook on the back of the door and lay on the bed with my book. I read the chapter on conversation. Each paragraph was headed by a maxim and I read them aloud to myself: 'The art of conversation is the art of being a good listener'; 'If you want to meet a person, first you must meet their gaze'; 'Respect their space'; 'Reinforce, don't compete'; 'When in doubt, talk shop'; 'Yes, not yes but . . .'

My mate Ben's uncle had put me in touch with a major refurbishment going on across the river in Camberwell. Two days after I moved in, I went down there and wandered round it with the guy who had been hired to do it. It was a fairly basic job, it was cash in hand and it was going to take at least three months. It was all so easy. It was early evening when I got back to Maitland Road. I wasn't exactly sure what being a good housemate was like but I could avoid being a bad one. Don't use up the hot water. I had a shower that lasted about a minute. I came downstairs and found

Pippa alone, reading a magazine. Don't be an obvious free-loader, especially at first.

'I bought some wine,' I said. 'Would you like a glass?'

'Sure,' said Pippa. 'Red or white?'

'Whichever you like,' I said. 'I got both.'

'Well, you can stay,' she said cheerfully. 'White, then.'

I poured two glasses and sat along the sofa from her, respecting her space. Be a good listener.

'I'm sure this is going to come out sounding wrong,' I said, 'but you don't look like a solicitor.'

'That's a relief,' she said, sipping her drink.

'So what kind of stuff do you do?'

She was really quite funny as she talked about the characters in her office and her strange, demanding clients. I was such a good listener. The book had said that in conversation men compete and women support. So I was really a woman. A really terrific woman. Yeah, yeah, that's right, I said. I see what you mean. Yeah, right, absolutely. Oh, that's fantastic. I can't believe it, you really did it? So what did he say? Bloody hell, what an idiot. I kept topping up the wine. I looked her in the eyes. I didn't invade her personal space. I reached for the bottle to fill her glass again but it was empty.

'Shall we move on to the red?' I said.

She slid along the sofa and invaded my personal space. She put her hand on my forearm.

'You know what one of the big problems with sharing a house is?' she said.

'No.'

'No, you don't, but I'm going to tell you. It's the sexual tension. It ruins the friendships and it causes problems.'

'I see what you mean.'

'You can't, because I haven't said it yet. When we're together, there's all this ridiculous flirtation and will-they-

or-won't-they?, and then there's probably some terrible break-up. It's dreadful for the couple and almost as bad for everybody else. You probably know about Astrid and poor Miles.'

'Not exactly.'

'Basically they got together and it was hopeless and she dumped him and he's been mooning around ever since.'

'I'm sorry.'

'It was so boring. It *is* so boring. Now he's got some new girlfriend. She's like a weapon for him to brandish at Astrid. There. Look what you made me do.'

Pippa stroked my arm reflectively and then continued: 'Now you're here, there'll be all this new tension.'

'You reckon?'

'It's unavoidable. We'll be brushing up against each other. We'll bump into each other wrapped in towels on our way from the shower.'

'I don't want to complicate things,' I said.

She ignored me and moved even closer. 'The only way to deal with it is to get it out of the way at the beginning.'

'How do you mean?'

She stroked my face and gave a slow, lazy smile. 'You know,' she said.

'What? Now?' I felt her nuzzling against me.

'It's not compulsory,' she said, 'but it'd be fun. And then we can go on to being friends.'

'But where?'

She pulled a face. 'Well, not here. Someone might come home. Let's go to my room.'

'Shall I bring the wine?'

'No, we'll have it later.'

She took my hand and led me upstairs, talking as she did so. It was something about household routines or someone's bad habits. But I couldn't concentrate on the details. The blood was rushing in my ears. I could hear it. I felt hot. The situation had moved beyond my control and I wasn't sure how it was going to end up. She led me into the room at the front of the house by the front door. Suddenly it all seemed to be happening to somebody else, or at least to somebody else as well as me. I could imagine that somebody else might find her room charming in its disorder, the clothes tossed everywhere, the bed unmade, the curtains closed. There was a clash of smells: perfume and deodorant and soap. I was repelled by it. I wanted to sweep it off the floor and throw open the windows, let in light and fresh air.

Pippa took hold of her T-shirt and pulled it over her head, revealing a black bra covering her small breasts. She kicked off her shoes and unfastened the buttons on the front of her jeans. She sat on the bed and leaned back.

'Pull them off,' she said.

She was as matter-of-fact as if we were going to play squash. I took the bottom of each leg of the jeans and pulled. She lifted herself off the bed and I eased them off. With expert speed she unclipped her bra, pulled down her panties, got into the bed and pulled the duvet over her. I glimpsed her dark nipples and her neatly trimmed pubic hair. Someone else would find this beautiful. They wouldn't believe their luck.

'Now it's your turn,' she said.

I took my clothes off with the grim feeling I had been tricked into going somewhere I didn't want to go. I couldn't think of a way to make it work. I got into the bed next to her and she pushed her face against me. I kissed her. I could taste the wine on her tongue. I had the uncomfortable sensation of being on the wrong side of her, like a left-handed person trying to do something right-handed.

She put a hand on my arm and ran down it, across on to my chest and down, down my stomach. 'Oh,' she said.

'I'm sorry,' I said. 'I'm not ... I don't ...'

'No, it's all right.'

'No, I mean I ...'

'It's all right,' she said, grinning. 'There's no hurry.'

She kissed my chest and then began to move downwards, kissing me as she went. I grabbed her shoulders. 'No,' I said.

'Relax.'

'No.'

I pushed her away and got out of the bed. I had to look around for my clothes. For a desperate moment I thought they might have disappeared irretrievably into the chaos of her room. But I found them and pulled on my underpants, standing stupidly on one leg, then the other. As I pulled my jeans on, I saw her staring at me, amused. 'It's all right,' she said.

'Of course it's all right,' I said.

'I mean, it's not a big deal.'

'That's easy for you to say. I suppose you do this with loads of guys.'

Now she looked puzzled, though still amused. 'What's *that* about?'

She was sitting up in the bed. She hadn't pulled her duvet up, the way actresses do in PG films to cover their breasts. It was probably the last time I'd ever see them. I walked over to her, shrivelled, humiliated, the blood burning in my face. 'If you tell anyone ...' I said.

'You'll what?' said Pippa.

'Just don't,' I said.

'Oh, don't be silly, Davy. Why would I?'

I stamped my feet and walked out of her room and straight

out of the house on to the street, where an icy drizzle soon soaked through my clothes. My eyes were aching. I felt furious with her for forcing herself on me like that, for not giving me a proper chance. And furious with myself for my failure. It wasn't just that there'd been a battle between us and she had won, dominated me and humiliated me. Humiliated me in front of myself. But here in this house, where I was going to start again, become a new person. Already I'd dragged myself down. She'd tell the others. I'd heard the way she gossiped. She wouldn't be able to resist it. Or maybe she would, because it would make her look like a slut, jumping into the pants of a guy who had just walked in off the street.

I was so lost in all of this that I collided with someone and had to reach out to stop her falling. But she dropped her shopping bags, and cans rolled out and a bag of rice split on the pavement. I looked at her in shock, as if I'd been unconscious and suddenly brought round and didn't know where I was.

'I'm so sorry,' I said. 'That was completely my fault. Let me help you.'

'Oh dear,' she said, flustered. 'Look at the mess.' The rice had scattered around us, and several green apples were rolling across the pavement towards the road. 'But it was probably me. I'm terribly clumsy. My husband's always scolding me.'

I bent down and started to replace the shopping. 'I'll buy you another bag of rice. Let's see. Basmati.'

'You really don't need to. It was a mistake. Most people wouldn't even have stopped. They'd have shouted something and rushed on.'

'I'm glad I'm not most people, then. These apples are bruised, I'm afraid. I'll buy some more of them as well.'

'Please don't.'

'At least let me carry them for you. Do you live near here?'

'Just a few yards away. Number fifty-four.'

'I live at seventy-two. We're neighbours!' I moved the bags to my left hand and held out the right.

The woman blushed and shook it. 'Hello,' she said shyly. 'I wish more people on this road were like you.'

'I've just moved in. My name's David.'

'I'm Margaret,' she said, 'but friends call me Peggy.'

Chapter Twenty-eight

We walked down the road together, and I noticed how she patted her hair surreptitiously and straightened her thick jacket as we did so. She was nervous of me. I'd been bad after Pippa. A feeling had been starting in my head. Now it was lifting.

Her house was smaller than the one I'd moved into, and in a much better state of repair. The window-frames were newly painted, the front door a smooth dark green. When she unlocked it and pushed it open, I could see that inside it was also tidy. Too tidy. Madly tidy. Even from here, I could smell the detergent and polish and loneliness.

'Thank you so much.'

'It was my pleasure, Peggy,' I said. 'I'll look out for you on the street.'

'Would you like a cup of coffee? Or we could have some wine, I suppose. It's after six o'clock.'

'I'd love a cup of coffee.' I stepped over the threshold with the bags.

'You would?'

'I don't know anyone round here,' I said. 'You're the first friendly face I've met.'

She nodded.

There wasn't a speck of dirt in the kitchen. Even the dozens of porcelain figurines on the dresser were clean. Peggy put on an apron – as if you really needed to put on an apron to make coffee – and filled the kettle. I sat at the small round table and looked at her. She was quite short, and not slim but not plump either. Compact. Her hair was cut in a bob and a glossy dark brown that looked natural to me. She had pink cheeks and her skin was still quite smooth, although I saw that there were tiny lines above her mouth and under her eyes, but when I examined her neck I estimated that she must be in her mid-fifties, about the same as my mother. Under her jacket she wore a powder-blue turtleneck, and a calf-length blue skirt that she ran her hands down anxiously, making sure it wasn't wrinkled or rising up. She wore sensible shoes and through her tights I saw the first traces of varicose veins.

'So, Peggy,' I said, 'how long have you lived in Maitland Road, then?'

She arranged biscuits on a plate. 'Nearly twenty-seven years.'

'You were here as a child, then?'

'No!' Her pink cheeks became pinker. 'You're teasing me. No, we bought this house just after we got married. It was different then. My husband says we should move. He doesn't like the way it's going.'

'What way is that?'

'The kind of people who live round here.'

'Do you want to move?'

'I don't know. I like the house.'

'It's lovely.'

'But I don't really feel I belong here. We're not like the other people on the road. Here, do you take milk?'

'Just a bit. No sugar. What do you mean, the other people?'

'Well, your house, for instance. Everyone in it is so . . .' She hesitated.

'Go on.'

Her eyes narrowed. 'They're the sort of people who come

for a bit,' she said, 'and then go. Move on. Not like real neighbours. That what the road's like.'

'I think I know how you feel,' I said.

'Do you?'

'The thing is, Peggy, I've only been in London a short while. I grew up in a small village, where everyone knew everyone else and looked out for each other. It was a real community. If someone was in trouble, they would be helped. If someone did wrong, they would be discovered. That's just the way it was there. And since Mum died –' I stopped abruptly.

'Yes?' she probed softly.

'I don't usually talk about it. My father died when I was little, I can hardly remember him now, and a few months ago my mother died of cancer. She'd been ill for a very long time and I stayed there so I could look after her and be with her. I was her only child. She didn't have anyone else.' I looked into Peggy's eyes. 'Neither did I.'

'You poor thing.'

'I'm all right, really. Just a bit sad still. These things take time. Maybe I'm telling you all of this because you remind me of her.'

'Do I?'

'In a way. Do you have children, Peggy?'

'No. It didn't happen,' she said simply.

'I'm sorry. That must have been hard.'

'It's a long time ago now.'

'Of course.'

We sat drinking our coffee. I ate two biscuits, at her insistence, and she told me which shops to use and which to avoid. There were five cards standing on the window-sill and in a pause I asked her when her birthday was.

'Two days ago. I don't really make any fuss about it nowadays. It's not something you want to remember.'

'Two days ago. You mean last Thursday?'

'Yes.'

'But that's my birthday too.'

'No! What an extraordinary coincidence.'

'Amazing,' I said. 'We must have been fated to meet.'

I told myself to make a note of the date of last Thursday before I forgot it and slipped up. Peggy excused herself and left the kitchen. I waited a few seconds, and when I heard her going up the stairs, I leaned forward and pulled her bag towards me. There were several notes folded in her wallet. I took out a ten, then pushed the bag back where it had been. After all, I was out of pocket with all the wine I'd been buying for the house, and I could spend a small part of the money on the Basmati rice I'd promised her. That would please her.

That Saturday night, the house was almost empty. Pippa wasn't there when I returned, and I met Astrid coming down the stairs as I went up, obviously on her way somewhere. It was the first time I had seen her wearing a dress: a short, simple red silk shift. With her long golden legs and slim tanned arms, her dark hair brushed back and her lips painted scarlet, she looked astonishing. I tried not to stare at her, but my chest felt uncomfortably tight.

'Hi, Davy, how's it going?' she asked.

'Fine,' I replied. 'I'm glad to be here.'

'We're glad to have you. I'll see you later, then.'

'Maybe we can have coffee together tomorrow?'

'Sure,' she said lightly.

And so, with a backward wave, she was gone. I was beginning to get the hang of the people in this house. You couldn't be too earnest or oppressive. People here were free in a way I hadn't come across before.

Miles was out as well, and Owen – though not with Astrid, I was glad to know. That left only Dario – who was lying in a stoned stupor in the basement kitchen – and Mick, who was in his room with the door shut and probably locked. I decided to risk it.

I started with Miles's room. It was the best in the house by far and it annoyed me that he had done so little to make the most of it. The large bay windows looked out on to the street, and one side of the room was entirely lined with a large cupboard. I pulled open one of the doors and peered inside. As well as towels and sheets, there were several cardboard boxes, filled with old music magazines, academic quarterlies, Ordnance Survey maps and files, which, on further scrutiny, turned out to be full of bills and letters. I didn't have time to read any now, but I promised myself I would later. I closed the cupboards and turned my attention to the rest of the room. There were no real surprises. The wardrobe contained suits and shirts, all of which looked quite expensive. I pulled open the drawers of the chest and found nothing interesting except a pack of condoms among the underwear. Time to move on.

I went quietly into Pippa's room, stepping over the mess and trying not to disturb it. You'd think it would be impossible for her to notice any changes, but even chaos like this had its own order. I saw a bottle of nail varnish standing on the floor, and then I remembered her, sitting in the bed, breasts half uncovered and an amused smile on her face. I unscrewed the top and tipped it over with my foot so it spread over a delicate shirt. I found several pairs of tights and dragged my fingernails down them to create ladders. I spat into a little pot of lip balm. There.

I went up the stairs as quietly as I could, so that Mick didn't hear me, and opened the door to Astrid's room. For a few seconds I just stood in the centre, relishing the quiet of her space. It occurred to me that her room was the twin of mine, which was on the floor above and also looked over the street. But this one was freshly painted, and it smelled of coconut, citrus fruit and lavender. I took the few steps to where her toiletries stood on a shelf and sniffed them in turn, learning them. It was clean, tidy and peaceful, just as I like rooms to be. I flicked through the clothes hanging in her wardrobe. There weren't many – Pippa probably owned ten times more – but I liked what there was. Nothing frilly or fussy, nothing shoddily made. I put my face among the hanging folds and breathed in her scent. Then I turned to the chest, opening each drawer in turn and rummaging through the contents. I put a pair of black knickers in my pocket. She had very little makeup. I took one lip-gloss.

I thought I heard a sound coming from Mick's room above, so I went out and stood in the hallway, listening. Nothing. I pushed open the door to Owen's room and stood at its threshold. Photographs were stacked against every wall, some with their backs turned to me but others in plain view. Women's faces in four-colour black stared sightlessly at me and suddenly my limbs were heavy and my skin prickled. It was starting in my head. I was under water, with things wavering around me, not holding their proper shape.

I heard the front door open. I backed out and pulled the door shut quietly, then turned, went into my own room and lay on my bed, waiting for the ticking in my left eye to go away. I heard voices. Miles, I thought, and someone else: a woman, but not Astrid or Pippa. I don't know how long I lay there, whether or not I slept, but when I went downstairs Dario was awake, sitting on the sofa smoking a cigarette, and Mick was frying eggs at the stove. The smell made me feel sick again. Miles was there, and so, too, was the woman whose voice I had heard. She was tall and striking and had flawless skin, but her face was discontented and her smile didn't quite reach her eyes. She reminded me of a bird of prey, a hawk perhaps. I told myself I had to be careful.

Chapter Twenty-nine

Mick was sitting at the table and Astrid was at the stove. She was wearing blue jeans and a light brown T-shirt. She was barefooted again, leaning up to reach a saucepan down from a high shelf. The effort pulled her shirt up, exposing the smooth brown skin of her lower back.

'Sorry,' I said, turning to go.

'That's all right,' said Astrid. 'Join us.'

I thought of my instruction manual. 'Is there anything I can do to help?'

She laughed. 'I'm cooking one of my special recipes. Pasta accompanied by spicy red pesto bought from a deli, sprinkled with cheese, plus red wine.'

'Sounds fantastic,' I said.

'It is,' said Astrid. 'Even I can't fuck it up.'

I found Mick disconcerting. He was like a smooth wall that provided no fingerholds. He didn't seem to find it awkward to stay silent. He looked at me for a moment, then got up and collected plates, forks and glasses, three of each. He took a bottle of red wine from a carrier-bag on the floor, opened it and poured some into each glass. I picked up mine.

'Cheers,' I said, too quickly. Astrid was stirring pasta in the saucepan and Mick just stared at his glass. It felt like an awkward moment but then Astrid smiled, picked up hers and took a gulp from it.

'Mick and I were talking about travelling,' she said. 'Have you done much, Davy?'

Lying is like a really good tool. It's a tool for manipulating people, for controlling them. You can tell them what they want to hear; you can make them think you're a particular person. The point of lying is to have different lies for different people. Different people *need* different lies, the way that different jobs need different tools. If you have just one lie for everyone, you might as well tell the truth because the truth is much easier. If you're telling the truth, you don't need to think because the truth automatically fits together neatly. Lies aren't like that. You have to make them fit. And you have to remember which lie you're telling at any particular time, and to whom, and if it fits with every other lie you've told and whether anything could happen, today, tomorrow or the day after to expose it. Knowing when not to lie is part of the skill. I knew, I just knew, that Mick and Astrid were talking about travelling because they had both done a lot. And I would so much like to have said yes, so that I would have been part of the club. But then they would ask where and I would name some place, and it would turn out that one of them had been there and it would go terribly wrong. It would only take something as small as that to ruin everything in the house and force me to leave.

'No,' I said. 'Where have you been?'

'Round Europe mainly,' said Astrid. 'India, a bit in the Far East, Australia. Nothing like Mick.'

'Where have you been, then?' I said to Mick.

He made a dismissive gesture. 'I just got back from Latin America,' he said. 'I was there a couple of years.'

I thought of my book, my manual on how to be a real person. Bring people out, it advised. There's no such thing as a bore. All a good talker needs is a good listener.

'What's the best place you went to?' I asked Mick. 'Where would you really recommend?'

He thought for a moment. 'Brazil,' he said.

'Why?'

'Number one.' He held up one finger. 'The rainforest. Two: the Amazon. Three: big, noisy, exciting cities. Four: the dancing. Five: the *cachasa*.' He started on the fingers of his other hand. 'Six: the music. Seven: the beaches. Eight: excellent dope.' This was the most I'd ever heard Mick say, but he continued. 'Then there's the women.'

'Number nine on your list,' I said lightly, pleased to see Astrid grinning, but Mick scowled as if I was mocking him.

'They're the most amazing women in the world. Present company excepted.'

'Oh, shut up, Mick,' said Astrid, heaping pasta on to the plates.

'And it's cheap.'

'Sounds great,' I said. 'How's your Spanish?'

Mick looked at Astrid.

'Portuguese, in fact,' said Astrid. 'Chile and Peru and the rest speak Spanish.'

'Yes, I knew that,' I said. 'I meant when you were travelling round the rest of South America. Actually, I was thinking of learning Portuguese.'

'Really?' said Astrid. 'Everyone says it's a lovely language.'

Fuck, I thought. Fuck fuck fuck fuck. I'd told the truth to stop myself looking stupid and I'd made myself look stupid anyway.

The next day I went to the bookshop and found a guidebook to South America. Brazil really did look good. Ten days later, I was sitting in a class at an institute in Clapton with several businessmen, a few white-haired retired men and women and a couple of younger people I couldn't make

263

out. Introductory Portuguese taught by a middle-aged woman, fat, bespectacled, Portuguese, but not at all the kind of woman Mick had been talking about. Week four. It was late March by now and I'd missed weeks one, two and three but I told the woman in the office I'd catch up.

Several days later, when I met Mick in the hall, I said in a cheery voice, '*Bom dia.*'

He looked startled. 'Is this for real?'

'I told you I was planning to learn.'

'Spanish is really more useful,' he said. 'Unless you're planning to go to Brazil. Or Angola or Mozambique.'

'Or Portugal,' I said.

'Yeah,' he said, sounding doubtful. 'Was it the women? I may have exaggerated about them.'

'No,' I said. 'I like the sound of the language.'

Mick's expression relaxed. 'I do too,' he said. 'I'm sorry. I'm not taking the piss. *Boa sorte.*'

'What?'

'Good luck.'

For the next few weeks, I lived my life happily in compartments. There was the Portuguese compartment, where I was a person planning a project in Brazil. There was the work compartment. Down in Camberwell I was the young apprentice, eager to learn. It was always good to pretend to know less than you really did. I could clearly see that Dario was taking the housemates at Maitland Road for a ride. He was allegedly paying his rent in kind, by doing the house up. It was mainly painting, but he also did a bit of electrics, a bit of carpentry, even some plastering and plumbing. It was a botch job. When he painted a room, he couldn't be bothered to tape up the wood frames. I mentioned it once but he said it was a waste of time. All that was needed was a steady hand. The result was paint speckles on the woodwork. His carpentry was all ragged edges, protruding screws and ill-fitting joints. If his electrical work was of the same standard, there was probably a risk of fire.

I thought of mentioning it to Miles and provoking a row, but that didn't fit with the role I was creating. For the moment, I was the perfect housemate, the one who did the washing-up and patched over disagreements. It was always useful to have ammunition that could be used later.

I wanted to get to know the housemates individually. One evening I wandered out into the garden to get a shirt off the line and found Dario in a corner, smoking a joint. He offered it to me and I took a puff.

'It's good stuff, isn't it?' he said.

It never had much effect on me. I'd always found it difficult to see why it meant so much to other people, why they gave it so much attention. 'Yes,' I said. 'It's really good stuff.'

I handed it back to Dario who took a fearsome drag on it, the tip flaming up.

'I can get some for you, if you want,' he said. 'For a good price. Just say the word.'

I didn't reply. So that was how he earned his pocket money.

'But don't mention it to Miles,' said Dario, dropping the roach and stamping on it. 'He's a bit paranoid about it.'

In the early days, I phoned Astrid's mobile on a Friday afternoon about some shopping that needed to be done. She suggested we meet up at a pub where she went at the end of the week. When I arrived at the Horse and Jockey, it was full of other despatch riders, spilling out of the doors, overflowing from the pavement on to the road. It was like a huge, bustling party that I hadn't been invited to, except that I had. I wandered around and found Astrid sitting with a black guy, in his thirties, strongly built, wearing jeans and a T-shirt, head completely shaved. I wondered if he was another boyfriend, but she introduced him to me as Campbell, her 'so-called boss'. I bought a drink for her and for him, and for another man sitting at her other side and one for myself, and they made room for me at the table. I enjoyed sitting there, watching this strange breed. There were riders in bright yellow tops, like competitors in the Tour de France, and there were scruffy young men in cut-off jeans and vests, and older men, grizzled, deeply tanned, with long hair in dreadlocks or ponytails. I sat and sipped my drink while they joshed each other, gossiped and complained about their clients.

'The problem,' said Campbell, returning with another round of drinks, 'is that they spend their lives cycling from rich person to rich person. They step through the door and they look at these people with their servants and their posh hallway, and then they get back on their bike.'

'So, do you really hate the people you deliver to?' I asked Astrid.

She laughed, eyes sparkling, and began to answer, but she was interrupted by Neil, the other man at the table. 'Basically we're offering a service, and they're free to use that service in any way they choose, whether it be to deliver a consignment of valuables or to fetch a hot dog for them.'

Astrid laughed again. 'And we're free to say they're stuck-up bastards with too much money.'

'Valuables?' I said.

'Documents, mainly,' she said, and winked at Neil. Could he have been another ex-boyfriend?

And then there was Peggy. I treated her as an exercise, a bit like the homework I brought back from my Portuguese class. I found her boring and unattractive, and I wondered what she thought of me. Did she see me as the son she'd never had? Or did she even see me as a fantasy young lover? It was a grotesque thought, but not impossible. Or maybe it was a combination of the two. Mothers often flirt with their sons, although they'd be shocked if you pointed it out to them. And it's possible that old women don't see themselves as old. They still have the fantasy that a young man might be attracted to them, that he would see through what they've become to what they once were. I found it terrible to think that women like Astrid turned into women like Peggy.

I decided that I would talk to Peggy as if she was a young woman like Astrid, not the old woman she was. I met her in the street a few times over those weeks, and usually she invited me in for tea. The third time, I accepted her offer of a glass of wine. She took a half-full bottle from the fridge. We drank it in her garden because it was warm and the evenings were becoming lighter with each passing day. I sat quite close to her, touching her sometimes as we talked, the way young people do, a hand on an arm to make a point. I saw a glitter in her eyes when I did it, a yes. The funny thing was that when I talked to Peggy pretending she was a young woman, I did better than when I talked to actual young women. It occurred to me that I should talk to young women pretending I was talking to an old woman pretending she was a young woman. Life is complicated.

Each time, when she left me alone in her kitchen for a few minutes, I helped myself to some money. I saw it as a contribution to my other role of generous housemate, coming home with bottles of wine. The third time, on that May evening, I thought we were getting on so well, that she was so grateful for my attention, that I took a bit too much: twenty or thirty pounds. But I thought she wouldn't mind. It was like a fee for giving her a good time.

I liked the idea of these different lives I was leading, and all the time I felt I was gaining power. The housemates had known each other for longer than I had but I knew so much they didn't. I had watched them. I had seen inside their rooms. I knew what Dario was doing to the house. I knew what kind of photographs Owen was taking. I knew Margaret Farrell. None of the rest of them knew her or knew I knew her. I had seen Pippa naked. She had seen me naked. That hadn't worked out. Did it matter? When I met her afterwards, she was exactly as friendly as she had been before. There seemed nothing between us. Had it made her feel sympathy for me? Pity? Contempt? Or did she feel nothing? Certainly there had been other men since me and I doubted that they had failed where I had. I was just another name on the list, except that I wasn't properly on it. I wondered if I should try to take another chance with her. Except that I might fail again. It was easier for women.

Chapter Thirty

It was weird seeing Astrid fly through the air, and in spite of everything that happened later, the sight remained vivid in my memory: the way she held her hands in front of her as she took off from her bike, as if she was about to do a racing dive into water, and then the way in which she instinctively curled her body, just as parachute jumpers are trained to do before impact. She didn't look surprised at all; there was just a small frown on her face, as though she had been given a thorny mathematical problem to solve. Even after she hit the road, and her body twisted, her limbs splayed awkwardly and her cheek smashed into the tarmac, her expression remained oddly unflustered. It was as though she was still waiting for the thing that had already happened. For one moment, she closed her eyes and lay quite still in the middle of the road, her bike a tangled mess behind her. I could imagine what she would look like dead.

I had been sitting on the front steps with Dario and a mate of his. It was one of those hot evenings that you know will turn into a hot night, and I had half closed my eyes. I was pretending to be in another world while I listened to Dario haggle – if you can haggle in a whisper – with the other man over the price of whatever it was he had in the plastic bag that he thought I hadn't noticed under his jacket. I knew Astrid was coming round the corner even before I saw her. And there she was, crouching low on her saddle. And there was Peggy Farrell sitting in her parked car, probably listening to the end of some boring programme on the radio, just a few yards from where I was sitting. She caught sight of me and a curious expression crossed her face, half furtive and half beseeching. It made me feel itchy with irritation and I pretended not to see her. She swung open her door. It was a perfect hit. Astrid: like a bird in the air, like a piece of meat on the ground.

Dario and I rushed over, Dario uttering high-pitched shrieks, but Peggy was there before us. She was apologizing away, while Astrid groaned things like 'Fuck' and 'Leave me alone'. Peggy was about to say something to me, but I stared at her as if she was a stranger and her face crumpled. I bent over Astrid, who looked dazed and was going on about her bike while blood trickled down her face. I wanted to pick her up and hold her, but I knew that even when she was injured she would probably resent this or make me feel stupid and clumsy, so I simply asked her how she was. I put on my most sympathetic face, even though I quickly saw it wasn't serious. She wouldn't be rushed off to A and E or bed-ridden and helpless for days, just a bit sore. I knew Peggy was staring at me, waiting for me to acknowledge her, but I continued to behave as if she wasn't there.

Astrid raised herself, ignoring my outstretched hand, and Dario picked up the battered bike. I saw that Peggy was having difficulty getting the bent door of her car shut. She looked at me for help but I let my contempt show on my face. A red flush stained her cheeks and she looked old and foolish. I turned my back on her and put an arm very carefully round Astrid. She didn't push me away. She leaned on me. Her hair brushed against my cheek and her blood was on my new white shirt. I could smell her sweat and her shampoo. Dario's druggie friend walked past us and raised a hand in greeting, and Dario muttered something under his breath.

'Who's that?' asked Astrid.

'Nobody,' said Dario. 'How's your head?' Then he threw me a furious glance and started going on about how he and I had been sitting on the steps together when she'd had her accident. So Astrid didn't know that Dario dealt drugs, which meant that probably no one else in the house did either.

We stumbled towards the house, Dario with the bike, me with Astrid, both of us calling out for Miles, who appeared at the front door. To see the stricken expression on his face, you'd have thought I was carrying Astrid's corpse. But anyway, we bundled her inside and she was swept up amid exclamations of horror, and I was left standing by the open door with the bike, feeling pissed off with everyone for taking over like that. I tried to hang the bike up on the hook but it was buckled and wouldn't fit. Pippa came downstairs just as I was saying something about the bike needing some work on it and told me it was Astrid who needed looking after, not the bike, before waltzing off down the stairs with the others to look after the invalid, leaving me on my own. The tightness in my chest increased and I felt the familiar buzzing behind my eyes. Then I saw Peggy coming up the steps.

'David,' she said.

'What?' I couldn't be bothered to be polite to her. But instead of looking flustered and embarrassed, as she would normally have done, her chin went up and her expression became stubborn. 'I need to speak to you.'

'I don't have the time,' I said, and was about to shut the door on her, but she put a hand out and stopped it.

'I said I need to talk to you.'

From downstairs came the sound of laughter. I looked at Peggy and said, 'What's this about?'

'The other day,' she said. 'In my house.'

So she'd seen me take her money. My headache intensified. I felt oppressed and hemmed in, and I grabbed her by the arm and said, 'Not out here. Come in.' I pulled her through the door and steered her into Miles's room, where we wouldn't be heard, shutting the door behind us.

'You should have asked me, if you needed money,' she said.

'I don't know what you're going on about.'

'I thought you liked my company,' she said. 'Stupid of me.'

I told myself to be charming. I tried to speak, but her face, all hurt and spiteful, swam in front of me.

'You've taken money before, haven't you?' She didn't wait for an answer but went on: 'My husband will think I'm so stupid when I tell him about it, which I've decided I must do. He'll think it serves me right.'

She was going on and on and on about it. I just wanted to shut her up, the gabby, interfering busybody. It was all her fault. Thinking I was the son she'd never had, thinking I found her attractive, thinking I wanted to sit in her dreary little kitchen making eyes at her, believing that was all I was good for and that my life was as petty and wretched as hers. What had she expected would happen? What had she hoped for? What? My grip tightened.

There was still a red mist in front of my eyes and a roaring in my head, but at least her voice had stopped. At least she was limp and I could take my hands away from her throat and lay her on the floor where she gazed up at me, her purple face and glassy eyes, her mouth half open so I could see the fillings in her teeth. Her skirt had ridden up and I bent down to tug it back over her knees.

I heard panting, like the sound made by a thirsty dog, and I realized it was coming from me. I was shivering, almost shaking. I sat down on Miles's bed and made myself take deep breaths. I had to keep calm. I had to think clearly. I was in Miles's room and at any moment he might walk in. But if I dragged Peggy's body out into the hall any of them could come across me. I glanced around: the large cupboards. That was it, I had to put her in there until I had a chance to get rid of the body properly.

Now that I had a plan, I felt quite strong and steady. I could feel the ache in my head receding, like wisps of fog being blown away. Other people would collapse and panic if they found themselves in a situation like this, but I could do it. I opened the cupboard door and pushed the piles of towels and sheets out of the way. I put my hands under Peggy's armpits and started to drag her across the floor. She was heavy, as if death had climbed into her body and was squatting there. Her shoe caught on the floorboards and spun off. Her head lolled. The most difficult bit was getting her into the cupboard. I had to push her in from behind and her limbs got caught in the doorway and her skirt acted as friction, making her hard to slide. But eventually I did it. I pulled the towels and sheets over her, although even a quick glance would show there was something bulky underneath.

As I shut the door and stood up, the sound of voices and footsteps outside the room made me freeze. But they continued up the next flight of stairs. I waited until I was sure no one was there, then opened the door and slipped out. As soon as I had left, though, I had the feeling I'd forgotten something. Had I put the shoe that had fallen off her foot in with the body? I was almost sure I had but had to fight the temptation to go back in to check. Had I shut the door properly, or would it swing open to reveal the body? Was there anything on me to give me away? I glanced down at my white shirt. There were streaks of oil from the bike. I stood in front of the mirror in the hall. I was impressed by how normal I seemed. I looked good. Fresh-faced and clear-eyed, relaxed. I smiled at myself and went up the stairs to my room. As I passed the bathroom, I could hear taps running and guessed Astrid must be taking a bath. I had a few minutes before I needed to face anyone.

I changed my shirt and splashed aftershave on my face. I took a few deep breaths. There. I thought of Peggy's body in Miles's bedroom. Miles, who was nervous about dope being smoked on the premises. It was almost funny. Not almost. It *was* funny. Of course, Miles would only have to open the cupboard and everything would be ruined. But he used it for general storage. I was probably safe for a bit. As soon as possible I had to find a way of getting the body out of the cupboard and out of the house. This was the evening for our long-planned meeting, so I would have to do it somehow while everyone was here. But maybe that was a good thing.

I went up to visit Astrid. There were several people in the room, and I pushed the door and slid quietly in. She was lying down in jogging pants and a T-shirt and Dario was sitting at the bottom of her bed. Mick stood by the window. Pippa was yelling something from the bathroom. There was a party atmosphere, which increased when Miles joined us, sitting by Astrid's side, his hand not quite touching hers, and Dario lit up a giant spliff.

'It was all in slow motion,' said Astrid.

'You must have fallen in a really natural way,' I said. 'That's why you didn't get seriously injured. It's the way they train paratroopers. But you did it naturally.'

Dario took a huge drag of his joint and I watched as the column of ash grew, then crumbled on to the floor, where he put his foot on top of it, grinding it surreptitiously into the carpet.

They were all talking. Mick sat on the bed to examine her. Pippa came in with a bottle of disinfectant. I heard myself saying things. But all the time I was thinking. I felt alert, powerful.

'I'll open some wine,' I said. 'We should celebrate being together for once.' I smiled at them all, thinking how amazing, how glorious it was that I had killed someone and hidden her body in the cupboard downstairs and none of them had the slightest idea that anything was wrong. 'I can't tell you how happy I am that I'm living here with you all.'

Astrid smiled up at me from the bed, her big, dark eyes glowing. 'Davy,' she said, 'you're the perfect housemate.'

I gave a little bow. 'That's me,' I said.

Chapter Thirty-one

The evening was like a dream. I was there and I wasn't there. Surely they could see the difference in me, the glow in my eyes, the consciousness of power, the knowledge. But I realized they couldn't, and that increased my sense of control. When Owen arrived with the food, I saw his shock at Astrid's appearance, but all he said was 'You get into a fight?'

He walked across to her, too close. She made an effort to seem casual about it. I went and sat beside her.

'She's being brave,' I said, then felt embarrassed. Did it look as if I was competing with Owen for her attention? I had to be careful. In all my excitement, the blood rushing through my body, I was in danger of overplaying this. I had to calm down. Fortunately nobody seemed to notice. Astrid was still the centre of attention. When I started concentrating again, they were dealing out the food and comparing themselves to the Seven Dwarfs. It made me feel angry. I was forgotten as they jokingly and affectionately allocated different dwarfs to Pippa and Mick and Dario and Miles. It reminded me of those times in the playground when they had picked teams and what it felt like to be left until last, the one nobody wanted. So I made a joke about it and took Bashful for myself, the one nobody would want to be. Bashful. What did they know?

I pushed forkfuls of food into my mouth, not tasting it. I let the conversation wash over me. Sometimes I managed a sentence. I smiled at things that were meant to be jokes.

I even smiled at Pippa and she smiled back. I looked around the table. These were friends, but how many of them really liked each other? I noticed that Astrid wasn't speaking or eating. I looked at Miles, who had a sudden businesslike expression on his face.

'Listen,' he said. 'I hate to break into this, but it's very rare that we're all together like this. Just the seven of us. Don't you dare start again, Dario.'

Suddenly it all became clear to me. That was how to do it.

'You're right,' I said. 'It *is* rare. Why don't we have a group photo to mark it?'

Miles nodded. 'We even have an official photographer,' he said.

Fuck, I thought. I'd forgotten about Owen. But I'd also forgotten his arrogance. He prattled about not taking snaps and Astrid teased him about being an artist.

'I'll take it,' I said.

'My camera's in the drawer over there,' said Miles.

Was God deliberately tormenting me? I jumped up and opened the drawer. Miles's digital camera was lying on top. I covered it with the stuff in the drawer, the brochures, menus and catalogues. 'It's not here. You must have moved it.'

'Someone's nabbed it, more like, and forgotten to put it back.'

'I've got one upstairs,' I said, and ran out before anything else could go wrong.

It was all so simple. I couldn't even allow myself to think of the possibility of being caught. I opened the cupboard door, pulled off the coverings and saw the empty eyes staring up at me. I felt nothing. I knelt down, took her arm, pulled her over my shoulder and raised myself slowly, the joints in my knees cracking. I kicked the cupboard door shut, then turned to check there was nothing stupid like a hat or a handbag to ruin my perfect crime. As I moved out into the hallway I even smiled at the idea of one of the housemates catching me like this. I walked smoothly upstairs, to the first floor, then the second. I pulled out the bed a little way and laid her down behind it so that she was invisible from the doorway. That was enough. Nobody would come into my room tonight.

I ran softly down the stairs. It was so simple. Before I entered the kitchen, I stopped. The camera. I'd forgotten it. I ran back up and down so that by the time I appeared I was panting with the effort. None of them noticed, though.

After the photograph, after Miles had kindly provided the distraction of telling everyone they would be ejected from the house, after the foil containers were cleared away, the washing-up done, I went upstairs, lay down on my bed without taking off my shoes, Peggy on the floor beside me, and waited for the house to grow quiet. I heard footsteps on stairs, floorboards creaking, water running, doors slamming, toilets flushing, but by twelve thirty it had all stopped. I forced myself to be patient. I looked at my watch again. One o'clock.

An idea came to me. I felt through her pockets and found a purse. I removed the ornate little watch from her wrist and unclipped her necklace. That might make the death look like a robbery.

I glanced at my watch. One fifteen. Time was moving in starts, not smoothly. As quietly as I could, I left my room and walked downstairs. I put my ears to the various doors and heard nothing. The last was Pippa's on the ground floor. That, too, was silent. I was free to act, but as I started up the stairs, I heard voices. They were from outside the front door. I assumed they were passers-by but then I heard the scrape of a key in the lock.

I ran up the stairs to the half-way landing, out of sight. The door opened and I heard footsteps. Pippa's voice and someone else's, a man's. What was wrong with her? 'Straight in here,' she said, leading him into her room. 'You want a drink? I'll bring something up.'

I waited until she returned. I heard the clink of glasses and her door closing. I sat on the upper stairs in half-darkness. I could see the old patterned wallpaper, peeling away and showing the plaster underneath but I couldn't make out its colour. After a few minutes I heard murmuring sounds from Pippa's room. If I acted quickly, I should be safe. I padded back upstairs. As I stood in my room, the risks of what I was attempting became clear to me for the first time. There were six – no, seven – other people in the house. They often stayed up late, left their rooms for a drink, a bath or a piss. It would take just one. I only needed a clear couple of minutes, but would God give them to me? I hoisted Peggy over my shoulder, walked out of the room and down the stairs, feeling every creak run through my body.

I hadn't even thought of what I would find out on the street. I eased the front door open and edged outside, hidden in the shadows of the porch. There was nobody. Twenty paces and I would be free. I stepped on to the pavement as if I was walking on to a stage, a stage surrounded by dark windows. Someone could be standing behind any of them, looking out. I counted the paces. It took twenty-seven and I reached her door. I walked down the steps to where the bins were and let her slip gently on to the cement. I pulled her behind the bins and covered her with bags of garbage. She might not be found for days.

Chapter Thirty-two

When I was still at school and went by the name of David, not Davy, teachers treated me as if I was stupid. My English teacher, who was tall, flat-chested and in love with dead writers, said I lacked imagination and my creative writing was plodding. My French teacher didn't even know who I was. I was one of the people at the back of the class, not noticed. My science teacher called me 'conscientious', my Design and Technology teacher called me 'competent', and my maths teacher said I was 'an average student'. Well, I wasn't average now, not average at all. I was one in a million.

It took me a time to get the hang of it. That night I hardly slept, and when I did I had strange, crowded dreams. My entire body felt unnaturally alert and vibrant: every creak or rustle made me start. I listened to footsteps on the road outside and waited, skin prickling, to hear if they would stop at our door. I couldn't tell if the feeling throbbing heavily inside me and pulsing behind my eyes was excitement or fear. I was awake at dawn, and ready for the day ahead, way before anyone else in the house, but I didn't go downstairs for a long time. I stood in front of the mirror in a clean blue shirt and jeans, and patted aftershave on my cheeks, practising my modest, boyish smile. I sat on the bed with my hands on my knees and my back quite straight, and breathed in and out, in and out. I heard Astrid in the room beneath get up and use the bathroom, then go downstairs. Very faintly, I heard sounds of voices from the kitchen: hers, Pippa's, someone else's, presumably the man Pippa was with last night. I got up and positioned myself beside the window so that I saw Astrid leave. Although she was limping slightly and I could see even from the top floor that her face was bruised, she still had that light-footed gait and held her head high. She walked down the street. She reached Peggy's house. She didn't hesitate but went on by.

I stayed where I was. The postman was coming up the road, very slowly, stopping at each door. I held my breath and watched as he fumbled in his mailbag, pulled out a couple of envelopes, then pushed open the gate to number fifty-four. Past the rubbish bins, scratching his head in the warmth, pushing the letters through the letterbox, out onto the road again. I saw him yawn and felt a smile spread across my face. I had to stop myself snorting out loud: he'd been just a few inches from her body and seen nothing, smelled nothing, noticed nothing. Next door, Mick coughed, groaned. The walls were too thin in that house.

I don't usually like breakfast, but that morning I was hungry. Pippa and a tall man with a bony face were in the kitchen when I came downstairs. He was dressed in a smart suit and was fiddling neurotically with his tie, repeatedly pulling the knot tight, then loosening it. Married, I thought. Married and feeling furtive; he was more nervous than I was. Pippa looked as though she'd slept like a baby for hours. She was wearing a grey suit whose skirt finished just above her knees, a white shirt with one button too many undone so I could see the frilly top of her bra, and her hair was coiled on top of her head, with artful stray locks framing her face. She gave me a bright smile from her painted lips and introduced me to the man, who turned out to be Jeff and on his way out.

'It was a bit rowdy during the night, wasn't it?' I said, to test them, but Pippa didn't react and Jeff blushed scarlet; he must have thought I was referring to them. I found half a packet of bacon in the fridge, and a couple of eggs left in the carton, past their sell-by date, so I made myself a fry-up, with baked beans as well, and fried bread, plus a big cup of milky coffee. It was the best breakfast I'd ever had and by the time I was half-way through, Mick was downstairs and Owen too, looking dishevelled and unshaven, but in a deliberate, self-conscious sort of way. Nobody said much but, then, they never do in the morning. I could tell that not one of them was suspicious and I wanted to say something to shake them out of their smug complacency.

When I left for work, I walked past number fifty-four as slowly as I could, glancing across at the bins. It was frustrating to think that I wouldn't be around when she was discovered, and when I got to the end of the road I turned and went back to the house again, as if I'd left something behind, so that I could once more pass the hidden body. All day long, the secret of her tingled in me and I left work early, excited as any lover. Until Peggy was discovered, it was like writing a letter that might change your life but not posting it.

At half past five, I got off the bus at the end of our road and it was then I saw the dustmen and stopped dead in my tracks, my heart swelling in my chest, my mouth dry, the road seeming to shrink, then expand in front of my eyes. There were two of them on the pavement, hauling bins and fitting them to the back of the vehicle, which the third was driving. They had only got to number twenty-eight. In the heat of the day, you could smell the rubbish. I would never do that job. You'd have to be desperate to deal with rotten meat and babies' nappies. They seemed cheerful enough. One was whistling.

I stayed where I was and lit a cigarette. I don't usually smoke when I'm alone, just offer fags to other people, but this seemed like a special occasion and I needed to do something with my hands. When the refuse collectors got to number fifty-two, I started to walk slowly along the road again, until I was near enough to make out what was happening. Then I halted, and pretended to tie up my shoelace. Number fifty-four. This was it. Two bins, one green for the recycled stuff and one blue for ordinary rubbish, were pulled out on to the pavement and hoisted up on to the dustcart. A few bits of paper spilled on to the tarmac, and an empty shampoo bottle. Nobody shouted or cried out. A group of youths swaggered past.

One of the men turned back to collect the bags of garbage that I'd pulled into place last night. He put both hands round the neck of a bag and hoisted it up on his shoulder. It was almost comical. He stopped, stared for a long time, then called his workmate over, gesturing. I could see one of Peggy's legs now, and then the figure of the driver swinging from his seat. There was shouting and commotion.

It's magic how quickly news spreads. In a matter of a minute or so, thirty or forty people were standing in a semi-circle around the body, everyone yelling and staring and punching numbers into their phones. They seemed to come from nowhere, and although they crowded up against each other, nobody got too close. It was as if there was an invisible line they couldn't cross, dividing the living from the dead. Except I'd crossed that line. I joined the crowd and stood at the back, peering over the shoulders of the others to see what they were seeing. Really, she didn't look much different from when I'd left her last night. A little less like a woman and more like a thing.

When I heard sirens, I sauntered off and sat in the little café that Astrid sometimes went to with Pippa, and I drank a mug of tea. Tea is a peaceful drink.

It was like being a conductor of an orchestra. I told Dario, when I got home, that something was going on in the street and he told Mick, and then the pair of them went to have a look and came back infected with the excitement of the crowd.

'I think someone's been mugged or something,' said Dario, and I made clucking noises.

'Or worse,' said Mick. 'That's what they're saying in the street. Murdered.' I covered my mouth with my hand, the way people do in films when they hear bad news.

'In our street?' I said.

Was I overdoing it? It didn't seem so. I thought I'd burst if I didn't tell someone myself. Who? Astrid, of course: I had to be the one who broke the news to her, so I called her mobile. She was at the Horse and Jockey, but I told her maybe she should come back. I didn't say why. I wanted to see her face when she heard. But Astrid came in and then, shortly after, she went out again, as if she wasn't very excited by what was going on, and I was left with a sour feeling, as if it hadn't worked properly. When Miles came back I persuaded him and Pippa to come with me to have a look at the house, which was now cordoned off. There were still police cars there, though the ambulance had gone, and I walked up to a young officer and asked what was going on.

'An incident,' he said.

'Has someone been murdered? That's what everyone's saying.'

He just looked at me.

'Who is it? Who lives here? We live up the road, so we're neighbours of whoever it is.'

'There's been an incident,' he said, and that was all. An incident.

'Come on, Davy, we'll know soon enough,' said Pippa, tucking her hand through my arm and tugging me away. 'You're living in London now, not a small town. This is the kind of thing that happens. You'll get used to it.'

'But it's hard to believe, isn't it?' I said. 'Right under our noses.'

The three police officers who came to the house made me feel safe, especially the one who was in charge, PC Prebble. Jim, he said his name was, smiling at all of us as if he wanted to be our friend. He was plump with a round face and a big, squashed nose. I could tell at once he liked me. I was personable and trying to be helpful, while the others – well, it was obvious he found them an odd lot, and not surprising, really. Dario was shrill and twitchy. Mick was silent to the point of being rude. Miles seemed bored. Pippa overdid her flirtatious act so that at one point I saw Prebble exchange a glance with one of his colleagues. Leah, Miles's girlfriend, arrived just after them and acted as if they were invisible, which was quite hard when the downstairs room was so crowded. I offered them tea and then they sat at the table with their notebooks and asked us if we had heard anything unusual last night.

'Nothing,' said Dario. 'Nothing at all.'

'It's always pretty noisy round here,' added Pippa.

'I heard people shouting in the night,' I said.

'When would this be?'

'I don't know. I'm sorry. I just know I woke and there were noises, but it didn't seem that remarkable. As Pippa says, it's not a quiet street. All I can say is that it was dark.'

'Dark,' said Prebble, gloomily, and doodled in his book. 'And it was just the seven of of you?'

'Not me,' said Leah. 'I don't live here.'

'Yet,' said Dario, under his breath, then gave a nervous giggle.

'Astrid was here too,' I said. 'She's out at the moment. And also . . .' I stopped and looked at Pippa.

'That's all,' she said defiantly. 'We were having a house meeting until quite late.' She smiled at me, daring me to contradict her, and I smiled reassuringly back. Her secret was safe with nice, reliable Davy.

'And nobody noticed anything unusual?'

'No,' said Mick. I think that was the only word he uttered the entire time the police were with us.

'Who's dead?' asked Owen.

'A Mrs Margaret Farrell. Did any of you know her?'

We all exchanged enquiring looks then shook our heads. No, we didn't know a Mrs Margaret Farrell.

'It's depressing, isn't it?' I said. 'That someone can live just a few doors down and we don't even know her name? Until she dies, that is.' I shook my head sorrowfully.

'Is it true what they're saying?' said Pippa. 'That she was killed and put behind her rubbish bins?'

'I'm afraid so.'

'How horrible.'

'But you'll catch them,' I said.

'We'll do our best.' He closed his notebook and stood up. 'The other officers will take your names and phone numbers. If anything occurs to you, please don't hesitate to get in touch.' He pulled out a card and put it on the table.

'Good luck,' I said. 'I hope you find them very soon.'

*　　*　　*

286

The best bit of the evening came later. Astrid was back and Owen had disappeared somewhere. We were all sitting downstairs, aimless but unwilling to go to bed yet. I sat on the sofa next to Astrid and every so often shifted position so that my arm brushed against her bare, golden one. I pretended to study my Portuguese, Astrid flicked through a magazine, Miles turned on the telly and we watched the end of some programme about decorating your house, and then the beginning of another of those cookery programmes where this smiling woman was making a fancy dish and letting her long hair fall over the ingredients. Miles changed channels and some film was just starting, which none of us wanted to watch but no one could be bothered to turn off. Dario ran into the room, excited, like a child.

'Turn the TV on!'

'It *is* on,' said Miles.

'. . . the body of fifty-seven-year-old Margaret Farrell was found yesterday evening. Police have begun a murder inquiry . . .'

I needed to time this right. I waited, and Pippa said: 'Margaret Farrell – she's Peggy!'

'Peggy!' echoed Astrid.

So then I spoke, lowering my voice in awe. 'We saw her last night. Me and Dario and Astrid. We saw her.'

I have to say I did it perfectly. People who play tennis talk about the sweet spot on the racquet, the thrill of the perfect shot. It felt so natural, as if I could do no wrong. I moved a bit and felt Astrid's warm, living flesh pressed against mine and her sweet-smelling hair brush my cheek. I closed my eyes and savoured the moment.

Chapter Thirty-three

'Fancy a drink?' said Ross.

'Sure,' I said.

'I'll catch you later, then,' he said.

Ross had arrived on the job a few days before. He was good-looking, with just the right confident carelessness about his hair and clothes. I couldn't work out what he was doing with work like this. Probably just earning some cash before taking off. The day he arrived I tried to make conversation with him. He looked at me curiously and I babbled some nonsense. I felt myself go red and hated myself for it – hated him as well. For the days after that we worked in separate parts of the house and ignored each other. I was on the wiring, the plumbing, the plastering. He was painting and doing the finishing touches. He had lost interest in me.

The most important rule, said Petra Davies, author of *Success in Friendship: A User's Manual*, is to care about other people. Petra Davies was wrong. She was as wrong as it is possible to be. The secret, as I was discovering, is *not* to care. I'd found this in the days at work after the murder. Everything seemed unimportant now, a charade, with nobody in on the joke except me. My head was buzzing with thoughts about Peggy dead and Peggy alive, about the police, about the guys in the house, and I worked without thought or interest. But I noticed from little murmurs and nods of approval that I was working faster and more effectively than before. I plastered one of the walls in what was going to be the master bedroom. I was so preoccupied with my thoughts that I hardly knew where I was or what I was doing. But when I finished, I stepped back and was startled by what I had done. It was a beautiful piece of work, smooth and level across the whole wall.

I wasn't interested in Ross now. It seemed a thousand years ago that I'd cared what he thought of me. One time I helped him with a cornice that needed fixing, but apart from that we hardly exchanged a word. So when he asked me out for a drink, it seemed like a joke. He'd actually sought me out.

We weren't able to do anything more than rinse our hands but that was all right, and it was even better when we arrived in the garden of the pub where Ross was meeting his girl-friend, Laura. She and her little friend, Melanie, worked in a gallery and the contrast between us, the neatly pressed and coiffured young women and the dusty, dirty men, seemed hugely comic. Laura, in particular, who sounded as if she had just arrived from a horse show, was loudly amused at the idea of having a boyfriend who was a grimy builder and stroked his hair in mock dismay. 'I'm really surprised they let you two in here,' she said. 'Isn't there some sign up forbidding builders and gypsies?'

'I'll get the drinks,' I said.

I went inside and returned with a cool, damp bottle of wine and a clump of glasses. They talked about people and places I didn't know. There was a pause and Laura looked me up and down appraisingly, like something in her stable. 'So how did you meet this one?' she said.

'He's the expert,' said Ross. 'He's the man.'

I didn't simper. I didn't blush and say, oh, well, not really. I was looking closely at Laura, so closely that I could see the fur on her cheek, the strands of hair that had escaped and blown across her forehead.

289

'Really?' she said. 'Have you got work set up after this job?'

'Not yet,' I said.

'Good,' she said. 'I'll bear you in mind.'

'Careful,' said Ross, and he and Laura laughed. He looked at his watch and then at her.

'Yes,' she said. 'Ross and I have to . . . you know . . .'

'Sure,' I said. 'I'll see you, then.'

As I started to get up, I looked at Laura's friend for the first time. She had hardly spoken. She was clearly in her friend's shadow. She had dark brown hair that she hadn't done much with. That and her dark eyes made her skin seem pale. As I looked at her and she noticed me looking at her, the blood rushed to her cheeks. I wasn't attracted to her in any way and suddenly I was intrigued by that. Nothing mattered, nothing was at stake.

'Mel,' I said.

'It's Melanie, really.'

'Would you like to go and get something to eat?' I said.

She murmured something, blushed and murmured something else, then said, 'Sure, yes, all right.' She stood up and I saw for the first time what she was wearing: a short-sleeved pale green top with a white frilly collar, a long white skirt and sandals, all very light, summery and girlish.

'I've got to go home and shower and change,' I said. 'But you can come along and meet the people I live with.'

On the tube I told her about the people in the house, exaggerating things about them, so that I made her laugh. I told her that things were a bit delicate because we were all about to be thrown out. I told her about the murder and the involvement of the police and saw her eyes widen.

'Did you know her?' she said.

'It's funny, isn't it?' I said. 'Murder victims are like famous people. People like to know them. Or to know someone who knows them.'

'I'm sorry,' she said. 'I didn't mean that.'

Petra Davies would have told me to reassure Melanie, to say, 'Of course, you didn't.' I said nothing; I just looked at her. Suddenly I wondered if I'd made a mistake. Did I really want to spend an entire evening with this woman, then another and another until after about four we could have awkward, unsatisfactory sex?

As I opened the door at Maitland Road, I met the whole group in the hallway, with carrier-bags and bottles. They all looked at Melanie. I felt for a moment like someone bringing his first girlfriend back to meet the parents. 'This is Mel,' I said.

There was a rush of greetings that almost overwhelmed her.

'Come for a picnic,' said Astrid.

Melanie looked alarmed. 'We were going out to eat,' she said.

That did it. 'Great idea,' I said. 'It's an initiation rite, but I'll protect you. Let me have a shower first.'

We were a strange group, marching over to the park. It made me think of excursions from school, walking in a crocodile, shepherded along the street. They were all there, except Owen. And Pippa was with a guy in a suit, who seemed even more ill at ease than Melanie.

As we settled down on the grass, Owen arrived, hovering around with his camera, taking pictures. I poured a plastic cup of wine for Melanie and one for myself.

'I haven't been to a picnic for years,' she murmured. She moved close, her shoulder against me.

'Ants,' I said, 'and nowhere to sit properly. You can't hold your food and drink at the same time.'

'I like it,' she said.

I filled her plate for her. I dipped a slice of carrot into a tub of hummus and fed it to her. I caught Astrid's eye on me. I could see what she was thinking. Oh, how sweet, little Davy's found a girlfriend. Still, at least I was showing them I wasn't some weird loner. I was stroking Melanie's hair when I sensed someone beside me. Astrid. I looked at Melanie. 'Will you excuse us?' I said.

'Oh, all right,' she said, and edged away to sit on her own, pretending to sip at her wine.

Astrid moved close to me and spoke in what was little more than a whisper. I thought of Melanie looking at us. She probably thought we were ex-lovers. Astrid was in a bit of a state because she'd been questioned again by the police. At first I thought she might have suspicions but I discovered she had a dim memory that someone else had been on the step when she had her accident. I forced myself to think clearly. Would it be better to tell her straight away or allow him to be a mysterious suspect dimly in the background? I was angry with myself for not thinking about this in advance. I decided to be transparently evasive on Dario's behalf. It would muddy things up a bit but I wasn't sure it was the best plan.

'Maybe there was someone,' I said. 'But if there was, Dario's the one you should ask.'

Astrid wasn't fooled for a second. Or, rather, she was. So Dario's customer would be forced into the light. The only disaster would be if he had seen Peggy follow me, but I was almost certain he'd scarpered before then. Astrid had clearly been brooding on matters because now she turned her attention to Pippa, claiming that Jeff should come forward and tell all. It was funny to see Pippa squirming, like a beetle with a needle pushed through it.

'It's not really a good idea,' she said.

It wasn't part of my strategy, but I couldn't resist it. 'Married, by any chance?' I said. She gave me an angry look but I returned it blandly.

'It would be awkward,' she said.

The evening turned golden, the shadows lengthened. I watched Astrid and Owen and it seemed to grow colder, and then Miles arrived and started to moan about the events he had set in motion, and it felt colder still. The magic had gone and people stirred and gathered together the stained, sticky remnants of the picnic. As we walked back, I thought about what was to come and whether there was anything I needed to worry about.

'I probably ought to go home,' said a voice beside me.

I looked down. I had almost forgotten about Melanie. I shook my head. 'There's something I want to show you,' I said.

We didn't speak again until we arrived back at the house. As the rest of them headed downstairs for coffee and a smoke, I took Melanie's hand and led her upstairs and into my room. I took her towards my bed, then placed my hands on her shoulders, positioning her just so, and looking into her large eyes. The collar of her shirt was tied with a white silk ribbon in a bow. If I could unfasten it easily, that would be proof that God wanted me to fuck her. She started to say something but I shook my head. I took one end of the ribbon and pulled. It came undone like a badly tied shoelace. I took the bottom of her shirt and lifted it over her head. She had to raise her arms to help me. I unclipped her bra and let it fall. I pulled her skirt and knickers down in a single movement. She had to lift her sandalled feet to step out of them. I sat her on the bed and pulled off her sandals.

At first, when I pushed myself inside her, I imagined that

I was fucking Pippa and I pushed harder and harder, and heard Melanie cry out under me. Then I thought of Astrid. I imagined her face on Melanie's body.

And then at the very moment I came, from the very first moment I started to come, I regretted everything: meeting Melanie, spending the evening with her, bringing her back here, having her in my bed. I felt her hands on my shoulders, her heels on the back of my thighs. She held me close inside her.

'Davy,' she said, after a long time. 'I've never ever done anything like this.' And then I heard a snuffling sound and saw that she was crying.

After she went to sleep I got up and went to the bathroom. I pulled up the blind and stared into the garden. Something was moving and it took me some time to make out what it was. What they were. What they were doing. I knew it. I don't know how, but I fucking knew it. Astrid and Owen, like animals, not caring who saw them. The tick in my eye, getting stronger. I tasting something sour in the back of my throat, as if I was about to be sick.

Chapter Thirty-four

I saw Owen's photographs before Astrid. I let myself in
one day when Dario was asleep and everyone else was out.
I wasn't working myself now. It took too much time and
the money wasn't good enough. I made up some of the
difference from people's carelessness. Pippa was the best.
She left notes lying around in her room and never noticed
if they disappeared. Since Peggy's death, I'd collected forty
pounds from her. And twenty from Miles, when he left
his wallet at home one day by mistake. A few coins from
Astrid, so far. Mick and Owen were trickier, and Dario
never seemed to have any money on him. One time,
though, I lifted some weed from his room and sold it back
to him. I said someone had given it to me at work and I
didn't want it, but I thought he might. He insisted on giving
me something for it, and I could tell he felt a bit guilty
that he was ripping me off.

For me the crunch had come when we were finishing the
work on the house, which the landlord was doing up before
selling. While we were adding the last touches – painting
the walls, laying down the last skirting-boards – this couple
had come to look at it. They weren't that old, in their early
thirties perhaps, but it was obvious they were stinking rich.
They had an air of smug wealth about them. Their hair
gleamed as if every strand had been buffed. Their skin
glowed. There was a kind of carelessness about them, as if
they were so far above normal people that they didn't even
need to show it. We were invisible to them, workers with

rough hands and plaster in our hair, who, for all they knew, didn't even understand English. And if we did understand, what did it matter? What did *we* matter? In loud, drawly voices, they said that if they bought the place, they'd start again. Their words: start again. Some of the decoration wasn't to their taste. They'd obviously have to rip out the kitchen units and get an architect in to have a look at the layout of the ground floor. The bathrooms were cheap and nasty. I stood and listened to them and felt a fluttering in my chest, as if a moth was trapped in there. A band tightened round my head. Ticking in both eyes.

I laid down my paintbrush, walked into the garden, where I could escape what they were saying, and made a promise to myself. I was going to get some proper money together and I was going to leave. Leave London, leave the UK, go to a new life where people would treat me with respect and I would be the one calling the tunes. I saw the beaches of Brazil, the beautiful women gazing up at me adoringly. For a few moments, I even saw Astrid beside me, hanging off my arm, laughing at what I was saying, pressing her slim, strong body against mine.

I left that day, after collecting what was owed to me, and I didn't go back, and I didn't answer the messages that were left on my mobile. I didn't tell the Maitland Road lot, of course, which meant that each morning I would leave the house at the usual time, and each afternoon return as if from a hard day at work. Now I had time to make plans and time to investigate the people I was living with.

Which was how I knew that Pippa had fucked poor old Mick, one more scalp to add to her collection. And then – much better, much more interesting, something to make my spine tingle – I came into the kitchen and saw Pippa saying something to Owen. She laughed and put her hand on his arm, and he went red and stepped back and I knew, I just knew, that they had done it as well. Pippa and Owen. Could no one else tell? I looked at them when they were all together and it was obvious that they were like blind people. Even Astrid.

One rainy day I was in Owen's room again, examining his photographs, which I'd been thinking about ever since I'd had that glimpse of them. All of them were black-and-white. Some were blurred and arty and pretentious, water and burned trees and posters half ripped off walls. The women were different. I could hardly move and my breath rasped in my throat. Owen, I thought, you bastard. You're not so different from me, after all. You think you're making art but really you're making pornography. Just because there's no colour doesn't mean that blood isn't blood, flesh isn't flesh. It made me laugh. He'd got some woman to take her clothes off by telling her it was art. Then I came across the woman with the mutilated face. I picked it up and held it in front of the window to see it more clearly. He was good, I had to admit it. He really was good. I felt envious of him. I touched each slash with my fingers. Now I know you, I thought. I know you, but you don't know me.

I heard the downstairs door open and the sound of voices: Astrid and Owen. I put the picture back, stepped quickly out of the room and went upstairs to my own, where I lay on my bed. I could hear them talking in low voices in the hallway, then their footsteps mounting the stairs together. I folded my arms round my body and screwed my eyes shut. Rain rattled against the window in waves with the wind but it felt as if it was inside my brain. The pair of them were going into Owen's room, where they would be together, surrounded by those images. I saw the naked bodies of

Owen's women, and then I saw Astrid and Owen naked too and it felt like something swelling in my head. I crept down one flight of stairs and listened outside their door. Astrid was saying something. What? I put my ear against the door.

'Your women don't have faces.'

So he was showing her the pictures. I couldn't hear what they were saying next; just murmurs, his voice, then hers. And then there was silence. Fucking silence. Except the roaring in my head.

Sometimes things come together, as if they were meant. You don't make plans, but you make yourself ready and available and plans come to you, falling into your lap like a gift.

The next day, I just happened to find myself near the Horse and Jockey at around the time I knew Astrid usually finished work, so I went in, scanning the room for a glimpse of her. She wasn't there and I turned to go.

'Davy. Over here, mate!'

It was one of her biker friends. I couldn't remember his name, though I'd met him there several times and he always treated me as if we'd been friends for years.

I walked over to the group.

'Looking for Astrid?' he said.

'I was just passing.'

'Yeah?' He grinned knowingly. 'She's not here. Have a drink, though.'

'Why so generous all of a sudden?' asked one of the other bikers, who had a shaved head and a ring through his nose.

'I got a tip today from Queen Ingrid. Can you imagine?'

'Queen Ingrid?' asked Buzzcut.

'You know. That bloody de Soto woman up in the fortified palace in Highgate.'

'The tan's real – she has lots of holidays.'

'And you got a tip? What was it? Additional services?'

There were smirks all around, even from a couple of the girls.

'No such luck. She needed a bit of furniture moving. So what'll you have, Davy?'

'Half of lager,' I said. 'Don't they have servants for that sort of thing?'

'Didn't seem to be anybody around.'

I sat in the warm fug, sipping slowly, smiling when they smiled and laughing when they laughed, keeping half an eye out for Astrid, my mind ticking away.

Early the next morning I bought an *A–Z* at the newsagent up the road, took the Underground to Highgate and walked the rest of the way, map in hand, like a tourist. The walk was all uphill. At the end, I felt I'd arrived at a place that looked down on the rest of us, scrabbling around in the heat of the city.

Century Road was just off the main street, and I needn't have worried about picking out the de Soto house: set back from the road, behind an iron fence, a burglar alarm blinking above its porched door, its tall windows glinting in the morning sun. Two cars were parked in the forecourt, a Jaguar and a Range Rover. His and hers. I looked around, suddenly feeling self-conscious. It seemed stupidly suspicious to be standing on a residential street staring at an expensive house. I walked along the road and through a square until I got to a shopping street. I returned to Century Road with a newspaper and a cup of coffee. I sat on the kerb, sipped coffee and pretended to read the paper. Now I looked like a dozen boring, explainable, forgettable people.

At twenty to eight a man in a suit came out of the house, got into the car, drove out and away, down the hill. I sipped at my now empty cup and actually began to read the paper. A bomb blast in a Baghdad market. A train crash in Egypt. At twenty-five past eight the postman walked through the gate and up the drive. He pressed a button and spoke into a small grille. After a few seconds the door opened and he stepped forward. He had a package in his hand, but whoever had answered was lost in the shadows. He turned round and I saw a glimpse of a woman disappearing inside, back into that world where she felt so safe. The door closed.

It was obvious that I couldn't break into a house like that. There were probably alarms of a kind I knew nothing about. I needed to be invited in and I needed to be sure that she was alone, with no builders, butlers or gardeners. That was the challenge. I thought for a moment, then felt excitement ripple through me. I stood up and carefully crammed the newspaper and the coffee cup into a bin. People noticed litterers.

Now that I had decided, I was burning to act but I had a whole day and night to get through. It took about an hour to reach the gallery where Melanie and Laura worked. I pushed the door open and entered the hushed, cool interior. There were no customers, but Laura and Melanie were there. Melanie was wearing a flowery cotton dress that Astrid wouldn't have been seen dead in. She had pink lips and looked like a child about to go off to a birthday party.

'Davy.' She blushed and put up a hand to check her hair. 'I wasn't expecting you!'

'Why would you be?' I asked rudely. 'Hi, Laura.'

'Hello, Davy.' She looked at me appraisingly and I felt my anger mount.

'These are a bit expensive, aren't they?' I said, flicking my hand dismissively at a canvas.

'Well, not if you —'

'Is there somewhere we can talk privately?'

'You can go to the stock room,' said Laura. 'It's not as if we're rushed off our feet.'

Melanie led me into the back. Through the frosted-glass door I could see Laura's shape moving around the gallery and I could hear her as well, the clack her shoes made on the wooden floor.

'Are you all right, Davy?' asked Melanie.

'Why not?'

'I didn't think I'd hear from you again.'

'Well, here I am.'

'I was worried.' As she spoke, she took a step forward and lifted her face. Her expression was anxious and hopeful. I knew she wanted me to kiss her, a chaste and tender kiss to reassure her of my affection.

I didn't kiss her, but there under the naked bulb, among the box files, pressed against the computer that beeped and whirred, I pulled up her flowery dress and pulled down her demure white knickers, pulled them over her sensible shoes and put them into my jacket pocket. I pushed my hand between her legs. She tried to stop me. Her eyes were wild and she struggled silently, looking over my shoulder at the door. Then she stopped struggling and I unzipped my flies and pushed myself inside her. When I'd finished — it didn't take long — she put her arms round my neck and pressed her face into my chest and told me it was all right and she understood and she loved me and she was so happy I'd tracked her down. She kissed me on the mouth, called me 'darling', and led me back into the shop by the hand, looking mussed and proud.

I'd tried nice. I'd tried considerate. And it hadn't worked. But when you were cruel, when you were indifferent, they liked you for it. If you treated them really badly, they fell in love with you. It was their own fault.

Chapter Thirty-five

Making up the package was fun. It was almost a pity that nobody but me would ever see it. I collected a packet of condoms I'd taken from Owen's room, a thong of Pippa's, a scarf Mel had left behind, and the lip-gloss I'd nabbed from Astrid's room. I'd also taken a padded envelope from a pile in Astrid's room, small enough to fit through the letterbox. I addressed it to Jonathan Whiteley, the boy I'd been best friends with at school, at Century Road but a different number. The de Sotos lived at number twenty-seven. I wrote number seven. Far enough away so that she probably wouldn't know who lived there, similar enough to be an understandable mistake by the postman.

Also, on the way back from seeing Melanie, I had gone to a shop I'd seen just off Brick Lane. It sold catapults and flick-knives to survivalists and fantasists. I chose a knife with a large, serrated blade. It needed to look scary. The man behind the counter was largely bald at the front but with a long grey ponytail behind. Who was he trying to fool? He put the knife into a paper bag. 'Good for cutting up deer,' he said.

'See many deer in the East End?' I said.

'I seen some in the Lea Valley,' he said.

It should have been impossible for me to sleep that night. I should have gone over and over it in my head, checking and rechecking that it could possibly work. But when my alarm went off at six, I felt as if I was being dragged out of a deep pit of sleep. At first I didn't recognize where I was and thought I was back at home, as if London had been a dream.

As I came down the stairs of the sleeping house, I met Astrid in the hall. 'You're early,' I said.

'I've got to fill in for someone,' she said, with a groan. 'You?'

'Same,' I said. 'More or less.'

I couldn't afford to loiter outside the house this time. It wasn't necessary either. I waited at the other end of the street for the postman to arrive. From a distance I saw Mr de Soto's Jaguar pull out of his drive and felt a lurch in my stomach. This was what it must feel like to be a boxer about to enter the ring, a rock star making his way to the stage. That feeling of a humming, expectant crowd out there, waiting for you to deliver an experience to them. Except in this case the audience didn't know they were going to be an audience. They didn't know their life was going to be changed.

The postman appeared in the road just after eight. It was as if I was pushing them around like counters on a board. It was going to be so simple: just get into the house, check she's alone. If she isn't, leave, no harm done, try again somewhere else. If she's alone, threaten her, immobilize her, steal what I want at leisure. Walk away, untraceable.

The postman went from house to house, up and down the paths, up, down, up, down. What a job. A job, you can't do well or badly. Just deliver the mail or don't deliver it, that's all.

I waited until he was a couple of houses away, then started to walk up the street. As I walked, I pulled on my surgical gloves and took the package from the plastic carrier-bag. I timed it perfectly. The postman emerged from the de Soto drive and turned away from me. I waited until he had disappeared round the corner. Then I walked quickly up the drive and pushed the package through the letterbox. It just fitted. No turning back now. I walked to the road, pulling off the gloves. I needed to give it ten minutes to make it took convincing. I glanced at my watch. Exactly eight twenty-seven. I timed myself walking away from the house. At eight thirty-two and thirty seconds I turned and walked purpose-fully back to the house. I pressed the doorbell. Time to go onstage.

There was a buzz and a crackle. 'Hello?'

'Hi,' I said, smiling into the little lens above the speaker.
'Yes?'

'Hi, my name's Jonathan Whiteley. I'm from number seven. I was just talking to the postman about a package and he said he might have delivered it to you by mistake.'

'Oh, God,' the crackly voice said. 'Was that you? Hang on.'

As the door opened, I stepped forward and inside.

Ingrid de Soto was lovely. That was what money did for you. She didn't live on the same planet as the rest of us. Her expensive hair was pulled tight into a bunch. She was wearing a blue silk dressing-gown and under it I could see the swell of her breasts, the flash of a gold necklace, thin as a wire round her neck, another round one wrist, a watch. In comparison, Pippa was shabbily dressed, Astrid was dishevelled, Melanie seemed cheap. But I was on her planet now. I looked around. She was clearly alone.

'I'm so sorry,' she said. 'I was confused. Sorry, I made a stupid mistake.' She smiled at me apologetically, with her beautiful, expensive teeth.

Now I was the one to be confused. 'What do you mean?' I said. Had I slipped up?

'Don't worry,' she said. 'Here.' She handed me the package.

I forced a smile. 'No, really,' I said. 'What mistake?'

She laughed. 'It's ridiculous,' she said. 'We get lots of deliveries in envelopes like those. I thought it was one of those sent to the wrong address. I just rang up the courier to collect it.' She checked her watch. 'Bloody hell, they'll be here in a moment.' She smiled again. 'It's not your problem.'

I punched her, hard, and she fell to the floor. As I grabbed her by the neck, much of the ferocity was really against myself. I'd made this brilliant arrangement to rob someone with whom I had no connection and the result was that a courier was about to arrive and catch me in the act. I was so furious with my own stupidity that I hardly felt the flailings of her arms and hands against me and hardly heard the gurgling and choking. I forced her down, banged her head against the floor and tightened my hands around her throat until I saw that her eyes weren't looking back at me, or at anything. I let her go.

'You bloody idiot,' I said, and I didn't know if I was talking to her or to myself.

I was standing over her, panicking. She lay sprawled beneath me on the floor, hands splayed. I looked at my watch and made myself breathe slowly and calmly. Eight thirty-five. I could give myself two minutes. That was all. I looked around. It was everything I had imagined, everything I had dreamed of. But to escape now I had to do the opposite of what I'd planned. I had to make this *not* look like a robbery. I had to make it look as if I was insane. What did insane people do when they killed women? I thought of Owen and his fucking photographs, and it seemed like a private joke. I took the knife from inside my jacket and unsheathed it. I held Ingrid de Soto's head steady, then cut bold strokes on her cheeks and forehead, the way I remembered from Owen's photograph. The incisions didn't bleed. I took one of her earrings between my fingers, pulled it clean out of her perfectly shaped earlobe and put it in my pocket. Suddenly it was a horrible sight, the blank dead jelly eyes. I turned her over, face down, staring into the floor. I checked my watch. Time up.

I walked to the front door. I just needed to get to the gate, and then to the other side of the road, and I would be free. Then I remembered: the bloody package. I couldn't just leave it there, could I, the thong and the condoms and scarf? I turned back, stepped over the sprawled body and looked around. There it was, on the shelf of a dresser by the door. I picked it up. A thought came to me and I also picked up an oval glass paperweight with spiralling patterns on it and an invitation on thick white card. I returned to the door, my shoes clicking on the tiles, echoing. I stepped outside, pulled the front door behind me and heard it click shut. I walked along the path, hearing the gravel under my feet. Don't run. People would remember someone running. Out of the gate, not looking to either side. I crossed the road. What now? Concealing myself, I rested my forehead against the trunk of a tree, feeling the roughness of the bark. It was alive and that woman was dead. Then a sudden thought came into my mind: Why did I kill her? To protect myself, because it had gone wrong? No, I said, that's not true. All you needed to do was take your package and leave. She would have apologized to the messenger. That would have been that.

It had been a stupid mistake. I hadn't had time to think about it, I'd been in a fog of panic, and made the wrong decision. Maybe that would protect me as well. I didn't even have a real motive. That woman was lying dead on the floor quite unnecessarily – perhaps I'd left my fingerprints everywhere. I looked warily round the tree-trunk, poised to return, and then – I guess I should have expected it, really, because it was turning into a farce – a bike came into view and, of course, Astrid was riding it. She was a distance away but I could see her face glistening with the effort of cycling up the hill, but she wasn't panting heavily. She was used to this. She looked wonderful. Why do you always end up with the one you don't really want? Melanie thought of me as her boyfriend. That woman was dead by mistake. That was the way life worked out.

Astrid swung off her bike in a single movement and pulled it over the gravel. It was like watching someone at school trying to solve a difficult problem. She rang the bell, then rang it again. She took out her phone and made a call. She peered through the letterbox. She'd seen something. I could watch her thinking. She looked around. I shrank further behind the tree. I heard her talking into her phone again. I couldn't make out the words but I could hear the urgency, the hysteria almost, in her tone. This might be an ambulance or even the police. Time to go.

I edged away and walked along the other side of Century Road. Before I turned the corner I heard the loud sound of a smashing window. That Astrid. Wonderful.

Chapter Thirty-six

It wasn't a coincidence. It was meant to be. She might not know it yet, but I did, and once I knew it the whole world looked different. I sat in the park and took out the paperweight. When I looked at it, following the lines of colour into the clear, glowing centre, it almost felt as if I was seeing my own life. I had killed Peggy, and Astrid had been there. I had killed Ingrid, and once again Astrid was there. She was my witness, my audience, and I was doing it for her. Everyone else receded and it was just the two of us. Astrid with her laughing eyes.

I don't know how long I sat there. The sun rose higher in the sky. The colours deepened and the shadows became shorter. I wasn't hungry or anxious or tired. I could feel my heart beating at just the right speed, and the blood pumping round my body. I clenched my fists and felt the muscles in my forearm tighten. I sat up straight on the park bench and my body felt as it was meant to be, light and powerful. I glanced around me and my eyes took in everything: the tall trees, the sweep of the path, a woman pushing a buggy with a little frown on her face, a child with a lollipop stuck into its mouth, the three ducks waddling behind, the single cloud puffing along on the horizon, the litter lifted up on a curl of wind, the man with a tattoo on his forearm. The world was entering my skull and I could keep it there. All that I saw, all that I heard, tasted, touched, could be held inside me. I smiled and felt the smile on my face. I blinked and my eyes were a camera focusing, clicking on the image I wanted to catch.

I walked from the park and into a shop where I bought a large bottle of water, which I drank on the spot, every last drop. I could feel the cold liquid running into me. I started to walk back towards the house, but I knew it would be some time before the police were finished with her, so I changed my mind and went to Melanie's gallery instead, to kill time. She couldn't believe it when I pushed the door open and went inside. The second day in a row! Her face lit up with a kind of dazed happiness that made her look even younger than she was. She didn't struggle this time, even though I was rough with her. There were red marks and bruises on her skin when I'd finished. I closed my eyes so I didn't have to see her looking at me. I left before she'd finished buttoning her shirt.

They should have listened to themselves and then they'd have realized how stupid they sound. Yabber, yabber, yabber. Miles being pompous and wounded all at once, and Pippa going on about tenants' rights. Dario whining between toxic clouds of smoke, Mick grunting, Leah putting in her poisonous remarks. Owen didn't really say anything, but that was probably because he was so busy trying to look like a film star who'd wandered into the wrong movie and now had to sit it out. I was Mr Nice Guy, of course, but I didn't put much effort into it. My mouth smiled, my eyes made contact with the others round the table, I nodded in agreement, frowned in thought. Every so often I heard myself saying bland, reasonable phrases, but it was all happening at a great distance from me.

Because I was waiting for Astrid. Every cell in my body was alert, each little sound vibrated through me. I heard every car that slowed down as it passed the house, every door that slammed, each footstep falling on the pavement outside.

At last it was her. Nobody else seemed to notice that the front door had opened, then closed softly. I strained my ears but could hear nothing. She must be standing in the hall, hesitating, wondering whether to go to her room or to come down and face us. Perhaps she wouldn't come downstairs at all. I didn't think I could stand that.

'You're behaving like a silly little schoolboy,' Leah snapped at Dario.

I nudged Pippa. 'I think I heard Astrid come in,' I whispered. 'Should we ask her to join us?'

'Astrid? Is that you?' she yelled immediately. Her voice was surprisingly loud for such a willowy girl. 'Come here, will you? We need you.'

'Bollocks to you,' roared Dario. 'You're deliberately twisting things, but you won't get away with it, you know.'

Her footsteps were light on the stairs. I tried not to stare at the doorway where she would appear so at first I caught only a burning glimpse of her, bundled up in oversized jeans and a large blue jumper. Like a waif. Like an orphan. I allowed myself to look properly as she came across and sank into the large armchair, mumbling something inane to cover my stare. Her face was pale, her dark eyes enormous. There was a pulse in her throat and a tiny blue vein in her temple, just visible behind her black hair. She'd never looked more beautiful; it was all I could do to stop myself going over to her and taking her in my arms. But everybody else was so caught up in the quarrel that they hardly took any notice of her. Blind, deaf fools, all of them. She just sat there, silent and blank, listening to them baying at each other. I saw how she put up one hand and brushed the hair away from her face. She had long, slender fingers, bare of rings. Her nails were cut very short. Every so often, she closed her eyes briefly. Her thick lashes lay against her smooth skin.

What was going through her head? Finally I couldn't bear it any longer. I went over to her, squatting down near enough to breathe in the smell of her, and asked her if she was all right. She turned her head and half smiled at me. Our eyes met, and I was looking right into her, deep down, and I knew then that if she didn't understand the connection between us yet, one day she would.

When she spoke at last, her words cut through the noise. 'What a cunt you are,' she said to Leah. She said she didn't care about the money. She made everyone ashamed of themselves. And then she told them. I watched her. The way her fists clenched when she spoke. The little lights in her pupils. How she bit her lip before giving details. Everyone gathered round but I had been there first. In all the excited clamour, I let myself reach out a hand and touch her shoulder, where the jersey stopped and her skin began. Mine, mine, mine.

Sometimes it's too easy. Like when I told Leah about Pippa and Owen. I was in the kitchen when she came in, and without asking her, I handed her a cup of coffee, black and no sugar, the way she liked it, then sliced up a mango for her: she didn't eat things like bread or cereal, but she liked fruit, I'd noticed.

'You look a bit tired,' I said to her. She didn't, really: she looked glitteringly awake and elegant as ever, but the sympathy in my voice softened her.

'I am, I guess,' she said, sliding a slice of mango into her mouth, then dabbing her lips with a tissue.

'It must be hard for you, Leah.'

'What must be?'

'This house. I mean, it's hard for me, and I'm just a tenant, not the landlord's boyfriend. For what it's worth, I think you're being very impressive.'

'Do you?'

'I do,' I said solemnly.

'To be honest, sometimes I feel like throwing in the towel and leaving Miles to sort out his own stupid mess.'

'I can imagine.'

'Why do you find it hard, though? You seem to get on so well with everyone.'

'I think I do. But it's all so complicated, isn't it?'

'You can say that again.'

'Like, I can't quite get the hang of who goes with who. Pippa, for instance.'

'Ha – that's easy. She goes with everyone.'

'Yeah, well, I know about Mick.'

'You mean she's . . . ?'

'And then there was Owen, of course.'

'Owen!'

'Yeah – you knew about that, didn't you? No? Oh, God, I've put my foot in it, haven't I? I thought people knew. It was only a fling, I'm sure of it.'

'So, Pippa and Owen.' I could see her eyes gleam.

'You won't mention it, will you? Especially not to Astrid. I think Astrid and Owen, you know . . . But I shouldn't have mentioned it.' I struck the side of my head lightly. 'Stupid me.'

She put a hand on my shoulder. Her manicured nails shone scarlet on my blue shirt. 'Not stupid at all, my dear Davy.'

I gave Pippa's thong and Astrid's lip-gloss from the parcel to Melanie, who behaved as though I'd given her a diamond ring. I decided I'd use Owen's condoms. And I started to watch everyone in the house with a new vigilance. I saw that everything was gathering to a head. The police wouldn't think it was a coincidence that Astrid was at both murders. They wouldn't understand how that had come about, how she had become my fate, my beloved destiny. But they would scrutinize her and everyone in her life. I had to be ahead of them.

Above all, I watched Astrid until I felt that there was nothing I didn't know about her. What was in her drawers, what texts were on her mobile, how many times a week she washed her hair, what shampoo and conditioner she used, what deodorant and face cream, whom she met after work, what vegetables she planted in her garden and how many times a day she watered and weeded the small plot. Once or twice, while looking in her purse, I helped myself to some money. I knew her gestures and habits: the way she pushed her hair back impatiently, the way her nose crinkled when she laughed, how she would kick off her shoes and tuck her long legs under her on the armchair, how she would blow on her coffee twice before sipping it, the colour of the varnish on her toenails. I stored every piece of information inside me. I had to be ready.

Chapter Thirty-seven

A couple of days later I was lying on my bed, entangled with Melanie, when there was a frantic knocking at the door. 'Yes?' I said.

'Wait,' said Melanie, but it was too late. The door opened and Dario came in. He didn't pay any attention to her attempts to rearrange her clothing.

'Have you heard?' he said.

'What?'

'There's a detective,' he said. 'He's in the kitchen talking to Astrid.'

I didn't answer. I was trying to think of some mistake I'd made, some connection I'd forgotten. That was the problem with lying. You had to remember how it all fitted together. Reality was easy. It took care of itself. But then I looked at Dario, sweating, eyes wide, and relaxed. Leah, Owen, Pippa, Mick, Miles, even Astrid. We all had our secrets. I felt Melanie's arm slip through mine.

'So, what's the problem?' she said.

'I'm going downstairs,' said Dario. 'We should all act as if nothing's wrong.'

'But nothing *is* wrong,' said Melanie.

'That's right,' said Dario, half to himself. 'Nothing's wrong. Everything's fine.'

'Dario,' I said, 'have you been smoking?'

I hardly needed to ask. His pupils were like black pinpricks.

'Just to settle myself,' he said.

He disappeared down the stairs. Melanie's face nuzzled into my neck.

'Shall we go down?' she said, with a smile.

I looked at her. 'Neaten yourself up a bit first,' I said.

'Yes, of course,' she said. 'Sorry. I was going to.'

When we walked into the kitchen, arms round each other in our swinging lovers' pose, it looked as if a party was getting going. At the centre of things, seated at the table, was the detective. He was wearing a suit with the tie loosened and the top button of his shirt undone. His greying hair was brushed back over his head. His face was narrow, with quick, smiling eyes that darted round the room observing everyone, taking everything in. I disliked him immediately. Distrusted him. Be careful, I told myself. Mustn't put a step wrong. Melanie and I sat at the table and grabbed a glass each of the wine Pippa was pouring. Melanie immediately started talking in a flirtatious, blushing way to him. I asked him if he was here to take statements. He looked at me properly for the first time, sizing me up. 'Why?' he said. 'Have you got something you want to say?'

Fuck, I thought. Fuck, fuck. I'd been trying to blend into the crowd and now I'd drawn attention to myself. 'Not exactly,' I stammered.

'But some people have,' said Leah.

I had to stop myself grinning. The attention had shifted to other people's secrets and it was all my doing. Leah was like an evil little toy I had wound up and set going and now she was trundling around stirring things up and generally muddying the water. It culminated wonderfully with her dropping a bag of Dario's weed on the table in front of Detective Chief Inspector Paul Kamsky. The evening went downhill from there.

The only good news was that Kamsky left without

arresting Dario, or even cautioning him. But from then on it was meltdown.

Over the next day and the next I was a spectator as the house started to pull itself apart. I could hardly go anywhere without seeing people whispering together, making plans about people who used to be friends or lovers. Sometimes it was just cold stares across the kitchen. The best was when one of Pippa's ex-lovers came and shouted on the doorstep, then threw a brick through the window at Leah. One by one, the secrets that had been suppressed so that these people could put up with each other were exposed for everyone to see.

Mostly I found it funny to watch what they were doing to each other but sometimes it got too much to bear and I felt as if it was happening inside my head, as if Dario had drawn a line across my brain, as if Leah's manipulations and Pippa's negotiations with Miles and whatever Astrid was up to with Owen and Mick and all of them, as if they were just voices jabbering away at each other. I felt like I should get drunk to shut them up and give me some peace, except I knew I had to think clearly. A single mistake, one word said in the wrong place, and I'd be done for.

Instead I left the house and walked away through street after street until I got to a park where I looked at couples arm in arm and mothers pushing buggies and a small boy failing to fly a kite. I felt like trying to help him because it irritated me, the way he was jerking the strings at the wrong moment, but then I remembered bad things happened to people who went up to small children in parks. I wondered how the two murder investigations were going. I tried to remember what Kamsky had said, or what people said he had said, and then I tried to make myself stop thinking about it. Because it was like dealing with women. The way

317

to get away with it was not to care. Thinking too much was the way to get caught. But thinking was how I'd get myself out of this. Get to Brazil where the sun shone. That was the really stupid thing. I'd done a murder for money and got no money from it. No money, just this anxiety and the tightness in my head.

When I arrived back at the house, I felt worse than I had before. My brain was buzzing with the thoughts I was trying to suppress. I ran up the stairs and walked into my room. Melanie was there. She gave a little jump. She gave me an uncertain smile. I looked around. The room seemed different.

'You startled me,' she said.

'What are you doing here?'

'Dario let me in,' she said.

'But what are you doing here?'

'Look,' she said, handing me some tickets. 'They're tickets for the Chelsea Flower Show. Someone at work gave them to me. We could go.'

I stared at them blankly. 'Why would I want to go to a flower show?'

'I don't know,' she said. 'I thought . . .'

I looked again at the room. 'What have you done?'

She started to stammer. 'I brought some things round. Wind chimes. Some flowers. I did a bit of tidying, got some things out.'

I walked over to her and put my right hand round her neck, quite gently. I pushed her backwards slowly. Then, when she was close to the wall, I gave her a shove, so that she banged her head. Not so that any damage was done but quite hard. Her eyes became wet with tears. I did it again.

'Davy,' she said, barely able to speak.

'Don't,' I said.

I let her go and she started to cough.

'Get out,' I said.

'No, Davy, please.'

Now I spoke more quietly, touching her cheek as I did so in very gentle slaps, little more than a whisper against her flesh. 'You don't touch my stuff.' Slap. 'You don't come in without asking me.' Slap. 'Understand?' Slap.

She nodded.

'Now get out. I'll call you.'

Almost in a dream she left and I heard her footsteps on the stairs. I lay down on the bed but jumped up almost immediately when there was a sharp knock on the door. I opened it. Astrid was standing there. She was wearing three-quarter-length brown jeans and a red top. She looked concerned. 'I saw Mel on the stairs,' she said. 'Is anything wrong?'

'No,' I said. 'Come in.'

She stepped inside and prowled round the room, looking as if she was scarcely conscious of where she was.

'Are *you* all right?' I said.

'I've just been seeing a mad psychiatrist,' she said.

I tried to look sympathetic. 'Is there a problem?'

'The police sent me. He's supposed to be an expert at profiling murderers.'

I felt a shiver. I tried to think of how an averagely interested person would respond. 'How did he ...' I began. 'I mean what does he think?'

'A scarred leather worker,' she said. 'If you meet one, let me know.'

I almost laughed with relief, then looked at my left hand. I was still holding the stupid tickets. Astrid was the only person I knew who was interested in gardens. 'I've got something for you,' I said. 'I thought it might cheer you up.'

I made up a story about having been given the tickets at

work. She seemed about as unexcited by it as I had been when Melanie gave them to me, but she was quite polite. She asked if she needed to wear a hat, as if she were looking for an excuse to get out of it. Then she gave an obviously forced smile and leaned forward and gave me a kiss on the cheek, the sort you might give an old aunt, and said thank you. I knew she wouldn't go. She'd find an excuse. It was probably for the best. What if she met Melanie and mentioned it to her? I wondered if it would have been different if I'd been disdainful of Astrid. Would that have made her want me? The trouble is, it doesn't work like that. You have to really not care about them to make them like you. If I had pretended not to like Astrid, she would have been exactly as she was now: treating me as part of the scenery. She would be nice enough to me but she wouldn't notice if I wasn't there.

As she walked round the room, she touched things and commented on them. She flicked at the wind chimes, she picked up a silk scarf Melanie had left and ran it through her fingers. She stopped in front of the mantelpiece and only at that moment did I notice that, in tidying my room, Melanie had found the glass paperweight I had taken from Ingrid de Soto's house. She had taken it from the drawer and put it in full view. All I needed was for Astrid to move on and I could put it back out of sight. But she stopped in front of it, as if lost in thought. I was about to say her name, to distract her, but before I could speak she picked it up and rotated it in her hand, holding it up to the light, as if fixing it for ever in her memory. The colours shimmered.

'Paperweights never have paper underneath them, do they?'

I mumbled something noncommittal. We talked nonsense

320

for a few seconds. I think she said something about looking for a place to live. I couldn't really hear. The words were drowned by the hiss of static in my head. She handed me the paperweight and I put it back carefully on the mantelpiece, her eyes on it all the time. She said she was going dancing.

'Nice,' I said, and stayed silent. I wanted to tell her that she mustn't let Owen touch her again. Not a kiss. Not a caress. Nothing. Or else.

I was left alone, staring at the paperweight. Melanie wouldn't remember it, but Astrid would. It wasn't fair. This wasn't the way I'd planned it. I wasn't like this. I wasn't really a murderer. All I ever wanted was to begin again, and be allowed to be myself at last. No, it wasn't fair.

Chapter Thirty-eight

There was so much to do and so many small details to attend to. It was my job to hold everything together in my head, and I knew that if I let one thing slip, that could be my undoing. And once I had started, the clock was ticking and I couldn't stop it. I found that I was good in a crisis.

As the household fell apart, it became comically easy to carry out what I had planned without being noticed. I was invisible. Leah was glaring at Miles. Miles was looking at Astrid and trying not to pay any attention to Leah. Owen was looking at Astrid too. Astrid was looking back at Owen and, although she didn't yet know it, she was also witnessing the spectacle that was being played out in front of her eyes. Pippa was watching herself, as usual. Dario wasn't looking at all, and when he was he clearly wasn't noticing. He was even worse after he was beaten up. Fear made him even more addled. Who knew what Mick saw? Mel was looking at me, all right, but Mel was a fool: she only saw what she wanted to see. I was looking at everything, at everyone. I was waiting, poised to strike when the time was right. In the meantime, it was me who called the journalists about Astrid, me who stirred up Leah's hatred. I was calling the shots now.

On the evening of the house sale, it seemed to me that everything was working out. I provoked some suspicion here and created some hostility there, all the while pretending to be nice Davy, peacemaker Davy, dull, dependable, sweet Davy. I almost felt like telling them the truth, just to see the expressions on their faces. I was like a magician who wanted to show them how the trick was done, how easily they had been fooled.

I steered Pippa towards Leah's bag of clothes and Dario towards Miles's shoes. As the noise grew and the violence started to turn ugly, I casually pushed Astrid's bike into the middle of the yard, where it was whisked away. As an after-thought, I stuffed the takings into my pocket – much more than I'd expected, thanks to the run on Leah's clothes – and threw the box into the bushes.

In front of the house where the sale was out of control, it felt like a forest fire. I just had to stand back. Leah strug-gled with a large black woman in the middle of a crowd. Dario and Pippa watched her, enjoying the disaster. Owen was taking photographs. I stepped forward and put my hand on Leah's shoulder, Davy, trying to help. I felt something jingle at my feet and looked down. Carefully I knelt and picked up the bunch of keys Leah had dropped. I put them into my pocket. Now, what could I do with them?

It got better. Because Leah told Astrid about Pippa and Owen. Right in front of everybody. Like a little bomb tossed into the already maimed and dazed group. And when Astrid walked out of the room (chin up, that's my girl), with every-one's eyes following her, I knew now was the time to strike.

That night I didn't sleep, couldn't sleep, didn't want to. I knew that this was a watershed in my life, and that after tomorrow everything would be different. I needed to savour the moment and not waste it in unconsciousness. After I had made everyone large mugs of tea and told them it would be all right, we just needed to take a step back from what had happened, they wandered off to their rooms one by one, shamefaced and miserable. I heard them shuffling along corridors, gargling and coughing in the bathroom, tossing and snuffling like animals in their beds. I heard Miles snoring. I heard – much later – Astrid returning. She came up the stairs quickly and lightly, and I could imagine her face, serious but not distraught, her jaw firm. For an instant I considered joining her. Perhaps she would tell me her feelings and weep on my shoulder. I could hold her against me and kiss her at last along her jaw line or that small hollow of her neck. Slender neck. No, it wouldn't do.

At last the house was dark and silent, and I could tell that only I was left awake, sitting upright on my bed with my hands in my lap, my breath steady, and my eyes fixed on a point on my wall, just above the door. I could feel myself growing taller and stronger as I sat there, each breath making me more powerful, readying me. My past self was dropping away: the Davy whose dad didn't want to know him, who was bullied at school, who had flattered his cow-eyed mother, who was eager to please, who had been humiliated by Pippa, who went out with someone like Melanie rather than someone like Astrid, who had to pretend all the time to be someone else. Those days were ending.

At dawn, I washed and shaved carefully. I went downstairs and made myself a piece of toast, but after one bite I threw it in the bin. No more food and no more sleep until this thing was done. Usually Astrid was the first up, and so it was this morning.

'Coffee?' I asked her, as she came into the kitchen. Her dark hair was still damp from her shower, but she was already dressed for work in her shorts and singlet. Her face glowed, clean of any makeup, and her long legs were tanned. I could see the muscles in her calves. My eyes burned just to look at her. My cheeks already stung with the tears I would cry, when it was done.

'Thanks, Davy. You're up early.'

'I couldn't sleep.'

'Me neither. At least it's Friday.' She went over and pushed open the door leading into the garden. 'It's going to be a lovely day.'

'Is it?'

'Sure. Look at the way the mist's burning off the grass. This is the best time of year.'

I could tell she was making an effort to be cheerful after the calamity of yesterday evening, but I gave her a chance anyway. 'I'm so sorry about what happened last night, Astrid.' She shrugged, but I kept on: 'If you want to know, I think Owen was an idiot and –'

'But I don't want to know,' she said firmly, coolly.

There. Her last chance was gone. She didn't realize what she had done. My cheeks flushed.

'Toast?' I managed to say.

'I'll grab something later. Have a good day.'

'Right. Um, you too, Astrid. Take care on that bike of yours.'

'I don't have a bike any more,' she said. 'Remember?'

'Sorry,' I said. 'What are you going to do?'

'Borrow Campbell's. Again.'

'I'm going to do some shopping and then I'm seeing Mel,' I said. 'Do you need anything?'

She laughed and shook her head. 'Sorry if I snapped just then.' She smiled at me sweetly, and then she was gone, striding out of the kitchen and taking the stairs two at a time. I heard her opening the door, then closing it behind her.

I stayed where I was. I saw Miles leave, without even his usual cup of tea. I made coffee for Pippa when she emerged, dainty and demure. Leah strode into the room, all business and briskness: dark brown wrap dress, discreet eyeshadow, slim briefcase, generally contemptuous.

'Good morning,' I said.

She paid no attention.

'Coffee? No milk, right?'

She started slicing an apple into a bowl, then added a handful of bran and a spoonful of yoghurt.

'Healthy,' I said.

She didn't reply.

'Busy day at the office today, then, Leah?'

'Very,' she said, despatching the sawdusty mess into her mouth.

'There all day?'

'Yes.'

'Are you all right about yesterday?'

She stopped and looked at me. 'How could I possibly be?'

'Right,' I said.

'Don't get me started,' she said, standing up and rinsing her bowl in the sink. 'I'll be off, then.'

'See you later.'

'Maybe.'

And she was gone too.

I went back upstairs. Dario and Mick were still in bed, but I could hear Owen moving around in his room – which was probably lucky for him, because, in my mood, I could have changed my mind and chosen him instead, to pay him back for getting his grubby hands on my Astrid. I put on my gloves and rummaged in the back of my underwear drawer for the little tissue parcel of Ingrid de Soto's earring. I took out the paperweight and Ingrid's invitation, and pulled Peggy Farrell's dainty watch and necklace from a balled-up pair of black socks in the same drawer. So much information. All these carrots that I was dangling in front of their stupid noses. I polished them with a tissue, wiping them clean. I went down the stairs as silently as possible and entered Miles's room, closing the door behind me. I shook the earring into a matchbox with only a few matches in it and put it on his mantelpiece; pushed Peggy's stuff into a pair of his socks instead. Nice symmetry, I thought. I put the paperweight inside one of his shoes. I heard Owen coming down the stairs towards the kitchen and stayed still for a moment. By the bed was a black notebook. I knew it was Miles's address book because I had copied Leah's address out of it days earlier. I tucked Ingrid de Soto's invitation into it, like a bookmark. Was it too blatant? When I was confident that nobody was around, I returned to my room to collect my jacket, checking to make sure that Leah's key was in the pocket. Time to go.

Leah's house was already up for sale. To my irritation, the nearest public phone box wasn't working, so I had to walk for about ten minutes to find another one. I called Campbell at his office and when he answered, said, 'Hello, is this the messenger service?'

'That's right. How can we help?'

'I looked you up in the *Yellow Pages*. I want a parcel collected, please. As quickly as possible.'

'Where are you?'

I gave him Leah's address.

'And where's it going to?'

'Holborn,' I said, feeling the cogs in my brain spinning.

'House or flat?'

'House. There's a bell. But I have a request to make. I won't be there, I've got to leave at once, but my wife will be in. Now I hope you don't think this is odd, but she hasn't been well, and I think she'd feel much safer if you could send a female messenger. Would that be possible?'

Campbell was clearly irritated by this and tried to insist it didn't matter but I played the part of the neurotically concerned husband, and I was the customer and the customer is always right, and Campbell finally admitted that, yes, he did have a female messenger and, yes, he would send her. My wife would have to wait a bit longer. That would be fine, I said, fine. My wife had nothing else to do.

Chapter Thirty-nine

Leah lived in a terraced house in Kentish Town. It was smaller than the house in Maitland Road but it still looked too big for one person. As I let myself in, I wondered if I'd made a mistake. Could there be lodgers? House guests? But I knew there weren't. She'd talked about living alone. Miles had talked about her rattling around in her huge empty mansion. How could she afford it? Where did these people get their money from? Rich parents, probably. It didn't matter. I had other things to think about.

I looked around her hallway. I needed to find something heavy. Astrid wasn't like Ingrid de Soto. She was tall and strong, stronger than me, probably. But a blow from a heavy object would take anyone down.

Leah was in the process of moving out. Paintings had been taken down and were leaning on the walls ready to be hung in Maitland Road. I walked through to the kitchen at the back of house. There was a small patio behind. I pulled open a couple of drawers and found a breadknife. That would do for afterwards. But I couldn't find the right heavy object. I walked back and into the living room. A rug was rolled up. On a coffee-table there was a piece of lined paper headed 'To Do', followed by a list of items, each one neatly ticked off. Bloody Leah.

On the mantelpiece I found what I was looking for. There was a small symbolic-looking sculpture, a rock with a hole in it and in the hole was a bronze figurine. I weighed it in my palm, felt its cool, rough mass. It was perfect.

I returned to the hallway and sat on the stairs. I placed the breadknife on the step and balanced the sculpture in my hands, moving it from one to the other, and waited. I could feel my heart beating fast, I could feel it in my chest and arms and legs and throbbing through my ears. All it would take was this one decisive act, the removal of the person who could betray me, and I'd be free.

I had little sense of time passing, but it felt quicker than I'd expected when I heard footsteps outside and saw an outline through the frosted glass of the front door. I stepped forward, holding the sculpture in my right hand. There would be a ring at the door, I'd open it with my left hand from behind the door so Astrid wouldn't see me, she'd step inside, push the door shut, a single blow.

But the bell didn't ring. I heard some fumbling and then there was the rattle of a key in the lock. I froze. I was unable to think or move. The door opened and Leah stepped inside. She shut the door, turned, saw me, and gave a start that was almost comic. Her eyes widened.

'Davy?' she said. 'What ... ?'

She couldn't even think of an adequate question to ask.

I started to babble. 'I found your keys,' I said. 'I brought them back.'

Even as I spoke, I knew it made no sense, that it wouldn't stand up to more than a moment's consideration.

Leah spoke to me like someone in a dream. 'I've a spare key,' she said, as if she needed to explain. 'But what are you doing here? Why the ... ?'

And then she saw the sculpture and she never finished the sentence. I brought it round with the force of all my anger, at Leah, a bit, for coming here and ruining everything, but also at life, at the world, for being so messy and complicated. The granite caught her on the side of the temple, full on, with a crunch. Her knees gave way and she fell down sideways, scraping against the wall as she did so. She lay on the ground, her legs flapping noisily. It seemed like a mercy to bend down and hold her throat with my gloved hands to make it stop and go away. I reached for the breadknife and marked her face, as I'd planned to do to Astrid. It was the first time I'd seen how pretty she was.

At that moment, of all moments, I started thinking in the funniest way. My mind was both clear and unclear. I saw myself, as if from above, standing over this dead woman with bubbling red incisions on her face. People would think of the person who had done this as a madman who killed women and mutilated them. A psychopath. But it wasn't really like that. That's not who I am.

I couldn't work out what was best to do. Should I wait for Astrid and go through with my plan? I considered the knife. No. I laid it down carefully. I looked around. Was there anything I needed to take away with me? Had I brought anything? I couldn't remember. Was it better to take the knife or leave it? I picked it up again. I ran to the kitchen and rinsed it under the tap. I ripped off a few sheets of kitchen roll and wrapped them round the blade. I put the bundle into a plastic shopping bag and rolled it up. Was there anything I was forgetting?

A dim fragment of my plan came back into my mind. Melanie. For my alibi. I needed an alibi, especially now. I stared blindly about me, my mind churning uselessly, and then I saw on the hall table a shallow, dark-blue cardboard box lined with pink tissue paper. Leah had been buying herself expensive lingerie. I snatched up the box and held it against my chest, taking a last look at Leah, who was staring at me glassily. Was I imagining it, or was there a contemptuous curl on her lips? I kicked at her, then went through the front door and outside. Astrid could arrive at any moment, but I had no thought now of staying to watch her. I had to get away. Was there blood on my clothes? I made myself look. Not that I could see. Just leave. Slowly. Walk, don't run.

I pushed the door shut but it wouldn't close. Something was resting against it, blocking it. Leah, of course. I wasn't good at this any more.

My forehead prickled with sweat and I felt dizzy and slightly sick, so I when I got to Regent's Park I stopped for a few minutes and sat on a bench just inside the gates. A busload of small schoolchildren swarmed by, chattering excitedly. Presumably they were on the way to the zoo. I stared at them as they passed, holding hands with each other, swinging their plastic lunchboxes. I felt tears stinging my eyes. It was all right for them.

I made myself revisit what had just happened. Had I left anything incriminating behind? No, I didn't think so. Could I have done anything else? No. It wasn't my fault Leah had come home. She had said she was going to work, hadn't she? I couldn't have known she'd change her mind like that. Stupid, stupid, stupid. I could feel the beginnings of a migraine stirring. That was all I needed. First, having to kill Leah like that, and now a bloody headache that would prevent me protecting myself properly. I pulled myself up from the bench, squinting against the sunlight, which jabbed into me, and made it across the road to a pharmacy where I bought some tablets and a bottle of water. I washed down three pills with several gulps of water, then splashed more water over my face. I tried to breathe calmly while I waited for the pain to recede. I didn't have much time.

It didn't take me long to get to Melanie's gallery. Laura

was there with a middle-aged man whose popping eyes made him look as if he was being strangled by the ridiculous cravat tied round his neck.

'Davy?' Laura looked at me with barely concealed displeasure. She was wearing a shirt with ruffles and a skirt with a large bow tied at the waist – like a parcel done up for Christmas.

'Hello, Laura.' I tried to smile at her, felt my lips dragging back over my teeth. My head was pounding viciously. 'Is Mel here?'

'She's in the back room. She's quite busy, as a matter of –'

'Thanks. I know the way.'

I pushed past them both and into the back, where Mel was sitting in front of the computer. She was frowning slightly and her lips were pursed, but when she saw me she jumped up hastily, pushing her hands through her hair and smiling anxiously. 'I wasn't expecting . . .'

'Sssh,' I said. I laid the box on the small table, walked up to her, put my arms round her and kissed her full on the lips. I was definitely feeling sick now. Sick, clammy and feverish. I kept my eyes fixed on a point over her shoulder. 'I've been thinking of you,' I said, when I let her go.

'Oh, Davy!' She stared at me, biting her lip and putting up a hand to brush my hair from my forehead. I forced myself not to flinch. 'I've been worrying about you.'

'No need. See? Instead of going to work this morning, like I should have done, I went shopping. Take a look.' I handed her the box.

Her eyes widened. 'Lolita's?' she said. 'You've bought me something from there? Why, it must have cost you a fortune.'

'You're worth it,' I said.

She lifted the lid, gave a little gasp, and drew out a lacy black négligée. Definitely not her style.

'Why, it's –'

'Do you like it? Hang on. You don't want to know the price!' I leaned forward, snatched the receipt out of the box and crumpled it in my hand. I was definitely slipping. She could have looked at it and seen it wasn't bought today, after all.

'Like it? Nobody's ever given me anything like this before.'

'I should hope not. You're my girl.'

She threw her arms round me once more, but I disengaged myself. 'I should go,' I said. 'I'll be in trouble at work as it is.'

'You mean, you've just come to give me this and now you're going all the way back?'

'I wanted to see you,' I said. 'Shall we meet later?'

'Oh, yes,' she said exultantly. 'Yes. Thank you, Davy. I'm bowled over, honestly. I can't believe it. And just when I was thinking you'd gone off me.'

I left the gallery. One more thing. I passed several shops, then entered a pâtisserie I had noticed earlier. There were fruit cakes, birthday cakes, cakes with teddy bears and cartoon characters. All the sugar and bright colours made me feel nauseous. I chose a chocolate cake, heavy and rich and thick with shavings of chocolate on top; chocolate with added chocolate. Just the thing for a celebration.

Chapter Forty

When I arrived home, Miles was there, which was definitive proof that there was a God. Or definitive proof that there wasn't a God. One of the two. He was sitting in the kitchen writing urgently on a scrap of paper. He looked up absently. 'Hi, Davy,' he said.

'I thought you and Leah were at work,' I said.

'I changed my mind. And she had to fetch something from her place,' he said. 'I think she was going to her office after that, though.'

Even better. He knew she was going home and nobody else did. The cardboard box containing the cake was fastened with golden ribbon that curled at the end. The knot was too tight to unravel, so I cut it with kitchen scissors. I placed the cake on a plate. Miles pulled a face. 'What the hell's that?'

'I saw it in a shop window,' I said. 'I couldn't resist it. People might like it with their coffee. You want some coffee?'

'If you're making it.'

I filled the kettle and switched it on. I had brought the knife with me and now I unwrapped it, then placed it next to the cake. I saw it was still marked with Leah's blood. I tore off two sheets of kitchen roll. With one I held the handle and with the other I wiped it so that most of the dark stain was removed, but not all. I took the packet of ground coffee from the fridge and spooned it into the cafetière. When the coffee was made, I took two mugs to the table and sat opposite Miles. 'What are you doing?' I asked.

'There's all sorts of stuff to sort out with the house,' he said. He gulped at the coffee. 'Thanks.'

'Where's Mick?' I asked.

'I haven't seen him,' said Miles.

'There doesn't seem to be anybody around,' I said.

I needed to know if Miles had seen anybody who could give him a solid alibi. 'I think I heard Dario upstairs,' he said. 'Everybody else is out.'

He carried on writing, columns of figures, then he sighed and drew a line through them.

'I'm sorry if I'm interrupting you,' I said.

'No, it's not that,' he said. 'It's the money. Maybe you can sort it out between yourselves.'

'I don't think I'll be getting much,' I said.

Miles gave an unhappy shrug. He got up and walked round the kitchen. 'It wasn't meant to happen this way,' he said, 'but I don't know how to stop it. Everything I do seems to make it worse.'

'Have a slice of cake,' I said. 'That'll make you feel better.'

He managed a sort of laugh. 'It's a bit early for me,' he said.

'That's not very grateful of you,' I said.

'Later, maybe,' he said distractedly. 'I mean, you know that Astrid and I have a history. And Leah's not exactly a diplomat.'

'While you're over there could you cut *me* a slice?' I said, breaking his flow.

'What?'

'Cake.'

Miles looked confused. 'Oh, all right.' He picked up the

knife and cut me a slice, then one for himself. 'You've tempted me.' He took a bite and pulled a face. 'Bloody hell, that's rich.'

'Good, though,' I said.

A few minutes later Miles left the kitchen and I heard the front door slam. I wiped the chocolate cake from the blade of the knife and put it back in the plastic bag. There was no sign of Dario or Mick. Miles's room was a mess. Leah had been moving in while everybody else was moving out. There were piles of her clothing on the floor, makeup and little glass and plastic bottles on every surface. I pulled some drawers open in Miles's desk. The bottom one contained old photographs and postcards, a tennis trophy from his schooldays, a couple of old electric plugs. In the end, I pushed the carrier-bag containing the knife between the two mattresses, which is where people hide things in films and where they always get found.

After I left Miles's room I phoned Melanie at work. I told her I loved her, that I wanted to see her and that she should come straight over here after work. I wanted to see her and talk to her about things. She was so happy and excited that she was almost laughing and crying at the same time. I could hear sounds coming from Dario's room but I didn't want to talk to anybody at that moment so I went upstairs and lay on my bed. For a few hours I had felt completely focused. Now I felt the way I did when I came back from the dentist and the anaesthetic was wearing off. For hours there had been a numbness but now there was a prickly feeling in my head as the real world forced its way in.

By now Astrid would know. The police would know. If I'd done something really, really, obviously stupid, if I'd dropped something, left something of myself, it was too late to do anything and soon there'd be a knock on the door.

Now the police were investigating three murders and it was going to be a huge deal. My head hurt. There was what had happened and there was what I had made it look like. I had to keep them separate. Now experts would be picking over every detail, every thread. I had only one advantage. They would be looking for something clever, something logical, or perhaps something insane that linked them. But I wasn't clever and I wasn't logical and I wasn't insane. They were just linked by bad luck. Had I blunderingly created a trail that was impossible to follow? Except for Astrid. It always came back to her.

I felt so tired. I just wanted to go back in time to before I'd done all this. But I couldn't go back in time, so I would need to draw a line under it, get away and start again. Start again. Again. In the meantime, I would have to live through the pantomime once more. How would it happen? Who would find out first? I imagined that Astrid would get her one phone call and would ring up the house. Mick or Dario would answer and they would spread it with that excitement, that sparkle in the eyes, that jolt of electricity people have when they've got really bad news to tell you. Suddenly I realized I had to get out of the house. I couldn't be here when the first news arrived, when people were huddling around, snatching at fragments, speculating about what exactly might have happened.

I ran down the stairs, nodding at Dario on the way. He asked me if I could give him a hand. I shook my head. I told him somebody had rung me. I had urgent work to attend to.

'This is going so badly,' he said.

I said I'd catch him later. As I walked away from the house, I phoned Melanie at work again.

'You're stalking me,' she said.

338

It was the first time she had ever teased me. Was I seeming needy? Putting myself in a position of weakness? 'Is it a problem?' I asked.

'No, no, course not,' she said.

I told her I'd pick her up from work. There was something I needed to talk to her about. She left her gallery at ten past five. I had more than four hours to kill and nothing to do. The day passed in a fuzzy rush. I wandered the streets looking at passers-by, men in stained trousers drinking lager and talking to themselves, people with headphones, busy shoppers. Everybody inching their way through a crowd of strangers. What did it matter if one or two or three of them disappeared? In a hundred years there'd still be a crowd here, winos talking to themselves, busy shoppers, but they'd be new. The old ones would be dead.

I took Melanie for a coffee. I dropped hints about us all having to leave the house and she blushed and smiled and said maybe we could think of looking for somewhere together, and I nodded and smiled and said we should think about it and maybe we should head home.

As I opened the door, Dario was standing in the hall, wild-eyed. He walked over to us and spoke quietly. 'Davy,' he said. 'Mel.'

At that moment I needed Melanie the way people some-times need a cigarette. It's not that you particularly want a smoke. It just gives you something to do with your hands. When you do all the stuff like taking the cigarette out of the packet, putting it into your mouth and playing with lighters or matches, it stops you feeling self-conscious. When Melanie was there, draped around me, doing what I said, agreeing with me, I turned into a new creature: Davy-and-Mel. So sweet, so young and in love. People stopped paying attention. Best of all, she could do the reacting for both of us. I pretended to be numbed by the news, so shocked that I couldn't even speak. And I watched Melanie as if she was an actress giving a performance. And what a performance. Her pretty pale face flushed, tears filled her eyes, she stammered and asked questions and said she couldn't believe it and held my arm tight and tried to remember when she had last seen Leah and what Leah had said. I stayed close, my arm round her, silent. I could smell her smooth, newly washed hair.

Pippa heard us and came out of her room. She seemed the most composed of anyone. Suddenly I saw how ridiculous Melanie looked, her cheeks streaked with black, weeping for somebody she hardly knew and couldn't have cared for.

'What's going to happen?' I asked.

'How should I know?' she said. 'Miles is downstairs. Go and see him.'

'Wouldn't it be better if you did?'

She smiled. 'No,' she said.

So the two young lovers went downstairs and found Miles sitting alone at the table staring into the air. We made tea and opened tins of biscuits and sat and held hands and murmured and nodded while Miles babbled and cried and talked aimlessly. There was too much talk. It was too confusing, too much to keep in mind. I was worried I would say the wrong thing but I couldn't think of an excuse to get up and leave him there. And then Astrid came in. She was wearing strange rough clothes: tracksuit bottoms and a T-shirt that clearly weren't hers. She looked exhausted and rumpled, yet she had the glow about her of someone who had been close to the action.

'Was it horrible?' I asked, then realized how fatuous that sounded and Astrid instantly told me so. Miles got up and

I could see that he felt more intimate with Astrid than he had with us. He had made do with us because there was nobody else to talk to. He might as well have been talking to himself. Now, with Astrid, he let his guard down and hugged her and talked in a new, raw tone. We watched them curiously.

'I've got something for you,' he said, then looked round at us awkwardly and said he'd talk to her outside.

They left the kitchen and Melanie turned to me. 'What was that?'

'I don't know. Let's go upstairs.'

As we walked up, I saw Miles and Astrid in a conspiratorial huddle on the stairs. I heard – thought I heard – Astrid saying, 'I can't take twenty thousand in cash, Miles!' But they looked round, saw me and feel silent. Shutting me out. We eased past them.

'Everything all right?' I asked.

Astrid turned away from me. 'I'll tell you later,' she said.

'If there's anything . . .'

'Yes,' she said. 'Yes, thanks.'

But I saw the money in her hands.

Chapter Forty-one

Maybe it could be all right. Maybe I could get what I had wanted, after all. I had to keep calm, that was the main thing. Very calm. Not a single wrong move. I was scared to open my mouth in case I said something that would trip me up, and I had to force myself to meet anyone's gaze because I thought they'd be able to see the thoughts that were swarming in my head. I could barely smile or grimace without worrying that it would be my undoing. It was hard to breathe steadily. Footsteps on the stairs made me giddy. Coming to get me. Knock on the door, hand on the shoulder. No solid ground under my feet. No clear view in front of me. But if I could grope my way through the darkness, if I could only keep my balance, I could still get out of this mess.

I had done all this, killed all these women – no, that wasn't me, not the real me; it wasn't my fault, just a stupid accident – and each time come away empty-handed. But now Astrid had all that money. I had seen her go upstairs with it. Twenty thousand pounds in cash. Astrid was in my way and Astrid had the money. My head still hurt, but it also felt as if there was an itch inside it that I couldn't get at. Get rid of Astrid, take the money. But everything was the wrong way round now, because at any minute the police would descend on the house and they'd find the stuff in Miles's room and I couldn't blame *another* death on him, could I, not if he was in the police station? Shit, shit, shit. Why hadn't I thought of that? Find another person as well. Owen. That was it. Serve him right. Get him out of the way. Me and Astrid in Brazil. But even through the wild duststorm of my thoughts I could see that it would be pushing it to try to find another fall-guy as well as Miles. Two killers in one house. No. It wouldn't do.

Chaos in my mind; chaos in the house. People were packing and crying. Dario was bumping a large cardboard box down the stairs and talking to himself. Pippa was throwing clothes out of her door, until the threshold of her room was strewn with them. I opened my window and pushed my head outside, and I could hear voices filtering towards me from Owen's room. Astrid was in there. She really shouldn't do that: it only made me angrier. I couldn't hear everything, only fragments of their talk. Something about leaving. Something about photographs. *Photographs.* I strained to make out more. Their voices dropped, then rose again. Something about Pippa. That was good. However much time passed, Pippa would always be there, that first lie in the relationship.

The photograph. I wiped my forehead with the back of my hand and swallowed hard. He was going to the police with the photograph, that was it. Everything closing in. I couldn't breathe. No air left for me. Had to keep calm. Now their voices dropped again. A low murmur. I couldn't make out the words. Silence. Were they kissing? Touching? Fucking? Were they? Who cared? It didn't really matter any more. That was all going to come to an end.

Melanie came into the room carrying a mug of tea. Kind, sweet Melanie, sweet enough to make me gag. A look of womanly concern on her face, but she was happy now, I could tell that. She sat beside me on the bed and I buried my face on her shoulder because if I saw her expression of sympathetic tenderness I would have to hit her to make it go away.

'Here, my love, drink this.'

'Thanks.'

'Everyone's in shock.'

I muttered something. My mind was whirling. Astrid. Money. Brazil. I wanted the money. Anyone would want the money. That was it. She was everyone's target now. Yes. The hiss in my head subsided, like static being gradually tuned out. Stir up the mud, I thought. Stir up the fear. Make sure everyone else felt the confusion and terror I was feeling now.

'Come on,' I said, jumping up from the bed and taking Melanie's hand.

'What?'

'Let's go downstairs.'

'But I made you a cup of tea.'

'I can't just sit here.'

I pulled her downstairs, meeting Dario coming up. I nodded at him. 'The police will be here soon,' I said in a whisper. 'You'd better be ready. They'll take your room apart, you know.'

His eyes widened and he stared wildly at me, then ran up the stairs.

Melanie and I went into the kitchen and I sat her at the table. I could hear Miles weeping in his room. Yes, mate, weep. You don't get it yet.

'Mel,' I said loudly.

'Yes?'

'Do you understand why I'm so upset?'

'Of course,' she said excitedly. 'You wouldn't be human if you weren't shocked by what's happened. Leah practically lived in this house. And in spite of everyone's difficulties, she was so full of –'

344

'No,' I said, cutting into her drivel. 'I mean, do you under-stand?'

I could hear footsteps coming down the stairs. Just from their light swiftness, I knew it was Astrid.

'Don't you get it yet, Mel?' I continued even louder. 'They think it's one of us.'

I heard Astrid come to a halt outside the door. That's right, my girl. You stay there and listen, the way I want you to. Call yourself free? Nobody's free. They're all part of a plan.

'And that's not all,' I went on, over Mel's wail of protest. 'That's why Owen's packing his bag. That's why Dario's running round like a headless chicken. That's why Miles was throwing up in the bathroom and putting those letters from Leah into the garbage before he's marched off to the police station. That's why Astrid looks completely distraught.'

When Astrid finally entered, Mel had her fingers in her ears like a toddler, blocking out what she couldn't bear to hear. I smiled sadly at Astrid. I was the reluctant truth-teller, the loyal good friend. I was the one who saw what no one else could bear to look at.

The police arrived like an army, some in plain clothes and some in uniform, carrying bags and cameras. My hands weren't steady so I put an arm round Melanie. My heart pounded so hard that it hurt in my chest. I could feel beads of sweat prickling my forehead and points of light jabbed behind my eyes. It was hard to make sense of the sounds around me, separate them out into words.

'Could you show us your room, sir?'

He was talking to me. I made myself look at the face that loomed towards me. I nodded gravely. 'Of course.'

I led him up the stairs, and his footsteps fell heavily behind me. Was I about to find out that I had made some terrible mistake?

'Here,' I said. My voice sounded quite natural.

'Thank you.'

'I – er – I'll wait downstairs, shall I? I'm not sure how this kind of thing works.'

A hint of a smile on his stiff face. I left him and went into the kitchen. Astrid was outside with Kamsky. They were standing by her vegetable garden and she was looking up at him with the expression of frankness I knew so well. I watched her. I went on watching her as a police officer strode past me and pushed his way out into the garden. He almost ran towards them. When Kamsky stepped forward to join him, I could see his face tensing. He turned back to Astrid and said something to her, then left her there. For several moments, she didn't move, but she put her hand against her heart as if it was hurting her. Then she walked towards the kitchen and when she lifted her head her gaze went right through me. As if I wasn't there at all.

If you can get through a door just as it's banging shut. If you can find the one gap in the fast-moving traffic and make it to the other side. If you can time it just right. Too soon and you'll expose yourself. Too late and you'll be trapped. One moment. I had to get it right.

When the police interviewed me, I could tell they weren't really interested in me. They didn't fire questions at me and try to trip me up. They just wanted to know stupidly easy things like my movements yesterday morning. Who had I seen in the house when I returned from my shopping expedition for Melanie? Now, let me think. Hmm. Well, I'd seen Miles. That's right. Miles. I'd thought it strange that he wasn't at work. What did he say? Ah, let me think: yes, he had said he knew Leah was going back to her house to get something. I was certain, yes. Was he upset? Oh, yes, Officer, he was very nervous and jumpy indeed. And that was before he heard about Leah's death? Oh, yes, Officer, even before that he was noticeably agitated. But – sudden frown – why are you asking me that? Surely you can't think it was Miles? Yes, Officer, I'm afraid Miles had argued with Leah. Absolutely. Yes, I don't want to betray house confidences, but he seemed obsessed with Astrid.

Out on to the street at last, into the drizzle. Pippa was there already and we sat on the low wall. She put her arm through mine and leaned her head on my shoulder. 'What a fucking nightmare,' she said.

'Yes,' I said. I kissed the top of her head.

'Isn't it horrible when everything you've done or said becomes suspicious? I tell you what, I'll be better at my job after this.'

So she didn't know yet.

Owen joined us and I could tell he didn't know either. He stood moodily in front of us, kicking bits of gravel on the pavement, his hands stuffed deep into his pockets. He scowled at Pippa when she reached out a hand, and moved a step backwards, then sat on the wall on the other side of me. She shrugged, stood up and pulled her mobile out of her pocket. Dario reeled out of the police station. His hair stuck up in orange peaks and his face was a chalky white. 'I wanted to confess,' he said, 'just to stop them. To make it all go away. Is there a word for it, feeling guilty for something you didn't do?'

'Shut up,' said Owen, who was rolling himself a cigarette.

'Right,' said Dario, as if Owen had given him useful advice.

347

He started pacing up and down, muttering to himself.

Then Astrid arrived. She was pale and the spring had gone out of her step. She sat between me and Owen. Owen passed her the cigarette. I put an arm round her. She let her weight rest on me. Her hair was against my cheek. I could feel her breathing. I could feel the crisp thickness of the cash in her jacket.

'OK?' I said.

She just turned and looked at me.

Dario padded towards us. 'Who are we waiting for?' he asked.

'Just Mick and Miles. I'm sure they'll be out soon.' I said it casually but Astrid jolted out of my embrace and stared at me, her eyes huge in her face.

'Don't you know?'

I looked at everyone else, as if they were the ones performing, not me. Mick walking down the steps towards us. People holding up their hands, shaking their heads in horrified denial, mouths open, weeping and wailing, arms round each other. I was at the centre of it. I got my arms round Astrid before Owen could, and I heard words coming out of my mouth and I thought they were the right words, the ones that wouldn't be noticed by anyone. Mick was going on about tissue and hairs. I hugged Dario as well, feeling how sharp his bones were and how his flesh was chilly; his breath smelled of garlic. We were all wet from the drizzle. Our clothes clung to us. Raindrops ran down our faces. I said stuff like 'Miles, Christ!' and 'Three women!' It didn't really matter. No one was listening to anyone else, we were all tottering around uselessly on the pavement, not knowing what to do next.

Dario suggested going to the pub. That wasn't good. That wasn't in my plan. We needed to go our separate ways now.

There wasn't much time. Everyone else thought it was a good idea so of course I agreed and we made our way along the pavement, Astrid pushing her bike. I didn't feel so well. There was a hissing in my head and my throat was like sandpaper. My eyes ached.

I don't know what everyone talked about. I could hear the words and I knew how to respond every so often so that it appeared I was part of the frantic emotions that were surging round the group, but I wasn't. I was thinking. I was waiting. I was feeling the minutes tick by. I was swallowing my nausea. I was stopping myself imagining what would happen if things went wrong.

When we finished our first drinks I offered to get the next round. But I went outside first. I got my penknife out of my pocket and sliced through both of the tyres on Astrid's bike. You won't get home on that, Astrid. You'll have to go a different way. I went back into the heat and the noise and the glaring light, collected the drinks and returned to the table.

Astrid was fumbling inside her jacket. 'This is probably evidence of some kind,' she said. 'Before the police grab it, we should share it out.'

'No,' I said, blood pounding in my ears so I could barely hear myself speak. 'For goodness' sake, Astrid, people are already looking at us. Don't flash money around in a place like this.'

I looked round nervously. It seemed a feeble excuse but Astrid nodded. Perhaps it provided reason for them not to let go of each other finally, not to drift apart.

'I'll do the maths,' said Pippa. 'Then we can arrange to meet tomorrow somewhere a bit more salubrious. It'll be an excuse for another farewell drink.'

'OK,' I said. I was steaming in the muggy heat of the pub. Drops of sweat prickled down my neck like dozens of small flies.

At last Pippa said she needed to make a move and everyone else was standing up, putting on their jackets. Astrid was standing up. She was pulling on her coat, tying its belt. We trooped outside, into the cool night, to discover her ripped tyres. How mean is that? Never mind. Walk to the Underground. Collect it later. She said we'd all meet tomorrow. Yes. Dream on, my darling. Dream on.

She gripped my arm as she said goodbye and her touch burned through my clothes. I swear I could feel it like a brand on my skin. She kissed Pippa. Now she was speaking to Owen in a low undertone. He was speaking to her. Their heads were close together, nearly touching. She took his hand. Let it go. Now. Let it go. Stand away. This mustn't happen. Don't let them go off together. They couldn't. I screwed my hands into fists and thought I'd have to scream out loud at any moment, to provide relief from the unbearable pressure building inside me. I would explode. Come apart. My head hammered.

'Right, then.'

Astrid stood back from Owen at last, and I felt relief flood through me, leaving me dizzy and weak as a kitten.

At last she left, raising one hand in farewell as she went. Give her a count of ten before following. I got to six, then worried about losing her. Nobody was looking at me anyway. I saw Astrid walking along the pavement. Stay close, wait for somewhere isolated. I felt in my pocket. The penknife I had used on her bike tyres. The cool weight of a spanner. A blow from behind. She wouldn't even know.

'Mr Gifford?'

I looked round. I was so taken by surprise that it took

me a few seconds to realize it was Detective Chief Inspector Kamsky.

'Who? Me?' I said stupidly. Ahead, Astrid disappeared round a bend in the road.

'Could we have a word?'

Chapter Forty-two

It had all gone wrong. Of course. I had dropped something somewhere, forgotten a detail. There was always a loose end, however much care you took. Even so, I hung on. I thought about how to be innocent. Ask questions, be puzzled. I could feel my face burning and there was a twitch at the side of my mouth that I couldn't control, but somehow I managed not to collapse. I told myself it was all right to be a bit rattled. The police made ordinary people nervous. Only real criminals are casual and amused about being arrested. Kamsky barely spoke on the drive to the police station.

'Is there a problem?' I asked, hearing how my voice came out a bit cracked and hoarse. I gave a sharp cough to clear my throat. 'Is there something more you need to ask me?'

'There's someone who wants a word with you.'

'Who?' I asked.

'You'll see.'

'Is it someone I know?'

Kamsky paused for a moment, as if trying to make up his mind. 'You'll see,' he repeated finally.

I was thinking so desperately that I hardly noticed as the driver pulled into a car park behind the police station and I was led across the cracked tarmac, through a back door, along a narrow corridor into a room and left alone to walk up and down. I'd only left it a couple of hours earlier but it wasn't like before. Nobody offered me tea. I didn't know if it was the same room. It felt darker. I tried to compose myself. But not too much. I mustn't seem defensive. The news wasn't entirely bad. No. If they were simply arresting me, they would have done it immediately. I would have been warned. Wasn't that the way it happened?

Kamsky came into the room, carrying a cassette tape-recorder. Behind him was another man in a suit. He was heavily built with grey hair that looked as if it had just been combed, too hard, against his skull. Kamsky motioned to me to sit at the table. The two pulled chairs to the other side and sat down. Kamsky placed the tape-recorder on the table and looked at it for a moment but didn't switch it on. 'I'd like to introduce you to my colleague, Bill Pope,' he said.

'What's this about?' I said. I could feel the spanner in my pocket.

'DI Pope came down this morning from Sheffield.'

I clenched my fists, then relaxed them, hearing my knuckles crack. I tried to make myself appear alarmed but not too alarmed. I felt my features twist into an expression but I had no idea how I must look to an outsider.

'Has something happened?' I asked. Bees inside my skull. Buzz, buzz.

Pope took a notebook from a pocket and opened it. He put on a pair of rimless glasses and peered down at it. 'David Michael Gifford,' he said.

'Yes,' I said. 'What is it?'

'You used to live at fourteen Donegal Close.'

'That's right. Has something happened?'

'When were you last there?'

'I don't know,' I said. Was that my voice? Yes. 'Five or six months ago.'

'Who lives there now?'

'My mum, I suppose.'

Pope frowned. 'You suppose?'

'I haven't been in touch for a while.'

'Why?'

I gave a shrug. 'When I came down to London, I wanted to make a new start.'

'What for?'

There was a pause as I tried to think how a person who didn't know what was going on would respond. 'I'm sorry,' I said. 'What's this about? Has something happened?'

Pope clicked and unclicked the pen he was holding. 'Why?' he said. 'Should it have?'

'Please,' I said, in a tone that was meant to sound distressed and confused. 'I don't know what you're talking about.'

'Why did you leave Sheffield?' Pope asked.

'Look, what's all this . . .' I stopped. Get it right, Davy. Hang on. 'I always knew I wanted to go to London. I got the offer of a job in London. It seemed the right time. Please could you tell me what this is about? You're alarming me.' I tried to smile at him. I couldn't. The skin on my face was stiff like cardboard.

Pope closed his notebook and leaned back in his chair.

'Concerns were expressed by residents of Donegal Close. Two days ago police officers forced entry to the premises and a body was found.'

This was it. This was the big moment on which everything would depend. I'd thought about it for a long time. 'Is it my mum?' I asked.

'The body had been there for some time. Months. But we managed to find out by . . . Well, we've confirmed it's the body of Mary Gifford.'

I could feel them staring at me. Their gaze on my face was hot like the sun.

'Dead?' I said. 'What happened? How could she . . . ? I mean, why did nobody find her?'

354

I wasn't able to cry but I rubbed my eyes hard and murmured unintelligible things. For a moment I put my face in my hands, shutting out their gaze and giving myself time to think. Then I looked up again. The two detectives stared at me impassively.

'I'm sorry,' I said. 'I should have been in touch. I didn't call. I didn't see her all the time I was away. But I never thought ... I never imagined ...' I rubbed my eyes hard again, and let a few whimpers escape.

'The officers talked to neighbours,' said Pope. 'They mentioned her son. They hadn't seen you for some time. Or her.'

'She wasn't well,' I said. 'She wasn't very mobile.'

'Her body was in the bed.'

'Bed,' I said numbly. 'She lay there a lot in the day.'

'Nobody knew where you'd gone,' said Pope. 'But then your name popped up on the computer. Imagine our surprise. I thought I'd better come and see you.'

'I'd have come up,' I said. 'Are you sure? My mother? Mum? She's really dead?'

'We need to ask some further questions,' said Pope. 'I now need to warn you that, in the case of charges being brought, what you say could be used as evidence in court. I should say also that you have the right to a lawyer present. If necessary, we can obtain one for you. Do you understand?'

'No,' I said slowly, as if in deep shock. 'I don't understand. Was there a crime?'

'That's what I'm here to consider.'

'Was she burgled? She wasn't ... Was she attacked?'

'Did you understand my warning? Do you want a lawyer?'

I'd thought about this carefully in advance and I knew what I was going to say. 'A lawyer? What for?'

'It's up to you,' said Kamsky.

'My mother's dead,' I said. 'I loved her. I should never have left her alone. I'll answer anything you want. I'll do anything I can to help.'

Kamsky switched the tape on and announced the date, the time and the place, the names of the officers present, my full name and that I had been told my rights and had agreed to be interviewed without a lawyer present. They began to ask me questions, but really over the next hour or so I learned far more than they did. I was deliberately vague and fumbling in my answers. After all, I was a son who had just been told his mother was dead and, despite his distress, was trying to do his best to help. If I had been precise in every detail about my movements and motives and what I had been doing in the weeks before I came to London and why I hadn't returned or even been in touch, that's what would have been suspicious.

It became clear that, after the heat of the last few weeks, the body had been so decayed that it had been difficult enough to make an identification and impossible to find out anything else significant. I could imagine the sequence. First the flies, then the maggots, a boiling carpet of maggots, scouring everything away. It was obvious that they didn't have anything but they'd brought me in to look at me, to jolt a reaction out of me. I didn't need to be clever. The more confused and helpless the better.

'I feel so terrible,' I said at one point. 'I thought her friends would look after her. I don't know what could have happened.'

'Did she have many friends?' asked Pope.

'A few,' I said. 'Less since she'd got ill.'

'How ill was she?'

'I don't know what was wrong with her but I think she

was sometimes in pain,' I said, glassy-eyed. 'I know she tried to keep it from me. But she was so brave about it. Maybe she tried to do too much.'

I wanted to keep on playing stupid. I knew it was the right thing to do. But I couldn't resist it. I had to know. I waited until the questions seemed to come to a halt.

'I don't understand,' I said. 'Why are you both here?'

'I need to consider all possibilities,' said Kamsky.

'My mother was found dead in her bed. In Sheffield. What do you mean, possibilities?'

'I hate this case,' Kamsky said.

It was my own fault. I'd gone through that door. I decided it was time to get angry. 'What do you mean, this fucking case?' I said. 'What case? You've just told me my mum's dead. What are you talking about? You've arrested fucking Miles. What are you after? Ask me anything you want. I don't care. But don't fuck me around.'

Too many fucks. That wasn't how Davy talked. It sounded like play-acting. I gave a hoarse sob to make up for it.

'Calm down,' said Pope, in a more soothing tone. 'Tell me about your mother. Were you close to her?'

They tried to probe my psychology but it was going nowhere. I was able to bore them into submission. I sniffled a bit, and stammered. I went round in aimless circles. I did some more dry sobbing. I did some more hiding my head in my hands. Finally there was a pause and Kamsky looked at Pope, nodded, then leaned over and switched off the tape-recorder. They both seemed quietly irritated at the waste of time.

'Please accept my condolences,' said Pope.

I didn't reply. I was remembering the months of irritation with my mother that had built up like a noise inside my head. All it had taken was a pillow over her face and the noise had gone away. It had been so easy, as if I had just left her sleeping. Pope took the notebook and replaced it in his jacket pocket.

'You'll be contacted about the inquest,' he said. 'You'll be wanting to arrange the funeral. And there's the house to be dealt with.'

The house. It had been there all this time, waiting for me.

'Did you hear me, Mr Gifford?'

'It's a bit sudden,' I said. 'I'm trying to take it in. Being an orphan. And all that.'

I looked at them in turn. It seemed to go down all right.

Chapter Forty-three

I had a house. They had no evidence against me and now I owned a house. Not a large one, not a lovely one, not one in a desirable area, not one I would ever want to live in. But mine. How much would it fetch? It had three bedrooms and a garden and I didn't believe in ghosts. The nasty smell could be scrubbed away. A hundred grand? I hardly needed the money in Astrid's jacket any more, but it wasn't to be sniffed at – it would still come in useful. Say, a hundred and twenty thousand pounds. Not bad, not bad at all. I could never have got that much from Ingrid de Soto's house. Funny how things turn out.

Or how things *could* turn out, I reminded myself. There were still things to do. Things in my way. There was the paperweight. Astrid just needed to hear about it, and to remember.

I had been scared and tired even before Kamsky had tapped me on the shoulder, but now all of that had gone. I was on top form again. I could feel my thoughts clearing in my head. I could feel my heart beating steadily again and my muzzy fatigue lifting, like the fog lifts in the morning.

I looked at my watch. It was well past midnight. It was too late to find Astrid now. She'd be asleep somewhere, tucked up in bed, those big eyes closed and those golden limbs relaxed under the sheets, not knowing what tomorrow would bring. It was too late, as well, for me to find somewhere to stay now. I briefly considered going round to Melanie's. She'd welcome me in, no matter how late it was. Indeed, she was probably lying awake, waiting for me to call or to come. But I couldn't go to Melanie's, not tonight, not ever again. She was history. I could hardly bring myself to remember her face, her dewy eyes, her frightened smile, her clutching hand.

I found a nasty little café with grimy windows, which was still open. There were only two people in it – an old man with long grey hair tied back in a greasy ponytail who was sitting at a table, stirring sugar into a cup of very milky coffee, and a young woman at the counter. She had spiky blonde hair and a sulky mouth.

'Are you still serving food?' I asked her.

'The chef's gone home. I could give you a sandwich, if you want.'

'OK.'

'Bacon?'

'OK.'

'But we close in a few minutes.'

'Right.'

The bread was stale. The bacon was tough, fatty and cold and bits stuck in my teeth. The woman turned chairs upside-down on tables and swept crumbs up round my feet. The man with greasy hair shuffled out. When I had my money, I would go to smart restaurants with clean windows and polished tables where waiters in dark suits would fill my wine glass and bend respectfully over me, calling me 'sir'. I chewed a few small mouthfuls very slowly, not hungry in the slightest but marking time, then ordered a coffee, though I didn't need it to keep me awake. I was already wide awake, fully charged. The next twenty-four hours lay in front of me like a road, clear and straight. I felt the spanner in my pocket. I checked my mobile to make sure it had enough battery. There were several missed calls from Melanie, but I ignored them.

At a little after one, the waitress slouched over to the door, turned the 'open' sign to 'closed' and asked me to leave.

I walked. Past queues outside nightclubs, past a group of drunken men in suits, past down-and-outs in doorways strewn with cigarette butts. Down to the river. I sat on a bench and looked at my watch. It was three o'clock. In two hours or so it would be light. I closed my eyes and went through everything in my mind. When I opened them, it was half past five and there was light on the horizon. I had no notion that any time had gone by and no memories of dreaming, but I supposed I must have slept. I stood up and stretched. I made sure all the buttons on my shirt were done up, took a comb out of my breast pocket and neatened my hair. Then I walked back the way I'd come. At twenty past seven, I stopped in a café and ordered a cup of tea, but I could only manage a few sips. My insides were burning. I bought freshmint chewing-gum from a newsagent: that would have to do this morning in the place of cleaning my teeth. I bought a bottle of water as well, and rinsed my mouth. I felt like a runner waiting to take his place on the starting blocks.

At half past eight, I went to a public pay phone, used my mobile to remind me of Astrid's number and punched it in.

'Hello?'

'Astrid! Did I wake you up?'

'Is that you, Davy?'

'Yes. My mobile's packed up and I'm in a phone booth.'

'I've been awake for ages.'

'Me too. Listen, I know we're meeting later with everyone, but I was really hoping I could come and see you before- hand. There's something I think you should know.'

I thought at least she'd ask me to explain, and I had my answer ready, but she didn't. Her voice was warm, natural. 'That'd be fine. Why don't you come here at – what? Ten, ten thirty? Then we can go on to Maitland Road together.'

'Great. You'd better tell me where "here" is, though.' If she was with a friend, I'd have to change plans.

'Oh, sorry.' She gave an odd little snort. 'I'm staying at my friend Saul's – you met him a couple of times. I'm feeding his cat and watering his plants for the next few weeks while he's away. Sorry. Too much information. It's Capulet Road, just off Stoke Newington Church Street. Number sixty-six A.'

It was so typical that it made me smile. I had spent a night wandering the streets while Astrid had already found somewhere to stay, with plants and a cat. I'd never become part of the world where people did things like that and knew other people who did it too.

I walked to Stoke Newington. It was just a couple of miles and it cleared my head. When I got to the main street, I went into a rather cool shop selling men's clothes and bought myself a new shirt. It was an olive-green colour and smelled cottony and clean. I looked at myself in the mirror and liked what I saw. I was pleased with the slim young man with honest grey eyes in a fresh face, and – I leaned forward and smiled at my reflection – oh, yes, a modest and endearing smile that said, 'You can trust me, you can lean on me, you can tell me what's troubling you. I won't let you down'. I wouldn't let myself down. I'd come this far and I was on the last leg of my journey.

At ten minutes to ten I turned off Stoke Newington Church Street and down Capulet Road. I passed sixty-six A but it was too early; I didn't look up but kept on walking. At three minutes to ten, I halted and put the last two sticks of chewing-gum into my mouth, chewed them vigorously, then spat them out on to the pavement. Then I went back up Capulet Road. I got to number sixty-six, a little cobbler's that looked like something out of medieval times. The dark blue door to the left said '66a', in gold. I stood in front of it for a few seconds. I straightened my jacket over my shirt. I took some deep breaths. I ran my fingers through my hair. I licked my lips, arranged my expression. And then I rang the bell.

It was only a few seconds before I heard the unmistakable sound of Astrid's footsteps running down the stairs: light and quick. She pulled open the door. Her feet were bare and she was wearing faded jeans and a high-necked green cardigan that was short enough to show a strip of her tanned stomach. We were co-ordinated, I thought, on this day of all days. But there was something different about her and it took me a few moments to understand what it was. She was smiling at me and seemed properly pleased that I was there. Of course, she had always been perfectly friendly and approachable before, but in Maitland Road we had rarely been alone and I had always felt I was on the sidelines of her life. Today it was simply me and her. Nobody had just left and nobody was about to arrive. Her eyes were fixed on mine; her expression was attentive. She put her hands on my shoulders and kissed me, first on one cheek, then the other. 'Hello, Davy,' she said. 'I'm really glad you're here. I've been feeling so cast down about everything.'

She didn't look cast down. Her face glowed with health and life. Her dark hair shone and her lips were glossy. She smelled of lemon and roses.

'Of course you have,' I said, stepping over the threshold and shutting the door behind me. I followed her up the stairs. The tendrils of hair at the nape of her neck were still damp; she must be fresh from a shower, I thought. Her back was slender. She led me into a room that served as kitchen and living room. It was all a bit higgledy-piggledy and cluttered. There were geraniums in the window box, and a ginger cat lay curled up and purring on the baggy corduroy sofa. It opened one yellow eye, examined me, then shut it again.

Astrid looked at me with concern. 'Where did you spend the night?'

I mumbled something about staying at a friend's.

'You look terrible.'

'Thanks,' I said.

'I was wondering if you'd like a shower or something.'

'I already had one.'

She laughed. 'It wasn't an accusation. Sit down. Try to ignore Saul's mess.' She hurled a coat and a bag off the sofa. 'Coffee? Tea? Juice? I think there's juice, anyway, I haven't really examined the fridge yet.'

'Coffee.' I wanted to prolong the moment; watch her as she served me, watch the way her cardigan tightened over her breasts as she reached up for cups.

'A small amount of milk and no sugar, right?'

'You remember.'

'Of course.' She smiled at me and I felt my throat thicken with desire.

'How long are you staying here for?'

'I don't know. A fortnight at least. I can't see beyond that. I've no idea what I'll do next. Maybe I should grow up and try to sort out my life. What do you think?'

'Think?'

'About what I should do next.'

I stared at her, memorizing every detail of her face. 'I don't think you should plan beyond the next few minutes at the moment, Astrid.'

She turned away and shovelled several spoonfuls of ground coffee into a cafetière and poured in boiling water, stirring vigorously. 'This might be a bit strong.'

She sat down on the sofa next to me, pushing the cat to the end without waking it. Her leg brushed my leg; her shoulder was a few millimetres from mine. When she bent her head to take a sip of her coffee, I gazed at the curve of her cheek, at her long dark lashes. Steam rose into her face, moistening her skin. 'You're trembling,' I said to her softly.

'Am I?' She held up her free hand. 'So I am. I'm tired, Davy. Tired, scared, lonely, at a loss.' She put the hand on my knee. 'Do you understand that feeling?'

I put my hand over hers. 'Do I understand it? Astrid, I've spent my whole life feeling like that.' Tears welled in my eyes but I didn't try to check them. I was done with pretending. This was my moment, my perfect day. I put down my coffee cup and picked up her hand between both my own.

'I should have paid more attention,' she said. She let me lift her hand to my lips and hold it there for a moment. 'You're the only person in the whole house to have come well out of all of this. Everyone else went to pieces or turned on other people, except you. You were always calm and kind. Especially to me. Do you think I didn't notice?'

'Do you know why, Astrid?'

'I think so.' She placed her hand against my cheek. She gazed at me, then leaned forward and, very lightly, kissed my lips. I pulled her to me. Her lips opened under mine, I felt her breasts against my chest. I pushed my hand into her hair and kissed her again, more roughly, tasting blood but that didn't matter. My Astrid. My destiny. My ending and my beginning.

I pushed her back on the sofa. I kissed her gently, then started to do things I'd wanted to do since the first moment I'd met her. I put a hand on her breast. She smiled blurrily at me and I moved my hand under her cardigan and felt her warm, smooth stomach, then the rough fabric of her bra. I wanted her. I wanted to do everything to her at once. I moved my hand down to her jeans and started to fumble with the button. 'Wait,' she said dreamily. 'We're got time, Davy. We've got all the time in the world.'

'I've waited so long,' I said.

'I know,' she said. 'I know.'

She sat up, stroked my hair and kissed me. 'I think I owe you,' she said.

'Owe me?' I was finding it difficult to speak.

She pulled my jacket off and very delicately undid the first button on my shirt. 'You got Miles out of the way for me, didn't you?'

'Maybe,' I said. 'What does it matter?'

She smiled at me and kissed me again. I could taste her, wet and sweet. She undid the second button. 'It matters to me,' she said, kissing my lips, my face. She kissed my ear and whispered, 'Tell me. I need to know. I want to know everything about you.'

'It was easy,' I said.

She undid the third button and pulled open my shirt. She put her lips against my neck. I moaned. I couldn't stop myself.

'So what did you do?'

She lay back on the sofa again. I bent over and kissed her lips. I kissed her hair, breathed it in. The clean soft smell was like a drug that made me feel dizzy and drunk with her. She gave a murmur.

'It was the paperweight,' I said.

'Mm?'

I put my fingers on the fastening of her jeans, and this time she didn't try to stop me. I undid the fastening, then drew down the zip. I saw her blue knickers, lacy at the top. I put my hand on them. I felt the hair through them, warm under my hand.

'Tell me,' she said.

'The paperweight.' I said the words to her between kisses. 'You saw it in my room. I just put it in Miles's room.' I pushed my hand deeper under her knickers.

'No,' she said. 'My top. Take it off first.'

I undid the first button. She lay back with her hands raised behind her head, open to me.

'Peggy was just a mistake,' I said, undoing the second button and the third. 'But it was in his room, so the traces were there already.'

'You?' she said.

'Yes,' I said.

'Perfect, Davy,' she said. 'Perfect.'

And I didn't know whether she meant me, stroking and kissing her beautiful body, or whether it was because now she finally understood it was me who knew everything and had done everything. I unfastened the last button and pulled the cardigan open and apart.

'No, it was a mistake. Leah and Ingrid.'

My hands moved to the blue filigreed covering of her bra.

'What's this?' I said, as I saw a black cord running along it and round under her back. I looked at her and her expression had changed suddenly, like a cloud covering the sun, and I knew what it was and I knew that bad things were going to happen. Everything was about to crumble. The darkness would cover everything, like an icy tide coming in.

367

I reached for my jacket, for the spanner in the pocket. I could take her with me. One blow. She would raise her hand. It would shatter her wrist. The next blow would hit her face, immobilize her. Then I could smash those glorious features to jelly. But the jacket was out of reach; the bitch had kicked it away.

I raised myself from the sofa, pushing her back with one hand so that her head knocked against its wooden arm, and then I heard a clatter outside, heavy footsteps. The door opened hard, banging against the wall, and there was a rush of bodies. I let myself be shoved backwards against a wall. They pushed me hard, so that something fell from a shelf and smashed. The pain in the back of my head was like cold water, but a trickle of clear thought seeped into the jumble of my mind.

'You're under arrest,' said a familiar voice. Kamsky. It was like a surprise party. You think you're having a night alone and suddenly all your friends jump out. You think no one can hear you and all the time they've been listening, snooping, prying, spying.

'No!' I said. 'Don't. Listen – listen, this is a mistake. A stupid mistake, I was just playing along with Astrid. I was talking dirty to excite her. You'd understand that. It was a joke.'

Astrid was sitting on the sofa with her head in her hands. Kamsky looked at her with concern. 'Are you all right?'

She stood up, then remembered the state she was in. She zipped up her jeans. A female officer stepped forward and removed the wire and microphone. She had to reach round Astrid's body and disentangle it from her bra. All the time, Astrid looked at me, with an almost speculative expression, as if she was staring at me through the bars of a cage. Her lips curled back.

'You . . .' she began, and then she stopped.

'You did well, Astrid,' said Kamsky. 'Really well, my dear.'

'He touched me,' she hissed. 'I let him. I *let* him.'

Her hand came to her mouth. Her eyes met mine for a second, then she ran from the room. I heard the sound of vomiting, again and again. Then the sound of a door being locked and then of a shower. Not very flattering. The officers started to get busy. There was rummaging in my pockets. Grubby fingers poking and prodding me. Dirty eyes staring. A nasty fluttering in my head. A nerve was jumping just above my lip. I tried to bite it still, but I couldn't stop it.

'You fucking piece of filth,' said a voice. A uniformed man brandished my spanner in front of my face. 'What the hell's this?'

'I'm a . . .' I couldn't remember the word. What was happening? Pieces of my brain falling off like flaking plaster; words and thoughts cascading away. 'A builder,' I managed at last. 'I keep tools in my pocket.'

'Admit what you did,' said Kamsky. 'Save us all a lot of trouble. Get your friend out of prison.'

I needed to look puzzled. I tried to pull my expression the right way. My face was rubber and cardboard. My mouth felt numb, as if I'd had a stroke or something.

'Get a guilty man out of prison?' I said at last. I laughed, tried to laugh. Kamsky drew back slightly. 'Why would I do that, mate?'

Kamsky's expression was partly anger and partly a kind of wonderment. 'You never give up, do you, your kind?'

My kind. What did that mean, 'my kind'? He didn't know anything at all about me and he never would. I didn't have a kind. I was someone else, someone different, and they'd never understand.

369

'All that stuff you said before,' I said, 'about what I say being used as evidence. I hope someone has noted down that I've kept trying to explain that you've made a mistake, that I'm completely innocent.'

'It's all on tape,' said Kamsky.

'I told you,' I said. 'I was playing along.'

'We've got you admitting it. You don't have an alibi. We've got the underwear you stole from Leah Peterson. That's right. We've been talking to your girlfriend. It seems she wasn't entirely convinced by your attempt at an alibi.'

'Silly little bitch,' I said. My tongue was thick. There was spit on my chin but I wiped it away. 'I got that underwear at the sale at our house.'

Kamsky smiled.

'Which is why Leah Peterson's credit-card payment is dated the day before she died. We've got you, Davy. You might as well tell us what you did. Spare the families of the people you killed.'

I was falling. A steel band was being drawn tight round my skull and no relief from it would ever come.

'No,' I said. 'No. No. You've got it all wrong. It wasn't me.'

Because it wasn't. Not really.

Epilogue

My mobile rang.

'Hi, Emlyn,' I said.

'What are you doing?'

'You know what I'm doing. I'm hacking some bushes down.'

'I know. But I like to hear you say it. It helps me imagine it.'

'Can't you ring a chatline for that sort of thing?'

'I've arranged for us to look at a house. The estate agent's meeting us there in half an hour.'

'A house? What for? We've already got a house.'

'Astrid. It's seventy-two Maitland Road. A friend of mind drove past and saw the for-sale sign.'

'Oh,' I said, and suddenly I felt cold and the garden turned from autumnal gold to grey. 'I didn't know he was selling it. He never said. But what did you arrange that for?'

'I'm curious to see it because of everything it's meant to you. And I want to see it with you. You always said you needed to go back one more time at least. But only if you want to.'

I paused for a moment.

'All right,' I said.

When we arrived the estate agent was already waiting on the pavement, a clipboard under his arm, a mobile phone at his ear. When we got out of the car, he held up his hand in acknowledgement of our presence but continued talking.

'Well, you know what they say about verbal agreements,' he said, and laughed. 'Cheers, mate. Catch you later.'

He put his phone into his pocket and turned to us. He seemed momentarily confused by our appearance. Emlyn was dressed in a grey suit with a blue open-necked shirt. I was doing my best impersonation of a landscape gardener who had been interrupted while at work.

'Sounds as if someone's being gazumped,' said Emlyn.

'I wouldn't say that,' said the agent. 'But the market's looking positive at the moment. Very positive.' He held out his hand. 'Mart Ponder,' he said.

'I'm Emlyn Kaplan,' said Emlyn, 'and this is Astrid Bell.'

'You've been told that the property's already under offer,' said Ponder, 'but the owner may be sympathetic to imaginative bids.'

'Clearly,' said Emlyn, giving me a sideways glance. 'In the meantime . . . ?'

'Yes, yes,' said Ponder. 'Let's go inside.'

He took a familiar key with an unfamiliar tag from his folder and opened the front door. I suddenly felt a stab of alarm. 'Is the owner around?'

'He's abroad and has been for quite some time,' said Ponder. 'The right cash offer and the buyer could move in tomorrow.'

I'd prepared myself to be shocked by the sight of bare boards and blank spaces on the walls but it wasn't exactly like that. Miles had never come back and finished the job of moving out. He hadn't been able to face the house again, so full of memories. There were still the familiar pictures on the wall. I could see a rug through the open door of Pippa's old room. Still, it was obvious that the house had been abandoned for months. There was a smell like from a cave or a cellar, damp and still, as if the air and the light had been shut out.

'You'll see the house needs some decoration,' said Ponder. He looked at the brackets on the wall just inside the door. 'Clearly someone used to hang his bike here. And he wasn't too careful about lifting it on or off.'

Emlyn raised an eyebrow and gave me an ironic smile. I didn't smile back. I felt suddenly as if I were a ghost coming back to haunt a house where I had once been happy, or at least where I had been young. A ghost in a house that already had its ghosts.

'Do you have a place of your own to sell?' asked Ponder. Emlyn shook his head. 'Well, good on you if you can afford this as your first buy.'

I felt he wasn't sure whether to be very dubious or very impressed.

'Let's start here,' he said, walking into Miles's old room. 'It's a bit rough but this place sells itself. Large rooms, big windows – look at that view out on to the garden. Plenty of original features, if that's what you like. I'll be honest, upstairs you'll find some pretty odd DIY that's been done, but you could easily rip it out.'

I opened a cupboard door. A coat and a jacket and a couple of familiar shirts still hung inside. I breathed in: behind the staleness and decay, I thought I could detect Miles's smell. Suddenly my eyes were full of tears. I blinked them away and turned back to the estate agent. 'Could we look round alone? It's easier to get a feel of a house like that.'

'No problemo. It's in need of a good clean, I'm afraid. Try to see beyond that to the outstanding potential. And give me a shout when you're ready.'

When he was gone, I sat on the bed – the bed Leah had

shared – and stared around me. Emlyn walked over to me and stroked my hair. 'Was this a bad idea?'

'Davy hasn't said anything, as far as I know, but they think that this is probably where he killed Peggy. That's the first woman. Well, the second, if you count his poor mother. He killed her here, stowed the body in the cupboard, then somehow dumped her out in the street.'

'Creepy,' said Emlyn.

'Mmm. She was a nice woman, I think. Decent. Lonely. Careless about opening car doors.' I stood up abruptly. 'Let's get out of here.'

'Where to next?'

'I'll give you the guided tour.'

Pippa's room, which used to be such a mess, was empty and bare, except for a tube of lipstick on the carpet near where her mirror used to stand. I pulled open her wardrobe, to the rattle of coat hangers, and found only a pair of red stilettos that she used to call her vamp shoes. I winced. For a moment, I could see her sitting cross-legged on her rug, surrounded by bright heaps of clothes and strewn with jewellery.

'It feels like the *Mary-Celeste*,' said Emlyn.

'We left in a hurry.'

I led him up the stairs. There were dustballs on the landing. The windows were smeared and one was newly cracked. A spider floated from the bulb in the bathroom. Our footsteps echoed tinnily.

'This was my room,' I said, pushing open the door and stepping inside. A rectangle of light lay on the carpet. 'It was nice when I was here. Simple.'

'You left some earrings,' said Emlyn, picking them up from the window-sill and holding them out in the palm of his hand: tiny silver bicycle wheels.

'Leave them,' I said. 'They belong here.'

'You don't have to do this, you know,' he said, as we left the room.

'But I want to. This way.

'Owen's,' I said, standing at the threshold.

'Your . . . ?'

'Yes.'

The photo of the woman swimming in a ripple of water still hung on the wall. I stood in front of it for a moment, in the fierce clutch of memory. How hungry and urgent we had been for each other once. How we'd clung to each other, for a while. Now he was a stranger again. One day I would barely be able to remember his face.

'Do you ever hear from him now?'

I shook my head. 'The thing is, I didn't actually like him very much. Whatever happened between us, he was never really my friend. So when it was over, and it was quite quickly over – well, that was it.'

'Out of here.' He tugged me from the room.

On the top floor I led him briefly into Dario's room, tripping over a grubby, ripped deck-chair that had somehow survived both the house sale and the skip, then into Mick's boxy, deserted space.

'Last but not least,' I said, standing in front of the closed door, 'that was where Davy was.'

'Do you want to go in?'

'No,' I said. There was an icy darkness behind that door. If I opened it, it would spill over me. 'No. I really don't want to go in.'

He took my hand and his fingers felt strong and warm on mine, full of life.

We went downstairs, where Ponder was waiting.

'Wait until you see this,' he said. 'Someone's going to spend some money on a new kitchen, sort out the french windows and they're going to have themselves something spectacular.'

'What's this?' said Emlyn. He walked across the kitchen, took a piece of paper from the wall and handed it to me. As I looked at it I felt an ache in my chest, a prickling behind my eyes. It was the photograph, the only photograph of us all together, the Seven Dwarfs. It had seemed hilariously bad when Davy printed it out; we were falling all over the place, hysterical, slightly drunk. But happy, yes, we looked happy then, squeezed into the frame, out of focus and pushed close up against each other, arms flailing, mouths open in merriment or scowls. Now when I looked at the picture I tried to see behind Davy's laughing eyes at what he knew and what we didn't, what he still knew and we didn't. How could he have done it, taken that group photograph, while the body of Peggy Farrell was lying upstairs? Was that his way of mocking us?

'Can we go into the garden?'

'No problemo,' said Ponder, unlocking the back door. 'Let me warn you, you're going to need to use your imagination a bit.'

We stepped outside into the late-autumn sunshine, warm on my cheeks. I looked at my garden and immediately felt the hot tears on my face. I had to take a tissue from my pocket and pretend I was sneezing. The vegetables, the peas, courgettes and potatoes, had bolted and collapsed, rotted and grown again haphazardly, then bolted again. There was a huge sinister bush of rhubarb. There were strings of old stalks winding along the ground.

'I don't know what this was supposed to be,' said Ponder, 'but the garden is a hundred feet long. Get in one of those designers, like the ones they have on TV, put in some paths, shape some borders – this could be a nice place for a barbecue.' There was a sudden electric tone of a pop song I could dimly recognize. Ponder took the mobile from his pocket. 'Excuse me.'

Emlyn was staring up at the exterior of the house. I walked over to him and kissed his cheek. 'Thank you.'

As we made our way closer to the house I saw a dark patch on the paving-stones. I knelt and touched it with my finger, then smelled it. Nothing. But I knew what it was: oil from when I'd fixed my bike out here. Emlyn looked questioningly at me. I just smiled and shook my head. Ponder snapped his phone shut. 'So, chaps, what do you think?'

'I hope somebody nice buys this,' I said. 'Someone with children. It's a place people should be happy in.'

'But not for you?'

'Not for me.'

'Fair enough.'

'Come on, my friend,' I said to Emlyn. 'My love.'

I put my hand in his and led him from there, the place where I'd once lived, in a different world. There were faces at the windows and voices in the silence. There were stories in the shadows. My house of memories; my house of ghosts. I wouldn't go there again.

So Emlyn and I walked along the road together and I didn't look back, because it was over. I was in a different story now.